Bramble-bees and Others

J. Henri Fabre

Contents

BRAMBLE-BEES
AND OTHERS

BY

J. Henri Fabre

TRANSLATOR'S NOTE.

In this volume I have collected all the essays on Wild Bees scattered through the "Souvenirs entomologiques," with the exception of those on the Chalicodomae, or Mason-bees proper, which form the contents of a separate volume entitled "The Mason-bees."

The first two essays on the Halicti (Chapters 12 and 13) have already appeared in an abbreviated form in "The Life and Love of the Insect," translated by myself and published by Messrs. A. & C. Black (in America by the Macmillan Co.) in 1911. With the greatest courtesy and kindness, Messrs. Black have given me their permission to include these two chapters in the present volume; they did so without fee or consideration of any kind, merely on my representation that it would be a great pity if this uniform edition of Fabre's Works should be rendered incomplete because certain essays formed part of volumes of extracts previously published in this country. Their generosity is almost unparalleled in my experience; and I wish to thank them publicly for it in the name of the author, of the French publishers and of the English and American publishers, as well as in my own.

Of the remaining chapters, one or two have appeared in the "English Review" or other magazines; but most of them now see the light in English for the first time.

I have once more, as in the case of "The Mason-bees," to thank Miss Frances Rodwell for the help which she has given me in the work of translation and research; and I am also grateful for much kind assistance received from the staff of the Natural History Museum and from Mr. Geoffrey Meade-Waldo in particular.

ALEXANDER TEIXEIRA DE MATTOS.
Chelsea, 1915.

CHAPTER 1. BRAMBLE-DWELLERS.

The peasant, as he trims his hedge, whose riotous tangle threatens to encroach upon the road, cuts the trailing stems of the bramble a foot or two from the ground and leaves the root-stock, which soon dries up. These bramble-stumps, sheltered and protected by the thorny brushwood, are in great demand among a host of Hymenoptera who have families to settle. The stump, when dry, offers to any one that knows how to use it a hygienic dwelling, where there is no fear of damp from the sap; its soft and abundant pith lends itself to easy work; and the top offers a weak spot which makes it possible for the insect to reach the vein of least resistance at once, without cutting away through the hard ligneous wall. To many, therefore, of the Bee and Wasp tribe, whether honey-gatherers or hunters, one of these dry stalks is a valuable discovery when its diameter matches the size of its would-be inhabitants; and it is also an interesting subject of study to the entomologist who, in the winter, pruning-shears in hand, can gather in the hedgerows a faggot rich in small industrial wonders. Visiting the bramble-bushes has long been one of my favourite pastimes during the enforced leisure of the wintertime; and it is seldom but some new discovery, some unexpected fact, makes up to me for my torn fingers.

My list, which is still far from being complete, already numbers nearly thirty species of bramble-dwellers in the neighbourhood of my house; other observers, more assiduous than I, exploring another region and one covering a wider range, have counted as many as fifty. I give at foot an inventory of the species which I have noted.

(Bramble-dwelling insects in the neighbourhood of Serignan [Vaucluse]:

1. MELLIFEROUS HYMENOPTERA.
Osmia tridentata, DUF. and PER.
Osmia detrita, PEREZ.
Anthidium scapulare, LATR.
Heriades rubicola, PEREZ.
Prosopis confusa, SCHENCK.
Ceratina chalcites, GERM.
Ceratina albilabris, FAB.
Ceratina callosa, FAB.
Ceratina coerulea, VILLERS.

2. HUNTING HYMENOPTERA.
Solenius vagus, FAB. (provisions, Diptera).
Solenius lapidarius, LEP. (provisions, Spiders?).
Cemonus unicolor, PANZ. (provisions, Plant-lice).
Psen atratus (provisions, Black Plant-lice).
Tripoxylon figulus, LIN. (provisions, Spiders).
A Pompilus, unknown (provisions, Spiders).
Odynerus delphinalis, GIRAUD.

3. PARASITICAL HYMENOPTERA.
A Leucopsis, unknown (parasite of Anthidium scapulare).
A small Scoliid, unknown (parasite of Solenius vagus).
Omalus auratus (parasite of various bramble-dwellers).
Cryptus bimaculatus, GRAV. (parasite of Osmia detrita).
Cryptus gyrator, DUF. (parasite of Tripoxylon figulus).
Ephialtes divinator, ROSSI (parasite of Cemonus unicolor).
Ephialtes mediator, GRAV. (parasite of Psen atratus).
Foenus pyrenaicus, GUERIN.
Euritoma rubicola, J. GIRAUD (parasite of Osmia detrita).

4. COLEOPTERA.
Zonitis mutica, FAB. (parasite of Osmia tridentata).

They include members of very diverse corporations. Some, more industrious and equipped with better tools, remove the pith from the dry stem and thus obtain a vertical cylindrical gallery, the length of which may be nearly a cubit. This sheath is next divided, by partitions, into more or less numerous storeys, each of which forms the cell of a larva. Others, less well-endowed with strength and implements, avail themselves of the old galleries of other insects, galleries that have been abandoned after serving as a home for their builder's family. Their only work is to make some slight repairs in the ruined tenement, to clear the channel of its lumber, such as the remains of cocoons and the litter of shattered ceilings, and lastly to build new partitions, either with a plaster made of clay or with a concrete formed of pith-scrapings cemented with a drop of saliva.

You can tell these borrowed dwellings by the unequal size of the storeys. When the worker has herself bored the channel, she economizes her space: she knows how costly it is. The cells, in that case, are all alike, the proper size for the tenant, neither too large nor too small. In this box, which has cost weeks of labour, the insect has to house the largest possible number of larvae, while allotting the necessary amount of room to each. Method in the superposition of the floors and economy of space are here the absolute rule.

But there is evidence of waste when the insect makes use of a bramble hollowed by another. This is the case with Tripoxylon figulus. To obtain the storerooms wherein to deposit her scanty stock of Spiders, she divides her borrowed cylinder into very unequal cells, by means of slender clay partitions. Some are a centimetre (.39 inch.--Translator's Note.) deep, the proper size for the insect; others are as much as two inches. These spacious rooms, out of all proportion to the occupier, reveal the reckless extravagance of a casual proprietress whose title-deeds have cost her nothing.

But, whether they be the original builders or labourers touching up the work of others, they all alike have their parasites, who constitute the third class of bramble-dwellers. These have neither galleries to excavate nor victuals to provide; they lay their egg in a strange cell; and their grub feeds either on the provisions of the lawful owner's larva or on that larva itself.

At the head of this population, as regards both the finish and the magnitude of the structure, stands the Three-pronged Osmia (Osmia tridentata, DUF. and PER.), to whom this chapter shall be specially devoted. Her gallery, which has the diameter of a lead pencil, sometimes descends to a depth of twenty inches. It is at first almost exactly cylindrical; but, in the course of the victualling, changes occur which modify it slightly at geometrically determined distances. The work of boring possesses no great interest. In the month of July, we see the insect, perched on a bramble-stump, attack the pith and dig itself a well. When this is deep enough, the Osmia goes down, tears off a few particles of pith and comes up again to fling her load outside. This monotonous labour continues until the Bee deems the gallery long enough, or until, as often happens, she finds herself stopped by an impassable knot.

Next comes the ration of honey, the laying of the egg and the partitioning, the last a delicate operation to which the insect proceeds by degrees from the base to the top. At the bottom of the gallery, a pile of honey is placed and an egg laid upon the pile; then a partition is built to separate this cell from the next, for each larva must have its special chamber, about a centimetre and a half (.58 inch.--Translator's Note.) long, having no communication with the chambers adjoining. The materials employed for this partition are bramble-sawdust, glued into a paste with the insects' saliva. Whence are these materials obtained? Does the Osmia go outside, to gather on the ground the rubbish which she flung out when boring the cylinder? On the contrary, she is frugal of her time and has better things to do than to pick up the scattered particles from the soil. The channel, as I said, is at first uniform in size, almost cylindrical; its sides still retain a thin coating of pith, forming the reserves which the Osmia, as a provident builder, has economized wherewith to construct the partitions. So she scrapes away with her mandibles, keeping within a certain radius, a radius that corresponds with the dimensions of the cell which she is going to build next; moreover, she conducts her work in such a way as to hollow out more in the middle and leave the two ends contracted. In this manner, the cylindrical channel of the start is succeeded, in the worked portion, by an ovoid cavity flattened at both ends, a space resembling a little barrel. This space will form the second cell.

As for the rubbish, it is utilized on the spot for the lid or cover that serves as a ceiling for one cell and a floor for the next. Our own master-builders could not con-trive more successfully to make the best use of their labourers' time. On the floor thus obtained, a second ration of honey is placed; and an egg is laid on the surface of the paste. Lastly, at the upper end of the little barrel, a partition is built with the scrapings obtained in the course of the final work on the third cell, which itself is shaped like a flattened ovoid. And so the work goes on, cell upon cell, each sup-plying the materials for the partition separating it from the one below. On reach-ing the end of the cylinder, the Osmia closes up the case with a thick layer of the same mortar. Then that bramble-stump is done with; the Bee will not return to it. If her ovaries are not yet exhausted, other dry stems will be exploited in the same fashion.

The number of cells varies greatly, according to the qualities of the stalk. If the bramble-stump be long, regular and smooth, we may count as many as fifteen: that, at least, is the highest figure which my observations have supplied. To obtain a good idea of the internal distribution, we must split the stalk lengthwise, in the winter, when the provisions have long been consumed and when the larvae are wrapped in their cocoons. We then see that, at regular intervals, the case becomes slightly nar-rower; and in each of the necks thus formed a circular disk is fixed, a partition one or two millimetres thick. (.039 to.079 inch.--Translator's Note.) The rooms sepa-rated by these partitions form so many little barrels or kegs, each compactly filled with a reddish, transparent cocoon, through which the larva shows, bent into a fish-hook. The whole suggests a string of rough, oval amber beads, touching at their amputated ends.

In this string of cocoons, which is the oldest, which the youngest? The oldest is obviously the bottom one, the one whose cell was the first built; the youngest is the one at the top of the row, the one in the cell last built. The oldest of the larvae starts the pile, down at the bottom of the gallery; the latest arrival ends it at the top; and those in between follow upon one another, according to age, from base to apex.

Let us next observe that there is no room in the shaft for two Osmiae at a time on the same level, for each cocoon fills up the storey, the keg that belongs to it, without leaving any vacant space; let us also remark that, when they attain the stage of perfection, the Osmiae must all emerge from the shaft by the only orifice which the bramble-stem boasts, the orifice at the top. There is here but one obstacle, easy to overcome: a plug of glued pith, of which the insect's mandibles make short work. Down below, the stalk offers no ready outlet; besides, it is prolonged underground indefinitely by the roots. Everywhere else is the ligneous fence, generally too hard and thick to break through. It is inevitable therefore that all the Osmiae, when the time comes to quit their dwelling, should go out by the top; and, as the narrowness of the shaft bars the passage of the preceding insect as long as the next insect, the one above it, remains in position, the removal must begin at the top, extend from cell to cell and end at the bottom. Consequently, the order of exit is the converse to the order of birth: the younger Osmiae leave the nest first, their elders leave it last.

The oldest, that is to say, the bottom one, was the first to finish her supply of honey and to spin her cocoon. Taking precedence of all her sisters in the whole series of her actions, she was the first to burst her silken bag and to destroy the ceiling that closes her room: at least, that is what the logic of the situation takes for granted. In her anxiety to get out, how will she set about her release? The way is blocked by the nearest cocoons, as yet intact. To clear herself a passage through the string of those cocoons would mean to exterminate the remainder of the brood; the deliverance of one would mean the destruction of all the rest. Insects are notoriously obstinate in their actions and unscrupulous in their methods. If the Bee at the bottom of the shaft wants to leave her lodging, will she spare those who bar her road?

The difficulty is great, obviously; it seems insuperable. Thereupon we become suspicious: we begin to wonder if the emergence from the cocoon, that is to say, the hatching, really takes place in the order of primogeniture. Might it not be--by a very singular exception, it is true, but one which is necessary in such circumstances--that the youngest of the Osmiae bursts her cocoon first and the oldest last; in short, that the hatching proceeds from one chamber to the next in the inverse direction to that which the age of the occupants would lead us to presume? In that case, the whole difficulty would be removed: each Osmia, as she rent her silken prison, would find a clear road in front of her, the Osmiae nearer the outlet having gone out before her. But is this really how things happen? Our theories very often do not agree with the insect's practice; even where our reasoning seems most logical, we should be more prudent to see what happens before venturing on any positive statements. Leon Dufour was not so prudent when he, the first in the field, took this little problem in hand. He describes to us the habits of an Odynerus (Odynerus rubicola, DUF.) who piles up clay cells in the shaft of a dry bramble-stalk; and, full of enthusiasm for his industrious Wasp, he goes on to say:

'Picture a string of eight cement shells, placed end to end and closely wedged inside a wooden sheath. The lowest was undeniably made first and consequently contains the first-laid egg, which, according to rules, should give birth to the first winged insect. How do you imagine that the larva in that first shell was bidden to waive its right of primogeniture and only to complete its metamorphosis after all its juniors? What are the conditions brought into play to produce a result apparently so contrary to the laws of nature? Humble yourself in the presence of the reality and confess your ignorance, rather than attempt to hide your embarrassment under vain explanations!

'If the first egg laid by the busy mother were destined to be the first-born of the Odyneri, that one, in order to see the light immediately after achieving wings, would have had the option either of breaking through the double walls of his prison or of perforating, from bottom to top, the seven shells ahead of him, in order to emerge through the truncate end of the bramble-stem. Now nature, while refusing any way of escape laterally, was also bound to veto any direct invasion, the brutal gimlet-work which would inevitably have sacrificed seven members of one family for the safety of an only son. Nature is as ingenious in design as she is fertile in resource, and she must have foreseen and forestalled every difficulty. She decided that the last-built cradle should yield the first-born child; that this one should clear the road for his next oldest brother, the second for the third and so on. And this is the order in which the birth of our Odyneri of the Brambles actually takes place.'

Yes, my revered master, I will admit without hesitation that the bramble-dwellers leave their sheath in the converse order to that of their ages: the youngest first, the oldest last; if not invariably, at least very often. But does the hatching, by which I mean the emergence from the cocoon, take place in the same order? Does the evolution of the elder wait upon that of the younger, so that each may give those who would bar his passage time to effect their deliverance and to leave the road clear? I very much fear that logic has carried your deductions beyond the bounds of reality. Rationally speaking, my dear sir, nothing could be more accurate than your inferences; and yet we must forgo the theory of the strange inversion which you suggest. None of the Bramble-bees with whom I have experimented behaves after that fashion. I know nothing personal about Odynerus rubicola, who appears to be a stranger in my district; but, as the method of leaving must be almost the same when the habitation is exactly similar, it is enough, I think, to experiment with some of the bramble-dwellers in order to learn the history of the rest.

My studies will, by preference, bear upon the Three-pronged Osmia, who lends herself more readily to laboratory experiments, both because she is stronger and because the same stalk will contain a goodly number of her cells. The first fact to be ascertained is the order of hatching. I take a glass tube, closed at one end, open at the other and of a diameter similar to that of the Osmia's tunnel. In this I place, one above the other, exactly in their natural order, the ten cocoons, or thereabouts, which I extract from a stump of bramble. The operation is performed in winter. The larvae, at that time, have long been enveloped in their silken case. To separate the cocoons from one another, I employ artificial partitions consisting of little round disks of sorghum, or Indian millet, about half a centimetre thick. (About one-fifth of an inch.--Translator's Note.) This is a white pith, divested of its fibrous wrapper and easy for the Osmia's mandibles to attack. My diaphragms are much thicker than the natural partitions; this is an advantage, as we shall see. In any case, I could not well use thinner ones, for these disks must be able to withstand the pressure of the rammer which places them in position in the tube. On the other hand, the experiment showed me that the Osmia makes short work of the material when it is a case of drilling a hole through it.

To keep out the light, which would disturb my insects destined to spend their larval life in complete darkness, I cover the tube with a thick paper sheath, easy to remove and replace when the time comes for observation. Lastly, the tubes thus prepared and containing either Osmiae or other bramble-dwellers are hung vertically, with the opening at the top, in a snug corner of my study. Each of these appliances fulfils the natural conditions pretty satisfactorily: the cocoons from the same bramble-stick are stacked in the same order which they occupied in the native shaft, the oldest at the bottom of the tube and the youngest close to the orifice; they are isolated by means of partitions; they are placed vertically, head upwards; moreover, my device has the advantage of substituting for the opaque wall of the bramble a transparent wall which will enable me to follow the hatching day by day, at any moment which I think opportune.

The male Osmia splits his cocoon at the end of June and the female at the beginning of July. When this time comes, we must redouble our watch and inspect the tubes several times a day if we would obtain exact statistics of the births. Well, during the six years that I have studied this question, I have seen and seen again, ad nauseam; and I am in a position to declare that there is no order governing the sequence of hatchings, absolutely none. The first cocoon to burst may be the one at the bottom of the tube, the one at the top, the one in the middle or in any other part, indifferently. The second to be split may adjoin the first or it may be removed from it by a number of spaces, either above or below. Sometimes several hatchings occur on the same day, within the same hour, some farther back in the row of cells, some farther forward; and this without any apparent reason for the simultaneity. In short, the hatchings follow upon one another, I will not say haphazard--for each of them has its appointed place in time, determined by impenetrable causes--but at any rate contrary to our calculations, based on this or the other consideration.

Had we not been deceived by our too shallow logic, we might have foreseen this result. The eggs are laid in their respective cells at intervals of a few days, of a few hours. How can this slight difference in age affect the total evolution, which lasts a year? Mathematical accuracy has nothing to do with the case. Each germ, each grub has its individual energy, determined we know not how and varying in each germ or grub. This excess of vitality belongs to the egg before it leaves the ovary. Might it not, at the moment of hatching, be the cause why this or that larva takes precedence of its elders or its juniors, chronology being altogether a secondary consideration? When the hen sits upon her eggs, is the oldest always the first to hatch? In the same way, the oldest larva, lodged in the bottom storey, need not necessarily reach the perfect state first.

A second argument, had we reflected more deeply on the matter, would have shaken our faith in any strict mathematical sequence. The same brood forming the string of cocoons in a bramble-stem contains both males and females; and the two sexes are divided in the series indiscriminately. Now it is the rule among the Bees for the males to issue from the cocoon a little earlier than the females. In the case of the Three-pronged Osmia, the male has about a week's start. Consequently, in a populous gallery, there is always a certain number of males, who are hatched seven or eight days before the females and who are distributed here and there over the series. This would be enough to make any regular hatching-sequence impossible in either direction.

These surmises accord with the facts: the chronological sequence of the cells tells us nothing about the chronological sequence of the hatchings, which take place without any definite order. There is, therefore, no surrender of rights of primogeniture, as Leon Dufour thought: each insect, regardless of the others, bursts its cocoon when its time comes; and this time is determined by causes which escape our notice and which, no doubt, depend upon the potentialities of the egg itself. It is the case with the other bramble-dwellers which I have subjected to the same test (Osmia detrita, Anthidium scapulare, Solenius vagus, etc.); and it must also be the case with Odynerus rubicola: so the most striking analogies inform us. Therefore the singular exception which made such an impression on Dufour's mind is a sheer logical illusion.

An error removed is tantamount to a truth gained; and yet, if it were to end here, the result of my experiment would possess but slight value. After destruction, let us turn to construction; and perhaps we shall find the wherewithal to compensate us for an illusion lost. Let us begin by watching the exit.

The first Osmia to leave her cocoon, no matter what place she occupies in the series, forthwith attacks the ceiling separating her from the floor above. She cuts a fairly clean hole in it, shaped like a truncate cone, having its larger base on the side where the Bee is and its smaller base opposite. This conformation of the exit-door is a characteristic of the work. When the insect tries to attack the diaphragm, it first digs more or less at random; then, as the boring progresses, the action is concentrated upon an area which narrows until it presents no more than just the necessary passage. Nor is the cone-shaped aperture special to the Osmia: I have seen it made by the other bramble-dwellers through my thick disks of sorghum-pith. Under natural conditions, the partitions, which, for that matter, are very thin, are destroyed absolutely, for the contraction of the cell at the top leaves barely the width which the insect needs. The truncate, cone-shaped breach has often been of great use to me. Its wide base made it possible for me, without being present at the work, to judge which of the two neighbouring Osmiae had pierced the partition; it told me the direction of a nocturnal migration which I had been unable to witness.

The first-hatched Osmia, wherever she may be, has made a hole in her ceiling. She is now in the presence of the next cocoon, with her head at the opening of the hole. In front of her sister's cradle, she usually stops, consumed with shyness; she draws back into her cell, flounders among the shreds of the cocoon and the wreckage of the ruined ceiling; she waits a day, two days, three days, more if necessary. Should impatience gain the upper hand, she tries to slip between the wall of the tunnel and the cocoon that blocks the way. She even undertakes the laborious work of gnawing at the wall, so as to widen the interval, if possible. We find these attempts, in the shaft of a bramble, at places where the pith is removed down to the very wood, where the wood itself is gnawed to some depth. I need hardly say that, although these lateral inroads are perceptible after the event, they escape the eye at the moment when they are being made.

If we would witness them, we must slightly modify the glass apparatus. I line the inside of the tube with a thick piece of whity-brown packing-paper, but only over one half of the circumference; the other half is left bare, so that I may watch the Osmia's attempts. Well, the captive insect fiercely attacks this lining, which to its eyes represents the pithy layer of its usual abode; it tears it away by tiny particles and strives to cut itself a road between the cocoon and the glass wall. The males, who are a little smaller, have a better chance of success than the females. Flattening themselves, making themselves thin, slightly spoiling the shape of the cocoon, which, however, thanks to its elasticity, soon recovers its first condition, they slip through the narrow passage and reach the next cell. The females, when in a hurry to get out, do as much, if they find the tube at all amenable to the process. But no sooner is the first partition passed than a second presents itself. This is pierced in its turn. In the same way will the third be pierced and others after that, if the insect can manage them, as long as its strength holds out. Too weak for these repeated borings, the males do not go far through my thick plugs. If they contrive to cut through the first, it is as much as they can do; and, even so, they are far from always succeeding. But, in the conditions presented by the native stalk, they have only feeble tissues to overcome; and then, slipping, as I have said, between the cocoon and the wall, which is slightly worn owing to the circumstances described, they are able to pass through the remaining occupied chambers and to reach the outside first, whatever their original place in the stack of cells. It is just possible that their early eclosion forces this method of exit upon them, a method which, though often attempted, does not always succeed. The females, furnished with stronger tools, make greater progress in my tubes. I see some who pierce three or four partitions, one after the other, and are so many stages ahead before those whom they have left behind are even hatched. While they are engaged in this long and toilsome operation, others, nearer to the orifice, have cleared a passage whereof those from a distance will avail themselves. In this way, it may happen that, when the width of the tube permits, an Osmia in a back row will nevertheless be one of the first to emerge.

In the bramble-stem, which is of exactly the same diameter as the cocoon, this escape by the side of the column appears hardly practicable, except to a few males; and even these have to find a wall which has so much pith that by removing it they can effect a passage. Let us then imagine a tube so narrow as to prevent any exit save in the natural sequence of the cells. What will happen? A very simple thing. The newly-hatched Osmia, after perforating his partition, finds himself faced with an unbroken cocoon that obstructs the road. He makes a few attempts upon the sides and, realizing his impotence, retires into his cell, where he waits for days and days, until his neighbour bursts her cocoon in her turn. His patience is inexhaustible. However, it is not put to an over long test, for within a week, more or less, the whole string of females is hatched.

When two neighbouring Osmiae are released at the same time, mutual visits are paid through the aperture between the two rooms: the one above goes down to the floor below; the one below goes up to the floor above; sometimes both of them are in the same cell together. Might not this intercourse tend to cheer them and encourage them to patience? Meanwhile, slowly, doors are opening here and there through the separating walls; the road is cleared by sections; and a moment arrives when the leader of the file walks out. The others follow, if ready; but there are always laggards who keep the rear-ranks waiting until they are gone.

To sum up, first, the hatching of the larvae takes place without any order; secondly, the exodus proceeds regularly from summit to base, but only in consequence of the insect's inability to move forward so long as the upper cells are not vacated. We have here not an exceptional evolution, in the inverse ratio to age, but the simple impossibility of emerging otherwise. Should a chance occur of going out before its turn, the insect does not fail to seize it, as we can see by the lateral movements which send the impatient ones a few ranks ahead and even release the more favoured altogether. The only remarkable thing that I perceive is the scrupulous respect shown to the as yet unopened neighbouring cocoon. However eager to come out, the Osmia is most careful not to touch it with his mandibles: it is taboo. He will demolish the partition, he will gnaw the side-wall fiercely, even though there be nothing left but wood, he will reduce everything around him to dust; but touch a cocoon that obstructs his way? Never! He will not make himself an outlet by breaking up his sisters' cradles.

It may happen that the Osmia's patience is in vain and that the barricade that blocks the way never disappears at all. Sometimes, the egg in a cell does not mature; and the unconsumed provisions dry up and become a compact, sticky, mildewed plug, through which the occupants of the floors below could never clear themselves a passage. Sometimes, again, a grub dies in its cocoon; and the cradle of the deceased, now turned into a coffin, forms an everlasting obstacle. How shall the insect cope with such grave circumstances?

Among the many bramble-stumps which I have collected, some few have presented a remarkable peculiarity. In addition to the orifice at the top, they had at the side one and sometimes two round apertures that looked as though they had been punched out with an instrument. On opening these stalks, which were old, deserted nests, I discovered the cause of these very exceptional windows. Above each of them was a cell full of mouldy honey. The egg had perished and the provisions remained untouched: hence the impossibility of getting out by the ordinary road. Walled in by the unsurmountable obstacle, the Osmia on the floor below had contrived an outlet through the side of the shaft; and those in the lower storeys had benefited by this ingenious innovation. The usual door being inaccessible, a side-window had been opened by means of the insect's jaws. The cocoons, torn, but still in position in the lower rooms, left no doubt as to this eccentric mode of exit. The same fact, moreover, was repeated, in several bramble-stumps, in the case of Osmia tridentata; it was likewise repeated in the case of Anthidium scapulare. The observation was worth confirming by experiment.

I select a bramble-stem with the thinnest rind possible, so as to facilitate the Osmiae's work. I split it in half, thus obtaining a smooth-sided trough which will enable me to judge better of future exits. The cocoons are next laid out in one of the troughs. I separate them with disks of sorghum, covering both surfaces of the disk with a generous layer of sealing-wax, a material which the Osmia's mandibles are not able to attack. The two troughs are then placed together and fastened. A little putty does away with the joint and prevents the least ray of light from penetrating. Lastly, the apparatus is hung up perpendicularly, with the cocoons' heads up. We have now only to wait. None of the Osmiae can get out in the usual manner, because each of them is confined between two partitions coated with sealing-wax. There is but one resource left to them if they would emerge into the light of day, that is, for each of them to open a side-window, provided always that they possess the instinct and the power to do so.

In July, the result is as follows: of twenty Osmiae thus immured, six succeed in boring a round hole through the wall and making their way out; the others perish in their cells, without managing to release themselves. But, when I open the cylinder, when I separate the two wooden troughs, I realize that all have attempted to escape through the side, for the wall of each cell bears traces of gnawing concentrated upon one spot. All, therefore, have acted in the same way as their more fortunate sisters; they did not succeed, because their strength failed them. Lastly, in my glass tubes, part-lined with a thick piece of packing-paper, I often see attempts at making a window in the side of the cell: the paper is pierced right through with a round hole.

This then is yet another result which I am glad to record in the history of the bramble-dwellers. When the Osmia, the Anthidium and probably others are unable to emerge through the customary outlet, they take an heroic decision and perforate the side of the shaft. It is the last resource, resolved upon after other methods have been tried in vain. The brave, the strong succeed; the weak perish in the attempt.

Supposing that all the Osmiae possessed the necessary strength of jaw as well as the instinct for this sideward boring, it is clear that egress from each cell through a special window would be much more advantageous than egress through the common door. The Bee could attend to his release as soon as he was hatched, instead of postponing it until after the emancipation of those who come before him; he would thus escape long waits, which too often prove fatal. In point of fact, it is no uncommon thing to find bramble-stalks in which several Osmiae have died in their cells, because the upper storeys were not vacated in time. Yes, there would be a precious advantage in that lateral opening, which would not leave each occupant at the mercy of his environment: many die that would not die. All the Osmiae, when compelled by circumstances, resort to this supreme method; all have the instinct for lateral boring; but very few are able to carry the work through. Only the favourites of fate succeed, those more generously endowed with strength and perseverance.

If the famous law of natural selection, which is said to govern and transform the world, had any sure foundation; if really the fittest removed the less fit from the scene; if the future were to the strongest, to the most industrious, surely the race of Osmiae, which has been perforating bramble-stumps for ages, should by this time have allowed its weaker members, who go on obstinately using the common outlet, to die out and should have replaced them, down to the very last one, by the stalwart drillers of side-openings. There is an opportunity here for immense progress; the insect is on the verge of it and is unable to cross the narrow intervening line. Selection has had ample time to make its choice; and yet, though there be a few successes, the failures exceed them in very large measure. The race of the strong has not abolished the race of the weak: it remains inferior in numbers, as doubtless it has been since all time. The law of natural selection impresses me with the vastness of its scope; but, whenever I try to apply it to actual facts, it leaves me whirling in space, with nothing to help me to interpret realities. It is magnificent in theory, but it is a mere gas-bubble in the face of existing conditions. It is majestic, but sterile. Then where is the answer to the riddle of the world? Who knows? Who will ever know?

Let us waste no more time in this darkness, which idle theorizing will not dispel; let us return to facts, humble facts, the only ground that does not give way under our feet. The Osmia respects her neighbour's cocoon; and her scruples are so great that, after vainly trying to slip between that cocoon and the wall, or else to open a lateral outlet, she lets herself die in her cell rather than effect an egress by forcing her way through the occupied cells. When the cocoon that blocks the way contains a dead instead of a live grub, will the result be the same?

In my glass tubes, I let Osmia-cocoons containing a live grub alternate with Osmia-cocoons in which the grub has been asphyxiated by the fumes of sulphocarbonic acid. As usual, the storeys are separated by disks of sorghum. The anchorites, when hatched, do not hesitate long. Once the partition is pierced, they attack the dead cocoons, go right through them, reducing the dead grub, now dry and shrivelled, to dust, and at last emerge, after wrecking everything in their path. The dead cocoons, therefore, are not spared; they are treated as would be any other obstacle capable of attack by the mandibles. The Osmia looks upon them as a mere barricade to be ruthlessly overturned. How is she apprised that the cocoon, which has undergone no outward change, contains a dead and not a live grub? It is certainly not by sight. Can it be by sense of smell? I am always a little suspicious of that sense of smell of which we do not know the seat and which we introduce on the slightest provocation as a convenient explanation of that which may transcend our explanatory powers.

My next test is made with a string of live cocoons. Of course, I cannot take all these from the same species, for then the experiment would not differ from the one which we have already witnessed; I take them from two different species which leave their bramble-stem at separate periods. Moreover, these cocoons must have nearly the same diameter to allow of their being stacked in a tube without leaving an empty space between them and the wall. The two species adopted are Solenius vagus, which quits the bramble at the end of June, and Osmia detrita, which comes a little earlier, in the first fortnight of the same month. I therefore alternate Osmia-cocoons and Solenius-cocoons, with the latter at the top of the series, either in glass tubes or between two bramble-troughs joined into a cylinder.

The result of this promiscuity is striking. The Osmiae, which mature earlier, emerge; and the Solenius-cocoons, as well as their inhabitants, which by this time have reached the perfect stage, are reduced to shreds, to dust, wherein it is impossible for me to recognize a vestige, save perhaps here and there a head, of the exterminated unfortunates. The Osmia, therefore, has not respected the live cocoons of a foreign species: she has passed out over the bodies of the intervening Solenii. Did I say passed over their bodies? She has passed through them, crunched the laggards between her jaws, treated them as cavalierly as she treats my disks. And yet those barricades were alive. No matter: when her hour came, the Osmia went ahead, destroying everything upon her road. Here, at any rate, is a law on which we can rely: the supreme indifference of the animal to all that does not form part of itself and its race.

And what of the sense of smell, distinguishing the dead from the living? Here, all are alive; and the Bee pierces her way as through a row of corpses. If I am told that the smell of the Solenii may differ from that of the Osmiae, I shall reply that such extreme subtlety in the insect's olfactory apparatus seems to me a rather far-fetched supposition. Then what is my explanation of the two facts? The explanation? I have none to give! I am quite content to know that I do not know, which at least spares me many vain lucubrations. And so I do not know how the Osmia, in the dense darkness of her tunnel, distinguishes between a live cocoon and a dead cocoon of the same species; and I know just as little how she succeeds in recognizing a strange cocoon. Ah, how clearly this confession of ignorance proves that I am behind the times! I am deliberately missing a glorious opportunity of stringing big words together and arriving at nothing.

The bramble-stump is perpendicular, or nearly so; its opening is at the top. This is the rule under natural conditions. My artifices are able to alter that state of things; I can place the tube vertically or horizontally; I can turn its one orifice either up or down; lastly, I can leave the channel open at both ends, which will give two outlets. What will happen under these several conditions? That is what we shall examine with the Three-pronged Osmia.

The tube is hung perpendicularly, but closed at the top and open at the bottom; in fact, it represents a bramble-stump turned upside down. To vary and complicate the experiment, the strings of cocoons are arranged differently in different tubes. In some of them, the heads of the cocoons are turned downwards, towards the opening; in others, they are turned upwards, towards the closed end; in others again, the cocoons alternate in direction, that is to say, they are placed head to head and rear to rear, turn and turn about. I need not say that the separating floors are of sorghum.

The result is identical in all these tubes. If the Osmiae have their heads pointing upwards, they attack the partition above them, as happens under normal conditions; if their heads point downwards, they turn round in their cells and set to work as usual. In short, the general outward trend is towards the top, in whatever position the cocoon be placed.

We here see manifestly at work the influence of gravity, which warns the insect of its reversed position and makes it turn round, even as it would warn us if we ourselves happened to be hanging head downwards. In natural conditions, the insect has but to follow the counsels of gravity, which tells it to dig upwards, and it will infallibly reach the exit-door situated at the upper end. But, in my apparatus, these same counsels betray it: it goes towards the top, where there is no outlet. Thus misled by my artifices, the Osmiae perish, heaped up on the higher floors and buried in the ruins.

It nevertheless happens that attempts are made to clear a road downwards. But it is rare for the work to lead to anything in this direction, especially in the case of the middle or upper cells. The insect is little inclined for this progress, the opposite to that to which it is accustomed; besides, a serious difficulty arises in the course of this reversed boring. As the Bee flings the excavated materials behind her, these fall back of their own weight under her mandibles; the clearance has to be begun anew. Exhausted by her Sisyphean task, distrustful of this new and unfamiliar method, the Osmia resigns herself and expires in her cell. I am bound to add, however, that the Osmiae in the lower storeys, those nearest the exit--sometimes one, sometimes two or three--do succeed in escaping. In that case, they unhesitatingly attack the partitions below them, while their companions, who form the great majority, persist and perish in the upper cells.

It was easy to repeat the experiment without changing anything in the natural conditions, except the direction of the cocoons: all that I had to do was to hang up some bramble-stumps as I found them, vertically, but with the opening downwards. Out of two stalks thus arranged and peopled with Osmiae, not one of the insects succeeded in emerging. All the Bees died in the shaft, some turned upwards, others downwards. On the other hand, three stems occupied by Anthidia discharged their population safe and sound. The outgoing was effected at the bottom, from first to last, without the least impediment. Must we take it that the two sorts of Bees are not equally sensitive to the influences of gravity? Can the Anthidium, built to pass through the difficult obstacle of her cotton wallets, be better-adapted than the Osmia to make her way through the wreckage that keeps falling under the worker's feet; or, rather, may not this very cotton-waste put a stop to these cataracts of rubbish which must naturally drive the insect back? This is all quite possible; but I can say nothing for certain.

Let us now experiment with vertical tubes open at both ends. The arrangements, save for the upper orifice, are the same as before. The cocoons, in some of the tubes, have their heads turned down; others, up; in others again, their positions alternate. The result is similar to what we have seen above. A few Osmiae, those nearest the bottom orifice, take the lower road, whatever the direction first occupied by the cocoon; the others, composing by far the larger number, take the higher road, even when the cocoon is placed upside down. As both doors are free, the outgoing is effected at either end with success.

What are we to conclude from all these experiments? First, that gravity guides the insect towards the top, where the natural door is, and makes it turn in its cell when the cocoon has been reversed. Secondly, I seem to suspect an atmospheric influence and, in any case, some second cause that sends the insect to the outlet. Let us admit that this cause is the proximity of the outer air acting upon the anchorite through the partitions.

The animal then is subject, on the one hand, to the promptings of gravity, and this to an equal degree for all, whatever the storey inhabited. Gravity is the common guide of the whole series from base to top. But those in the lower boxes have a second guide, when the bottom end is open. This is the stimulus of the adjacent air, a more powerful stimulus than that of gravity. The access of the air from without is very slight, because of the partitions; while it can be felt in the nethermost cells, it must decrease rapidly as the storeys ascend. Wherefore the bottom insects, very few in number, obeying the preponderant influence, that of the atmosphere, make for the lower outlet and reverse, if necessary, their original position; those above, on the contrary, who form the great majority, being guided only by gravity when the upper end is closed, make for that upper end. It goes without saying that, if the upper end be open at the same time as the other, the occupants of the top storeys will have a double incentive to take the ascending path, though this will not prevent the dwellers on the lower floors from obeying, by preference, the call of the adjacent air and adopting the downward road.

I have one means left whereby to judge of the value of my explanation, namely, to experiment with tubes open at both ends and lying horizontally. The horizontal position has a twofold advantage. In the first place, it removes the insect from the influence of gravity, inasmuch as it leaves it indifferent to the direction to be taken, the right or the left. In the second place, it does away with the descent of the rubbish which, falling under the worker's feet when the boring is done from below, sooner or later discourages her and makes her abandon her enterprise.

There are a few precautions to be observed for the successful conduct of the experiment; I recommend them to any one who might care to make the attempt. It is even advisable to remember them in the case of the tests which I have already described. The males, those puny creatures, not built for work, are sorry labourers when confronted with my stout disks. Most of them perish miserably in their glass cells, without succeeding in piercing their partitions right through. Moreover, instinct has been less generous to them than to the females. Their corpses, interspersed here and there in the series of the cells, are disturbing causes, which it is wise to eliminate. I therefore choose the larger, more powerful-looking cocoons. These, except for an occasional unavoidable error, belong to females. I pack them in tubes, sometimes varying their position in every way, sometimes giving them all a like arrangement. It does not matter whether the whole series comes from one and the same bramble-stump or from several: we are free to choose where we please; the result will not be altered.

The first time that I prepared one of these horizontal tubes open at both ends, I was greatly struck by what happened. The series consisted of ten cocoons. It was divided into two equal batches. The five on the left went out on the left, the five on the right went out on the right, reversing, when necessary, their original direction in the cell. It was very remarkable from the point of view of symmetry; moreover, it was a very unlikely arrangement among the total number of possible arrangements, as mathematics will show us.

Let us take n to represent the number of Osmiae. Each of them, once gravity ceases to interfere and leaves the insect indifferent to either end of the tube, is capable of two positions, according as she chooses the exit on the right or on the left. With each of the two positions of this first Osmia can be combined each of the two positions of the second, giving us, in all, 2 x 2 = (2 squared) arrangements. Each of these (2 squared) arrangements can be combined, in its turn, with each of the two positions of the third Osmia. We thus obtain 2 x 2 x 2 = (2 cubed) arrangements with three Osmiae; and so on, each additional insect multiplying the previous result by the factor 2. With n Osmiae, therefore, the total number of arrangements is (2 to the power n.)

But note that these arrangements are symmetrical, two by two: a given arrangement towards the right corresponds with a similar arrangement towards the left; and this symmetry implies equality, for, in the problem in hand, it is a matter of indifference whether a fixed arrangement correspond with the right or left of the tube. The previous number, therefore, must be divided by 2. Thus, n Osmiae, according as each of them turns her head to the right or left in my horizontal tube, are able to adopt (2 to the power n - 1) arrangements. If n = 10, as in my first experiment, the number of arrangements becomes (2 to the power 9) = 512.

Consequently, out of 512 ways which my ten insects can adopt for their outgoing position, there resulted one of those in which the symmetry was most striking. And observe that this was not an effect obtained by repeated attempts, by haphazard experiments. Each Osmia in the left half had bored to the left, without touching the partition on the right; each Osmia in the right half had bored to the right, without touching the partition on the left. The shape of the orifices and the surface condition of the partition showed this, if proof were necessary. There had been a spontaneous decision, one half in favour of the left, one half in favour of the right.

The arrangement presents another merit, one superior to that of symmetry: it has the merit of corresponding with the minimum expenditure of force. To admit of the exit of the whole series, if the string consists of n cells, there are originally n partitions to be perforated. There might even be one more, owing to a complication which I disregard. There are, I say, at least n partitions to be perforated. Whether each Osmia pierces her own, or whether the same Osmia pierces several, thus relieving her neighbours, does not matter to us: the sum-total of the force expended by the string of Bees will be in proportion to the number of those partitions, in whatever manner the exit be effected.

But there is another task which we must take seriously into consideration, because it is often more troublesome than the boring of the partition: I mean the work of clearing a road through the wreckage. Let us suppose the partitions pierced and the several chambers blocked by the resulting rubbish and by that rubbish only, since the horizontal position precludes any mixing of the contents of different chambers. To open a passage for itself through these rubbish-heaps, each insect will have the smallest effort to make if it passes through the smallest possible number of cells, in short, if it makes for the opening nearest to it. These smallest individual efforts amount, in the aggregate, to the smallest total effort. Therefore, by proceeding as they did in my experiment, the Osmiae effect their exit with the least expenditure of energy. It is curious to see an insect apply the 'principle of least action,' so often postulated in mechanics.

An arrangement which satisfies this principle, which conforms to the law of symmetry and which possesses but one chance in 512, is certainly no fortuitous result. It is determined by a cause; and, as this cause acts invariably, the same arrangement must be reproduced if I renew the experiment. I renewed it, therefore, in the years that followed, with as many appliances as I could find bramble-stumps; and, at each new test, I saw once more what I had seen with such interest on the first occasion. If the number be even--and my column at that time consisted usually of ten--one half goes out on the right, the other on the left. If the number be odd-- eleven, for instance--the Osmia in the middle goes out indiscriminately by the right or left exit. As the number of cells to be traversed is the same on both sides, her expenditure of energy does not vary with the direction of the exit; and the principle of least action is still observed.

It was important to discover if the Three-pronged Osmia shared her capacity, in the first place, with the other bramble-dwellers and, in the second, with Bees differently housed, but also destined laboriously to cut a new road for themselves when the hour comes to quit the nest. Well, apart from a few irregularities, due either to cocoons whose larva perished in my tubes before developing, or to those inexperienced workers, the males, the result was the same in the case of Anthidium scapulare. The insects divided themselves into two equal batches, one going to the right, the other to the left. Tripoxylon figulus left me undecided. This feeble insect is not capable of perforating my partitions; it nibbles at them a little; and I had to judge the direction from the marks of its mandibles. These marks, which are not always very plain, do not yet allow me to pronounce an opinion. Solenius vagus, who is a skilful borer, behaved differently from the Osmia. In a column of ten, the whole exodus was made in one direction.

On the other hand, I tested the Mason-bee of the Sheds, who, when emerging under natural conditions, has only to pierce her cement ceiling and is not confronted with a series of cells. Though a stranger to the environment which I created for her, she gave me a most positive answer. Of a column of ten laid in a horizontal tube open at both ends, five made their way to the right and five to the left. Dioxys cincta, a parasite in the buildings of both species of Mason-bees, the Chalicodoma of the Sheds and the Chalicodoma of the Walls (Cf. "The Mason-bees" by J. Henri Fabre, translated by Alexander Teixeira de Mattos: passim.--Translator's Note.), provided me with no precise result. The Leaf-cutting Bee (Megachile apicalis, SPIN. (Cf. Chapter 8 of the present volume.--Translator's Note.)), who builds her leafy cups in the old cells of the Chalicodoma of the Walls, acts like the Solenius and directs her whole column towards the same outlet.

Incomplete as it is, this symmetry shows us how unwise it were to generalize from the conclusions to which the Three-pronged Osmia leads us. Whereas some Bees, such as the Anthidium and the Chalicodoma, share the Osmia's talent for using the twofold exit, others, such as the Solenius and the Leaf-cutter, behave like a flock of sheep and follow the first that goes out. The entomological world is not all of a piece; its gifts are very various: what one is capable of doing another cannot do; and penetrating indeed would be the eyes that saw the causes of these differences. Be this as it may, increased research will certainly show us a larger number of species qualified to use the double outlet. For the moment, we know three; and that is enough for our purpose.

I will add that, when the horizontal tube has one of its ends closed, the whole string of Osmiae makes for the open end, turning round to do so, if need be.

Now that the facts are set forth, let us, if possible, trace the cause. In a horizontal tube, gravity no longer acts to determine the direction which the insect will take. Is it to attack the partition on the right or that on the left? How shall it decide? The more I look into the matter, the more do my suspicions fall upon the atmospheric influence which is felt through the two open ends. Of what does this influence consist? Is it an effect of pressure, of hygrometry, of electrical conditions, of properties that escape our coarser physical attunement? He were a bold man who should undertake to decide. Are not we ourselves, when the weather is about to alter, subject to subtle impressions, to sensations which we are unable to explain? And yet this vague sensitiveness to atmospheric changes would not be of much help to us in circumstances similar to those of my anchorites. Imagine ourselves in the darkness and the silence of a prison-cell, preceded and followed by other similar cells. We possess implements wherewith to pierce the walls; but where are we to strike to reach the final outlet and to reach it with the least delay? Atmospheric influence would certainly never guide us.

And yet it guides the insect. Feeble though it be, through the multiplicity of partitions, it is exercised on one side more than on the other, because the obstacles are fewer; and the insect, sensible to the difference between those two uncertainties, unhesitatingly attacks the partition which is nearer to the open air. Thus is decided the division of the column into two converse sections, which accomplish the total liberation with the least aggregate of work. In short, the Osmia and her rivals 'feel' the free space. This is yet one more sensory faculty which evolution might well have left us, for our greater advantage. As it has not done so, are we then really, as many contend, the highest expression of the progress accomplished, throughout the ages, by the first atom of glair expanded into a cell?

CHAPTER 2. THE OSMIAE.

February has its sunny days, heralding spring, to which rude winter will reluctantly yield place. In snug corners, among the rocks, the great spurge of our district, the characias of the Greeks, the jusclo of the Provencals, begins to lift its drooping inflorescence and discreetly opens a few sombre flowers. Here the first Midges of the year will come to slake their thirst. By the time that the tip of the stalks reaches the perpendicular, the worst of the cold weather will be over.

Another eager one, the almond-tree, risking the loss of its fruit, hastens to echo these preludes to the festival of the sun, preludes which are too often treacherous. A few days of soft skies and it becomes a glorious dome of white flowers, each twinkling with a roseate eye. The country, which still lacks green, seems dotted everywhere with white-satin pavilions. 'Twould be a callous heart indeed that could resist the magic of this awakening.

The insect nation is represented at these rites by a few of its more zealous members. There is first of all the Honey-bee, the sworn enemy of strikes, who profits by the least lull of winter to find out if some rosemary is not beginning to open somewhere near the hive. The droning of the busy swarm fills the flowery vault, while a snow of petals falls softly to the foot of the tree.

Together with the population of harvesters there mingles another, less numerous, of mere drinkers, whose nesting-time has not yet begun. This is the colony of the Osmiae, with their copper-coloured skin and bright-red fleece. Two species have come hurrying up to take part in the joys of the almond-tree: first, the Horned Osmia, clad in black velvet on the head and breast and in red velvet on the abdomen; and, a little later, the Three-horned Osmia, whose livery must be red and red only. These are the first delegates despatched by the pollen-gleaners to ascertain the state of the season and attend the festival of the early blooms. 'Tis but a moment since they burst their cocoon, the winter abode: they have left their retreats in the crevices of the old walls; should the north wind blow and set the almond-tree shivering, they will hasten to return to them. Hail to you, O my dear Osmiae, who yearly, from the far end of the harmas (The piece of waste ground in which the author studied his insects in their natural state. Cf. "The Life of the Fly" by J. Henri Fabre, translated by Alexander Teixeira de Mattos: chapter 1.--Translator's Note.), opposite snow-capped Ventoux (A mountain in the Provencal Alps, near Carpentras and Serignan, 6,271 feet.--Translator's Note.), bring me the first tidings of the awakening of the insect world! I am one of your friends; let us talk about you a little.

Most of the Osmiae of my region have none of the industry of their kinswomen of the brambles, that is to say, they do not themselves prepare the dwelling destined for the laying. They want ready-made lodgings, such as the old cells and old galleries of Anthophorae and Chalicodomae. If these favourite haunts are lacking, then a hiding-place in the wall, a round hole in some bit of wood, the tube of a reed, the spiral of a dead Snail under a heap of stones are adopted, according to the tastes of the several species. The retreat selected is divided into chambers by partition-walls, after which the entrance to the dwelling receives a massive seal. That is the sum-total of the building done.

For this plasterer's rather than mason's work, the Horned and the Three-horned Osmia employ soft earth. This material is different from the Mason-bee's cement, which will withstand wind and weather for many years on an exposed pebble; it is a sort of dried mud, which turns to pap on the addition of a drop of water. The Mason-bee gathers her cementing-dust in the most frequented and driest portions of the road; she wets it with a saliva which, in drying, gives it the consistency of stone. The two Osmiae who are the almond-tree's early visitors are no chemists: they know nothing of the making and mixing of hydraulic mortar; they limit themselves to gathering natural soaked earth, mud in short, which they allow to dry without any special preparation on their part; and so they need deep and well-sheltered retreats, into which the rain cannot penetrate, or the work would fall to pieces.

While exploiting, in friendly rivalry with the Three-horned Osmia, the galleries which the Mason-bee of the Sheds good-naturedly surrenders to both, Latreille's

Osmia uses different materials for her partitions and her doors. She chews the leaves of some mucilaginous plant, some mallow perhaps, and then prepares a sort of green putty with which she builds her partitions and finally closes the entrance to the dwelling. When she settles in the spacious cells of the Masked Anthophora (Anthophora personata, ILLIG.), the entrance to the gallery, which is wide enough to admit one's finger, is closed with a voluminous plug of this vegetable paste. On the earthy banks, hardened by the sun, the home is then betrayed by the gaudy colour of the lid. It is as though the authorities had closed the door and affixed to it their great seals of green wax.

So far then as their building-materials are concerned, the Osmiae whom I have been able to observe are divided into two classes: one building compartments with mud, the other with a green-tinted vegetable putty. The first section includes the Horned Osmia and the Three-horned Osmia, both so remarkable for the horny tubercles on their faces.

The great reed of the south, the Arundo donax, is often used, in the country, for rough garden-shelters against the mistral or just for fences. These reeds, the ends of which are chopped off to make them all the same length, are planted perpendicularly in the earth. I have often explored them in the hope of finding Osmia-nests. My search has very seldom succeeded. The failure is easily explained. The partitions and the closing-plug of the Horned and of the Three-horned Osmia are made, as we have seen, of a sort of mud which water instantly reduces to pap. With the upright position of the reeds, the stopper of the opening would receive the rain and would become diluted; the ceilings of the storeys would fall in and the family would perish by drowning. Therefore the Osmia, who knew of these drawbacks before I did, refuses the reeds when they are placed perpendicularly.

The same reed is used for a second purpose. We make canisses of it, that is to say, hurdles, which, in spring, serve for the rearing of silk-worms and, in autumn, for the drying of figs. At the end of April and during May, which is the time when the Osmiae work, the canisses are indoors, in the silk-worm nurseries, where the Bee cannot take possession of them; in autumn, they are outside, exposing their layers of figs and peeled peaches to the sun; but by that time the Osmiae have long disappeared. If, however, during the spring, an old, disused hurdle is left out of doors, in a horizontal position, the Three-horned Osmia often takes possession of it and makes use of the two ends, where the reeds lie truncated and open.

There are other quarters that suit the Three-horned Osmia, who is not particular, it seems to me, and will make shift with any hiding-place, so long as it has the requisite conditions of diameter, solidity, sanitation and kindly darkness. The most original dwellings that I know her to occupy are disused Snail-shells, especially the house of the Common Snail (Helix aspersa). Let us go to the slope of the hills thick with olive-trees and inspect the little supporting-walls which are built of dry stones and face the south. In the crevices of this insecure masonry, we shall reap a harvest of old Snail-shells, plugged with earth right up to the orifice. The family of the Three-horned Osmia is settled in the spiral of those shells, which is subdivided into chambers by mud partitions.

Let us inspect the stone-heaps, especially those which come from the quarry-works. Here we often find the Field-mouse sitting on a grass mattress, nibbling acorns, almonds, olive-stones and apricot-stones. The Rodent varies his diet: to oily and farinaceous foods he adds the Snail. When he is gone, he has left behind him, under the overhanging stones, mixed up with the remains of other victuals, an assortment of empty shells, sometimes plentiful enough to remind me of the heap of Snails which, cooked with spinach and eaten country-fashion on Christmas Eve, are flung away next day by the housewife. This gives the Three-horned Osmia a handsome collection of tenements; and she does not fail to profit by them. Then again, even if the Field-mouse's conchological museum be lacking, the same broken stones serve as a refuge for Garden-snails who come to live there and end by dying there. When we see Three-horned Osmiae enter the crevices of old walls and of stone-heaps, there is no doubt about their occupation: they are getting free lodgings out of the old Snail-shells of those labyrinths.

The Horned Osmia, who is less common, might easily also be less ingenious, that is to say, less rich in varieties of houses. She seems to scorn empty shells. The only homes that I know her to inhabit are the reeds of the hurdles and the deserted cells of the Masked Anthophora.

All the other Osmiae whose method of nest-building I know work with green putty, a paste made of some crushed leaf or other; and none of them, except Latreille's Osmia, is provided with the horned or tubercled armour of the mud-kneaders. I should like to know what plants are used in making the putty; probably each species has its own preferences and its little professional secrets; but hitherto observation has taught me nothing concerning these details. Whatever worker prepare it, the putty is very much the same in appearance. When fresh, it is always a clear dark green. Later, especially in the parts exposed to the air, it changes, no doubt through fermentation, to the colour of dead leaves, to brown, to dull-yellow; and the leafy character of its origin is no longer apparent. But uniformity in the materials employed must not lead us to believe in uniformity in the lodging; on the contrary, this lodging varies greatly with the different species, though there is a marked predilection in favour of empty shells. Thus Latreille's Osmia, together with the Three-horned Osmia, uses the spacious structures of the Mason-bee of the Sheds; she likes the magnificent cells of the Masked Anthophora; and she is always ready to establish herself in the cylinder of any reed lying flat on the ground.

I have already spoken of an Osmia (O. cyanoxantha, PEREZ) who elects to make her home in the old nests of the Mason-bee of the Pebbles. (Cf. "The Mason-bees": chapter 10.--Translator's Note.) Her closing-plug is made of a stout concrete, consisting of fair-sized bits of gravel sunk in the green paste; but for the inner partitions she employs only unalloyed putty. As the outer door, situated on the curve of an unprotected dome, is exposed to the inclemencies of the weather, the mother has to think of fortifying it. Danger, no doubt, is the originator of that gritty concrete.

The Golden Osmia (O. aurulenta, LATR.) absolutely insists on an empty Snail-shell as her residence. The Brown or Girdled Snail, the Garden Snail and especially the Common Snail, who has a more spacious spiral, all scattered at random in the grass, at the foot of the walls and of the sun-swept rocks, furnish her with her usual dwelling-house. Her dried putty is a kind of felt full of short white hairs. It must come from some hairy-leaved plant, one of the Boragineae perhaps, rich both in mucilage and the necessary bristles.

The Red Osmia (O. rufo-hirta, LATR.) has a weakness for the Brown Snail and the Garden Snail, in whose shells I find her taking refuge in April when the north-wind blows. I am not yet much acquainted with her work, which should resemble that of the Golden Osmia.

The Green Osmia (O. viridana, MORAWITZ) takes up her quarters, tiny creature that she is, in the spiral staircase of Bulimulus radiatus. It is a very elegant, but very small lodging, to say nothing of the fact that a considerable portion is taken up with the green-putty plug. There is just room for two.

The Andrenoid Osmia (O. andrenoides, LATR.), who looks so curious, with her naked red abdomen, appears to build her nest in the shell of the Common Snail, where I discover her refuged.

The Variegated Osmia (O. versicolor, LATR.) settles in the Garden Snail's shell, almost right at the bottom of the spiral.

The Blue Osmia (O. cyanea, KIRB.) seems to me to accept many different quarters. I have extracted her from old nests of the Mason-bee of the Pebbles, from the galleries dug in a roadside bank by the Colletes (A short-tongued Burrowing-bee known also as the Melitta.--Translator's Note.) and lastly from the cavities made by some digger or other in the decayed trunk of a willow-tree.

Morawitz' Osmia (O. Morawitzi, PEREZ) is not uncommon in the old nests of the Mason-bee of the Pebbles, but I suspect her of favouring other lodgings besides.

The Three-pronged Osmia (O. tridentata, DUF. and PER.) creates a home of her own, digging herself a channel with her mandibles in dry bramble and sometimes in danewort. It mixes a few scrapings of perforated pith with the green paste. Its habits are shared by the Ragged Osmia (O. detrita, PEREZ) and by the Tiny Osmia (O. parvula, DUF.)

The Chalicodoma works in broad daylight, on a tile, on a pebble, on a branch in the hedge; none of her trade-practises is kept a secret from the observer's curiosity. The Osmia loves mystery. She wants a dark retreat, hidden from the eye. I would like, nevertheless, to watch her in the privacy of her home and to witness her work with the same facility as if she were nest-building in the open air. Perhaps there are some interesting characteristics to be picked up in the depths of her retreats. It remains to be seen whether my wish can be realized.

When studying the insect's mental capacity, especially its very retentive memory for places, I was led to ask myself whether it would not be possible to make a suitably-chosen Bee build in any place that I wished, even in my study. And I wanted, for an experiment of this sort, not an individual but a numerous colony. My preference leant towards the Three-horned Osmia, who is very plentiful in my neighbourhood, where, together with Latreille's Osmia, she frequents in particular the monstrous nests of the Chalicodoma of the Sheds. I therefore thought out a scheme for making the Three-horned Osmia accept my study as her settlement and build her nests in glass tubes, through which I could easily watch the progress. To these crystal galleries, which might well inspire a certain distrust, were to be added more natural retreats: reeds of every length and thickness and disused Chalicodoma-cells taken from among the biggest and the smallest. A scheme like this sounds mad. I admit it, while mentioning that perhaps none ever succeeded so well with me. We shall see as much presently.

My method is extremely simple. All I ask is that the birth of my insects, that is to say, their first seeing the light, their emerging from the cocoon, should take place on the spot where I propose to make them settle. Here there must be retreats of no matter what nature, but of a shape similar to that in which the Osmia delights. The first impressions of sight, which are the most long-lived of any, shall bring back my insects to the place of their birth. And not only will the Osmiae return, through the always open windows, but they will always nidify on the natal spot if they find something like the necessary conditions.

And so, all through the winter, I collect Osmia-cocoons, picked up in the nests of the Mason-bee of the Sheds; I go to Carpentras to glean a more plentiful supply in the nests of the Hairy-footed Anthophora, that old acquaintance whose wonderful cities I used to undermine when I was studying the history of the Oil-beetles. (This study is not yet translated into English; but cf. "The Life of the Fly": chapters 2 and 4.--Translator's Note.) Later, at my request, a pupil and intimate friend of mine, M. Henri Devillario, president of the civil court at Carpentras, sends me a case of fragments broken off the banks frequented by the Hairy-footed Anthophora and the Anthophora of the Walls, useful clods which furnish a handsome adjunct to my collection. Indeed, at the end, I find myself with handfuls of cocoons of the Three-horned Osmia. To count them would weary my patience without serving any particular purpose.

I spread out my stock in a large open box on a table which receives a bright diffused light but not the direct rays of the sun. The table stands between two windows facing south and overlooking the garden. When the moment of hatching comes, those two windows will always remain open to give the swarm entire liberty to go in and out as it pleases. The glass tubes and the reed-stumps are laid here and there, in fine disorder, close to the heap of cocoons and all in a horizontal position, for the Osmia will have nothing to do with upright reeds. The hatching of some of the Osmiae will therefore take place under cover of the galleries destined to be the building-yard later; and the site will be all the more deeply impressed on their memory. When I have made these comprehensive arrangements, there is nothing more to be done; and I wait patiently for the building-season to open.

My Osmiae leave their cocoons in the second half of April. Under the immediate rays of the sun, in well-sheltered nooks, the hatching would occur a month earlier, as we can see from the mixed population of the snowy almond-tree. The constant shade in my study has delayed the awakening, without, however, making any change in the nesting-period, which synchronizes with the flowering of the thyme. We now have, around my working-table, my books, my jars and my various appliances, a buzzing crowd that goes in and out of the windows at every moment. I enjoin the household henceforth not to touch a thing in the insects' laboratory, to do no more sweeping, no more dusting. They might disturb the swarm and make it think that my hospitality was not to be trusted. I suspect that the maid, wounded in her self-esteem at seeing so much dust accumulating in the master's study, did not always respect my prohibitions and came in stealthily, now and again, to give a little sweep of the broom. At any rate, I came across a number of Osmiae who seemed to have been crushed under foot while taking a sunbath on the floor in front of the window. Perhaps it was I myself who committed the misdeed in a heedless moment. There is no great harm done, for the population is a numerous one; and, notwithstanding those crushed by inadvertence, notwithstanding the parasites wherewith many of the cocoons are infested, notwithstanding those who may have come to grief outside or been unable to find their way back, notwithstanding the deduction of one-half which we must make for the males: notwithstanding all this, during four or five weeks I witness the work of a number of Osmiae which is much too large to allow of my watching their individual operations. I content myself with a few, whom I mark with different-coloured spots to distinguish them; and I take no notice of the others, whose finished work will have my attention later.

The first to appear are the males. If the sun is bright, they flutter around the heap of tubes as if to take careful note of the locality; blows are exchanged and the rival swains indulge in mild skirmishing on the floor, then shake the dust off their wings and fly away. I find them, opposite my window, in the refreshment-bar of the lilac-bush, whose branches bend with the weight of their scented panicles. Here the Bees get drunk with sunshine and draughts of honey. Those who have had their fill come home and fly assiduously from tube to tube, placing their heads in the orifices to see if some female will at last make up her mind to emerge.

One does, in point of fact. She is covered with dust and has the disordered toilet that is inseparable from the hard work of the deliverance. A lover has seen her, so has a second, likewise a third. All crowd round her. The lady responds to their advances by clashing her mandibles, which open and shut rapidly, several times in succession. The suitors forthwith fall back; and they also, no doubt to keep up their dignity, execute savage mandibular grimaces. Then the beauty retires into the arbour and her wooers resume their places on the threshold. A fresh appearance of the female, who repeats the play with her jaws; a fresh retreat of the males, who do the best they can to flourish their own pincers. The Osmiae have a strange way of declaring their passion: with that fearsome gnashing of their mandibles, the lovers look as though they meant to devour each other. It suggests the thumps affected by our yokels in their moments of gallantry.

The ingenious idyll is soon over. By turns greeting and greeted with a clash of jaws, the female leaves her gallery and begins impassively to polish her wings. The rivals rush forward, hoist themselves on top of one another and form a pyramid of which each struggles to occupy the base by toppling over the favoured lover. He, however, is careful not to let go; he waits for the strife overhead to calm down; and, when the supernumeraries realize that they are wasting their time and throw up the game, the couple fly away far from the turbulent rivals. This is all that I have been able to gather about the Osmia's nuptials.

The females, who grow more numerous from day to day, inspect the premises; they buzz outside the glass galleries and the reed dwellings; they go in, stay for a while, come out, go in again and then fly away briskly into the garden. They return, first one, then another. They halt outside, in the sun, on the shutters fastened back against the wall; they hover in the window-recess, come inside, go to the reeds and give a glance at them, only to set off again and to return soon after. Thus do they learn to know their home, thus do they fix their birthplace in their memory. The village of our childhood is always a cherished spot, never to be effaced from our recollection. The Osmia's life endures for a month; and she acquires a lasting remembrance of her hamlet in a couple of days. 'Twas there that she was born; 'twas there that she loved; 'tis there that she will return. Dulces reminiscitur Argos. ('Now falling by another's wound, his eyes He casts to heaven, on Argos thinks and dies.'--"Aeneid," Book 10 Dryden's translation.)

At last each has made her choice. The work of construction begins; and my expectations are fulfilled far beyond my wishes. The Osmiae build nests in all the retreats which I have placed at their disposal. The glass tubes, which I cover with a sheet of paper to produce the shade and mystery favourable to concentrated toil, do wonderfully well. All, from first to last, are occupied. The Osmiae quarrel for the possession of these crystal palaces, hitherto unknown to their race. The reeds and the paper tubes likewise do wonderfully. The number provided is too small; and I hasten to increase it. Snail-shells are recognized as excellent abodes, though deprived of the shelter of the stone-heap; old Chalicodoma-nests, down to those of the Chalicodoma of the Shrubs (Cf. "The Mason-bees": chapters 4 and 10.--Translator's Note.), whose cells are so small, are eagerly occupied. The late-comers, finding nothing else free, go and settle in the locks of my table-drawers. There are daring ones who make their way into half-open boxes containing ends of glass tubes in which I have stored my most recent acquisitions: grubs, pupae and cocoons of all kinds, whose evolution I wished to study. Whenever these receptacles have an atom of free space, they claim the right to build there, whereas I formally oppose the claim. I hardly reckoned on such a success, which obliges me to put some order into the invasion with which I am threatened. I seal up the locks, I shut my boxes, I close my various receptacles for old nests, in short I remove from the building-yard any retreat of which I do not approve. And now, O my Osmiae, I leave you a free field!

The work begins with a thorough spring-cleaning of the home. Remnants of cocoons, dirt consisting of spoilt honey, bits of plaster from broken partitions, remains of dried Mollusc at the bottom of a shell: these and much other insanitary refuse must first of all disappear. Violently the Osmia tugs at the offending object and tears it out; and then off she goes, in a desperate hurry, to dispose of it far away from the study. They are all alike, these ardent sweepers: in their excessive zeal, they fear lest they should block up the place with a speck of dust which they might drop in front of the new house. The glass tubes, which I myself have rinsed under the tap, are not exempt from a scrupulous cleaning. The Osmia dusts them, brushes them thoroughly with her tarsi and then sweeps them out backwards. What does she pick up? Not a thing. It makes no difference: as a conscientious housewife, she gives the place a touch of the broom nevertheless.

Now for the provisions and the partition-walls. Here the order of the work changes according to the diameter of the cylinder. My glass tubes vary greatly in dimensions. The largest have an inner width of a dozen millimetres (Nearly half an inch.--Translator's Note.); the narrowest measure six or seven. (About a quarter of an inch.--Translator's Note.) In the latter, if the bottom suit her, the Osmia sets to work bringing pollen and honey. If the bottom do not suit her, if the sorghum-pith plug with which I have closed the rear-end of the tube be too irregular and badly-joined, the Bee coats it with a little mortar. When this small repair is made, the harvesting begins.

In the wider tubes, the work proceeds quite differently. At the moment when the Osmia disgorges her honey and especially at the moment when, with her hind-tarsi, she rubs the pollen-dust from her ventral brush, she needs a narrow aperture, just big enough to allow of her passage. I imagine that, in a straitened gallery, the rubbing of her whole body against the sides gives the harvester a support for her brushing-work. In a spacious cylinder, this support fails her; and the Osmia starts with creating one for herself, which she does by narrowing the channel. Whether it be to facilitate the storing of the victuals or for any other reason, the fact remains that the Osmia housed in a wide tube begins with the partitioning.

Her division is made by a dab of clay placed at right angles to the axis of the cylinder, at a distance from the bottom determined by the ordinary length of a cell. This wad is not a complete round; it is more crescent-shaped, leaving a circular space between it and one side of the tube. Fresh layers are swiftly added to the dab of clay; and soon the tube is divided by a partition which has a circular opening at the side of it, a sort of dog-hole through which the Osmia will proceed to knead the Bee-bread. When the victualling is finished and the egg laid upon the heap, the hole is closed and the filled-up partition becomes the bottom of the next cell. Then the same method is repeated, that is to say, in front of the just completed ceiling a second partition is built, again with a side-passage, which is stouter, owing to its distance from the centre, and better able to withstand the numerous comings and goings of the housewife than a central orifice, deprived of the direct support of the wall, could hope to be. When this partition is ready, the provisioning of the second cell is effected; and so on until the wide cylinder is completely stocked.

The building of this preliminary party-wall, with a narrow, round dog-hole, for a chamber to which the victuals will not be brought until later is not restricted to the Three-horned Osmia; it is also frequently found in the case of the Horned Osmia and of Latreille's Osmia. Nothing could be prettier than the work of the last-named, who goes to the plants for her material and fashions a delicate sheet in which she cuts a graceful arch. The Chinaman partitions his house with paper screens; Latreille's Osmia divides hers with disks of thin green cardboard perforated with a serving-hatch which remains until the room is completely furnished. When we have no glass houses at our disposal, we can see these little architectural refinements in the reeds of the hurdles, if we open them at the right season.

By splitting the bramble-stumps in the course of July, we perceive also that the Three-pronged Osmia, notwithstanding her narrow gallery, follows the same practice as Latreille's Osmia, with a difference. She does not build a party-wall, which the diameter of the cylinder would not permit; she confines herself to putting up a frail circular pad of green putty, as though to limit, before any attempt at harvesting, the space to be occupied by the Bee-bread, whose depth could not be calculated afterwards if the insect did not first mark out its confines. Can there really be an act of measuring? That would be superlatively clever. Let us consult the Three-horned Osmia in her glass tubes.

The Osmia is working at her big partition, with her body outside the cell which she is preparing. From time to time, with a pellet of mortar in her mandibles, she goes in and touches the previous ceiling with her forehead, while the tip of her abdomen quivers and feels the pad in course of construction. One might well say that she is using the length of her body as a measure, in order to fix the next ceiling at the proper distance. Then she resumes her work. Perhaps the measure was not correctly taken; perhaps her memory, a few seconds old, has already become muddled. The Bee once more ceases laying her plaster and again goes and touches the front wall with her forehead and the back wall with the tip of her abdomen. Looking at that body trembling with eagerness, extended to its full length to touch the two ends of the room, how can we fail to grasp the architect's grave problem? The Osmia is measuring; and her measure is her body. Has she quite done, this time? Oh dear no! Ten times, twenty times, at every moment, for the least particle of mortar which she lays, she repeats her mensuration, never being quite certain that her trowel is going just where it should.

Meanwhile, amid these frequent interruptions, the work progresses and the partition gains in width. The worker is bent into a hook, with her mandibles on the inner surface of the wall and the tip of her abdomen on the outer surface. The soft masonry stands between the two points of purchase. The insect thus forms a sort of rolling-press, in which the mud wall is flattened and shaped. The mandibles tap and furnish mortar; the end of the abdomen also pats and gives brisk trowel-touches. This anal extremity is a builder's tool; I see it facing the mandibles on the other side of the partition, kneading and smoothing it all over, flattening the little lump of clay. It is a singular implement, which I should never have expected to see used for this purpose. It takes an insect to conceive such an original idea, to do mason's work with its behind! During this curious performance, the only function of the legs is to keep the worker steady by spreading out and clinging to the walls of the tunnel.

The partition with the hole in it is finished. Let us go back to the measuring of which the Osmia was so lavish. What a magnificent argument in favour of the reasoning-power of animals! To find geometry, the surveyor's art, in an Osmia's tiny brain! An insect that begins by taking the measurements of the room to be constructed, just as any master-builder might do! Why, it's splendid, it's enough to cover with confusion those horrible sceptics who persist in refusing to admit the animal's 'continuous little flashes of atoms of reason!'

O common-sense, veil your face! It is with this gibberish about continuous flashes of atoms of reason that men pretend to build up science to-day! Very well, my masters; the magnificent argument with which I am supplying you lacks but one little detail, the merest trifle: truth! Not that I have not seen and plainly seen all that I am relating; but measuring has nothing to do with the case. And I can prove it by facts.

If, in order to see the Osmia's nest as a whole, we split a reed lengthwise, taking care not to disturb its contents; or, better still, if we select for examination the string of cells built in a glass tube, we are forthwith struck by one detail, namely, the uneven distances between the partitions, which are placed almost at right angles to the axis of the cylinder. It is these distances which fix the size of the chambers, which, with a similar base, have different heights and consequently unequal holding-capacities. The bottom partitions, the oldest, are farther apart; those of the front part, near the orifice, are closer together. Moreover, the provisions are plentiful in the loftier cells, whereas they are niggardly and reduced to one-half or even one-third in the cells of lesser height.

Here are a few examples of these inequalities. A glass tube with a diameter of 12 millimetres (.468 inch.--Translator's Note.), inside measurement, contains ten cells. The five lower ones, beginning with the bottom-most, have as the respective distances between their partitions, in millimetres:

11, 12, 16, 13, 11. (.429,.468,.624,.507,.429 inch.--Translator's Note.)

The five upper ones measure between their partitions:

7, 7, 5, 6, 7. (.273,.273,.195,.234,.273 inch.--Translator's Note.)

A reed-stump 11 millimetres (.429 inch.--Translator's Note.) across the inside contains fifteen cells; and the respective distances between the partitions of those cells, starting from the bottom, are:

13, 12, 12, 9, 9, 11, 8, 8, 7, 7, 7, 6, 6, 6, 7. (.507,.468,.468, .351,.351,.429,.312,.312,.273,.273,.273,.234,.234,.234, .273 inch.--Translator's Note.)

When the diameter of the tunnel is less, the partitions can be still further apart, though they retain the general characteristic of being closer to one another the nearer they are to the orifice. A reed of five millimetres (.195 inch.--Translator's Note.) in diameter, gives me the following distances, always starting from the bottom:

22, 22, 20, 20, 12, 14. (.858,.858,.78,.78,.468,.546 inch.--Translator's Note.)

Another, of 9 millimetres (.351 inch.--Translator's Note.), gives me:

15, 14, 11, 10, 10, 9, 10. (.585,.546,.429,.39,.39,.351,.39 inch.--Translator's Note.)

A glass tube of 8 millimetres (.312 inch.--Translator's Note.) yields:

15, 14, 20, 10, 10, 10. (.585,.546,.78,.39,.39,.39 inch.--Translator's Note.).

I could fill pages and pages with such figures, if I cared to print all my notes. Do they prove that the Osmia is a geometrician, employing a strict measure based on the length of her body? Certainly not, because many of those figures exceed the length of the insect; because sometimes a higher number follows suddenly upon a lower; because the same string contains a figure of one value and another figure of but half that value. They prove only one thing: the marked tendency of the insect to shorten the distance between the party-walls as the work proceeds. We shall see later that the large cells are destined for the females and the small ones for the males.

Is there not at least a measuring adapted to each sex? Again, not so; for in the first series, where the females are housed, instead of the interval of 11 millimetres, which occurs at the beginning and the end, we find, in the middle of the series, an interval of 16 millimetres, while in the second series, reserved for the males, instead of the interval of 7 millimetres at the beginning and the end, we have an interval of 5 millimetres in the middle. It is the same with the other series, each of which shows a striking discrepancy in its figures. If the Osmia really studied the dimensions of her chambers and measured them with the compasses of her body, how could she, with her delicate mechanism, fail to notice mistakes of 5 millimetres, almost half her own length?

Besides, all idea of geometry vanishes if we consider the work in a tube of moderate width. Here, the Osmia does not fix the front partition in advance; she does not even lay its foundation. Without any boundary-pad, with no guiding mark for the capacity of the cell, she busies herself straightway with the provisioning. When the heap of Bee-bread is judged sufficient, that is, I imagine, when her tired body tells her that she has done enough harvesting, she closes up the chamber. In this case, there is no measuring; and yet the capacity of the cell and the quantity of the victuals fulfil the regular requirements of one or the other sex.

Then what does the Osmia do when she repeatedly stops to touch the front partition with her forehead and the back partition, the one in the course of building, with the tip of her abdomen? I have no idea what she does or what she has in view. I leave the interpretation of this performance to others, more venturesome than I. Plenty of theories are based on equally shaky foundations. Blow on them and they sink into the quagmire of oblivion.

The laying is finished, or perhaps the cylinder is full. A final partition closes the last cell. A rampart is now built, at the orifice of the tube itself, to forbid the ill-disposed all access to the home. This is a thick plug, a massy work of fortification, whereon the Osmia spends enough mortar to partition off any number of cells. A whole day is not too long for making this barricade, especially in view of the minute finishing-touches, when the Osmia fills up with putty every chink through which the least atom could slip. The mason completing a wall smooths his plaster and brings it to a fine surface while it is still wet; the Osmia does the same, or almost. With little taps of the mandibles and a continual shaking of her head, a sign of her zest for the work, she smooths and polishes the surface of the lid for hours at a time. After such pains, what foe could visit the dwelling?

And yet there is one, an Anthrax, A. sinuata (Cf. "The Life of the Fly": chapters 2 and 4.--Translator's Note.), who will come later on, in the height of summer, and succeed, invisible bit of thread that she is, in making her way to the grub through the thickness of the door and the web of the cocoon. In many cells, mischief of another kind has already been done. During the progress of the works, an impudent Midge, one of the Tachina-flies, who feeds her family on the victuals amassed by the Bee, hovers in front of the galleries. Does she penetrate to the cells and lay her eggs there in the mother's absence? I could never catch the sneak in the act. Does she, like that other Tachina who ravages cells stocked with game (The cells of the Hunting Wasps.--Translator's Note.), nimbly deposit her eggs on the Osmia's harvest at the moment when the Bee is going indoors? It is possible, though I cannot say for certain. The fact remains that we soon see the Midge's grub-worms swarming around the larva, the daughter of the house. There are ten, fifteen, twenty or more of them gnawing with their pointed mouths at the common dish and turning the food into a heap of fine, orange-coloured vermicelli. The Bee's grub dies of starvation. It is life, life in all its ferocity even in these tiny creatures. What an expenditure of ardent labour, of delicate cares, of wise precautions, to arrive at...what? Her offspring sucked and drained dry by the hateful Anthrax; her family sweated and starved by the infernal Tachina.

The victuals consist mostly of yellow flour. In the centre of the heap, a little honey is disgorged, which turns the pollen-dust into a firm, reddish paste. On this paste the egg is laid, not flat, but upright, with the fore-end free and the hind-end lightly held and fixed in the plastic mass. When hatched, the young grub, kept in its place by its rear-end, need only bend its neck a little to find the honey-soaked paste under its mouth. When it grows stronger, it will release itself from its support and eat up the surrounding flour.

All this is touching, in its maternal logic. For the new-born, dainty bread-and-honey; for the adolescent, dry bread. In cases where the provisions are all of a kind, these delicate precautions are superfluous. The victuals of the Anthophorae and the Chalicodomae consist of flowing honey, the same throughout. The egg is then laid at full length on the surface, without any particular arrangement, thus compelling the new-born grub to take its first mouthfuls at random. This has no drawback, as the food is of the same quality throughout. But, with the Osmia's provisions--dry powder on the edges, jam in the centre--the grub would be in danger if its first meal were not regulated in advance. To begin with pollen not seasoned with honey would be fatal to its stomach. Having no choice of its mouthfuls because of its immobility and being obliged to feed on the spot where it was hatched, the young grub must needs be born on the central mass, where it has only to bend its head a little way in order to find what its delicate stomach calls for. The place of the egg, therefore, fixed upright by its base in the middle of the red jam, is most judiciously chosen. What a contrast between this exquisite maternal forethought and the horrible destruction by the Anthrax and the Midge!

The egg is rather large for the size of the Osmia. It is cylindrical, slightly curved, rounded at both ends and transparent. It soon becomes cloudy, while remaining diaphanous at each extremity. Fine lines, hardly perceptible to the most penetrating lens, show themselves in transverse circles. These are the first signs of segmentation. A contraction appears in the front hyaline part, marking the head. An extremely thin opaque thread runs down either side. This is the cord of tracheae communicating between one breathing-hole and another. At last, the segments show distinctly, with their lateral pads. The grub is born.

At first, one would think that there was no hatching in the proper sense of the word--that is to say, no bursting and casting of a wrapper. The most minute attention is necessary to show that appearances are deceptive and that actually a fine membrane is thrown off from front to back. This infinitesimal shred is the shell of the egg.

The grub is born. Fixed by its base, it curves into an arc and bends its head, until now held erect, down to the red mass. The meal begins. Soon a yellow cord occupying the front two-thirds of the body proclaims that the digestive apparatus is swelling out with food. For a fortnight, consume your provender in peace, my child; then spin your cocoon: you are now safe from the Tachina! Shall you be safe from the Anthrax' sucker later on? Alack!

CHAPTER 3. THE DISTRIBUTION OF THE SEXES.

Does the insect know beforehand the sex of the egg which it is about to lay? When examining the stock of food in the cells just now, we began to suspect that it does, for each little heap of provisions is carefully proportioned to the needs at one time of a male and at another of a female. What we have to do is to turn this suspicion into a certainty demonstrated by experiment. And first let us find out how the sexes are arranged.

It is not possible to ascertain the chronological order of a laying, except by going to suitably-chosen species. Digging up the burrows of Cerceris-, Bembex- or Philanthus-wasps will never tell us that this grub has taken precedence of that in point of time nor enable us to decide whether one cocoon in a colony belongs to the same family as another. To compile a register of births is absolutely impossible here. Fortunately there are a few species in which we do not find this difficulty: these are the Bees who keep to one gallery and build their cells in storeys. Among the number are the different inhabitants of the bramble-stumps, notably the Three-pronged Osmiae, who form an excellent subject for observation, partly because they are of imposing-size--bigger than any other bramble-dwellers in my neighbourhood--partly because they are so plentiful.

Let us briefly recall the Osmia's habits. Amid the tangle of a hedge, a bramble-stalk is selected, still standing, but a mere withered stump. In this the insect digs a more or less deep tunnel, an easy piece of work owing to the abundance of soft pith. Provisions are heaped up right at the bottom of the tunnel and an egg is laid on the surface of the food: that is the first-born of the family. At a height of some twelve millimetres (About half an inch.--Translator's Note.), a partition is fixed, formed of bramble saw-dust and of a green paste obtained by masticating particles of the leaves of some plant that has not yet been identified. This gives a second storey, which in its turn receives provisions and an egg, the second in order of primogeniture. And so it goes on, storey by storey, until the cylinder is full. Then a thick plug of the same green material of which the partitions are formed closes the home and keeps out marauders.

In this common cradle, the chronological order of births is perfectly clear. The first-born of the family is at the bottom of the series; the last-born is at the top, near the closed door. The others follow from bottom to top in the same order in which they followed in point of time. The laying is numbered automatically; each cocoon tells us its respective age by the place which it occupies.

To know the sexes, we must wait for the month of June. But it would be unwise to postpone our investigations until that period. Osmia-nests are not so common that we can hope to pick one up each time that we go out with that object; besides, if we wait for the hatching-period before examining the brambles, it may happen that the order has been disturbed through some insects' having tried to make their escape as soon as possible after bursting their cocoons; it may happen that the male Osmiae, who are more forward than the females, are already gone. I therefore set to work a long time beforehand and devote my leisure in winter to these investigations.

The bramble-sticks are split and the cocoons taken out one by one and methodically transferred to glass tubes, of approximately the same diameter as the native cylinder. These cocoons are arranged one on top of the other in exactly the same order that they occupied in the bramble; they are separated from one another by a cotton plug, an insuperable obstacle to the future insect. There is thus no fear that the contents of the cells may become mixed or transposed; and I am saved the trouble of keeping a laborious watch. Each insect can hatch at its own time, in my presence or not: I am sure of always finding it in its place, in its proper order, held fast fore and aft by the cotton barrier. A cork or sorghum-pith partition would not fulfil the same purpose: the insect would perforate it and the register of births would be muddled by changes of position. Any reader wishing to undertake similar investigations will excuse these practical details, which may facilitate his work.

We do not often come upon complete series, comprising the whole laying, from the first-born to the youngest. As a rule, we find part of a laying, in which the number of cocoons varies greatly, sometimes falling as low as two, or even one. The mother has not deemed it advisable to confide her whole family to a single bramble-stump; in order to make the exit less toilsome, or else for reasons which escape me, she has left the first home and elected to make a second home, perhaps a third or more.

We also find series with breaks in them. Sometimes, in cells distributed at random, the egg has not developed and the provisions have remained untouched, but mildewed; sometimes, the larva has died before spinning its cocoon, or after spinning it. Lastly, there are parasites, such as the Unarmed Zonitis (Zonitis mutica, one of the Oil-beetles.--Translator's Note.) and the Spotted Sapyga (A Digger-wasp.--Translator's Note.), who interrupt the series by substituting themselves for the original occupant. All these disturbing factors make it necessary to examine a large number of nests of the Three-pronged Osmia, if we would obtain a definite result.

I have been studying the bramble-dwellers for seven or eight years and I could not say how many strings of cocoons have passed through my hands. During a recent winter, in view particularly of the distribution of the sexes, I collected some forty of this Osmia's nests, transferred their contents into glass tubes and made a careful summary of the sexes. I give some of my results. The figures start in their order from the bottom of the tunnel dug in the bramble and proceed upwards to the orifice. The figure 1 therefore denotes the first-born of the series, the oldest in date; the highest figure denotes the last-born. The letter M, placed under the corresponding figure, represents the male and the letter F the female sex.

1 2 3 4 5 6 7 8 9 10 11 12 13 14 15 F F M F M F M M F F F F M F M

This is the longest series that I have ever been able to procure. It is also complete, inasmuch as it comprises the entire laying of the Osmia. My statement requires explaining, otherwise it would seem impossible to know whether a mother whose acts one has not watched, nay more, whom one has never seen, has or has not finished laying her eggs. The bramble-stump under consideration leaves a free space of nearly four inches above the continuous string of cocoons. Beyond it, at the actual orifice, is the terminal stopper, the thick plug which closes the entrance to the gallery. In this empty portion of the tunnel there is ample accommodation for numerous cocoons. The fact that the mother has not made use of it proves that her ovaries were exhausted; for it is exceedingly unlikely that she has abandoned first-rate lodgings to go laboriously digging a new gallery elsewhere and there continue her laying.

You may say that, if the unoccupied space marks the end of the laying, nothing tells us that the beginning is actually at the bottom of the cul-de-sac, at the other end of the tunnel. You may also say that the laying is done in shifts, separated by intervals of rest. The space left empty in the channel would mean that one of these shifts was finished and not that there were no more eggs ripe for hatching. In answer to these very plausible explanations, I will say that, the sum of my observations-- and they have been extremely numerous--is that the total number of eggs laid not only by the Osmiae but by a host of other Bees fluctuates round about fifteen.

Besides, when we consider that the active life of these insects lasts hardly a month; when we remember that this period of activity is disturbed by dark, rainy or very windy days, during which all work is suspended; when lastly we ascertain, as I have done ad nauseam in the case of the Three-horned Osmia, the time required for building and victualling a cell, it becomes obvious that the total laying must be kept within narrow bounds and that the mother has no time to lose if she wishes to get fifteen cells satisfactorily built in three or four weeks interrupted by compulsory rests. I shall give some facts later which will dispel your doubts, if any remain.

I assume, therefore, that a number of eggs bordering on fifteen represents the entire family of an Osmia, as it does of many other Bees.

Let us consult some other complete series. Here are two:

1 2 3 4 5 6 7 8 9 10 11 12 13 F F M F M F M F M F F F F M F F M F F F M F F M F M

In both cases, the laying is taken as complete, for the same reasons as above.

We will end with some series that appear to me incomplete, in view of the small number of cells and the absence of any free space above the pile of cocoons:

1 2 3 4 5 6 7 8 M M F M M M M M M M F M F M M M F M F F M M M M F M F F F F M M M F M

These examples are more than sufficient. It is quite evident that the distribution of the sexes is not governed by any rule. All that I can say on consulting the whole of my notes, which contain a good many instances of complete layings-- most of them, unfortunately, spoilt through gaps caused by parasites, the death of the larva, the failure of the egg to hatch and other accidents--all that I can say in general is that the complete series begins with females and nearly always ends with males. The incomplete series can teach us nothing in this respect, for they are only fragments starting we know not whence; and it is impossible to tell whether they should be ascribed to the beginning, to the end, or to an intermediate period of the laying. To sum up: in the laying of the Three-pronged Osmia, no order governs the succession of the sexes; only, the series has a marked tendency to begin with females and to finish with males.

The brambles, in my district, harbour two other Osmiae, both of much smaller size: O. detrita, PEREZ, and O. parvula, DUF. The first is very common, the second very rare; and until now I have found only one of her nests, placed above a nest of O. detrita, in the same bramble. Here, instead of the lack of order in the distribution of the sexes which we find with O. tridentata, we have an order remarkable for consistency and simplicity. I have before me the list of the series of O. detrita collected last winter. Here are some of them:

1. A series of twelve: seven females, beginning with the bottom of the tunnel, and then five males.

2. A series of nine: three females first, then six males.

3. A series of eight: five females followed by three males.

4. A series of eight: seven females followed by one male.

5. A series of eight: one female followed by seven males.

6. A series of seven: six females followed by one male.

The first series might very well be complete. The second and fifth appear to be the end of layings, of which the beginning has taken place elsewhere, in another bramble-stump. The males predominate and finish off the series. Nos. 3, 4 and 6, on the other hand, look like the beginnings of layings: the females predominate and are at the head of the series. Even if these interpretations should be open to doubt, one result at least is certain: with O. detrita, the laying is divided into two groups, with no intermingling of the sexes; the first group laid yields nothing but females, the second, or more recent, yields nothing but males.

What was only a sort of attempt with the Three-pronged Osmia--who, it is true, begins with females and ends with males, but muddles up the order and mixes the two sexes anyhow between the extreme points--becomes a regular law with her kinswoman. The mother occupies herself at the start with the stronger sex, the more necessary, the better-gifted, the female sex, to which she devotes the first flush of her laying and the fullness of her vigour; later, when she is perhaps already at the end of her strength, she bestows what remains of her maternal solicitude upon the weaker sex, the less-gifted, almost negligible male sex.

O. parvula, of whom I unfortunately possess but one series, repeats what the previous witness has just shown us. This series, one of nine cocoons, comprises five females followed by four males, without any mixing of the sexes.

Next to these disgorgers of honey and gleaners of pollen-dust, it would be well to consult other Hymenoptera, Wasps who devote themselves to the chase and pile their cells one after the other, in a row, showing the relative age of the cocoons. The brambles house several of these: Solenius vagus, who stores up Flies; Psen atratus, who provides her grubs with a heap of Plant-lice; Trypoxylon figulus, who feeds them with Spiders.

Solenius vagus digs her gallery in a bramble-stick that is lopped short, but still fresh and green. The house of this Fly-huntress, therefore, suffers from damp, as the sap enters, especially on the lower floors. This seems to me rather insanitary. To avoid the humidity, or for other reasons which escape me, the Solenius does not dig very far into her bramble-stump and consequently can stack but a small number of cells in it. A series of five cocoons gives me first four females and then one male; another series, also of five, contains first three females, with two males following. These are the most complete that I have for the moment.

I reckoned on the Black Psen, or Psen atratus, whose series are pretty long; it is a pity that they are nearly always greatly interfered with by a parasite called Ephialtes mediator. (Cf. "The Life of the Fly": chapter 2.--Translator's Note.) I obtained only three series free from gaps: one of eight cocoons, comprising only females; one of six, likewise consisting wholly of females; lastly, one of eight, formed exclusively of males. These instances seem to show that the Psen arranges her laying in a succession of females and a succession of males; but they tell us nothing of the relative order of the two series.

From the Spider-huntress, Trypoxylon figulus, I learnt nothing decisive. She appeared to me to rove about from one bramble to the next, utilizing galleries which she has not dug herself. Not troubling to be economical with a lodging which it has cost her nothing to acquire, she carelessly builds a few partitions at very unequal heights, stuffs three or four compartments with Spiders and passes on to another bramble-stump, with no reason, so far as I know, for abandoning the first. Her cells, therefore, occur in series that are too short to give us any useful information.

This is all that the bramble-dwellers have to tell us; I have enumerated the list of the principal ones in my district. We will now look into some other Bees who arrange their cocoons in single files: the Megachiles (Cf. Chapter 8 of the present volume.--Translator's Note.), who cut disks out of leaves and fashion the disks into thimble-shaped receptacles; the Anthidia (Cf. Chapters 9 and 10 of the present volume.--Translator's Note.), who weave their honey-wallets out of cotton-wool and arrange their cells one after the other in some cylindrical gallery. In most cases, the home is the produce of neither the one nor the other. A tunnel in the upright, earthy banks, the old work of some Anthophora, is the usual dwelling. There is no great depth to these retreats; and all my searches, zealously prosecuted during a number of winters, procured me only series containing a small number of cocoons, four or five at most, often one alone. And, what is quite as serious, nearly all these series are spoilt by parasites and allow me to draw no well-founded deductions.

I remembered finding, at rare intervals, nests of both the Anthidium and the Megachile in the hollows of cut reeds. I thereupon installed some hives of a new kind on the sunniest walls of my enclosure. They consisted of stumps of the great reed of the south, open at one end, closed at the other by the natural knot and gathered into a sort of enormous pan-pipe, such as Polyphemus might have employed. The invitation was accepted: Osmiae, Anthidia and Megachiles came in fairly large numbers, especially the first, to benefit by the queer installation.

In this way I obtained some magnificent series of Anthidia and Megachiles, running up to a dozen. There was a melancholy side to this success. All my series, with not one exception, were ravaged by parasites. Those of the Megachile (M. sericans, FONSCOL), who fashions her goblets with robinia-, holm-, and terebinth-leaves, were inhabited by Coelioxys octodentata (A Parasitic Bee.--Translator's Note.); those of the Anthidium (A. florentinum, LATR.) were occupied by a Leucopsis. Both kinds were swarming with a colony of pigmy parasites whose name I have not yet been able to discover. In short, my pan-pipe hives, though very useful to me from other points of view, taught me nothing about the order of the sexes among the Leaf-cutters and the cotton-weavers.

I was more fortunate with three Osmiae (O. tricornis, LATR., O. cornuta,

LATR., and O. Latreillii, SPIN.), all of whom gave me splendid results, with reed-stumps arranged either against the walls of my garden, as I have just said, or near their customary abode, the huge nests of the Mason-bee of the Sheds. One of them, the Three-horned Osmia, did better still: as I have described, she built her nests in my study, as plentifully as I could wish, using reeds, glass tubes and other retreats of my selecting for her galleries.

We will consult this last, who has furnished me with documents beyond my fondest hopes, and begin by asking her of how many eggs her average laying consists. Of the whole heap of colonized tubes in my study, or else out of doors, in the hurdle-reeds and the pan-pipe appliances, the best-filled contains fifteen cells, with a free space above the series, a space showing that the laying is ended, for, if the mother had any more eggs available, she would have lodged them in the room which she leaves unoccupied. This string of fifteen appears to be rare; it was the only one that I found. My attempts at indoor rearing, pursued during two years with glass tubes or reeds, taught me that the Three-horned Osmia is not much addicted to long series. As though to decrease the difficulties of the coming deliverance, she prefers short galleries, in which only a part of the laying is stacked. We must then follow the same mother in her migration from one dwelling to the next if we would obtain a complete census of her family. A spot of colour, dropped on the Bee's thorax with a paint-brush while she is absorbed in closing up the mouth of the tunnel, enables us to recognize the Osmia in her various homes.

In this way, the swarm that resided in my study furnished me, in the first year, with an average of twelve cells. Next year, the summer appeared to be more favourable and the average became rather higher, reaching fifteen. The most numerous laying performed under my eyes, not in a tube, but in a succession of Snail-shells, reached the figure of twenty-six. On the other hand, layings of between eight and ten are not uncommon. Lastly, taking all my records together, the result is that the family of the Osmia fluctuates round about fifteen in number.

I have already spoken of the great differences in size apparent in the cells of one and the same series. The partitions, at first widely spaced, draw gradually nearer to one another as they come closer to the aperture, which implies roomy cells at the back and narrow cells in front. The contents of these compartments are no less uneven between one portion and another of the string. Without any exception known to me, the large cells, those with which the series starts, have more abundant provisions than the straitened cells with which the series ends. The heap of honey and pollen in the first is twice or even thrice as large as that in the second. In the last cells, the most recent in date, the victuals are but a pinch of pollen, so niggardly in amount that we wonder what will become of the larva with that meagre ration.

One would think that the Osmia, when nearing the end of the laying, attaches no importance to her last-born, to whom she doles out space and food so sparingly. The first-born receive the benefit of her early enthusiasm: theirs is the well-spread table, theirs the spacious apartments. The work has begun to pall by the time that the last eggs are laid; and the last-comers have to put up with a scurvy portion of food and a tiny corner.

The difference shows itself in another way after the cocoons are spun. The large cells, those at the back, receive the bulky cocoons; the small ones, those in front, have cocoons only a half or a third as big. Before opening them and ascertaining the sex of the Osmia inside, let us wait for the transformation into the perfect insect, which will take place towards the end of summer. If impatience gets the better of us, we can open them at the end of July or in August. The insect is then in the nymphal stage; and it is easy, under this form, to distinguish the two sexes by the length of the antennae, which are larger in the males, and by the glassy protuberances on the forehead, the sign of the future armour of the females. Well, the small cocoons, those in the narrow front cells, with their scanty store of provisions, all belong to males; the big cocoons, those in the spacious and well-stocked cells at the back, all belong to females.

The conclusion is definite: the laying of the Three-horned Osmia consists of two distinct groups, first a group of females and then a group of males.

With my pan-pipe apparatus displayed on the walls of my enclosure and with old hurdle-reeds left lying flat out of doors, I obtained the Horned Osmia in fair quantities. I persuaded Latreille's Osmia to build her nest in reeds, which she did with a zeal which I was far from expecting. All that I had to do was to lay some reed-stumps horizontally within her reach, in the immediate neighbourhood of her usual haunts, namely, the nests of the Mason-bee of the Sheds. Lastly, I succeeded without difficulty in making her build her nests in the privacy of my study, with glass tubes for a house. The result surpassed my hopes.

With both these Osmiae, the division of the gallery is the same as with the Three-horned Osmia. At the back are large cells with plentiful provisions and widely-spaced partitions; in front, small cells, with scanty provisions and partitions close together. Also, the larger cells supplied me with big cocoons and females; the smaller cells gave me little cocoons and males. The conclusion therefore is exactly the same in the case of all three Osmiae.

Before dismissing the Osmiae, let us devote a moment to their cocoons, a comparison of which, in the matter of bulk, will furnish us with fairly accurate evidence as to the relative size of the two sexes, for the thing contained, the perfect insect, is evidently proportionate to the silken wrapper in which it is enclosed. These cocoons are oval-shaped and may be regarded as ellipsoids formed by a revolution around the major axis. The volume of one of these solids is expressed in the following formula:

4 / 3 x pi x a x (b squared),

in which 2a is the major axis and 2b the minor axis.

Now, the average dimensions of the cocoons of the Three-horned Osmia are as follows:

2a = 13 mm. (.507 inch.--Translator's Note.), 2b = 7 mm. (.273 inch.--Translator's Note.) in the females;

2a = 9 mm. (.351 inch.--Translator's Note.), 2b = 5 mm. (.195 inch.--Translator's Note.) in the males.

The ratio therefore between 13 x 7 x 7 = 637 and 9 x 5 x 5 = 225 will be more or less the ratio between the sizes of the two sexes. This ratio is somewhere between 2 to 1 and 3 to 1. The females therefore are two or three times larger than the males, a proportion already suggested by a comparison of the mass of provisions, estimated simply by the eye.

The Horned Osmia gives us the following average dimensions:

2a = 15 mm. (.585 inch.--Translator's Note.), 2b = 9 mm. (.351 inch.--Translator's Note.) in the females;

2a = 12 mm. (.468 inch.--Translator's Note.), 2b = 7 mm. (.273 inch.--Translator's Note.) in the males.

Once again, the ratio between 15 x 9 x 9 = 1215 and 12 x 7 x 7 = 588 lies between 2 to 1 and 3 to 1.

Besides the Bees who arrange their laying in a row, I have consulted others whose cells are grouped in a way that makes it possible to ascertain the relative order of the two sexes, though not quite so precisely. One of these is the Mason-bee of the Walls. I need not describe again her dome-shaped nest, built on a pebble, which is now so well-known to us. (Cf. "The Mason-bees": chapter 1.--Translator's Note.)

Each mother chooses her stone and works on it in solitude. She is an ungracious landowner and guards her site jealously, driving away any Mason who even looks as though she might alight on it. The inhabitants of the same nest are therefore always brothers and sisters; they are the family of one mother.

Moreover, if the stone presents a large enough surface--a condition easily fulfilled--the Mason-bee has no reason to leave the support on which she began her laying and go in search of another whereon to deposit the rest of her eggs. She is too thrifty of her time and of her mortar to involve herself in such expenditure except for grave reasons. Consequently, each nest, at least when it is new, when the Bee herself has laid the first foundations, contains the entire laying. It is a different thing when an old nest is restored and made into a place for depositing the eggs. I shall come back later to such houses.

A newly-built nest then, with rare exceptions, contains the entire laying of one female. Count the cells and we shall have the total list of the family. Their maximum number fluctuates round about fifteen. The most luxuriant series will occasionally reach as many as eighteen, though these are very scarce.

When the surface of the stone is regular all around the site of the first cell, when the mason can add to her building with the same facility in every direction, it is obvious that the groups of cells, when finished, will have the oldest in the central portion and the more recent in the surrounding portion. Because of this juxtaposition of the cells, which serve partly as a wall to those which come next, it is possible to form some estimate of the chronological order of the cells in the Chalicodoma's nest and thus to discover the sequence of the two sexes.

In winter, by which time the Bee has long been in the perfect state, I collect Chalicodoma-nests, removing them bodily from their support with a few smart sideward taps of the hammer on the pebbles. At the base of the mortar dome the cells are wide agape and display their contents. I take the cocoon from its box, open it and take note of the sex of the insect enclosed.

I should probably be accused of exaggeration if I mentioned the total number of the nests which I have gathered and the cells which I have inspected by this method during the last six or seven years. I will content myself with saying that the harvest of a single morning sometimes consisted of as many as sixty nests of the Mason-bee. I had to have help in carrying home my spoils, even though the nests were removed from their stones on the spot.

From the enormous number of nests which I have examined, I am able to state that, when the cluster is regular, the female cells occupy the centre and the male cells the edges. Where the irregularity of the pebble has prevented an even distribution around the initial point, the same rule has been observed. A male cell is never surrounded on every side by female cells: either it occupies the edges of the nest, or else it adjoins, at least on some sides, other male cells, of which the last form part of the exterior of the cluster. As the surrounding cells are obviously of a later date than the inner cells, it follows that the Mason-bee acts like the Osmiae: she begins her laying with females and ends it with males, each of the sexes forming a series of its own, independent of the other.

Some further circumstances add their testimony to that of the surrounded and surrounding cells. When the pebble projects sharply and forms a sort of dihedral angle, one of whose faces is more or less vertical and the other horizontal, this angle is a favourite site with the Mason, who thus finds greater stability for her edifice in the support given her by the double plane. These sites appear to me to be in great request with the Chalicodoma, considering the number of nests which I find thus doubly supported. In nests of this kind, all the cells, as usual, have their foundations fixed to the horizontal surface; but the first row, the row of cells first built, stands with its back against the vertical surface.

Well, these older cells, which occupy the actual edge of the dihedral angle, are always female, with the exception of those at either end of the row, which, as they belong to the outside, may be male cells. In front of this first row come others. The female cells occupy the middle portion and the male the ends. Finally, the last row, closing in the remainder, contains only male cells. The progress of the work is very visible here: the Mason has begun by attending to the central group of female cells, the first row of which occupies the dihedral angle, and has finished her task by distributing the male cells round the outside.

If the perpendicular face of the dihedral angle be high enough, it sometimes happens that a second row of cells is placed above the first row backing on to that plane; a third row occurs less often. The nest is then one of several storeys. The lower storeys, the older, contain only females; the upper, the more recent storey, contains none but males. It goes without saying that the surface layer, even of the lower storeys, can contain males without invalidating the rule, for this layer may always be looked upon as the Chalicodoma's last work.

Everything therefore contributes to show that, in the Mason-bee, the females take the lead in the order of primogeniture. Theirs is the central and best-protected part of the clay fortress; the outer part, that most exposed to the inclemencies of the weather and to accidents, is for the males.

The males' cells do not differ from the females' only by being placed at the outside of the cluster; they differ also in their capacity, which is much smaller. To estimate the respective capacities of the two sorts of cells, I go to work as follows: I fill the empty cell with very fine sand and pour this sand back into a glass tube measuring 5 millimetres (.195 inch.--Translator's Note.) in diameter. From the height of the column of sand we can estimate the comparative capacity of the two kinds of cells. I will take one at random among my numerous examples of cells thus gauged.

It comprises thirteen cells and occupies a dihedral angle. The female cells give me the following figures, in millimetres, as the height of the columns of sand:

40, 44, 43, 48, 48, 46, 47 (1.56, 1.71, 1.67, 1.87, 1.87, 1.79, 1.83 inches.--Translator's Note.),

averaging 45. (1.75 inches.--Translator's Note.)

The male cells give me:

32, 35, 28, 30, 30, 31 (1.24, 1.36, 1.09, 1.17, 1.17, 1.21 inches.--Translator's Note.),

averaging 31. (1.21 inches.--Translator's Note.)

The ratio of the capacity of the cells for the two sexes is therefore roughly a ratio of 4 to 3. The actual contents of the cell being proportionate to its capacity, the above ratio must also be more or less the ratio of provisions and sizes between females and males. These figures will assist us presently to tell whether an old cell, occupied for a second or third time, belonged originally to a female or a male.

The Chalicodoma of the Sheds cannot give us any information on this matter. She builds under the same eaves, in excessively populous colonies; and it is impossible to follow the labours of any single Mason, whose cells, distributed here and there, are soon covered up with the work of her neighbours. All is muddle and confusion in the individual output of the swarming throng.

I have not watched the work of the Chalicodoma of the Shrubs with close enough attention to be able to state definitely that this Bee is a solitary builder. Her nest is a ball of clay hanging from a bough. Sometimes, this nest is the size of a large walnut and then appears to be the work of one alone; sometimes, it is the size of a man's fist, in which case I have no doubt that it is the work of several. Those bulky nests, comprising more than fifty cells, can tell us nothing exact, as a number of workers must certainly have collaborated to produce them.

The walnut-sized nests are more trustworthy, for everything seems to indicate that they were built by a single Bee. Here females are found in the centre of the group and males at the circumference, in somewhat smaller cells, thus repeating what the Mason-bee of the Pebbles has told us.

One clear and simple rule stands out from this collection of facts. Apart from the strange exception of the Three-pronged Osmia, who mixes the sexes without any order, the Bees whom I studied and probably a crowd of others produce first a continuous series of females and then a continuous series of males, the latter with less provisions and smaller cells. This distribution of the sexes agrees with what we have long known of the Hive-bee, who begins her laying with a long sequence of workers, or sterile females, and ends it with a long sequence of males. The analogy continues down to the capacity of the cells and the quantities of provisions. The real females, the Queen-bees, have wax cells incomparably more spacious than the cells of the males and receive a much larger amount of food. Everything therefore demonstrates that we are here in the presence of a general rule.

But does this rule express the whole truth? Is there nothing beyond a laying in two series? Are the Osmiae, the Chalicodomae and the rest of them fatally bound by this distribution of the sexes into two distinct groups, the male group following upon the female group, without any mixing of the two? Is the mother absolutely powerless to make a change in this arrangement, should circumstances require it?

The Three-pronged Osmia already shows us that the problem is far from being solved. In the same bramble-stump, the two sexes occur very irregularly, as though at random. Why this mixture in the series of cocoons of a Bee closely related to the Horned Osmia and the Three-horned Osmia, who stack theirs methodically by separate sexes in the hollow of a reed? What the Bee of the brambles does cannot her kinswomen of the reeds do too? Nothing, so far as I know, can explain this difference in a physiological act of primary importance. The three Bees belong to the same genus; they resemble one another in general outline, internal structure and habits; and, with this close similarity, we suddenly find a strange dissimilarity.

There is just one thing that might possibly arouse a suspicion of the cause of this irregularity in the Three-pronged Osmia's laying. If I open a bramble-stump in the winter to examine the Osmia's nest, I find it impossible, in the vast majority of cases, to distinguish positively between a female and a male cocoon: the difference in size is so small. The cells, moreover, have the same capacity: the diameter of the cylinder is the same throughout and the partitions are almost always the same distance apart. If I open it in July, the victualling-period, it is impossible for me to distinguish between the provisions destined for the males and those destined for the females. The measurement of the column of honey gives practically the same depth in all the cells. We find an equal quantity of space and food for both sexes.

This result makes us foresee what a direct examination of the two sexes in the adult form tells us. The male does not differ materially from the female in respect of size. If he is a trifle smaller, it is scarcely noticeable, whereas, in the Horned Osmia and the Three-horned Osmia, the male is only half or a third the size of the female, as we have seen from the respective bulk of their cocoons. In the Mason-bee of the Walls there is also a difference in size, though less pronounced.

The Three-pronged Osmia has not therefore to trouble about adjusting the dimensions of the dwelling and the quantity of the food to the sex of the egg which she is about to lay; the measure is the same from one end of the series to the other. It does not matter if the sexes alternate without order: one and all will find what they need, whatever their position in the row. The two other Osmiae, with their great disparity in size between the two sexes, have to be careful about the twofold consideration of board and lodging. And that, I think, is why they begin with spacious cells and generous rations for the homes of the females and end with narrow, scantily-provisioned cells, the homes of the males. With this sequence, sharply defined for the two sexes, there is less fear of mistakes which might give to one what belongs to another. If this is not the explanation of the facts, I see no other.

The more I thought about this curious question, the more probable it appeared to me that the irregular series of the Three-pronged Osmia and the regular series of the other Osmiae, of the Chalicodomae and of the Bees in general were all traceable to a common law. It seemed to me that the arrangement in a succession first of females and then of males did not account for everything. There must be something more. And I was right: that arrangement in series is only a tiny fraction of the reality, which is remarkable in a very different way. This is what I am going to prove by experiment.

CHAPTER 4. THE MOTHER DECIDES THE SEX OF THE EGG.

I will begin with the Mason-bee of the Pebbles. (This is the same insect as the Mason-bee of the Walls. Cf. "The Mason-bees": passim.--Translator's Note.) The old nests are often used, when they are in good enough repair. Early in the season the mothers quarrel fiercely over them; and, when one of the Bees has taken possession of the coveted dome, she drives any stranger away from it. The old house is far from being a ruin, only it is perforated with as many holes as it once had occupants. The work of restoration is no great matter. The heap of earth due to the destruction of the lid by the outgoing tenant is taken out of the cell and flung away at a distance, atom by atom. The remnants of the cocoon are also thrown away, but not always, for the delicate silken wrapper sometimes adheres closely to the masonry.

The victualling of the renovated cell is now begun. Next comes the laying; and lastly the orifice is sealed with a mortar plug. A second cell is utilized in the same way, followed by a third and so on, one after the other, as long as any remain unoccupied and the mother's ovaries are not exhausted. Finally, the dome receives, mainly over the apertures already plugged, a coat of plaster which makes the nest look like new. If she has not finished her laying, the mother goes in search of other old nests to complete it. Perhaps she does not decide to found a new establishment except when she can find no second-hand dwellings, which mean a great economy of time and labour. In short, among the countless number of nests which I have collected, I find many more ancient than recent ones.

How shall we distinguish one from the other? The outward aspect tells you nothing, owing to the great care taken by the Mason to restore the surface of the old dwelling equal to new. To resist the rigours of the winter, this surface must be impregnable. The mother knows that and therefore repairs the dome. Inside, it is another matter: the old nest stands revealed at once. There are cells whose provisions, at least a year old, are intact, but dried up or musty, because the egg has never developed. There are others containing a dead larva, reduced by time to a blackened, curled-up cylinder. There are some whence the perfect insect was never able to issue: the Chalicodoma wore herself out in trying to pierce the ceiling of her chamber; her strength failed her and she perished in the attempt. Others again and very many are occupied by ravagers, Leucopses (Cf. "The Mason-bees": chapter 11.--Translator's Note.) and Anthrax-flies, who will come out a good deal later, in July. Altogether, the house is far from having every room vacant; there are nearly always a considerable number occupied either by parasites that were still in the egg-stage at the time when the Mason-bee was at work or by damaged provisions, dried grubs or Chalicodomae in the perfect state who have died without being able to effect their deliverance.

Should all the rooms be available, a rare occurrence, there still remains a method of distinguishing between an ancient nest and a recent one. The cocoon, as I have said, adheres pretty closely to the walls; and the mother does not always take away this remnant, either because she is unable to do so, or because she considers the removal unnecessary. Thus the base of the new cocoon is set in the bottom of the old cocoon. This double wrapper points very clearly to two generations, two separate years. I have even found as many as three cocoons fitting one into another at their bases. Consequently, the nests of the Mason-bee of the Pebbles are able to do duty for three years, if not more. Eventually they become utter ruins, abandoned to the Spiders and to various smaller Bees or Wasps, who take up their quarters in the crumbling rooms.

As we see, an old nest is hardly ever capable of containing the Mason-bee's entire laying, which calls for some fifteen apartments. The number of rooms at her disposal is most unequal, but always very small. It is saying much when there are enough to receive about half the laying. Four or five cells, sometimes two or even one: that is what the Mason usually finds in a nest that is not her own work. This large reduction is explained when we remember the numerous parasites that live upon the unfortunate Bee.

Now, how are the sexes distributed in those layings which are necessarily broken up between one old nest and another? They are distributed in such a way as utterly to upset the idea of an invariable succession first of females and then of males, the idea which occurs to us on examining the new nests. If this rule were a constant one, we should be bound to find in the old domes at one time only females, at another only males, according as the laying was at its first or at its second stage. The simultaneous presence of the two sexes would then correspond with the transition period between one stage and the next and should be very unusual. On the contrary, it is very common; and, however few cells there may be, we always find both females and males in the old nests, on the sole condition that the compartments have the regulation holding-capacity, a large capacity for the females, a lesser for the males, as we have seen.

The old male cells can be recognized by their position on the outer edges and by their capacity, measuring on an average the same as a column of sand 31 millimetres high in a glass tube 5 millimetres wide. (1.21 x.195 inches.--Translator's Note.) These cells contain males of the second or third generation and none but males. In the old female cells, those in the middle, whose capacity is measured by a similar column of sand 45 millimetres high (1.75 inches.--Translator's Note.), are females and none but females.

This presence of both sexes at a time, even when there are but two cells free, one spacious and the other small, proves in the plainest fashion that the regular distribution observed in the complete nests of recent production is here replaced by an irregular distribution, harmonizing with the number and holding-capacity of the chambers to be stocked. The Mason-bee has before her, let me suppose, only five vacant cells: two larger and three smaller. The total space at her disposal would do for about a third of the laying. Well, in the two large cells, she puts females; in the three small cells, she puts males.

As we find the same sort of thing in all the old nests, we must needs admit that the mother knows the sex of the egg which she is going to lay, because that egg is placed in a cell of the proper capacity. We can go further and admit that the mother alters the order of succession of the sexes at her pleasure, because her layings, between one old nest and another, are broken up into small groups of males and females according to the exigencies of space in the actual nest which she happens to be occupying.

Just now, in the new nest, we saw the Mason-bee arranging her total laying into series first of females and next of males; and here she is, mistress of an old nest of which she has not the power to alter the arrangement, breaking up her laying into sections comprising both sexes just as required by the conditions imposed upon her. She therefore decides the sex of the egg at will, for, without this prerogative, she could not, in the chambers of the nest which she owes to chance, deposit unerringly the sex for which those chambers were originally built; and this happens however small the number of chambers to be filled.

When the nest is new, I think I see a reason why the Mason-bee should seriate her laying into females and then males. Her nest is a half-sphere. That of the Mason-bee of the Shrubs is very nearly a sphere. Of all shapes, the spherical shape is the strongest. Now these two nests require an exceptional power of resistance. Without protection of any kind, they have to brave the weather, one on its pebble, the other on its bough. Their spherical configuration is therefore very practical.

The nest of the Mason-bee of the Walls consists of a cluster of upright cells backing against one another. For the whole to take a spherical form, the height of the chambers must diminish from the centre of the dome to the circumference. Their elevation is the sine of the meridian arc starting from the plane of the pebble. Therefore, if they are to have any solidity, there must be large cells in the middle and small cells at the edges. And, as the work begins with the central chambers and ends with those on the circumference, the laying of the females, destined for the large cells, must precede that of the males, destined for the small cells. So the females come first and the males at the finish.

This is all very well when the mother herself founds the dwelling, when she lays the first rows of bricks. But, when she is in the presence of an old nest, of which she is quite unable to alter the general arrangement, how is she to make use of the few vacant rooms, the large and the small alike, if the sex of the egg be already irrevocably fixed? She can only do so by abandoning the arrangement in two consecutive rows and accommodating her laying to the varied exigencies of the home. Either she finds it impossible to make an economical use of the old nest, a theory refuted by the evidence, or else she determines at will the sex of the egg which she is about to lay.

The Osmiae themselves will furnish the most conclusive evidence on the latter point. We have seen that these Bees are not generally miners, who themselves dig out the foundation of their cells. They make use of the old structures of others, or else of natural retreats, such as hollow stems, the spirals of empty shells and various hiding-places in walls, clay or wood. Their work is confined to repairs to the house, such as partitions and covers. There are plenty of these retreats; and the insect would always find first-class ones if it thought of going any distance to look for them. But the Osmia is a stay-at-home: she returns to her birth-place and clings to it with a patience extremely difficult to exhaust. It is here, in this little familiar corner, that she prefers to settle her progeny. But then the apartments are few in number and of all shapes and sizes. There are long and short ones, spacious ones and narrow. Short of expatriating herself, a Spartan course, she has to use them all, from first to last, for she has no choice. Guided by these considerations, I embarked on the experiments which I will now describe.

I have said how my study, on two separate occasions, became a populous hive, in which the Three-horned Osmia built her nests in the various appliances which I had prepared for her. Among these appliances, tubes, either of glass or reed, predominated. There were tubes of all lengths and widths. In the long tubes, entire or almost entire layings, with a series of females followed by a series of males, were deposited. As I have already referred to this result, I will not discuss it again. The short tubes were sufficiently varied in length to lodge one or other portion of the total laying. Basing my calculations on the respective lengths of the cocoons of the two sexes, on the thickness of the partitions and the final lid, I shortened some of these to the exact dimensions required for two cocoons only, of different sexes.

Well, these short tubes, whether of glass or reed, were seized upon as eagerly as the long tubes. Moreover, they yielded this splendid result: their contents, only a part of the total laying, always began with female and ended with male cocoons. This order was invariable; what varied was the number of cells in the long tubes and the proportion between the two sorts of cocoons, sometimes males predominating and sometimes females.

The experiment is of paramount importance; and it will perhaps make the result clearer if I quote one instance from among a multitude of similar cases. I give the preference to this particular instance because of the rather exceptional fertility of the laying. An Osmia marked on the thorax is watched, day by day, from the commencement to the end of her work. From the 1st to the 10th of May, she occupies a glass tube in which she lodges seven females followed by a male, which ends the series. From the 10th to the 17th of May, she colonizes a second tube, in which she lodges first three females and then three males. From the 17th to the 25th of May, a third tube, with three females and then two males. On the 26th of May, a fourth tube, which she abandons, probably because of its excessive width, after laying one female in it. Lastly, from the 26th to the 30th of May, a fifth tube, which she colonizes with two females and three males. Total: twenty-five Osmiae, including seventeen females and eight males. And it will not be superfluous to observe that these unfinished series do not in any way correspond with periods separated by intervals of rest. The laying is continuous, in so far as the variable condition of the atmosphere allows. As soon as one tube is full and closed, another is occupied by the Osmia without delay.

The tubes reduced to the exact length of two cells fulfilled my expectation in the great majority of cases: the lower cell was occupied by a female and the upper by a male. There were a few exceptions. More discerning than I in her estimate of what was strictly necessary, better-versed in the economy of space, the Osmia had found a way of lodging two females where I had only seen room for one female and a male.

This experiment speaks volumes. When confronted with tubes too small to receive all her family, she is in the same plight as the Mason-bee in the presence of an old nest. She thereupon acts exactly as the Chalicodoma does. She breaks up her laying, divides it into series as short as the room at her disposal demands; and each series begins with females and ends with males. This breaking up, on the one hand, into sections in all of which both sexes are represented and the division, on the other hand, of the entire laying into just two groups, one female, the other male, when the length of the tube permits, surely provide us with ample evidence of the insect's power to regulate the sex of the egg according to the exigencies of space.

And besides the exigencies of space one might perhaps venture to add those connected with the earlier development of the males. These burst their cocoons a couple of weeks or more before the females; they are the first who hasten to the sweets of the almond-tree. In order to release themselves and emerge into the glad sunlight without disturbing the string of cocoons wherein their sisters are still sleeping, they must occupy the upper end of the row; and this, no doubt, is the reason that makes the Osmia end each of her broken layings with males. Being next to the door, these impatient ones will leave the home without upsetting the shells that are slower in hatching.

I experimented on Latreille's Osmia, using short and even very short stumps of reed. All that I had to do was to lay them just beside the nests of the Mason-bee of the Sheds, nests beloved by this particular Osmia. Old, disused hurdles supplied me with reeds inhabited from end to end by the Horned Osmia. In both cases I obtained the same results and the same conclusions as with the Three-horned Osmia.

I return to the latter, nidifying under my eyes in some old nests of the Mason-bee of the Walls, which I had placed within her reach, mixed up with the tubes. Outside my study, I had never yet seen the Three-horned Osmia adopt that domicile. This may be due to the fact that these nests are isolated one by one in the fields; and the Osmia, who loves to feel herself surrounded by her kin and to work in plenty of company, refuses them because of this isolation. But on my table, finding them close to the tubes in which the others are working, she adopts them without hesitation.

The chambers presented by those old nests are more or less spacious according to the thickness of the coat of mortar which the Chalicodoma has laid over the assembled chambers. To leave her cell, the Mason-bee has to perforate not only the plug, the lid built at the mouth of the cell, but also the thick plaster wherewith the dome is strengthened at the end of the work. The perforation results in a vestibule which gives access to the chamber itself. It is this vestibule which is sometimes longer and sometimes shorter, whereas the corresponding chamber is of almost constant dimensions, in the case of the same sex, of course.

We will first consider the short vestibule, at the most large enough to receive the plug with which the Osmia will close up the lodging. There is then nothing at her disposal except the cell proper, a spacious apartment in which one of the Osmia's females will find ample accommodation, for she is much smaller than the original occupant of the chamber, no matter the sex; but there is not room for two cocoons at a time, especially in view of the space taken up by the intervening partition. Well, in those large, well-built chambers, formerly the homes of Chalicodomae, the Osmia settles females and none but females.

Let us now consider the long vestibule. Here, a partition is constructed, encroaching slightly on the cell proper, and the residence is divided into two unequal storeys, a large room below, housing a female, and a narrow cabin above, containing a male.

When the length of the vestibule permits, allowing for the space required by the outer stopper, a third storey is built, smaller than the second; and another male is lodged in this cramped corner. In this way the old nest of the Mason-bee of the Pebbles is colonized, cell after cell, by a single mother.

The Osmia, as we see, is very frugal of the lodging that has fallen to her share; she makes the best possible use of it, giving to the females the spacious chambers of the Mason-bee and to the males the narrow vestibules, subdivided into storeys when this is feasible. Economy of space is the chief consideration, since her stay-at-home tastes do not allow her to indulge in distant quests. She has to employ the site which chance places at her disposal just as it is, now for a male and now for a female. Here we see displayed, more clearly than ever, her power of deciding the sex of the egg, in order to adapt it judiciously to the conditions of the house-room available.

I had offered at the same time to the Osmiae in my study some old nests of the Mason-bee of the Shrubs, which are clay spheroids with cylindrical cavities in them. These cavities are formed, as in the old nests of the Mason-bee of the Pebbles, of the cell properly so-called and of the exit-way which the perfect insect cut through the outer coating at the time of its deliverance. Their diameter is about seven millimetres (.273 inch.--Translator's Note.); their depth at the centre of the heap is 23 millimetres (.897 inch.--Translator's Note.); and at the edge averages 14 millimetres (.546 inch.--Translator's Note.)

The deep central cells receive only the females of the Osmia; sometimes even the two sexes together, with a partition in the middle, the female occupying the lower and the male the upper storey. True, in such cases economy of space is strained to the utmost, the apartments provided by the Mason-bee of the Shrubs being very small as it is, despite their entrance-halls. Lastly, the deeper cavities on the circumference are allotted to females and the shallower to males.

I will add that a single mother peoples each nest and also that she proceeds from cell to cell without troubling to ascertain the depth. She goes from the centre to the edges, from the edges to the centre, from a deep cavity to a shallow cavity and vice versa, which she would not do if the sexes were to follow upon each other in a settled order. For greater certainty, I numbered the cells of one nest as each of them was closed. On opening them later, I was able to see that the sexes were not sub-jected to a chronological arrangement. Females were succeeded by males and these by females without its being possible for me to make out any regular sequence. Only--and this is the essential point--the deep cavities were allotted to the females and the shallow ones to the males.

We know that the Three-horned Osmia prefers to haunt the habitations of the Bees who nidify in populous colonies, such as the Mason-bee of the Sheds and the Hairy-footed Anthophora. Exercising the very greatest care, I broke up some great lumps of earth removed from the banks inhabited by the Anthophora and sent to me from Carpentras by my dear friend and pupil M. Devillario. I examined them conscientiously in the quiet of my study. I found the Osmia's cocoons arranged in short series, in very irregular passages, the original work of which is due to the An-thophora. Touched up afterwards, made larger or smaller, lengthened or shortened, intersected with a network of crossings by the numerous generations that had suc-ceeded one another in the same city, they formed an inextricable labyrinth.

Sometimes these corridors did not communicate with any adjoining apartment; sometimes they gave access to the spacious chamber of the Anthophora, which could be recognized, in spite of its age, by its oval shape and its coating of glazed stucco. In the latter case, the bottom cell, which once constituted, by itself, the chamber of the Anthophora, was always occupied by a female Osmia. Beyond it, in the narrow corridor, a male was lodged, not seldom two, or even three. Of course, clay partitions, the work of the Osmia, separated the different inhabitants, each of whom had his own storey, his own closed cell.

When the accommodation consisted of no more than a simple cylinder, with no state-bedroom at the end of it--a bedroom always reserved for a female--the contents varied with the diameter of the cylinder. The series, of which the longest were series of four, included, with a wider diameter, first one or two females, then one or two males. It also happened, though rarely, that the series was reversed, that is to say, it began with males and ended with females. Lastly, there were a good many isolated cocoons, of one sex or the other. When the cocoon was alone and occupied the Anthophora's cell, it invariably belonged to a female.

I have observed the same thing in the nests of the Mason-bee of the Sheds, but not so easily. The series are shorter here, because the Mason-bee does not bore galleries but builds cell upon cell. The work of the whole swarm thus forms a stratum of cells that grows thicker from year to year. The corridors occupied by the Osmia are the holes which the Mason-bee dug in order to reach daylight from the deep layers. In these short series, both sexes are usually present; and, if the Mason-bee's chamber is at the end of the passage, it is inhabited by a female Osmia.

We come back to what the short tubes and the old nests of the Mason-bee of the Pebbles have already taught us. The Osmia who, in tubes of sufficient length, divides her whole laying into a continuous sequence of females and a continuous sequence of males, now breaks it up into short series in which both sexes are present. She adapts her sectional layings to the exigencies of a chance lodging; she always places a female in the sumptuous chamber which the Mason-bee or the Anthophora occupied originally.

Facts even more striking are supplied by the old nests of the Masked Anthophora (A. personata, ILLIG.), old nests which I have seen utilized by the Horned Osmia and the Three-horned Osmia at the same time. Less frequently, the same nests serve for Latreille's Osmia. Let us first describe the Masked Anthophora's nests.

In a steep bank of sandy clay, we find a set of round, wide-open holes. There are generally only a few of them, each about half an inch in diameter. They are the entrance-doors leading to the Anthophora's abode, doors always left open, even after the building is finished. Each of them gives access to a short passage, sometimes straight, sometimes winding, nearly horizontal, polished with minute care and varnished with a sort of white glaze. It looks as if it had received a thin coat of whitewash. On the inner surface of this passage, in the thickness of the earthy bank, spacious oval niches have been excavated, communicating with the corridor by means of a narrow bottle-neck, which is closed, when the work is done, with a substantial mortar stopper. The Anthophora polishes the outside of this stopper so well, smooths its surface so perfectly, bringing it to the same level as that of the passage, is so careful to give it the white tint of the rest of the wall that, when the job is finished, it becomes absolutely impossible to distinguish the entrance-door corresponding with each cell.

The cell is an oval cavity dug in the earthy mass. The wall has the same polish, the same chalky whiteness as the general passage. But the Anthophora does not limit herself to digging oval niches: to make her work more solid, she pours over the walls of the chamber a salivary liquid which not only whitens and varnishes but also penetrates to a depth of some millimetres into the sandy earth, which it turns into a hard cement. A similar precaution is taken with the passage; and therefore the whole is a solid piece of work capable of remaining in excellent condition for years.

Moreover, thanks to the wall hardened by the salivary fluid, the structure can be removed from its matrix by chipping it carefully away. We thus obtain, at least in fragments, a serpentine tube from which hangs a single or double row of oval nodules that look like large grapes drawn out lengthwise. Each of these nodules is a cell, the entrance to which, carefully hidden, opens into the tube or passage. When she wishes to leave her cell, in the spring, the Anthophora destroys the mortar disk that closes the jar and thus reaches the general corridor, which is quite open to the outer air. The abandoned nest provides a series of pear-shaped cavities, of which the distended part is the old cell and the contracted part the exit-neck, rid of its stopper.

These pear-shaped hollows form splendid lodgings, impregnable strongholds, in which the Osmiae find a safe and commodious retreat for their families. The Horned Osmia and the Three-horned Osmia establish themselves there at the same time. Although it is a little too large for her, Latrielle's Osmia also appears very well satisfied with it.

I have examined some forty of the superb cells utilized by each of the first two. The great majority are divided into two storeys by means of a transversal partition. The lower storey includes the larger portion of the Anthophora's cell; the upper storey includes the rest of the cell and a little of the bottle-neck that surmounts it. The two-roomed dwelling is closed, in the passage, by a shapeless, bulky mass of dried mud. What a clumsy artist the Osmia is, compared with the Anthophora! Against the exquisite work of the Anthophora, partition and plug strike a note as hideously incongruous as a lump of dirt on polished marble.

The two apartments thus obtained are of a very unequal capacity, which at once strikes the observer. I measured them with my five-millimetre tube. On an average, the bottom one is represented by a column of sand 50 millimetres deep (1.95 inches.--Translator's Note.) and the top one by a column of 15 millimetres (.585 inch.--Translator's Note.). The holding-capacity of the one is therefore about three times as large as that of the other. The cocoons enclosed present the same disparity. The bottom one is big, the top one small. Lastly, the lower one belongs to a female Osmia and the upper to a male Osmia.

Occasionally the length of the bottle-neck allows of a fresh arrangement and the cavity is divided into three storeys. The bottom one, which is always the most spacious, contains a female; the two above, both smaller than the first and one smaller than the other, contain males.

Let us keep to the first case, which is always the most frequent. The Osmia is in the presence of one of these pear-shaped hollows. It is a find that must be employed to the best advantage: a prize of this sort is rare and falls only to fortune's favourites. To lodge two females in it at once is impossible; there is not sufficient room. To lodge two males in it would be undue generosity to a sex that is entitled to but the smallest consideration. Besides, the two sexes must be represented in almost equal numbers. The Osmia decides upon one female, whose portion shall be the better room, the lower one, which is larger, better-protected and more nicely polished, and one male, whose portion shall be the upper storey, a cramped attic, uneven and rugged in the part which encroaches on the bottle-neck. This decision is proved by numerous undeniable facts. Both Osmiae therefore can choose the sex of the egg about to be laid, seeing that they are now breaking up the laying into groups of two, a female and a male, as required by the conditions of the lodging.

I have only once found Latreille's Osmia established in the nest of the Masked Anthophora. She had occupied but a small number of cells, because the others were not free, being inhabited by the Anthophora. The cells in question were divided into three storeys by partitions of green mortar; the lower storey was occupied by a female, the two others by males, with smaller cocoons.

I came to an even more remarkable example. Two Anthidia of my district, A. septemdentatum, LATR., and A. bellicosum, LEP., adopt as the home of their off-spring the empty shells of different snails: Helix aspersa, H. algira, H. nemoralis, H. caespitum. The first-named, the Common Snail, is the most often used, under the stone-heaps and in the crevices of old walls. Both Anthidia colonize only the second whorl of the spiral. The central part is too small and remains unoccupied. Even so with the front whorl, the largest, which is left completely empty, so much so that, on looking through the opening, it is impossible to tell whether the shell does or does not contain the Bee's nest. We have to break this last whorl if we would perceive the curious nest tucked away in the spiral.

We then find first a transversal partition, formed of tiny bits of gravel cemented by a putty made from resin, which is collected in fresh drops from the oxycedrus and the Aleppo pine. Beyond this is a stout barricade made up of rubbish of all kinds: bits of gravel, scraps of earth, juniper-needles, the catkins of the conifers, small shells, dried excretions of Snails. Next come a partition of pure resin, a large cocoon in a roomy chamber, a second partition of pure resin and, lastly, a smaller cocoon in a narrow chamber. The inequality of the two cells is the necessary consequence of the shape of the shell, whose inner space gains rapidly in width as the spiral gets nearer to the orifice. Thus, by the mere general arrangement of the home and without any work on the Bee's part beyond some slender partitions, a large room is marked out in front and a much smaller room at the back.

By a very remarkable exception, which I have mentioned casually elsewhere, the males of the genus Anthidium are generally larger than the females; and this is the case with the two species in particular that divide the Snail's spiral with resin partitions. I collected some dozens of nests of both species. In at least half the cases, the two sexes were present together; the female, the smaller, occupied the front cell and the male, the bigger, the back cell. Other cells, which were smaller or too much obstructed at the back by the dried-up remains of the Mollusc, contained only one cell, occupied at one time by a female and at another by a male. A few, lastly, had both cells inhabited now by two males and now by two females. The most frequent arrangement was the simultaneous presence of both sexes, with the female in front and the male behind. The Anthidia who make resin-dough and live in Snail-shells can therefore alternate the sexes regularly to meet the exigencies of the spiral dwelling-house.

One more thing and I have done. My apparatus of reeds, fixed against the walls of the garden, supplied me with a remarkable nest of the Horned Osmia. The nest is established in a bit of reed 11 millimetres wide inside. (.429 inch--Translator's Note.) It comprises thirteen cells and occupies only half the cylinder, although the orifice is plugged with the usual stopper. The laying therefore seems here to be complete.

Well, this laying is arranged in a most singular fashion. There is first, at a suitable distance from the bottom or the node of the reed, a transversal partition, perpendicular to the axis of the tube. This marks off a cell of unusual size, in which a female is lodged. After that, in view of the excessive width of the tunnel, which is too great for a series in single file, the Osmia appears to alter her mind. She therefore builds a partition perpendicular to the transversal partition which she has just constructed and thus divides the second storey into two rooms, a larger room, in which she lodges a female, and a smaller, in which she lodges a male. She next builds a second transversal partition and a second longitudinal partition perpendicular to it. These once more give two unequal chambers, stocked likewise, the large one with a female, the smaller one with a male.

From this third storey onwards, the Osmia abandons geometrical accuracy; the architect seems to be a little out in her reckoning. The transversal partitions become more and more slanting and the work grows irregular, but always with a sprinkling of large chambers for the females and small chambers for the males. Three females and two males are housed in this way, the sexes alternating.

By the time that the base of the eleventh cell is reached, the transversal partition is once more almost perpendicular to the axis. Here what happened at the bottom is repeated. There is no longitudinal partition; and the spacious cell, covering the whole diameter of the cylinder, receives a female. The edifice ends with two transversal partitions and one longitudinal partition, which mark out, on the same level, chambers twelve and thirteen, both of which contain males.

There is nothing more curious than this mixing of the two sexes, when we know with what precision the Osmia separates them in a linear series, where the narrow width of the cylinder demands that the cells shall be set singly, one above the other. Here, the Bee is making use of a tube whose diameter is not suited to her work; she is constructing a complex and difficult edifice, which perhaps would not possess the necessary solidity if the ceilings were too broad. The Osmia therefore supports these ceilings with longitudinal partitions; and the unequal chambers resulting from the introduction of these partitions receive females at one time and males at another, according to their capacity.

CHAPTER 5. PERMUTATIONS OF SEX.

The sex of the egg is optional. The choice rests with the mother, who is guided by considerations of space and, according to the accommodation at her disposal, which is frequently fortuitous and incapable of modification, places a female in this cell and a male in that, so that both may have a dwelling of a size suited to their unequal development. This is the unimpeachable evidence of the numerous and varied facts which I have set forth. People unfamiliar with insect anatomy--the public for whom I write--would probably give the following explanation of this marvellous prerogative of the Bee: the mother has at her disposal a certain number of eggs, some of which are irrevocably female and the others irrevocably male: she is able to pick out of either group the one which she wants at the actual moment; and her choice is decided by the holding capacity of the cell that has to be stocked. Everything would then be limited to a judicious selection from the heap of eggs.

Should this idea occur to him, the reader must hasten to reject it. Nothing could be more false, as the merest reference to anatomy will show. The female reproductive apparatus of the Hymenoptera consists generally of six ovarian tubes, something like glove-fingers, divided into bunches of three and ending in a common canal, the oviduct, which carries the eggs outside. Each of these glove-fingers is fairly wide at the base, but tapers sharply towards the tip, which is closed. It contains, arranged in a row, one after the other, like beads on a string, a certain number of eggs, five or six for instance, of which the lower ones are more or less developed, the middle ones half-way towards maturity, and the upper ones very rudimentary. Every stage of evolution is here represented, distributed regularly from bottom to top, from the verge of maturity to the vague outlines of the embryo. The sheath clasps its string of ovules so closely that any inversion of the order is impossible.

Besides, an inversion would result in a gross absurdity: the replacing of a riper egg by another in an earlier stage of development.

Therefore, in each ovarian tube, in each glove-finger, the emergence of the eggs occurs according to the order governing their arrangement in the common sheath; and any other sequence is absolutely impossible. Moreover, at the nesting period, the six ovarian sheaths, one by one and each in its turn, have at their base an egg which in a very short time swells enormously. Some hours or even a day before the laying, that egg by itself represents or even exceeds in bulk the whole of the ovigenous apparatus. This is the egg which is on the point of being laid. It is about to descend into the oviduct, in its proper order, at its proper time; and the mother has no power to make another take its place. It is this egg, necessarily this egg and no other, that will presently be laid upon the provisions, whether these be a mess of honey or a live prey; it alone is ripe, it alone is at the entrance to the oviduct; none of the others, since they are farther back in the row and not at the right stage of development, can be substituted at this crisis. Its birth is inevitable.

What will it yield, a male or a female? No lodging has been prepared, no food collected for it; and yet both food and lodging have to be in keeping with the sex that will proceed from it. And here is a much more puzzling condition: the sex of that egg, whose advent is predestined, has to correspond with the space which the mother happens to have found for a cell. There is therefore no room for hesitation, strange though the statement may appear: the egg, as it descends from its ovarian tube, has no determined sex. It is perhaps during the few hours of its rapid development at the base of its ovarian sheath, it is perhaps on its passage through the oviduct that it receives, at the mother's pleasure, the final impress that will produce, to match the cradle which it has to fill, either a female or a male.

Thereupon the following question presents itself. Let us admit that, when the normal conditions remain, a laying would have yielded m females and n males. Then, if my conclusions are correct, it must be in the mother's power, when the conditions are different, to take from the m group and increase the n group to the same extent; it must be possible for her laying to be represented as $m-1$, $m-2$, $m-3$, etc. females and by $n+1$, $n+2$, $n+3$, etc. males, the sum of $m+n$ remaining constant, but one of the sexes being partly permuted into the other. The ultimate conclusion even cannot be disregarded: we must admit a set of eggs represented by $m-m$, or zero, females and of n+m males, one of the sexes being completely replaced by the other. Conversely, it must be possible for the feminine series to be augmented from the masculine series to the extent of absorbing it entirely. It was to solve this question and some others connected with it that I undertook, for the second time, to rear the Three-horned Osmia in my study.

The problem on this occasion is a more delicate one; but I am also better-equipped. My apparatus consists of two small, closed packing-cases, with the front side of each pierced with forty holes, in which I can insert my glass tubes and keep them in a horizontal position. I thus obtain for the Bees the darkness and mystery which suit their work and for myself the power of withdrawing from my hive, at any time, any tube that I wish, with the Osmia inside, so as to carry it to the light and follow, if need be with the aid of the lens, the operations of the busy worker. My investigations, however frequent and minute, in no way hinder the peaceable Bee, who remains absorbed in her maternal duties.

I mark a plentiful number of my guests with a variety of dots on the thorax, which enables me to follow any one Osmia from the beginning to the end of her laying. The tubes and their respective holes are numbered; a list, always lying open on my desk, enables me to note from day to day, sometimes from hour to hour, what happens in each tube and particularly the actions of the Osmiae whose backs bear distinguishing marks. As soon as one tube is filled, I replace it by another. Moreover, I have scattered in front of either hive a few handfuls of empty Snail-shells, specially chosen for the object which I have in view. Reasons which I will explain later led me to prefer the shells of Helix caespitum. Each of the shells, as and when stocked, received the date of the laying and the alphabetical sign corresponding with the Osmia to whom it belonged. In this way, I spent five or six weeks in continual observation. To succeed in an enquiry, the first and foremost condition is patience. This condition I fulfilled; and it was rewarded with the success which I was justified in expecting.

The tubes employed are of two kinds. The first, which are cylindrical and of the same width throughout, will be of use for confirming the facts observed in the first year of my experiments in indoor rearing. The others, the majority, consist of two cylinders which are of very different diameters, set end to end. The front cylinder, the one which projects a little way outside the hive and forms the entrance-hole,

varies in width between 8 and 12 millimetres. (Between.312 to .468 inch.--Transla-
tor's Note.) The second, the back one, contained entirely within my packing-case, is
closed at its far end and is 5 to 6 millimetres (.195 to.234 inch.--Translator's Note.)
in diameter. Each of the two parts of the double-galleried tunnel, one narrow and
one wide, measures at most a decimetre (3.9 inches.--Translator's Note.) in length.
I thought it advisable to have these short tubes, as the Osmia is thus compelled to
select different lodgings, each of them being insufficient in itself to accommodate
the total laying. In this way I shall obtain a greater variety in the distribution of the
sexes. Lastly, at the mouth of each tube, which projects slightly outside the case,
there is a little paper tongue, forming a sort of perch on which the Osmia alights
on her arrival and giving easy access to the house. With these facilities, the swarm
colonized fifty-two double-galleried tubes, thirty-seven cylindrical tubes, seventy-
eight Snail-shells and a few old nests of the Mason-bee of the Shrubs. From this rich
mine of material I will take what I want to prove my case.

Every series, even when incomplete, begins with females and ends with males.
To this rule I have not yet found an exception, at least in galleries of normal diameter. In each new abode, the mother busies herself first of all with the more important sex. Bearing this point in mind, would it be possible for me, by manoeuvring,
to obtain an inversion of this order and make the laying begin with males? I think
so, from the results already ascertained and the irresistible conclusions to be drawn
from them. The double-galleried tubes are installed in order to put my conjectures
to the proof.

The back gallery, 5 or 6 millimetres (.195 to.234 inch.--Translator's Note.)
wide, is too narrow to serve as a lodging for normally developed females. If, therefore, the Osmia, who is very economical of her space, wishes to occupy them, she
will be obliged to establish males there. And her laying must necessarily begin here,
because this corner is the rear-most part of the tube. The foremost gallery is wide,
with an entrance-door on the front of the hive. Here, finding the conditions to
which she is accustomed, the mother will go on with her laying in the order which
she prefers.

Let us now see what has happened. Of the fifty-two double galleried tubes,
about a third did not have their narrow passage colonized. The Osmia closed its aperture communicating with the large passage; and the latter alone received the eggs.

This waste of space was inevitable. The female Osmiae, though nearly always larger than the males, present marked differences among one another: some are bigger, some are smaller. I had to adjust the width of the narrow galleries to Bees of average dimensions. It may happen therefore that a gallery is too small to admit the large-sized mothers to whom chance allots it. When the Osmia is unable to enter the tube, obviously she will not colonize it. She then closes the entrance to this space which she cannot use and does her laying beyond it, in the wide tube. Had I tried to avoid these useless apparatus by choosing tubes of larger calibre, I should have encountered another drawback: the medium-sized mothers, finding themselves almost comfortable, would have decided to lodge females there. I had to be prepared for it: as each mother selected her house at will and as I was unable to interfere in her choice, a narrow tube would be colonized or not, according as the Osmia who owned it was or was not able to make her way inside.

There remain some forty pairs of tubes with both galleries colonized. In these there are two things to take into consideration. The narrow rear tubes of 5 or 5 1/2 millimetres (.195 to.214 inch.--Translator's Note.)--and these are the most numerous--contain males and males only, but in short series, between one and five. The mother is here so much hampered in her work that they are rarely occupied from end to end; the Osmia seems in a hurry to leave them and to go and colonize the front tube, whose ample space will leave her the liberty of movement necessary for her operations. The other rear tubes, the minority, whose diameter is about 6 millimetres (.234 inch.--Translator's Note.), contain sometimes only females and sometimes females at the back and males towards the opening. One can see that a tube a trifle wider and a mother slightly smaller would account for this difference in the results. Nevertheless, as the necessary space for a female is barely provided in this case, we see that the mother avoids as far as she can a two-sex arrangement beginning with males and that she adopts it only in the last extremity. Finally, whatever the contents of the small tube may be, those of the large one, following upon it, never vary and consist of females at the back and males in front.

Though incomplete, because of circumstances very difficult to control, the result of the experiment is none the less very striking. Twenty-five apparatus contain only males in their narrow gallery, in numbers varying from a minimum of one to a maximum of five. After these comes the colony of the large gallery, beginning with females and ending with males. And the layings in these apparatus do not always belong to late summer or even to the intermediate period: a few small tubes contain the earliest eggs of the Osmiae. A couple of Osmiae, more forward than the others, set to work on the 23rd of April. Both of them started their laying by placing males in the narrow tubes. The meagre supply of provisions was enough in itself to show the sex, which proved later to be in accordance with my anticipations. We see then that, by my artifices, the whole swarm starts with the converse of the normal order. This inversion is continued, at no matter what period, from the beginning to the end of the operations. The series which, according to rule, would begin with females now begins with males. Once the larger gallery is reached, the laying is pursued in the usual order.

We have advanced one step and that no small one: we have seen that the Osmia, when circumstances require it, is capable of reversing the sequence of the sexes. Would it be possible, provided that the tube were long enough, to obtain a complete inversion, in which the entire series of the males should occupy the narrow gallery at the back and the entire series of the females the roomy gallery in front? I think not; and I will tell you why.

Long and narrow cylinders are by no means to the Osmia's taste, not because of their narrowness but because of their length. Remember that for each load of honey brought the worker is obliged to move backwards twice. She enters, head first, to begin by disgorging the honey-syrup from her crop. Unable to turn in a passage which she blocks entirely, she goes out backwards, crawling rather than walking, a laborious performance on the polished surface of the glass and a performance which, with any other surface, would still be very awkward, as the wings are bound to rub against the wall with their free end and are liable to get rumpled or bent. She goes out backwards, reaches the outside, turns round and goes in again, but this time the opposite way, so as to brush off the load of pollen from her abdomen on to the heap. If the gallery is at all long, this crawling backwards becomes troublesome after a time; and the Osmia soon abandons a passage that is too small to allow of free movement. I have said that the narrow tubes of my apparatus are, for the most part, only very incompletely colonized. The Bee, after lodging a small number of males in them, hastens to leave them. In the wide front gallery, she can stay where she is and still be able to turn round easily for her different manipulations; she will avoid those two long journeys backwards, which are so exhausting and so bad for her wings.

Another reason no doubt prompts her not to make too great a use of the narrow passage, in which she would establish males, followed by females in the part where the gallery widens. The males have to leave their cells a couple of weeks or more before the females. If they occupy the back of the house, they will die prisoners or else they will overturn everything on their way out. This risk is avoided by the order which the Osmia adopts.

In my tubes with their unusual arrangement, the mother might well find the dilemma perplexing: there is the narrowness of the space at her disposal and there is the emergence later on. In the narrow tubes, the width is insufficient for the females; on the other hand, if she lodges males there, they are liable to perish, since they will be prevented from issuing at the proper moment. This would perhaps explain the mother's hesitation and her obstinacy in settling females in some of my apparatus which looked as if they could suit none but males.

A suspicion occurs to me, a suspicion aroused by my attentive examination of the narrow tubes. All, whatever the number of their inmates, are carefully plugged at the opening, just as separate tubes would be. It might therefore be the case that the narrow gallery at the back was looked upon by the Osmia not as the prolongation of the large front gallery, but as an independent tube. The facility with which the worker turns as soon as she reaches the wide tube, her liberty of action, which is now as great as in a doorway communicating with the outer air, might well be misleading and cause the Osmia to treat the narrow passage at the back as though the wide passage in front did not exist. This would account for the placing of the female in the large tube above the males in the small tube, an arrangement contrary to her custom.

I will not undertake to decide whether the mother really appreciates the danger of my snares, or whether she makes a mistake in considering only the space at her disposal and beginning with males. At any rate, I perceive in her a tendency to deviate as little as possible from the order which safeguards the emergence of the two sexes. This tendency is demonstrated by her repugnance to colonizing my narrow tubes with long series of males. However, so far as we are concerned, it does not matter much what passes at such times in the Osmia's little brain. Enough for us to know that she dislikes narrow and long tubes, not because they are narrow, but because they are at the same time long.

And, in fact, she does very well with a short tube of the same diameter. Such are the cells in the old nests of the Mason-bee of the Shrubs and the empty shells of the Garden Snail. With the short tube, the two disadvantages of the long tube are avoided. She has very little of that crawling backwards to do when she has a Snail-shell for the home of her eggs and scarcely any when the home is the cell of the Mason-bee. Moreover, as the stack of cocoons numbers two or three at most, the deliverance will be exempt from the difficulties attached to a long series. To persuade the Osmia to nidify in a single tube long enough to receive the whole of her laying and at the same time narrow enough to leave her only just the possibility of admittance appears to me a project without the slightest chance of success: the Bee would stubbornly refuse such a dwelling or would content herself with entrusting only a very small portion of her eggs to it. On the other hand, with narrow but short cavities, success, without being easy, seems to me at least quite possible. Guided by these considerations, I embarked upon the most arduous part of my problem: to obtain the complete or almost complete permutation of one sex with the other; to produce a laying consisting only of males by offering the mother a series of lodgings suited only to males.

Let us in the first place consult the old nests of the Mason-bee of the Shrubs. I have said that these mortar spheroids, pierced all over with little cylindrical cavities, are adopted pretty eagerly by the Three-horned Osmia, who colonizes them before my eyes with females in the deep cells and males in the shallow cells. That is how things go when the old nest remains in its natural state. With a grater, however, I scrape the outside of another nest so as to reduce the depth of the cavities to some ten millimetres. (About two-fifths of an inch.--Translator's Note.) This leaves in each cell just room for one cocoon, surmounted by the closing stopper. Of the fourteen cavities in the nests, I leave two intact, measuring fifteen millimetres in depth. (.585 inch.--Translator's Note.) Nothing could be more striking than the result of this experiment, made in the first year of my home rearing. The twelve cavities whose depth had been reduced all received males; the two cavities left untouched received females.

A year passes and I repeat the experiment with a nest of fifteen cells; but this time all the cells are reduced to the minimum depth with the grater. Well, the fifteen cells, from first to last, are occupied by males. It must be quite understood that, in each case, all the offspring belonged to one mother, marked with her distinguishing spot and kept in sight as long as her laying lasted. He would indeed be difficult to please who refused to bow before the results of these two experiments. If, however, he is not yet convinced, here is something to remove his last doubts.

The Three-horned Osmia often settles her family in old shells, especially those of the Common Snail (Helix aspersa), who is so common under the stone-heaps and in the crevices of the little unmortared walls that support our terraces. In this species, the spiral is wide open, so that the Osmia, penetrating as far down as the helical passage permits, finds, immediately above the point which is too narrow to pass, the space necessary for the cell of a female. This cell is succeeded by others, wider still, always for females, arranged in a line in the same way as in a straight tube. In the last whorl of the spiral, the diameter would be too great for a single row. Then longitudinal partitions are added to the transverse partitions, the whole resulting in cells of unequal dimensions in which males predominate, mixed with a few females in the lower storeys. The sequence of the sexes is therefore what it would be in a straight tube and especially in a tube with a wide bore, where the partitioning is complicated by subdivisions on the same level. A single Snail-shell contains room for six or eight cells. A large, rough earthen stopper finishes the nest at the entrance to the shell.

As a dwelling of this sort could show us nothing new, I chose for my swarm the Garden Snail (Helix caespitum), whose shell, shaped like a small, swollen Ammonite, widens by slow degrees, the diameter of the usable portion, right up to the mouth, being hardly greater than that required by a male Osmia-cocoon. Moreover, the widest part, in which a female might find room, has to receive a thick stopping-plug, below which there will often be a free space. Under all these conditions, the house will hardly suit any but males arranged one after the other.

The collection of shells placed at the foot of each hive includes specimens of different sizes. The smallest are 18 millimetres (.7 inch.--Translator's Note.) in diameter and the largest 24 millimetres (.936 inch.--Translator's Note.) There is room for two cocoons, or three at most, according to their dimensions.

Now these shells were used by my visitors without any hesitation, perhaps even with more eagerness than the glass tubes, whose slippery sides might easily be a little annoying to the Bee. Some of them were occupied on the first few days of the laying; and the Osmia who had started with a home of this sort would pass next to a second Snail-shell, in the immediate neighbourhood of the first, to a third, a fourth and others still, always close to one another, until her ovaries were emptied. The whole family of one mother would thus be lodged in Snail-shells which were duly marked with the date of the laying and a description of the worker. The faithful adherents of the Snail-shell were in the minority. The greater number left the tubes to come to the shells and then went back from the shells to the tubes. All, after filling the spiral staircase with two or three cells, closed the house with a thick earthen stopper on a level with the opening. It was a long and troublesome task, in which the Osmia displayed all her patience as a mother and all her talents as a plasterer. There were even some who, scrupulous to excess, carefully cemented the umbilicus, a hole which seemed to inspire them with distrust as being able to give access to the interior of the dwelling. It was a dangerous-looking cavity, which for the greater safety of the family it was prudent to block up.

When the pupae are sufficiently matured, I proceed to examine these elegant abodes. The contents fill me with joy: they fulfil my anticipations to the letter. The great, the very great majority of the cocoons turn out to be males; here and there, in the bigger cells, a few rare females appear. The smallness of the space has almost done away with the sixty-eight Snail-shells colonized. But, of this total number, I must use only those series which received an entire laying and were occupied by the same Osmia from the beginning to the end of the egg-season. Here are a few examples, taken from among the most conclusive.

From the 6th of May, when she started operations, to the 25th of May, the date at which her laying ceased, the Osmia occupied seven Snail-shells in succession. Her family consists of fourteen cocoons, a number very near the average; and, of these fourteen cocoons, twelve belong to males and only two to females. These occupy the seventh and thirteenth places in chronological order.

Another, between the 9th and 27th of May, stocked six Snail-shells with a family of thirteen, including ten males and three females. The places occupied by the latter in the series were numbers 3, 4 and 5.

A third, between the 2nd and 29th of May, colonized eleven Snail-shells, a prodigious task. This industrious one was also exceedingly prolific. She supplied me with a family of twenty-six, the largest which I have ever obtained from one Osmia. Well, this abnormal progeny consisted of twenty-five males and one female, one alone, occupying place 17.

There is no need to go on, after this magnificent example, especially as the other series would all, without exception, give us the same result. Two facts are immediately obvious. The Osmia is able to reverse the order of her laying and to start with a more or less long series of males before producing any females. In the first case, the first female appears as number 7; in the third, as number 17. There is something better still; and this is the proposition which I was particularly anxious to prove: the female sex can be permuted with the male sex and can be permuted to the point of disappearing altogether. We see this especially in the third case, where the presence of a solitary female in a family of twenty-six is due to the somewhat larger diameter of the corresponding Snail-shell and also, no doubt, to some mistake on the mother's part, for the female cocoon, in a series of two, occupies the upper storey, the one next to the orifice, an arrangement which the Osmia appears to me to dislike.

This result throws so much light on one of the darkest corners of biology that I must attempt to corroborate it by means of even more conclusive experiments. I propose next year to give the Osmiae nothing but Snail-shells for a lodging, picked out one by one, and rigorously to deprive the swarm of any other retreat in which the laying could be effected. Under these conditions, I ought to obtain nothing but males, or nearly, for the whole swarm.

There would still remain the inverse permutation: to obtain only females and no males, or very few. The first permutation makes the second seem very probable, although I cannot as yet conceive a means of realizing it. The only condition which I can regulate is the dimensions of the home. When the rooms are small, the males abound and the females tend to disappear. With generous quarters, the converse would not take place. I should obtain females and afterwards an equal number of males, confined in small cells which, in case of need, would be bounded by numerous partitions. The factor of space does not enter into the question here. What artifice can we then employ to provoke this second permutation? So far, I can think of nothing that is worth attempting.

It is time to conclude. Leading a retired life, in the solitude of a village, having quite enough to do with patiently and obscurely ploughing my humble furrow, I know little about modern scientific views. In my young days I had a passionate longing for books and found it difficult to procure them; to-day, when I could almost have them if I wanted, I am ceasing to wish for them. It is what usually happens as life goes on. I do not therefore know what may have been done in the direction whither this study of the sexes has led us. If I am stating propositions that are really new or at least more comprehensive than the propositions already known, my words will perhaps sound heretical. No matter: as a simple translator of facts, I do not hesitate to make my statement, being fully persuaded that time will turn my heresy into orthodoxy. I will therefore recapitulate my conclusions.

Bees lay their eggs in series of first females and then males, when the two sexes are of different sizes and demand an unequal quantity of nourishment. When the two sexes are alike in size, the same sequence may occur, but less regularly.

This dual arrangement disappears when the place chosen for the nest is not large enough to contain the entire laying. We then see broken layings, beginning with females and ending with males.

The egg, as it issues from the ovary, has not yet a fixed sex. The final impress that produces the sex is given at the moment of laying or a little before.

So as to be able to give each larva the amount of space and food that suits it according as it is male or female, the mother can choose the sex of the egg which she is about to lay. To meet the conditions of the building, which is often the work of another or else a natural retreat that admits of little or no alteration, she lays either a male egg or a female egg as she pleases. The distribution of the sexes depends upon herself. Should circumstances require it, the order of the laying can be reversed and begin with males; lastly, the entire laying can contain only one sex.

The same privilege is possessed by the predatory Hymenoptera, the Wasps, at least by those in whom the two sexes are of a different size and consequently require an amount of nourishment that is larger in the one case than in the other. The mother must know the sex of the egg which she is going to lay; she must be able to choose the sex of that egg so that each larva may obtain its proper portion of food.

Generally speaking, when the sexes are of different sizes, every insect that collects food and prepares or selects a dwelling for its offspring must be able to choose the sex of the egg in order to satisfy without mistake the conditions imposed upon it.

The question remains how this optional assessment of the sexes is effected. I know absolutely nothing about it. If I should ever learn anything about this delicate point, I shall owe it to some happy chance for which I must wait, or rather watch, patiently. Towards the end of my investigations, I heard of a German theory which relates to the Hive-bee and comes from Dzierzon, the apiarist. (Johann Dzierzon, author of "Theorie und Praxis des neuen Bienenfreundes."--Translator's Note.) If I understand it aright, according to the very incomplete documents which I have before me, the egg, as it issues from the ovary, is said already to possess a sex, which is always the same; it is originally male; and it becomes female by fertilization. The males are supposed to proceed from non-fertilized eggs, the females from fertilized eggs. The Queen-bee would thus lay female eggs or male eggs according as she fertilized them or not while they were passing into her oviduct.

Coming from Germany, this theory cannot but inspire me with profound distrust. As it has been given acceptance, with rash precipitancy, in standard works, I will overcome my reluctance to devoting my attention to Teutonic ideas and will submit it not to the test of argument, which can always be met by an opposite argument, but to the unanswerable test of facts.

For this optional fertilization, determining the sex, the mother's organism requires a seminal reservoir which distils its drop of sperm upon the egg contained in the oviduct and thus gives it a feminine character, or else leaves it its original character, the male character, by refusing it that baptism. This reservoir exists in the Hive-bee. Do we find a similar organ in the other Hymenoptera, whether honey-gatherers or hunters? The anatomical treatises are either silent on this point or, without further enquiry, apply to the order as a whole the data provided by the Hive-bee, however much she differs from the mass of Hymenoptera owing to her social habits, her sterile workers and especially her tremendous fertility, extending over so long a period.

I at first doubted the universal presence of this spermatic receptacle, having failed to find it under my scalpel in my former investigations into the anatomy of the Sphex-wasps and some other game-hunters. But this organ is so delicate and so small that it very easily escapes the eye, especially when our attention is not specially directed in search of it; and, even when we are looking for it and it only, we do not always succeed in discovering it. We have to find a globule attaining in many cases hardly as much as a millimetre (About one-fiftieth of an inch.--Translator's Note.) in diameter, a globule headed amidst a tangle of air-ducts and fatty patches, of which it shares the colour, a dull white. Then again, the merest slip of the forceps is enough to destroy it. My first investigations, therefore, which concerned the reproductive apparatus as a whole, might very well have allowed it to pass unperceived.

In order to know the rights of the matter once and for all, as the anatomical treatises taught me nothing, I once more fixed my microscope on its stand and rearranged my old dissecting-tank, an ordinary tumbler with a cork disk covered with black satin. This time, not without a certain strain on my eyes, which are already growing tired, I succeeded in finding the said organ in the Bembex-wasps, the Halicti (Cf. Chapters 12 to 14 of the present volume.--Translator's Note.), the Carpenter-bees, the Bumble-bees, the Andrenae (A species of Burrowing Bees.--Translator's Note.) and the Megachiles. (Or Leaf-cutting Bees. Cf. Chapter 8 of the present volume.--Translator's Note.) I failed in the case of the Osmiae, the Chalicodomae and the Anthophorae. Is the organ really absent? Or was there want of skill on my part? I lean towards want of skill and admit that all the game-hunting and honey-gathering Hymenoptera possess a seminal receptacle, which can be recognized by its contents, a quantity of spiral spermatozoids whirling and twisting on the slide of the microscope.

This organ once accepted, the German theory becomes applicable to all the Bees and all the Wasps. When copulating, the female receives the seminal fluid and holds it stored in her receptacle. From that moment, the two procreating elements are present in the mother at one and the same time: the female element, the ovule; and the male element, the spermatozoid. At the egg-layer's will, the receptacle bestows a tiny drop of its contents upon the matured ovule, when it reaches the oviduct, and you have a female egg; or else it withholds its spermatozoids and you have an egg that remains male, as it was at first. I readily admit it: the theory is very simple, lucid and seductive. But is it correct? That is another question.

One might begin by reproaching it with making a singular exception to one of the most general rules. Which of us, casting his eyes over the whole zoological progression, would dare to assert that the egg is originally male and that it becomes female by fertilization? Do not the two sexes both call for the assistance of the fertilizing element? If there be one undoubted truth, it is certainly that. We are, it is true, told very curious things about the Hive-bee. I will not discuss them: this Bee stands too far outside the ordinary limits; and then the facts asserted are far from being accepted by everybody. But the non-social Bees and the predatory insects have nothing special about their laying. Then why should they escape the common rule, which requires that every living creature, male as well as female, should come from a fertilized ovule? In its most solemn act, that of procreation, life is one and uniform; what it does here it does there and there and everywhere. What! The sporule of a scrap of moss requires an antherozoid before it is fit to germinate; and the ovule of a Scolia, that proud huntress, can dispense with the equivalent in order to hatch and produce a male? These new-fangled theories seem to me to have very little value.

One might also bring forward the case of the Three-pronged Osmia, who distributes the two sexes without any order in the hollow of her reed. What singular whim is the mother obeying when, without decisive motive, she opens her seminal phial at haphazard to anoint a female egg, or else keeps it closed, also at haphazard, to allow a male egg to pass unfertilized? I could imagine impregnation being given or withheld for periods of some duration; but I cannot understand impregnation and non-impregnation following upon each other anyhow, in any sort of order, or rather with no order it all. The mother has just fertilized an egg. Why should she refuse to fertilize the next, when neither the provisions nor the lodgings differ in the smallest respect from the previous provisions and lodgings? These capricious alternations, so unreasonable and so exceedingly erratic, are scarcely appropriate to an act of such importance.

But I promised not to argue and I find myself arguing. My reasoning is too fine for dull wits. I will pass on and come to the brutal fact, the real sledge-hammer blow.

Towards the end of the Bee's operations, in the first week of June, the last acts of the Three-horned Osmia become so exceptionally interesting that I made her the object of redoubled observation. The swarm at this time is greatly reduced in numbers. I have still some thirty laggards, who continue very busy, though their work is in vain. I see some very conscientiously stopping up the entrance to a tube or a Snail-shell in which they have laid nothing at all. Others are closing the home after only building a few partitions, or even mere attempts at partitions. Some are placing at the back of a new gallery a pinch of pollen which will benefit nobody and then shutting up the house with an earthen stopper as thick, as carefully made as though the safety of a family depended on it. Born a worker, the Osmia must die working. When her ovaries are exhausted, she spends the remainder of her strength on useless works: partitions, plugs, pollen-heaps, all destined to be left unemployed. The little animal machine cannot bring itself to be inactive even when there is nothing more to be done. It goes on working so that its last vibrations of energy may be used up in fruitless labour. I commend these aberrations to the staunch supporters of reasoning-powers in the animal.

Before coming to these useless tasks, my laggards have laid their last eggs, of which I know the exact cells, the exact dates. These eggs, as far as the microscopes can tell, differ in no respect from the others, the older ones. They have the same dimensions, the same shape, the same glossiness, the same look of freshness. Nor are their provisions in any way peculiar, being very well suited to the males, who conclude the laying. And yet these last eggs do not hatch: they wrinkle, fade and wither on the pile of food. In one case, I count three or four sterile eggs among the last lot laid; in another, I find two or only one. Elsewhere in the swarm, fertile eggs have been laid right up to the end.

Those sterile eggs, stricken with death at the moment of their birth, are too numerous to be ignored. Why do they not hatch like the other eggs, which outwardly they resemble in every respect? They have received the same attention from the mother and the same portion of food. The searching microscope shows me nothing in them to explain the fatal ending.

To the unprejudiced mind, the answer is obvious. Those eggs do not hatch because they have not been fertilized. Any animal or vegetable egg that had not received the life-giving impregnation would perish in the same way. No other answer is possible. It is no use talking of the distant period of the laying: eggs of the same period laid by other mothers, eggs of the same date and likewise the final ones of a laying, are perfectly fertile. Once more, they do not hatch because they were not fertilized.

And why were they not fertilized? Because the seminal receptacle, so tiny, so difficult to see that it sometimes escaped me despite all my scrutiny, had exhausted its contents. The mothers in whom this receptacle retained a remnant of sperm to the end had their last eggs as fertile as the first; the others, whose seminal reservoir was exhausted too soon, had their last-born stricken with death. All this seems to me as clear as daylight.

If the unfertilized eggs perish without hatching, those which hatch and produce males are therefore fertilized; and the German theory falls to the ground.

Then what explanation shall I give of the wonderful facts which I have set forth? Why, none, absolutely none. I do not explain facts, I relate them. Growing daily more sceptical of the interpretations suggested to me and more hesitating as to those which I may have to suggest myself, the more I observe and experiment, the more clearly I see rising out of the black mists of possibility an enormous note of interrogation.

Dear insects, my study of you has sustained me and continues to sustain me in my heaviest trials. I must take leave of you for to-day. The ranks are thinning around me and the long hopes have fled. Shall I be able to speak to you again? (This is the closing paragraph of Volume 3 of the "Souvenirs entomologiques," of which the author has lived to publish seven more volumes, containing over 2,500 pages and nearly 850,000 words.--Translator's Note.)

CHAPTER 6. INSTINCT AND DISCERNMENT.

The Pelopaeus (A Mason-wasp forming the subject of essays which have not yet been published in English.--Translator's Note.) gives us a very poor idea of her intellect when she plasters up the spot in the wall where the nest which I have removed used to stand, when she persists in cramming her cell with Spiders for the benefit of an egg no longer there and when she dutifully closes a cell which my forceps has left empty, extracting alike germ and provisions. The Mason-bees (Cf. "The Mason-bees": chapter 7.--Translator's Note.), the caterpillar of the Great Peacock Moth (Cf. "Social Life in the Insect World" by J.H. Fabre, translated by Bernard Miall: chapter 14.--Translator's Note.) and many others, when subjected to similar tests, are guilty of the same illogical behaviour: they continue, in the normal order, their series of industrious actions, though an accident has now rendered them all useless. Just like millstones unable to cease revolving though there be no corn left to grind, let them once be given the compelling power and they will continue to perform their task despite its futility. Are they then machines? Far be it from me to think anything so foolish.

It is impossible to make definite progress on the shifting sands of contradictory facts: each step in our interpretation may find us embogged. And yet these facts speak so loudly that I do not hesitate to translate their evidence as I understand it. In insect mentality, we have to distinguish two very different domains. One of these is INSTINCT properly so called, the unconscious impulse that presides over the most wonderful part of what the creature achieves. Where experience and imitation are of absolutely no avail, instinct lays down its inflexible law. It is instinct and instinct alone that makes the mother build for a family which she will never see; that counsels the storing of provisions for the unknown offspring; that directs the sting towards the nerve-centres of the prey and skilfully paralyses it, so that the game may keep good; that instigates, in fine, a host of actions wherein shrewd reason and consummate science would have their part, were the creature acting through discernment.

This faculty is perfect of its kind from the outset, otherwise the insect would have no posterity. Time adds nothing to it and takes nothing from it. Such as it was for a definite species, such it is to-day and such it will remain, perhaps the most settled zoological characteristic of them all. It is not free nor conscious in its practice, any more than is the faculty of the stomach for digestion or that of the heart for pulsation. The phases of its operations are predetermined, necessarily entailed one by another; they suggest a system of clock-work wherein one wheel set in motion brings about the movement of the next. This is the mechanical side of the insect, the fatum, the only thing which is able to explain the monstrous illogicality of a Pelopaeus when misled by my artifices. Is the Lamb when it first grips the teat a free and conscious agent, capable of improvement in its difficult art of taking nourishment? The insect is no more capable of improvement in its art, more difficult still, of giving nourishment.

But, with its hide-bound science ignorant of itself, pure insect, if it stood alone, would leave the insect unarmed in the perpetual conflict of circumstances. No two moments in time are identical; though the background remain the same, the details change; the unexpected rises on every side. In this bewildering confusion, a guide is needed to seek, accept, refuse and select; to show preference for this and indifference to that; to turn to account, in short, anything useful that occasion may offer. This guide the insect undoubtedly possesses, to a very manifest degree. It is the second province of its mentality. Here it is conscious and capable of improvement by experience. I dare not speak of this rudimentary faculty as intelligence, which is too exalted a title: I will call it DISCERNMENT. The insect, in exercising its highest gifts, discerns, differentiates between one thing and another, within the sphere of its business, of course; and that is about all.

As long as we confound acts of pure instinct and acts of discernment under the same head, we shall fall back into those endless discussions which embitter controversy without bringing us one step nearer to the solution of the problem. Is the insect conscious of what it does? Yes and no. No, if its action is in the province of instinct; yes, if the action is in that of discernment. Are the habits of an insect capable of modification? No, decidedly not, if the habit in question belongs to the province of instinct; yes, if it belongs to that of discernment. Let us state this fundamental distinction more precisely by the aid of a few examples.

The Pelopaeus builds her cells with earth already softened, with mud. Here we have instinct, the unalterable characteristic of the worker. She has always built in this way and always will. The passing ages will never teach her, neither the struggle for life nor the law of selection will ever induce her to imitate the Mason-bee and collect dry dust for her mortar. This mud nest needs a shelter against the rain. The hiding-place under a stone suffices at first. But should she find something better, the potter takes possession of that something better and instals herself in the home of man. (The Pelopaeus builds in the fire-places of houses.--Translator's Note.) There we have discernment, the source of some sort of capacity for improvement.

The Pelopaeus supplies her larvae with provisions in the form of Spiders. There you have instinct. The climate, the longitude or latitude, the changing seasons, the abundance or scarcity of game introduce no modification into this diet, though the larva shows itself satisfied with other fare provided by myself. Its forebears were brought up on Spiders; their descendants consumed similar food; and their posterity again will know no other. Not a single circumstance, however favourable, will ever persuade the Pelopaeus that young Crickets, for instance, are as good as Spiders and that her family would accept them gladly. Instinct binds her down to the national diet.

But, should the Epeira (The Weaving or Garden Spider. Cf. "The Life of the Spider" by J. Henri Fabre translated by Alexander Teixeira de Mattos; chapters 9 to 14 and appendix.--Translator's Note.), the favourite prey, be lacking, must the Pelopaeus therefore give up foraging? She will stock her warehouses all the same, because any Spider suits her. There you have discernment, whose elasticity makes up, in certain circumstances, for the too-great rigidity of instinct. Amid the innumerable variety of game, the huntress is able to discern between what is Spider and what is not; and, in this way, she is always prepared to supply her family, without quitting the domain of her instinct.

The Hairy Ammophila gives her larva a single caterpillar, a large one, paralysed by as many pricks of her sting as it has nervous centres in its thorax and abdomen. Her surgical skill in subduing the monster is instinct displayed in a form which makes short work of any inclination to see in it an acquired habit. In an art that can leave no one to practise it in the future unless that one be perfect at the outset, of what avail are happy chances, atavistic tendencies, the mellowing hand of time? But the grey caterpillar, sacrificed one day, may be succeeded on another day by a green, yellow or striped caterpillar. There you have discernment, which is quite capable of recognizing the regulation prey under very diverse garbs.

The Megachiles build their honey-jars with disks cut out of leaves; certain Anthidia make felted cotton wallets; others fashion pots out of resin. There you have instinct. Will any rash mind ever conceive the singular idea that the Leaf-cutter might very well have started working in cotton, that the cotton-wool-worker once thought or will one day think of cutting disks out of the leaves of the lilac- and the rose-tree, that the resin-kneader began with clay? Who would dare to indulge in any such theories? Each Bee has her art, her medium, to which she strictly confines herself. The first has her leaves; the second her wadding; the third her resin. None of these guilds has ever changed trades with another; and none ever will. There you have instinct, keeping the workers to their specialities. There are no innovations in their workshops, no recipes resulting from experiment, no ingenious devices, no progress from indifferent to good, from good to excellent. To-day's method is the facsimile of yesterday's; and to-morrow will know no other.

But, though the manufacturing-process is invariable, the raw material is subject to change. The plant that supplies the cotton differs in species according to the locality; the bush out of whose leaves the pieces will be cut is not the same in the various fields of operation; the tree that provides the resinous putty may be a pine, a cypress, a juniper, a cedar or a spruce, all very different in appearance. What will guide the insect in its gleaning? Discernment.

These, I think, are sufficient details of the fundamental distinction to be drawn in the insect's mentality; the distinction, that is, between instinct and discernment. If people confuse these two provinces, as they nearly always do, any understanding becomes impossible; the last glimmer of light disappears behind the clouds of interminable discussions. From an industrial point of view, let us look upon the insect as a worker thoroughly versed from birth in a craft whose essential principles never vary; let us grant that unconscious worker a gleam of intelligence which will permit it to extricate itself from the inevitable conflict of attendant circumstances; and I think that we shall have come as near to the truth as the state of our knowledge will allow for the moment.

Having thus assigned a due share both to instinct and the aberrations of instinct when the course of its different phases is disturbed, let us see what discernment is able to do in the selection of a site for the nest and materials for building it; and, leaving the Pelopaeus, upon whom it is useless to dwell any longer, let us consider other examples, picked from among those richest in variations.

The Mason-bee of the Sheds (Chalicodoma rufitarsis, PEREZ) well deserves the name which I have felt justified in giving her from her habits: she settles in numerous colonies in our sheds, on the lower surface of the tiles, where she builds huge nests which endanger the solidity of the roof. Nowhere does the insect display a greater zeal for work than in one of these colossal cities, an estate which is constantly increasing as it passes down from one generation to another; nowhere does it find a better workshop for the exercise of its industry. Here it has plenty of room: a quiet resting-place, sheltered from damp and from excess of heat or cold.

But the spacious domain under the tiles is not within the reach of all: sheds with free access and the proper sunny aspect are pretty rare. These sites fall only to the favoured of fortune. Where will the others take up their quarters? More or less everywhere. Without leaving the house in which I live, I can enumerate stone, wood, glass, metal, paint and mortar as forming the foundation of the nests. The green-house with its furnace heat in the summer and its bright light, equalling that outside, is fairly well-frequented. The Mason-bee hardly ever fails to build there each year, in squads of a few dozen apiece, now on the glass panes, now on the iron bars of the framework. Other little swarms settle in the window embrasures, under the projecting ledge of the front door or in the cranny between the wall and an open shutter. Others again, being perhaps of a morose disposition, flee society and prefer to work in solitude, one in the inside of a lock or of a pipe intended to carry the rain-water from the leads; another in the mouldings of the doors and windows or in the crude ornamentation of the stone-work. In short, the house is made use of all round, provided that the shelter be an out-of-door one; for observe that the enterprising invader, unlike the Pelopaeus, never penetrates inside our dwellings. The case of the conservatory is an exception more apparent than real: the glass building, standing wide open throughout the summer, is to the Mason-bee but a shed a little lighter than the others. There is nothing here to arouse the distrust with which anything indoors or shut up inspires her. To build on the threshold of an outer door, or to usurp its lock, a hiding-place to her fancy, is all that she allows herself; to go any farther is an adventure repugnant to her taste.

Lastly, in the case of all these dwellings, the Mason-bee is man's free tenant; her industry makes use of the products of our own industry. Can she have no other establishments? She has, beyond a doubt; she possesses some constructed on the ancient plan. On a stone the size of a man's fist, protected by the shelter of a hedge, sometimes even on a pebble in the open air, I see her building now groups of cells as large as a walnut, now domes emulating in size, shape and solidity those of her rival, the Mason-bee of the Walls.

The stone support is the most frequent, though not the only one. I have found nests, but sparsely inhabited it is true, on the trunks of trees, in the seams of the rough bark of oaks. Among those whose support was a living plant, I will mention two that stand out above all the others. The first was built in the lobe of a torch-thistle as thick as my leg; the second rested on a stalk of the opuntia, the Indian fig. Had the fierce armour of these two stout cactuses attracted the attention of the insect, which looked upon their tufts of spikes as furnishing a system of defence for its nest? Perhaps so. In any case, the attempt was not imitated; I never saw another installation of the kind. There is one definite conclusion to be drawn from my two discoveries. Despite the oddity of their structure, which is unparalleled among the local flora, the two American importations did not compel the insect to go through an apprenticeship of groping and hesitation. The one which found itself in the presence of those novel growths, and which was perhaps the first of its race to do so, took possession of their lobes and stalks just as it would have done of a familiar site. From the start, the fleshy plants from the New World suited it as well as the trunk of a native tree.

The Mason-bee of the Pebbles (Chalicodoma parietina) has none of this elasticity in the choice of a site. In her case, the smooth stone of the parched uplands is the almost invariable foundation of her structures. Elsewhere, under a less clement sky, she prefers the support of a wall, which protects the nest against the prolonged snows. Lastly, the Mason-bee of the Shrubs (Chalicodoma rufescens, PEREZ) fixes her ball of clay to a twig of any ligneous plant, from the thyme, the rock-rose and the heath to the oak, the elm and the pine. The list of the sites that suit her would almost form a complete catalogue of the ligneous flora.

The variety of places wherein the insect instals itself, so eloquent of the part played by discernment in their selection, becomes still more remarkable when it is accompanied by a corresponding variety in the architecture of the cells. This is more particularly the case with the Three-horned Osmia, who, as she uses clayey materials very easily affected by the rain, requires, like the Pelopaeus, a dry shelter for her cells, a shelter which she finds ready-made and uses just as it is, after a few touches by way of sweeping and cleansing. The homes which I see her adopt are especially the shells of Snails that have died under the stone-heaps and in the low, unmortared walls which support the cultivated earth of the hills in shelves or terraces. The use of Snail-shells is accompanied by the no less active use of the old cells of both the Mason-bee of the Sheds and of certain Anthophorae (A. pilipes, A. parietina and A. personata).

We must not forget the reed, which is highly appreciated when--a rare find--it appears under the requisite conditions. In its natural state, the plant with the mighty hollow cylinders is of no possible use to the Osmia, who knows nothing of the art of perforating a woody wall. The gallery of an internode has to be wide open before the insect can take possession of it. Also, the clean-cut stump must be horizontal, otherwise the rain would soften the fragile edifice of clay and soon lay it low; also, the stump must not be lying on the ground and must be kept at some distance from the dampness of the soil. We see therefore that, without the intervention of man, involuntary in the vast majority of cases and deliberate only on the experimenter's part, the Osmia would hardly ever find a reed-stump suited to the installation of her family. It is to her a casual acquisition, a home unknown to her race before men took it into their heads to cut reeds and make them into hurdles for drying figs in the sun.

How did the work of man's pruning-knife bring about the abandonment of the natural lodging? How was the spiral staircase of the Snail-shell replaced by the cylindrical gallery of the reed? Was the change from one kind of house to another effected by gradual transitions, by attempts made, abandoned, resumed, becoming more and more definite in their results as generation succeeded generation? Or did the Osmia, finding the cut reed that answered her requirements, instal herself there straightway, scorning her ancient dwelling, the Snail-shell? These questions called for a reply; and they have received one. Let us describe how things happened.

Near Serignan are some great quarries of coarse limestone, characteristic of the miocene formation of the Rhone valley. These have been worked for many generations. The ancient public buildings of Orange, notably the colossal frontage of the theatre whither all the intellectual world once flocked to hear Sophocles' "Oedipus Tyrannus," derive most of their material from these quarries. Other evidence confirms what the similarity of the hewn stone tells us. Among the rubbish that fills up the spaces between the tiers of seats, they occasionally discover the Marseilles obol, a bit of silver stamped with the four-spoked wheel, or a few bronze coins bearing the effigy of Augustus or Tiberius. Scattered also here and there among the monuments of antiquity are heaps of refuse, accumulations of broken stones in which various Hymenoptera, including the Three-horned Osmia in particular, take possession of the dead Snail-shell.

The quarries form part of an extensive plateau which is so arid as to be nearly deserted. In these conditions, the Osmia, at all times faithful to her birth-place, has little or no need to emigrate from her heap of stones and leave the shell for another dwelling which she would have to go and seek at a distance. Since there are heaps of stone there, she probably has no other dwelling than the Snail-shell. Nothing tells us that the present-day generations are not descended in the direct line from the generations contemporary with the quarryman who lost his as or his obol at this spot. All the circumstances seem to point to it: the Osmia of the quarries is an inveterate user of Snail-shells; so far as heredity is concerned, she knows nothing whatever of reeds. Well, we must place her in the presence of these new lodgings.

I collect during the winter about two dozen well-stocked Snail-shells and instal them in a quiet corner of my study, as I did at the time of my enquiries into the distribution of the sexes. The little hive with its front pierced with forty holes has bits of reed fitted to it. At the foot of the five rows of cylinders I place the inhabited shells and with these I mix a few small stones, the better to imitate the natural conditions. I add an assortment of empty Snail-shells, after carefully cleaning the interior so as to make the Osmia's stay more pleasant. When the time comes for nest-building, the stay-at-home insect will have, close beside the house of its birth, a choice of two habitations: the cylinder, a novelty unknown to its race; and the spiral staircase, the ancient ancestral home.

The nests were finished at the end of May and the Osmiae began to answer my list of questions. Some, the great majority, settled exclusively in the reeds; the others remained faithful to the Snail-shell or else entrusted their eggs partly to the spirals and partly to the cylinders. With the first, who were the pioneers of cylindrical architecture, there was no hesitation that I could perceive: after exploring the stump of reed for a time and recognizing it as serviceable, the insect instals itself there and, an expert from the first touch, without apprenticeship, without groping, without any tendencies bequeathed by the long practice of its predecessors, builds its straight row of cells on a very different plan from that demanded by the spiral cavity of the shell which increases in size as it goes on.

The slow school of the ages, the gradual acquisitions of the past, the legacies of heredity count for nothing therefore in the Osmia's education. Without any novitiate on its own part or that of its forebears, the insect is versed straight away in the calling which it has to pursue; it possesses, inseparable from its nature, the qualities demanded by its craft: some which are invariable and belong to the domain of instinct; others, flexible, belonging to the province of discernment. To divide a free lodging into chambers by means of mud partitions; to fill those chambers with a heap of pollen-flour, with a few sups of honey in the central part where the egg is to lie; in short, to prepare board and lodging for the unknown, for a family which the mothers have never seen in the past and will never see in the future: this, in its essential features, is the function of the Osmia's instinct. Here, everything is harmoniously, inflexibly, permanently preordained; the insect has but to follow its blind impulse to attain the goal. But the free lodging offered by chance varies exceedingly in hygienic conditions, in shape and in capacity. Instinct, which does not choose, which does not contrive, would, if it were alone, leave the insect's existence in peril. To help her out of her predicament, in these complex circumstances, the Osmia possesses her little stock of discernment, which distinguishes between the dry and the wet, the solid and the fragile, the sheltered and the exposed; which recognizes the worth or the worthlessness of a site and knows how to sprinkle it with cells according to the size and shape of the space at disposal. Here, slight industrial variations are necessary and inevitable; and the insect excels in them without any apprenticeship, as the experiment with the native Osmia of the quarries has just proved.

Animal resources have a certain elasticity, within narrow limits. What we learn from the animals' industry at a given moment is not always the full measure of their skill. They possess latent powers held in reserve for certain emergencies. Long generations can succeed one another without employing them; but, should some circumstance require it, suddenly those powers burst forth, free of any previous attempts, even as the spark potentially contained in the flint flashes forth independently of all preceding gleams. Could one who knew nothing of the Sparrow but her nest under the eaves suspect the ball-shaped nest at the top of a tree? Would one who knew nothing of the Osmia save her home in the Snail-shell expect to see her accept as her dwelling a stump of reed, a paper funnel, a glass tube? My neighbour the Sparrow, impulsively taking it into her head to leave the roof for the plane-tree, the Osmia of the quarries, rejecting her natal cabin, the spiral of the shell, for my cylinder, alike show us how sudden and spontaneous are the industrial variations of animals.

CHAPTER 7. ECONOMY OF ENERGY.

What stimulus does the insect obey when it employs the reserve powers that slumber in its race? Of what use are its industrial variations? The Osmia will yield us her secret with no great difficulty. Let us examine her work in a cylindrical habitation. I have described in full detail, in the foregoing pages, the structure of her nests when the dwelling adopted is a reed-stump or any other cylinder; and I will content myself here with recapitulating the essential features of that nest-building.

We must first distinguish three classes of reeds according to their diameter: the small, the medium-sized and the large. I call small those whose narrow width just allows the Osmia to go about her household duties without discomfort. She must be able to turn where she stands in order to brush her abdomen and rub off its load of pollen, after disgorging the honey in the centre of the heap of flour already collected. If the width of the tube does not admit of this operation, if the insect is obliged to go out and then come in again backwards in order to place itself in a favourable posture for the discharge of the pollen, then the reed is too narrow and the Osmia is rather reluctant to accept it. The middle-sized reeds and a fortiori the large ones leave the victualler entire liberty of action; but the former do not exceed the width of a cell, a width agreeing with the bulk of the future cocoon, whereas the latter, with their excessive diameter, require more than one chamber on the same floor.

When free to choose, the Osmia settles by preference in the small reeds. Here, the work of building is reduced to its simplest expression and consists in dividing the tube by means of earthen partitions into a straight row of cells. Against the partition forming the back wall of the preceding cell the mother places first a heap of honey and pollen; next, when the portion is seen to be enough, she lays an egg in the centre of it. Then and then only she resumes her plasterer's work and marks out the length of the new cell with a mud partition. This partition in its turn serves as the rear-wall of another chamber, which is first victualled and then closed; and so on until the cylinder is sufficiently colonized and receives a thick terminal stopper at its orifice. In a word, the chief characteristic of this method of nest-building, the roughest of all, is that the partition in front is not undertaken so long as the victualling is still incomplete, or, in other words, that the provisions and the egg are deposited before the Bee sets to work on the partition.

At first sight, this latter detail hardly deserves attention: is it not right to fill the pot before we put a lid on? The Osmia who owns a medium-sized reed is not at all of this opinion; and other plasterers share her views, as we shall see when we watch the Odynerus building her nest. (A genus of Mason-wasps, the essays on which have not yet been translated into English.--Translator's Note.) Here we have an excellent illustration of one of those latent powers held in reserve for exceptional occasions and suddenly brought into play, although often very far removed from the insect's regular methods. If the reed, without being of inordinate width from the point of view of the cocoon, is nevertheless too spacious to afford the Bee a suitable purchase against the wall at the moment when she is disgorging honey and brushing off her load of pollen; the Osmia altogether changes the order of her work; she sets up the partition first and then does the victualling.

All round the inside of the tube she places a ring of mud, which, as the result of her constant visits to the mortar, ends by becoming a complete diaphragm minus an orifice at the side, a sort of round dog-hole, just large enough for the insect to pass through. When the cell is thus marked out and almost wholly closed, the Osmia attends to the storing of her provisions and the laying of her eggs. Steadying herself against the margin of the hole at one time with her fore-legs and at another with her hind-legs, she is able to empty her crop and to brush her abdomen; by pressing against it, she obtains a foothold for her little efforts in these various operations. When the tube was narrow, the outer wall supplied this foothold and the earthen partition was postponed until the heap of provisions was completed and surmounted by the egg; but in the present case the passage is too wide and would leave the insect floundering helplessly in space, so the partition with its serving-hatch takes precedence of the victuals. This method is a little more expensive than the other, first in materials, because of the diameter of the reed, and secondly in time, if only because of the dog-hole, a delicate piece of mortar-work which is too soft at first and cannot be used until it has dried and become harder. Therefore the Osmia, who is sparing of her time and strength, accepts medium-sized reeds only when there are no small ones available.

The large tubes she will use only in grave emergencies and I am unable to state exactly what these exceptional circumstances are. Perhaps she decides to make use of those roomy dwellings when the eggs have to be laid at once and there is no other shelter in the neighbourhood. While my cylinder-hives gave me plenty of well-filled reeds of the first and second class, they provided me with but half-a-dozen at most of the third, notwithstanding my precaution to furnish the apparatus with a varied assortment.

The Osmia's repugnance to big cylinders is quite justified. The work in fact is longer and more costly when the tubes are wide. An inspection of a nest constructed under these conditions is enough to convince us. It now consists not of a string of chambers obtained by simple transverse partitions, but of a confused heap of clumsy, many-sided compartments, standing back to back, with a tendency to group themselves in storeys without succeeding in doing so, because any regular arrangement would mean that the ceilings possessed a span which it is not in the builder's power to achieve. The edifice is not a geometrical masterpiece and it is even less satisfactory from the point of view of economy. In the previous constructions, the sides of the reed supplied the greater part of the walls and the work was limited to one partition for each cell. Here, except at the actual periphery, where the tube itself supplies a foundation, everything has to be obtained by sheer building: the floor, the ceiling, the walls of the many-sided compartment are one and all made of mortar. The structure is almost as costly in materials as that of the Chalicodoma or the Pelopaeus.

It must be pretty difficult, too, when one thinks of its irregularity. Fitting as best she can the projecting angles of the new cell into the recessed corners of the cell already built, the Osmia runs up walls more or less curved, upright or slanting, which intersect one another at various points, so that each compartment requires a new and complicated plan of construction, which is very different from the circular-partition style of architecture, with its row of parallel dividing-disks. Moreover, in this composite arrangement, the size of the recesses left available by the earlier work to some extent decides the assessment of the sexes, for, according to the dimensions of those recesses, the walls erected take in now a larger space, the home of a female, and now a smaller space, the home of a male. Roomy quarters therefore have a double drawback for the Osmia: they greatly increase the outlay in materials; and also they establish in the lower layers, among the females, males who, because of their earlier hatching, would be much better placed near the mouth of the nest. I am convinced of it: if the Osmia refuses big reeds and accepts them only in the last resort, when there are no others, it is because she objects to additional labour and to the mixture of the sexes.

The Snail-shell, then, is but an indifferent home for her, which she is quite ready to abandon should a better offer. Its expanding cavity represents an average between the favourite small cylinder and the unpopular large cylinder, which is accepted only when there is no other obtainable. The first whorls of the spiral are too narrow to be of use to the Osmia, but the middle ones have the right diameter for cocoons arranged in single file. Here things happen as in a first-class reed, for the helical curve in no way affects the method of structure employed for a rectilinear series of cells. Circular partitions are erected at the required distances, with or without a serving-hatch, according to the diameter. These mark out the first cells, one after the other, which are reserved solely for the females. Then comes the last whorl, which is much too wide for a single row of cells; and here we once more find, exactly as in a wide reed, a costly profusion of masonry, an irregular arrangement of the cells and a mixture of the sexes.

Having said so much, let us go back to the Osmia of the quarries. Why, when I offer them simultaneously Snail-shells and reeds of a suitable size, do the old frequenters of the shells prefer the reeds, which in all probability have never before been utilized by their race? Most of them scorn the ancestral dwelling and enthusiastically accept my reeds. Some, it is true, take up their quarters in the Snail-shell; but even among these a goodly number refuse my new shells and return to their birth-place, the old Snail-shell, in order to utilize the family property, without much labour, at the cost of a few repairs. Whence, I ask, comes this general preference for the cylinder, never used hitherto? The answer can be only this: of two lodgings at her disposal the Osmia selects the one that provides a comfortable home at a minimum outlay. She economizes her strength when restoring an old nest; she economizes it when replacing the Snail-shell by the reed.

Can animal industry, like our own, obey the law of economy, the sovran law that governs our industrial machine even as it governs, at least to all appearances, the sublime machine of the universe? Let us go deeper into the question and bring other workers into evidence, those especially who, better equipped perhaps and at any rate better fitted for hard work, attack the difficulties of their trade boldly and look down upon alien establishments with scorn. Of this number are the Chalicodomae, the Mason-bees proper.

The Mason-bee of the Pebbles does not make up her mind to build a brand-new dome unless there be a dearth of old and not quite dilapidated nests. The mothers, sisters apparently and heirs-at-law to the domain, dispute fiercely for the ancestral abode. The first who, by sheer brute force, takes possession of the dome, perches upon it and, for long hours, watches events while polishing her wings. If some claimant puts in an appearance, forthwith the other turns her out with a volley of blows. In this way the old nests are employed so long as they have not become uninhabitable hovels.

Without being equally jealous of the maternal inheritance, the Mason-bee of the Sheds eagerly uses the cells whence her generation issued. The work in the huge city under the eaves begins thus: the old cells, of which, by the way, the good-natured owner yields a portion to Latreille's Osmia and to the Three-horned Osmia alike, are first made clean and wholesome and cleared of broken plaster and then provisioned and shut. When all the accessible chambers are occupied, the actual building begins with a new stratum of cells upon the former edifice, which becomes more and more massive from year to year.

The Mason-bee of the Shrubs, with her spherical nests hardly larger than walnuts, puzzled me at first. Does she use the old buildings or does she abandon them for good? To-day perplexity makes way for certainty: she uses them very readily. I have several times surprised her lodging her family in the empty rooms of a nest where she was doubtless born herself. Like her kinswoman of the Pebbles, she returns to the native dwelling and fights for its possession. Also, like the dome-builder, she is an anchorite and prefers to cultivate the lean inheritance alone. Sometimes, however, the nest is of exceptional size and harbours a crowd of occupants, who live in peace, each attending to her business, as in the colossal hives in the sheds. Should the colony be at all numerous and the estate descend to two or three generations in succession, with a fresh layer of masonry each year, the normal walnut-sized nest becomes a ball as large as a man's two fists. I have gathered on a pine-tree a nest of the Mason-bee of the Shrubs that weighed a kilogram (2.205 pounds avoirdupois.--Translator's Note.) and was the size of a child's head. A twig hardly thicker than a straw served as its support. The casual sight of that lump swinging over the spot on which I had sat down made me think of the mishap that befell Garo. (The hero of La Fontaine's fable, "Le Gland et la Citrouille," who wondered why acorns grew on such tall trees and pumpkins on such low vines, until he fell asleep under one of the latter and a pumpkin dropped upon his nose.--Translator's Note.) If such nests were plentiful in the trees, any one seeking the shade would run a serious risk of having his head smashed.

After the Masons, the Carpenters. Among the guild of wood-workers, the most powerful is the Carpenter-bee (Xylocopa violacea (Cf. "The Life of the Spider": chapter 1.--Translator's Note.)), a very large Bee of formidable appearance, clad in black velvet with violet-coloured wings. The mother gives her larvae as a dwelling a cylindrical gallery which she digs in rotten wood. Useless timber lying exposed to the air, vine-poles, large logs of fire-wood seasoning out of doors, heaped up in front of the farmhouse porch, stumps of trees, vine-stocks and big branches of all kinds are her favourite building-yards. A solitary and industrious worker, she bores, bit by bit, circular passages the width of one's thumb, as clear-cut as though they were made with an auger. A heap of saw-dust accumulates on the ground and bears witness to the severity of the task. Usually, the same aperture is the entrance to two or three parallel corridors. With several galleries there is accommodation for the entire laying, though each gallery is quite short; and the Bee thus avoids those long series which always create difficulties when the moment of hatching arrives. The laggards and the insects eager to emerge are less likely to get in each other's way.

After obtaining the dwelling, the Carpenter-bee behaves like the Osmia who is in possession of a reed. Provisions are collected, the egg is laid and the chamber is walled in front with a saw-dust partition. The work is pursued in this way until the two or three passages composing the house are completely stocked. Heaping up provisions and erecting partitions are an invariable feature of the Xylocopa's programme; no circumstance can release the mother from the duty of providing for the future of her family, in the matter both of ready-prepared food and of separate compartments for the rearing of each larva. It is only in the boring of the galleries, the most laborious part of the work, that economy can occasionally be exercised by a piece of luck. Well, is the powerful Carpenter, all unheeding of fatigue, able to take advantage of such fortunate occasions? Does she know how to make use of houses which she has not tunnelled herself? Why, yes: a free lodging suits her just as much as it does the various Mason-bees. She knows as well as they the economic advantages of an old nest that is still in good condition: she settles down, as far as possible, in her predecessors' galleries, after freshening up the sides with a superficial scraping. And she does better still. She readily accepts lodgings which have never known a drill, no matter whose. The stout reeds used in the trellis-work that supports the vines are valuable discoveries, providing as they do sumptuous galleries free of cost. No preliminary work or next to none is required with these. Indeed, the insect does not even trouble to make a side-opening, which would enable it to occupy the cavity contained within two nodes; it prefers the opening at the end cut by man's pruning-knife. If the next partition be too near to give a chamber of sufficient length, the Xylocopa destroys it, which is easy work, not to be compared with the labour of cutting an entrance through the side. In this way, a spacious gallery, following on the short vestibule made by the pruning-knife, is obtained with the least possible expenditure of energy.

Guided by what was happening on the trellises, I offered the black Bee the hospitality of my reed-hives. From the very beginning, the insect gladly welcomed my advances; each spring, I see it inspect my rows of cylinders, pick out the best ones and instal itself there. Its work, reduced to a minimum by my intervention, is limited to the partitions, the materials for which are obtained by scraping the inner sides of the reed.

As first-rate joiners, next to the Carpenter-bees come the Lithurgi, of whom my district possesses two species: L. cornutus, FAB., and L. chrysurus, BOY. By what aberration of nomenclature was the name of Lithurgus, a worker in stone, given to insects which work solely in wood? I have caught the first, the stronger of the two, digging galleries in a large block of oak that served as an arch for a stable-door; I have always found the second, who is more widely distributed, settling in dead wood--mulberry, cherry, almond, poplar--that was still standing. Her work is exactly the same as the Xylocopa's, on a smaller scale. A single entrance-hole gives access to three or four parallel galleries, assembled in a serried group; and these galleries are subdivided into cells by means of saw-dust partitions. Following the example of the big Carpenter-bee, Lithurgus chrysurus knows how to avoid the laborious work of boring, when occasion offers: I find her cocoons lodged almost as often in old dormitories as in new ones. She too has the tendency to economize her strength by turning the work of her predecessors to account. I do not despair of see-ing her adopt the reed if, one day, when I possess a large enough colony, I decide to try this experiment on her. I will say nothing about L. cornutus, whom I only once surprised at her carpentering.

The Anthophorae, those children of the precipitous earthy banks, show the same thrifty spirit as the other members of the mining corporation. Three species, A. parietina, A. personata and A. pilipes, dig long corridors leading to the cells, which are scattered here and there and one by one. These passages remain open at all seasons of the year. When spring comes, the new colony uses them just as they are, provided that they are well preserved in the clayey mass baked by the sun; it increases their length if necessary, runs out a few more branches, but does not decide to start boring in new ground until the old city, which, with its many labyrinths, resembles some monstrous sponge, is too much undermined for safety. The oval niches, the cells that open on those corridors, are also profitably employed. The Anthophora restores their entrance, which has been destroyed by the insect's recent emergence; she smooths their walls with a fresh coat of whitewash, after which the lodging is fit to receive the heap of honey and the egg. When the old cells, insufficient in number and moreover partly inhabited by diverse intruders, are all occupied, the boring of new cells begins, in the extended sections of the galleries, and the rest of the eggs are housed. In this way, the swarm is settled at a minimum of expense.

To conclude this brief account, let us change the zoological setting and, as we have already spoken of the Sparrow, see what he can do as a builder. The simplest form of his nest is the great round ball of straw, dead leaves and feathers, in the fork of a few branches. It is costly in material, but can be set up anywhere, when the hole in the wall or the shelter of a tile are lacking. What reasons induced him to give up the spherical edifice? To all seeming, the same reasons that led the Osmia to abandon the Snail-shell's spiral, which requires a fatiguing expenditure of clay, in favour of the economical cylinder of the reed. By making his home in a hole in the wall, the Sparrow escapes the greater part of his work. Here, the dome that serves as a protection from the rain and the thick walls that offer resistance to the wind both become superfluous. A mere mattress is sufficient; the cavity in the wall provides the rest. The saving is great; and the Sparrow appreciates it quite as much as the Osmia.

This does not mean that the primitive art has disappeared, lost through neglect; it remains an ineffaceable characteristic of the species, ever ready to declare itself should circumstances demand it. The generations of to-day are as much endowed with it as the generations of yore; without apprenticeship, without the example of others, they have within themselves, in the potential state, the industrial aptitude of their ancestors. If aroused by the stimulus of necessity, this aptitude will pass suddenly from inaction to action. When, therefore, the Sparrow still from time to time indulges in spherical building, this is not progress on his part, as is sometimes contended; it is, on the contrary, a retrogression, a return to the ancient customs, so prodigal of labour. He is behaving like the Osmia who, in default of a reed, makes shift with a Snail-shell, which is more difficult to utilize but easier to find. The cylinder and the hole in the wall stand for progress; the spiral of the Snail-shell and the ball-shaped nest represent the starting-point.

I have, I think, sufficiently illustrated the inference which is borne out by the whole mass of analogous facts. Animal industry manifests a tendency to achieve the essential with a minimum of expenditure; after its own fashion, the insect bears witness to the economy of energy. On the one hand, instinct imposes upon it a craft that is unchangeable in its fundamental features; on the other hand, it is left a certain latitude in the details, so as to take advantage of favourable circumstances and attain the object aimed at with the least possible expenditure of time, materials and work, the three elements of mechanical labour. The problem in higher geometry solved by the Hive-bee is only a particular case--true, a magnificent case,--of this general law of economy which seems to govern the whole animal world. The wax cells, with their maximum capacity as against a minimum wall-space, are the equivalent, with the superaddition of a marvellous scientific skill, of the Osmia's compartments in which the stonework is reduced to a minimum through the selection of a reed. The artificer in mud and the artificer in wax obey the same tendency: they economize. Do they know what they are doing? Who would venture to suggest it in the case of the Bee grappling with her transcendental problem? The others, pursuing their rustic art, are no wiser. With all of them, there is no calculation, no premeditation, but simply blind obedience to the law of general harmony.

CHAPTER 8. THE LEAF-CUTTERS.

It is not enough that animal industry should be able, to a certain extent, to adapt itself to casual exigencies when choosing the site of a nest; if the race is to thrive, something else is required, something which hide-bound instinct is unable to provide. The Chaffinch, for instance, introduces a great quantity of lichen into the outer layer of his nest. This is his method of strengthening the edifice and making a stout framework in which to place first the bottom mattress of moss, fine straw and rootlets and then the soft bed of feathers, wool and down. But, should the time-honoured lichen be lacking, will the bird refrain from building its nest? Will it forgo the delight of hatching its brood because it has not the wherewithal to settle its family in the orthodox fashion?

No, the chaffinch is not perplexed by so small a matter; he is an expert in materials, he understands botanical equivalents. In the absence of the branches of the evernias, he picks the long beards of the usneas, the wartlike rosettes of the parmelias, the membranes of the stictises torn away in shreds; if he can find nothing better, he makes shift with the bushy tufts of the cladonias. As a practical lichenologist, when one species is rare or lacking in the neighbourhood, he is able to fall back on others, varying greatly in shape, colour and texture. And, if the impossible happened and lichen failed entirely, I credit the Chaffinch with sufficient talent to be able to dispense with it and to build the foundations of his nest with some coarse moss or other.

What the worker in lichens tells us the other weavers of textile materials confirm. Each has his favourite flora, which hardly ever varies when the plant is easily accessible and which can be supplemented by plenty of others when it is not. The bird's botany would be worth examining; it would be interesting to draw up the industrial herbal of each species. In this connection, I will quote just one instance, so as not to stray too far from the subject in hand.

The Red-backed Shrike (Lanius collurio), the commonest variety in my district, is noteworthy because of his savage mania for forked gibbets, the thorns in the hedgerows whereon he impales the voluminous contents of his game-bag--little half-fledged birds, small Lizards, Grasshoppers, caterpillars, Beetles--and leaves them to get high. To this passion for the gallows, which has passed unnoticed by the country-folk, at least in my part, he adds another, an innocent botanical passion, which is so much in evidence that everybody, down to the youngest bird's-nester, knows all about it. His nest, a massive structure, is made of hardly any other materials than a greyish and very fluffy plant, which is found everywhere among the corn. This is the Filago spathulata of the botanists; and the bird also makes use, though less frequently, of the Filago germanica, or common cotton-rose. Both are known in Provencal by the name herbo dou tarnagas, or Shrike-herb. This popular designation tells us plainly how faithful the bird is to its plant. To have struck the agricultural labourer, a very indifferent observer, the Shrike's choice of materials must be remarkably persistent.

Have we here a taste that is exclusive? Not in the least. Though cotton-roses of all species are plentiful on level ground, they become scarce and impossible to find on the parched hills. The bird, on its side, is not given to journeys of exploration and takes what it finds to suit it in the neighbourhood of its tree or hedge. But on arid ground, the Micropus erectus, or upright micropus, abounds and is a satisfactory substitute for the Filago so far as its tiny, cottony leaves and its little fluffy balls of flowers are concerned. True, it is short and does not lend itself well to weaver's work. A few long sprigs of another cottony plant, the Helichrysum staechas, or wild everlasting, inserted here and there, will give body to the structure. Thus does the Shrike manage when hard up for his favourite materials: keeping to the same botanical family, he is able to find and employ substitutes among the fine cotton-clad stalks.

He is even able to leave the family of the Compositae and to go gleaning more or less everywhere. Here is the result of my botanizings at the expense of his nests. We must distinguish between two genera in the Shrike's rough classification: the cottony plants and the smooth plants. Among the first, my notes mention the following: Convolvulus cantabrica, or flax-leaved bindweed; Lotus symmetricus, or bird's-foot trefoil; Teucrium polium, or poly; and the flowery heads of the Phragmites communis, or common reed. Among the second are these: Medicago lupulina, or nonesuch; Trifolium repens, or white clover; Lathyrus pratensis, or meadow lathyrus; Capsella bursa pastoris, or shepherd's purse; Vicia peregrina, or broad-podded vetch; Convolvulus arvensis, or small bindweed; Pterotheca nemausensis, a sort of hawkweed; and Poa pratensis, or smooth-stalked meadow-grass. When it is downy, the plant forms almost the whole nest, as is the case with the flax-leaved bindweed; when smooth, it forms only the framework, destined to support a crumbling mass of micropus, as is the case with the small bindweed. When making this collection, which I am far from giving as the birds' complete herbarium, I was struck by a wholly unexpected detail: of the various plants, I found only the heads still in bud; moreover, all the sprigs, though dry, possessed the green colouring of the growing plant, a sign of swift desiccation in the sun. Save in a few cases, therefore, the Shrike does not collect the dead and withered remains: it is from the growing plants that he reaps his harvest, mowing them down with his beak and leaving the sheaves to dry in the sun before using them. I caught him one day hopping about and pecking at the twigs of a Biscayan bindweed. He was getting in his hay, strewing the ground with it.

The evidence of the Shrike, confirmed by that of all the other workers--weavers, basket-makers or woodcutters--whom we may care to call as witnesses, shows us what a large part must be assigned to discernment in the bird's choice of materials for its nest. Is the insect as highly gifted? When it works with vegetable matter, is it exclusive in its tastes? Does it know only one definite plant, its special province? Or has it, for employment in its manufactures, a varied flora, in which its discernment exercises a free choice? For answers to these questions we may look, above all, to the Leaf-cutting Bees, the Megachiles. Reaumur has told the story of their industry in detail; and I refer the reader who wishes for further particulars to the master's Memoirs.

The man who knows how to use his eyes in his garden will observe, some day or other, a number of curious holes in the leaves of his lilac- and rose-trees, some of them round, some oval, as if idle but skilful hands had been at work with the pinking-iron. In some places, there is scarcely anything but the veins of the leaves left. The author of the mischief is a grey-clad Bee, a Megachile. For scissors, she has her mandibles; for compasses, producing now an oval and anon a circle, she has her eye and the pivot of her body. The pieces cut out are made into thimble-shaped wallets, destined to contain the honey and the egg: the larger, oval pieces supply the floor and sides; the smaller, round pieces are reserved for the lid. A row of these thimbles, placed one on top of the other, up to a dozen or more, though often there are less: that is, roughly, the structure of the Leaf-cutter's nest.

When taken out of the recess in which the mother has manufactured it, the cylinder of cells seems to be an indivisible whole, a sort of tunnel obtained by lining with leaves some gallery dug underground. The real thing does not correspond with its appearance: under the least pressure of the fingers, the cylinder breaks up into equal sections, which are so many compartments independent of their neighbours as regards both floor and lid. This spontaneous break up shows us how the work is done. The method agrees with those adopted by the other Bees. Instead of a general scabbard of leaves, afterwards subdivided into compartments by transverse partitions, the Megachile constructs a string of separate wallets, each of which is finished before the next is begun.

A structure of this sort needs a sheath to keep the pieces in place while giving them the proper shape. The bag of leaves, in fact, as turned out by the worker, lacks stability; its numerous pieces, not glued together, but simply placed one after the other, come apart and give way as soon as they lose the support of the tunnel that keeps them united. Later, when it spins its cocoon, the larva infuses a little of its fluid silk into the gaps and solders the pieces to one another, especially the inner ones, so much so that the insecure bag in due course becomes a solid casket whose component parts it is no longer possible to separate entirely.

The protective sheath, which is also a framework, is not the work of the mother. Like the great majority of the Osmiae, the Megachiles do not understand the art of making themselves a home straight away: they want a borrowed lodging, which may vary considerably in character. The deserted galleries of the Anthophorae, the burrows of the fat Earth-worms, the tunnels bored in the trunks of trees by the larva of the Cerambyx-beetle (The Capricorn, the essay on which has not yet been published in English.--Translator's Note.), the ruined dwellings of the Mason-bee of the Pebbles, the Snail-shell nests of the Three-horned Osmia, reed-stumps, when these are handy, and crevices in the walls are all so many homes for the

Leaf-cutters, who choose this or that establishment according to the tastes of their particular genus.

For the sake of clearness, let us cease generalizing and direct our attention to a definite species. I first selected the White-girdled Leaf-cutter (Megachile albocincta, PEREZ), not on account of any exceptional peculiarities, but solely because this is the Bee most often mentioned in my notes. Her customary dwelling is the tunnel of an Earth-worm opening on some clay bank. Whether perpendicular or slanting, this tunnel runs down to an indefinite depth, where the climate would be too damp for the Bee. Besides, when the time comes for the hatching of the adult insect, its emergence would be fraught with peril if it had to climb up from a deep pit through crumbling rubbish. The Leaf-cutter, therefore, uses only the front portion of the Worm's gallery, two decimetres at most. (7.8 inches.--Translator's Note.) What is to be done with the rest of the tunnel? It is an ascending shaft, tempting to an enemy; and some underground ravager might come this way and destroy the nest by attacking the row of cells at the back.

The danger is foreseen. Before fashioning her first honey-bag, the Bee blocks the passage with a strong barricade composed of the only materials used in the Leaf-cutter's guild. Fragments of leaves are piled up in no particular order, but in sufficient quantities to make a serious obstacle. It is not unusual to find in the leafy rampart some dozens of pieces rolled into screws and fitting into one another like a stack of cylindrical wafers. For this work of fortification, artistic refinement seems superfluous; at any rate, the pieces of leaves are for the most part irregular. You can see that the insect has cut them out hurriedly, unmethodically and on a different pattern from that of the pieces intended for the cells.

I am struck with another detail in the barricade. Its constituents are taken from stout, thick, strong-veined leaves. I recognize young vine-leaves, pale-coloured and velvety; the leaves of the whitish rock-rose (Cistus albidus), lined with a hairy felt; those of the holm-oak, selected among the young and bristly ones; those of the hawthorn, smooth but tough; those of the cultivated reed, the only one of the Monocotyledones exploited, as far as I know, by the Megachiles. In the construction of cells, on the other hand, I see smooth leaves predominating, notably those of the wild briar and of the common acacia, the robinia. It would appear, therefore, that the insect distinguishes between two kinds of materials, without being an absolute purist and sternly excluding any sort of blending. The very much indented leaves, whose projections can be completely removed with a dexterous snip of the scissors, generally furnish the various layers of the barricade; the little robinia-leaves, with their fine texture and their unbroken edges, are better suited to the more delicate work of the cells.

A rampart at the back of the Earth-worm's shaft is a wise precaution and the Leaf-cutter deserves all credit for it; only it is a pity for the Megachiles' reputation that this protective barrier often protects nothing at all. Here we see, under a new guise, that aberration of instinct of which I gave some examples in an earlier chapter. My notes contain memoranda of various galleries crammed with pieces of leaves right up to the orifice, which is on a level with the ground, and entirely devoid of cells, even of an unfinished one. These were ridiculous fortifications, of no use whatever; and yet the Bee treated the matter with the utmost seriousness and took infinite pains over her futile task. One of these uselessly barricaded galleries furnished me with some hundred pieces of leaves arranged like a stack of wafers; another gave me as many as a hundred and fifty. For the defence of a tenanted nest, two dozen and even fewer are ample. Then what was the object of the Leaf-cutter's ridiculous pile?

I wish I could believe that, seeing that the place was dangerous, she made her heap bigger so that the rampart might be in proportion to the danger. Then, perhaps, at the moment of starting on the cells, she disappeared, the victim of an accident, blown out of her course by a gust of wind. But this line of defence is not admissible in the Megachile's case. The proof is palpable: the galleries aforesaid are barricaded up to the level of the ground; there is no room, absolutely none, to lodge even a single egg. What was her object, I ask again, when she persisted in obstinately piling up her wafers? Has she really an object?

I do not hesitate to say no. And my answer is based upon what the Osmiae taught me. I have described above how the Three-horned Osmia, towards the end of her life, when her ovaries are depleted, expends on useless operations such energy as remains to her. Born a worker, she is bored by the inactivity of retirement; her leisure requires an occupation. Having nothing better to do, she sets up partitions; she divides a tunnel into cells that will remain empty; she closes with a thick plug reeds containing nothing. Thus is the modicum of strength of her decline exhausted in vain labours. The other Builder-bees behave likewise. I see Anthidia laboriously provide numerous bales of cotton to stop galleries wherein never an egg was laid; I see Mason-bees build and then religiously close cells that will remain unvictualled and uncolonized.

The long and useless barricades then belong to the last hours of the Megachile's life, when the eggs are all laid; the mother, whose ovaries are exhausted, persists in building. Her instinct is to cut out and heap up pieces of leaves; obeying this impulse, she cuts out and heaps up even when the supreme reason for this labour ceases. The eggs are no longer there, but some strength remains; and that strength is expended as the safety of the species demanded in the beginning. The wheels of action go on turning in the absence of the motives for action; they continue their movement as though by a sort of acquired velocity. What clearer proof can we hope to find of the unconsciousness of the animal stimulated by instinct?

Let us return to the Leaf-cutter's work under normal conditions. Immediately after a protective barrier comes the row of cells, which vary considerably in number, like those of the Osmia in her reed. Strings of about a dozen are rare; the most frequent consist of five or six. No less subject to variation is the number of pieces joined to make a cell: pieces of two kinds, some, the oval ones, forming the honey-pot; others, the round ones, serving as a lid. I count, on an average, eight to ten pieces of the first kind. Though all cut on the pattern of an ellipse, they are not equal in dimensions and come under two categories. The larger, outside ones are each of them almost a third of the circumference and overlap one another slightly. Their lower end bends into a concave curve to form the bottom of the bag. Those inside, which are considerably smaller, increase the thickness of the sides and fill up the gaps left by the first.

The Leaf-cutter therefore is able to use her scissors according to the task before her: first, the large pieces, which help the work forward, but leave empty spaces; next, the small pieces, which fit into the defective portions. The bottom of the cell particularly comes in for after-touches. As the natural curve of the larger pieces is not enough to provide a cup without cracks in it, the Bee does not fail to improve the work with two or three small oval pieces applied to the imperfect joins.

Another advantage results from the snippets of unequal size. The three or four outer pieces, which are the first placed in position, being the longest of all, project beyond the mouth, whereas the next, being shorter, do not come quite up to it. A brim is thus obtained, a ledge on which the round disks of the lid rest and are prevented from touching the honey when the Bee presses them into a concave cover. In other words, at the mouth the circumference comprises only one row of leaves; lower down it takes two or three, thus restricting the diameter and securing an hermetic closing.

The cover of the pot consists solely of round pieces, very nearly alike and more or less numerous. Sometimes I find only two, sometimes I count as many as ten, closely stacked. At times, the diameter of these pieces is of an almost mathematical precision, so much so that the edges of the disk rest upon the ledge. No better result would be obtained had they been cut out with the aid of compasses. At times, again, the piece projects slightly beyond the mouth, so that, to enter, it has to be pressed down and curved cupwise. There is no variation in the diameter of the first pieces placed in position, those nearest to the honey. They are all of the same size and thus form a flat cover which does not encroach on the cell and will not afterwards interfere with the larva, as a convex ceiling would. The subsequent disks, when the pile is numerous, are a little larger; they only fit the mouth by yielding to pressure and becoming concave. The Bee seems to make a point of this concavity, for it serves as a mould to receive the curved bottom of the next cell.

When the row of cells is finished, the task still remains of blocking up the entrance to the gallery with a safety-stopper similar to the earthen plug with which the Osmia closes her reeds. The Bee then returns to the free and easy use of the scissors which we noticed at the beginning when she was fencing off the back part of the Earth-worm's too deep burrow; she cuts out of the foliage irregular pieces of different shapes and sizes and often retaining their original deeply-indented margins; and with all these pieces, very few of which fit at all closely the orifice to be blocked, she succeeds in making an inviolable door, thanks to the huge number of layers.

Let us leave the Leaf-cutter to finish depositing her eggs in other galleries, which will be colonized in the same manner, and consider for a moment her skill as a cutter. Her edifices consist of a multitude of fragments belonging to three categories: oval pieces for the sides of the cells; round pieces for the lids; and irregular pieces for the barricades at the front and back. The last present no difficulty: the

Bee obtains them by removing from the leaf some projecting portion, as it stands, a serrate lobe which, owing to its notches, shortens the insect's task and lends itself better to scissor-work. So far, there is nothing to deserve attention: it is unskilled labour, in which an inexperienced apprentice might excel.

With the oval pieces, it becomes another matter. What model has the Megachile when cutting her neat ellipses out of the delicate material for her wallets, the robinia-leaves? What mental pattern guides her scissors? What system of measurement tells her the dimensions? One would like to picture the insect as a living pair of compasses, capable of tracing an elliptic curve by a certain natural inflexion of its body, even as our arm traces a circle by swinging from the shoulder. A blind mechanism, the mere outcome of its organization, would alone be responsible for its geometry. This explanation would tempt me if the large oval pieces were not accompanied by much smaller ones, also oval, which are used to fill the empty spaces. A pair of compasses which changes its radius of its own accord and alters the curve according to the plan before it appears to me an instrument somewhat difficult to believe in. There must be something better than that. The circular pieces of the lid suggest it to us.

If, by the mere flexion inherent in her structure, the Leaf-cutter succeeds in cutting out ovals, how does she succeed in cutting out rounds? Can we admit the presence of other wheels in the machinery for the new pattern, so different in shape and size? Besides, the real point of the difficulty does not lie there. These rounds, for the most part, fit the mouth of the jar with almost exact precision. When the cell is finished, the Bee flies hundreds of yards away to make the lid. She arrives at the leaf from which the disk is to be cut. What picture, what recollection has she of the pot to be covered? Why, none at all: she has never seen it; she does her work underground, in utter darkness! At the utmost, she can have the indications of touch: not actual indications, of course, for the pot is not there, but past indications, useless in a work of precision. And yet the disk to be cut out must have a fixed diameter: if it were too large, it would not go in; if too small, it would close badly, it would slip down on the honey and suffocate the egg. How shall it be given its correct dimensions without a pattern? The Bee does not hesitate for a moment. She cuts out her disk with the same celerity which she would display in detaching any shapeless lobe that might do for a stopper; and that disk, without further measurement, is of the right size to fit the pot. Let whoso will explain this geometry, which in my opinion is inexplicable, even when we allow for memory begotten of touch and sight.

One winter evening, as we were sitting round the fire, whose cheerful blaze unloosed our tongues, I put the problem of the Leaf-cutter to my family:

'Among your kitchen-utensils,' I said, 'you have a pot in daily use; but it has lost its lid, which was knocked over and broken by the Tomcat playing among the shelves. To-morrow is market-day and one of you will be going to Orange to buy the week's provisions. Would she undertake, without a measure of any kind, with the sole aid of memory, which we would allow her to refresh before starting by a careful examination of the object, to bring back exactly what the pot wants, a lid neither too large nor too small, in short the same size as the top?'

It was admitted with one accord that nobody would accept such a commission without taking a measure with her, or at least a bit of string giving the width. Our memory for sizes is not accurate enough. She would come back from the town with something that 'might do'; and it would be the merest chance if this turned out to be the right size.

Well, the Leaf-cutter is even less well-off than ourselves. She has no mental picture of her pot, because she has never seen it; she is not able to pick and choose in the crockery-dealer's heap, which acts as something of a guide to our memory by comparison; she must, without hesitation, far away from her home, cut out a disk that fits the top of her jar. What is impossible to us is child's-play to her. Where we could not do without a measure of some kind, a bit of string, a pattern or a scrap of paper with figures upon it, the little Bee needs nothing at all. In housekeeping matters she is cleverer than we are.

One objection was raised. Was it not possible that the Bee, when at work on the shrub, should first cut a round piece of an approximate diameter, larger than that of the neck of the jar, and that afterwards, on returning home, she should gnaw away the superfluous part until the lid exactly fitted the pot? These alterations made with the model in front of her would explain everything.

That is perfectly true; but are there any alterations? To begin with, it seems to me hardly possible that the insect can go back to the cutting once the piece is detached from the leaf: it lacks the necessary support to gnaw the flimsy disk with any precision. A tailor would spoil his cloth if he had not the support of a table when cutting out the pieces for a coat. The Megachile's scissors, so difficult to wield on anything not firmly held, would do equally bad work.

Besides, I have better evidence than this for my refusal to believe in the existence of alterations when the Bee has the cell in front of her. The lid is composed of a pile of disks whose number sometimes reaches half a score. Now the bottom part of all these disks is the under surface of the leaf, which is paler and more strongly veined; the top part is the upper surface, which is smooth and greener. In other words, the insect places them in the position which they occupy when gathered. Let me explain. In order to cut out a piece, the Bee stands on the upper surface of the leaf. The piece detached is held in the feet and is therefore laid with its top surface against the insect's chest at the moment of departure. There is no possibility of its being turned over on the journey. Consequently, the piece is laid as the Bee has just picked it, with the lower surface towards the inside of the cell and the upper surface towards the outside. If alterations were necessary to reduce the lid to the diameter of the pot, the disk would be bound to get turned over: the piece, manipulated, set upright, turned round, tried this way and that, would, when finally laid in position, have its top or bottom surface inside just as it happened to come. But this is exactly what does not take place. Therefore, as the order of stacking never changes, the disks are cut, from the first clip of the scissors, with their proper dimensions. The insect excels us in practical geometry. I look upon the Leaf-cutter's pot and lid as an addition to the many other marvels of instinct that cannot be explained by mechanics; I submit it to the consideration of science; and I pass on.

The Silky Leaf-cutter (Megachile sericans, FONSCOL.; M. Dufourii, LEP.) makes her nests in the disused galleries of the Anthophorae. I know her to occupy another dwelling which is more elegant and affords a more roomy installation: I mean the old dwelling of the fat Capricorn, the denizen of the oaks. The metamorphosis is effected in a spacious chamber lined with soft felt. When the long-horned Beetle reaches the adult stage, he releases himself and emerges from the tree by following a vestibule which the larva's powerful tools have prepared beforehand. When the deserted cabin, owing to its position, remains wholesome and there is no sign of any running from its walls, no brown stuff smelling of the tan-yard, it is soon visited by the Silky Megachile, who finds in it the most sumptuous of the apartments inhabited by the Leaf-cutters. It combines every condition of comfort:

perfect safety, an even temperature, freedom from damp, ample room; and so the mother who is fortunate enough to become the possessor of such a lodging uses it entirely, vestibule and drawing-room alike. Accommodation is found for all her family of eggs; at least, I have nowhere seen nests as populous as here.

One of them provides me with seventeen cells, the highest number appearing in my census of the Megachile clan. Most of them are lodged in the nymphal chamber of the Capricorn; and, as the spacious recess is too wide for a single row, the cells are arranged in three parallel series. The remainder, in a single string, occupy the vestibule, which is completed and filled up by the terminal barricade. In the materials employed, hawthorn-and paliurus-leaves predominate. The pieces, both in the cells and in the barrier, vary in size. It is true that the hawthorn-leaves, with their deep indentations, do not lend themselves to the cutting of neat oval pieces. The insect seems to have detached each morsel without troubling overmuch about the shape of the piece, so long as it was big enough. Nor has it been very particular about arranging the pieces according to the nature of the leaf: after a few bits of paliurus come bits of vine and hawthorn; and these again are followed by bits of bramble and paliurus. The Bee has collected her pieces anyhow, taking a bit here and there, just as her fancy dictated. Nevertheless, paliurus is the commonest, perhaps for economical reasons.

I notice, in fact, that the leaves of this shrub, instead of being used piecemeal, are employed whole, when they do not exceed the proper dimensions. Their oval form and their moderate size suit the insect's requirements; and there is therefore no necessity to cut them into pieces. The leaf-stalk is clipped with the scissors and, without more ado, the Megachile retires the richer by a first-rate bit of material.

Split up into their component parts, two cells give me altogether eighty-three pieces of leaves, whereof eighteen are smaller than the others and of a round shape. The last-named come from the lids. If they average forty-two each, the seventeen cells of the nest represent seven hundred and fourteen pieces. These are not all: the nest ends, in the Capricorn's vestibule, with a stout barricade in which I count three hundred and fifty pieces. The total therefore amounts to one thousand and sixty-four. All those journeys and all that work with the scissors to furnish the deserted chamber of the Cerambyx! If I did not know the Leaf-cutter's solitary and jealous disposition, I should attribute the huge structure to the collaboration of several

mothers; but there is no question of communism in this case. One dauntless creature and one alone, one solitary, inveterate worker, has produced the whole of the
prodigious mass. If work is the best way to enjoy life, this one certainly has not been
bored during the few weeks of her existence.

I gladly award her the most honourable of eulogies, that due to the industrious; and I also compliment her on her talent for closing the honey-pots. The pieces
stacked into lids are round and have nothing to suggest those of which the cells
and the final barricade are made. Excepting the first, those nearest the honey, they
are perhaps cut a little less neatly than the disks of the White-girdled Leaf-cutter;
no matter: they stop the jar perfectly, especially when there are some ten of them
one above the other. When cutting them, the Bee was as sure of her scissors as a
dressmaker guided by a pattern laid on the stuff; and yet she was cutting without
a model, without having in front of her the mouth to be closed. To enlarge on this
interesting subject would mean to repeat oneself. All the Leaf-cutters have the same
talent for making the lids of their pots.

A less mysterious question than this geometrical problem is that of the materials. Does each species of Megachile keep to a single plant, or has it a definite botanical domain wherein to exercise its liberty of choice? The little that I have already
said is enough to make us suspect that the insect is not restricted to one plant; and
this is confirmed by an examination of the separate cells, piece by piece, when we
find a variety which we were far from imagining at first. Here is the flora of the
Megachiles in my neighbourhood, a very incomplete flora and doubtless capable of
considerable amplification by future researches.

The Silky Leaf-cutter gathers the materials for her pots, her lids and her barricades from the following plants: paliurus, hawthorn, vine, wild briar, bramble,
holm-oak, amelanchier, terebinthus, sage-leaved rock-rose. The first three supply
the greater part of the leaf-work; the last three are represented only by rare fragments.

The Hare-footed Leaf-cutter (Megachile lagopoda, LIN.) which I see very busy
in my enclosure, though she only collects her materials there, exploits the lilac and
the rose-tree by preference. From time to time, I see her also cutting bits out of the
robinia, the quince-tree and the cherry-tree. In the open country, I have found her
building with the leaves of the vine alone.

The Silvery Leaf-cutter (Megachile argentata, FAB.), another of my guests, shares the taste of the aforesaid for the lilac and the rose, but her domain includes in addition the pomegranate-tree, the bramble, the vine, the common dogwood and the cornelian cherry.

The White-girdled Leaf-cutter likes the robinia, to which she adds, in lavish proportions, the vine, the rose and the hawthorn and sometimes, in moderation, the reed and the whitish-leaved rock-rose.

The Black-tipped Leaf-cutter (Megachile apicalis, SPIN.) has for her abode the cells of the Mason-bee of the Pebbles and the ruined nests of the Osmiae and Anthidia in the Snail-shells. I have not known her to use any other materials than the wild briar and the hawthorn.

Incomplete though it be, this list tells us that the Megachiles do not have exclusive botanical tastes. Each species manages extremely well with several plants differing greatly in appearance. The first condition to be fulfilled by the shrub exploited is that it be near the nest. Frugal of her time, the Leaf-cutter declines to go on distant expeditions. Whenever I come upon a recent Megachile-nest, I am not long in finding in the neighbourhood, without much searching, the tree or shrub from which the Bee has cut her pieces.

Another main condition is a fine and supple texture, especially for the first disks used in the lid and for the pieces which form the lining of the wallet. The rest, less carefully executed, allows of coarser stuff; but even then the piece must be flexible and lend itself to the cylindrical configuration of the tunnel. The leaves of the rock-roses, thick and roughly fluted, fulfil this condition unsatisfactorily, for which reason I see them occurring only at very rare intervals. The insect has gathered pieces of them by mistake and, not finding them good to use, has ceased to visit the unprofitable shrub. Stiffer still, the leaf of the holm-oak in its full maturity is never employed: the Silky Leaf-cutter uses it only in the young state and then in moderation; she can get her velvety pieces better from the vine. In the lilac-bushes so zealously exploited before my eyes by the Hare-footed Leaf-cutter occur a medley of different shrubs which, from their size and the lustre of their leaves, should apparently suit that sturdy pinker. They are the shrubby hare's-ear, the honeysuckle, the prickly butcher's-broom, the box. What magnificent disks ought to come from the hare's-ear and the honeysuckle! One could get an excellent piece, without further labour, by merely cutting the leaf-stalk of the box, as Megachile sericans does with her paliurus. The lilac-lover disdains them absolutely. For what reason? I fancy that she finds them too stiff. Would she think differently if the lilac-bush were not there? Perhaps so.

In short, apart from the questions of texture and proximity to the nest, the Megachile's choice, it seems to me, must depend upon whether a particular shrub is plentiful or not. This would explain the lavish use of the vine, an object of wide-spread cultivation, and of the hawthorn and the wild briar, which form part of all our hedges. As these are to be found everywhere, the fact that the different Leaf-cutters make use of them is no reflection upon a host of equivalents varying according to the locality.

If we had to believe what people tell us about the effects of heredity, which is said to hand down from generation to generation, ever more firmly established, the individual habits of those who come before, the Megachiles of these parts, experienced in the local flora by the long training of the centuries, but complete novices in the presence of plants which their race encounters for the first time, ought to refuse as unusual and suspicious any exotic leaves, especially when they have at hand plenty of the leaves made familiar by hereditary custom. The question was deserving of separate study.

Two subjects of my observations, the Hare-footed and the Silvery Leaf-cutter, both of them inmates of my open-air laboratory, gave me a definite answer. Knowing the points frequented by the two Megachiles, I planted in their work-yard, overgrown with briar and lilac, two outlandish plants which seemed to me to fulfil the required conditions of suppleness of texture, namely, the ailantus, a native of Japan, and the Virginian physostegia. Events justified the selection: both Bees exploited the foreign flora with the same assiduity as the local flora, passing from the lilac to the ailantus, from the briar to the physostegia, leaving the one, going back to the other, without drawing distinctions between the known and the unknown. Inveterate habit could not have given greater certainty, greater ease to their scissors, though this was their first experience of such a material.

The Silvery Leaf-cutter lent herself to an even more conclusive test. As she readily makes her nest in the reeds of my apparatus, I was able, up to a certain point, to create a landscape for her and select its vegetation myself. I therefore moved the reed-hive to a part of the enclosure stocked chiefly with rosemary, whose scanty foliage is not adapted for the Bee's work, and near the apparatus I arranged an exotic shrubbery in pots, including notably the smooth lopezia, from Mexico, and the long-fruited capsicum, an Indian annual. Finding close at hand the wherewithal to build her nest, the Leaf-cutter went no further afield. The lopezia suited her especially, so much so that almost the whole nest was composed of it. The rest had been gathered from the capsicum.

Another recruit, whose co-operation I had in no way engineered, came spontaneously to offer me her evidence. This was the Feeble Leaf-cutter (Megachile imbecilla, GERST.). Nearly a quarter of a century ago, I saw her, all through the month of July, cutting out her rounds and ellipses at the expense of the petals of the Pelargonium zonale, the common geranium. Her perseverance devastated--there is no other word for it--my modest array of pots. Hardly was a blossom out, when the ardent Megachiles came and scalloped it into crescents. The colour was indifferent to her: red, white or pink, all the petals underwent the disastrous operation. A few captures, ancient relics of my collecting-boxes by this time, indemnified me for the pillage. I have not seen this unpleasant Bee since. With what does she build when there are no geranium-flowers handy? I do not know; but the fact remains that the fragile tailoress used to attack the foreign flower, a fairly recent acquisition from the Cape, as though all her race had never done anything else.

These details leave us with one obvious conclusion, which is contrary to our original ideas, based on the unvarying character of insect industry. In constructing their jars, the Leaf-cutters, each following the taste peculiar to her species, do not make use of this or that plant to the exclusion of the others; they have no definite flora, no domain faithfully transmitted by heredity. Their pieces of leaves vary according to the surrounding vegetation; they vary in different layers of the same cell. Everything suits them, exotic or native, rare or common, provided that the bit cut out be easy to employ. It is not the general aspect of the shrub, with its fragile or bushy branches, its large or small, green or grey, dull or glossy leaves, that guides the insect: such advanced botanical knowledge does not enter into the question at all. In the thicket chosen as a pinking-establishment, the Megachile sees but one thing: leaves useful for her work. The Shrike, with his passion for plants with long, woolly sprigs, knows where to find nicely-wadded substitutes when his favourite growth, the cotton-rose, is lacking; the Megachile has much wider resources: indifferent to the plant itself, she looks only into the foliage. If she finds leaves of the proper size, of a dry texture capable of defying the damp and of a suppleness favourable to cylindrical curving, that is all she asks; and the rest does not matter. She has therefore an almost unlimited field for her labour.

These sudden and wholly unprovoked changes give cause for reflection. When my geranium-flowers were devastated, how had the obtrusive Bee, untroubled by the profound dissimilarity between the petals, snow-white here, bright scarlet there, how had she learnt her trade? Nothing tells us that she herself was not for the first time exploiting the plant from the Cape; and, if she really did have predecessors, the habit had not had time to become inveterate, considering the modern importation of the geranium. Where again did the Silvery Megachile, for whom I created an exotic shrubbery, make the acquaintance of the lopezia, which comes from Mexico? She certainly is making a first start. Never did her village or mine possess a stalk of that chilly denizen of our hot-houses. She is making a first start; and behold her straightway a graduate, versed in the art of carving unfamiliar foliage.

People often talk of the long apprenticeships served by instinct, of its gradual acquirements, of its talents, the laborious work of the ages. The Megachiles affirm the exact opposite. They tell me that the animal, though invariable in the essence of its art, is capable of innovation in the details; but at the same time they assure me that any such innovation is sudden and not gradual. Nothing prepares the innovations, nothing improves them or hands them down; otherwise a selection would long ago have been made amid the diversity of foliage; and the shrub recognized as the most serviceable, especially when it is also plentiful, would alone supply all the building-materials needed. If heredity transmitted industrial discoveries, a Megachile who thought of cutting her disks out of pomegranate-leaves and found them satisfactory ought to have instilled a liking for similar materials into her descendants; and we should this day find Leaf-cutters faithful to the pomegranate-leaves, workers who remained exclusive in their choice of the raw material. The facts refute these theories.

People also say:

'Grant us a variation, however small, in the insect's industry; and that variation, accentuated more and more, will produce a new race and finally a fixed species.'

This trifling variation is the fulcrum for which Archimedes clamoured in order to lift the world with his system of levers. The Megachiles offer us one and a very great one: the indefinite variation of their materials. What will the theorists' levers lift with this fulcrum? Why, nothing at all! Whether they cut the delicate petals of the geranium or the tough leaves of the lilac-bushes, the Leaf-cutters are and will be what they were. This is what we learn from the persistence of each species in its structural details, despite the great variety of the foliage employed.

CHAPTER 9. THE COTTON-BEES.

The evidence of the Leaf-cutters proves that a certain latitude is left to the insect in its choice of materials for the nest; and this is confirmed by the testimony of the Anthidia, the cotton-manufacturers. My district possesses five: A. Florentinum, LATR., A. diadema, LATR., A. manicatum, LATR., A. cingulatum, LATR., A. scapulare, LATR. None of them creates the refuge in which the cotton goods are manufactured. Like the Osmiae and the Leaf-cutters, they are homeless vagrants, adopting, each to her own taste, such shelter as the work of others affords. The Scapular Anthidium is loyal to the dry bramble, deprived of its pith and turned into a hollow tube by the industry of various mining Bees, among which figure, in the front rank, the Ceratinae, dwarf rivals of the Xylocopa, or Carpenter-bee, that mighty driller of rotten wood. The spacious galleries of the Masked Anthophora suit the Florentine Anthidium, the foremost member of the genus so far as size is concerned. The Diadem Anthidium considers that she has done very well if she inherits the vestibule of the Hairy-footed Anthophora, or even the ordinary burrow of the Earth-worm. Failing anything better, she may establish herself in the dilapidated dome of the Mason-bee of the Pebbles. The Manicate Anthidium shares her tastes. I have surprised the Girdled Anthidium cohabiting with a Bembex-wasp. The two occupants of the cave dug in the sand, the owner and the stranger, were living in peace, both intent upon their business. Her usual habitation is some hole or other in the crevices of a ruined wall. To these refuges, the work of others, we can add the stumps of reeds, which are as popular with the various cotton-gatherers as with the Osmiae; and, after we have mentioned a few most unexpected retreats, such as the sheath provided by a hollow brick or the labyrinth furnished by the lock of a gate, we shall have almost exhausted the list of domiciles.

Like the Osmiae and the Leaf-cutters, the Anthidium shows an urgent need of a ready-made home. She never houses herself at her own expense. Can we discover the reason? Let us first consult a few hard workers who are artificers of their own dwellings. The Anthophora digs corridors and cells in the road-side banks hardened by the sun; she does not erect, she excavates; she does not build, she clears. Toiling away with her mandibles, atom by atom, she manages to contrive the passages and chambers necessary for her eggs; and a huge business it is. She has, in addition, to polish and glaze the rough sides of her tunnels. What would happen if, after obtaining a home by dint of long-continued toil, she had next to line it with wadding, to gather the fibrous down from cottony plants and to felt it into bags suitable for the honey-paste? The hard-working Bee would not be equal to producing all these refinements. Her mining calls for too great an expenditure of time and strength to leave her the leisure for luxurious furnishing. Chambers and corridors, therefore, will remain bare.

The Carpenter-bee gives us the same answer. When with her joiner's wimble she has patiently bored the beam to a depth of nine inches, would she be able to cut out and place in position the thousand and one pieces which the Silky Leaf-cutter employs for her nest? Time would fail her, even as it would fail a Megachile who, lacking the Capricorn's chamber, had herself to dig a home in the trunk of the oak. Therefore the Carpenter-bee, after the tedious work of boring, gets the installation done in the most summary fashion, simply running up a sawdust partition.

The two things, the laborious business of obtaining a lodging and the artistic work of furnishing, seem unable to go together. With the insect as with man, he who builds the house does not furnish it, he who furnishes it does not build it. To each his share, because of lack of time. Division of labour, the mother of the arts, makes the workman excel in his department; one man for the whole work would mean stagnation, the worker never getting beyond his first crude attempts. Animal industry is a little like our own: it does not attain its perfection save with the aid of obscure toilers, who, without knowing it, prepare the final masterpiece. I see no other reason for this need of a gratuitous lodging for the Megachile's leafy basket or the Anthidia's cotton purses. In the case of other artists who handle delicate things that require protection, I do not hesitate to assume the existence of a ready-made home. Thus Reaumur tells us of the Upholsterer-bee, Anthocopa papaveris, who fashions her cells with poppy-petals. I do not know the flower-cutter, I have never seen her; but her art tells me plainly enough that she must establish herself in some gallery wrought by others, as, for instance, in an Earth-worm's burrow.

We have but to see the nest of a Cotton-bee to convince ourselves that its builder cannot at the same time be an indefatigable navvy. When and newly-felted and not yet made sticky with honey, the wadded purse is by far the most elegant known specimen of entomological nest-building, especially where the cotton is of a brilliant white, as is frequently the case in the manufacturers of the Girdled Anthidium. No bird's-nest, however deserving of our admiration, can vie in fineness of flock, in gracefulness of form, in delicacy of felting with this wonderful bag, which our fingers, even with the aid of tools, could hardly imitate, for all their dexterity. I abandon the attempt to understand how, with its little bales of cotton brought up one by one, the insect, no otherwise gifted than the kneaders of mud and the makers of leafy baskets, manages to felt what it has collected into a homogeneous whole and then to work the product into a thimble-shaped wallet. Its tools as a master-fuller are its legs and its mandibles, which are just like those possessed by the mortar-kneaders and Leaf-cutters; and yet, despite this similarity of outfit, what a vast difference in the results obtained!

To see the Cotton-bees' talents in action seems an undertaking fraught with innumerable difficulties: things happen at a depth inaccessible to the eye; and to persuade the insect to work in the open does not lie in our power. One resource remained and I did not fail to turn to it, though hitherto I have been wholly unsuccessful. Three species, Anthidium diadema, A. manicatum and A. florentinum--the first-named in particular--show themselves quite ready to take up their abode in my reed-apparatus. All that I had to do was to replace the reeds by glass tubes, which would allow me to watch the work without disturbing the insect. This stratagem had answered perfectly with the Three-horned Osmia and Latreille's Osmia, whose little housekeeping-secrets I had learnt thanks to the transparent dwelling-house. Why should it not answer for its Cotton-bees and, in the same way, with the Leaf-cutters? I almost counted on success. Events betrayed my confidence. For four years I supplied my hives with glass tubes and not once did the Cotton-weavers or the Leaf-cutters condescend to take up their quarters in the crystal palaces. They always preferred the hovel provided by the reed. Shall I persuade them one day? I do not abandon all hope.

Meanwhile, let me describe the little that I saw. More or less stocked with cells, the reed is at last closed, right at the orifice, with a thick plug of cotton, usually coarser than the wadding of the honey-satchels. It is the equivalent of the Three-horned Osmia's barricade of mud, of the leaf-putty of Latreille's Osmia, of the Megachiles' barrier of leaves cut into disks. All these free tenants are careful to shut tight the door of the dwelling, of which they have often utilized only a portion. To watch the building of this barricade, which is almost external work, demands but a little patience in waiting for the favourable moment.

The Anthidium arrives at last, carrying the bale of cotton for the plugging. With her fore-legs she tears it apart and spreads it out; with her mandibles, which go in closed and come out open, she loosens the hard lumps of flock; with her forehead she presses each new layer upon the one below. And that is all. The insect flies off, returns the richer by another bale and repeats the performance until the cotton barrier reaches the level of the opening. We have here, remember, a rough task, in no way to be compared with the delicate manufacturer of the bags; nevertheless, it may perhaps tell us something of the general procedure of the finer work. The legs do the carding, the mandibles the dividing, the forehead the pressing; and the play of these implements produces the wonderful cushioned wallet. That is the mechanism in the lump; but what of the artistry?

Let us leave the unknown for facts within the scope of observation. I will question the Diadem Anthidium in particular, a frequent inmate of my reeds. I open a reed-stump about two decimetres long by twelve millimetres in diameter. (About seven and three-quarter inches by half an inch.--Translator's Note.) The end is occupied by a column of cotton-wool comprising ten cells, without any demarcation between them on the outside, so that their whole forms a continuous cylinder. Moreover, thanks to a close felting, the different compartments are soldered together, so much so that, when pulled by the end, the cotton edifice does not break into sections, but comes out all in one piece. One would take it for a single cylinder, whereas in reality the work is composed of a series of chambers, each of which has been constructed separately, independently of the one before, except perhaps at the base.

For this reason, short of ripping up the soft dwelling, still full of honey, it is impossible to ascertain the number of storeys; we must wait until the cocoons are woven. Then our fingers can tell the cells by counting the knots that resist pressure under the cover of wadding. This general structure is easily explained. A cotton bag is made, with the sheath of the reed as a mould. If this guiding sheath were lacking, the thimble shape would be obtained all the same, with no less elegance, as is proved by the Girdled Anthidium, who makes her nest in some hiding-place or other in the walls or the ground. When the purse is finished, the provisions come and the egg, followed by the closing of the cell. We do not here find the geometrical lid of the Leaf-cutters, the pile of disks tight-set in the mouth of the jar. The bag is closed with a cotton sheet whose edges are soldered by a felting-process to the edges of the opening. The soldering is so well done that the honey-pouch and its cover form an indivisible whole. Immediately above it, the second cell is constructed, having its own base. At the beginning of this work, the insect takes care to join the two storeys by felting the ceiling of the first to the floor of the second. Thus continued to the end, the work, with its inner solderings, becomes an unbroken cylinder, in which the beauties of the separate wallets disappear from view. In very much the same fashion, but with less adhesion among the different cells, do the Leaf-cutters act when stacking their jars in a column without any external division into storeys.

Let us return to the reed-stump which gives us these details. Beyond the cotton-wool cylinder wherein ten cocoons are lodged in a row comes an empty space of half a decimetre or more. (About two inches.--Translator's Note.) The Osmiae and the Leaf-cutters are also accustomed to leave these long, deserted vestibules. The nest ends, at the orifice of the reed, with a strong plug of flock coarser and less white than that of the cells. This use of closing-materials which are less delicate in texture but of greater resisting-power, while not an invariable characteristic, occurs frequently enough to make us suspect that the insect knows how to distinguish what is best suited now to the snug sleeping-berth of the larvae, anon to the defensive barricade of the home. Sometimes the choice is an exceedingly judicious one, as is shown by the nest of the Diadem Anthidium. Time after time, whereas the cells were composed of the finest grade of white cotton, gathered from Centaurea solsticialis, or St. Barnaby's thistle, the barrier at the entrance, differing from the rest of the work in its yellow colouring, was a heap of close-set bristles supplied by the scallop-leaved mullein. The two functions of the wadding are here plainly marked. The delicate skin of the larvae needs a well-padded cradle; and the mother collects the softest materials that the cottony plants provide. Rivalling the bird, which furnishes the inside of the nest with wool and strengthens the outside with sticks, she reserves for the grubs' mattress the finest down, so hard to find and collected with such patience. But, when it becomes a matter of shutting the door against the foe, then the entrance bristles with forbidding caltrops, with stiff, prickly hairs.

This ingenious system of defence is not the only one known to the Anthidia. More distrustful still, the Manicate Anthidium leaves no space in the front part of the reed. Immediately after the column of cells, she heaps up, in the uninhabited vestibule, a conglomeration of rubbish, whatever chance may offer in the neighbourhood of the nest: little pieces of gravel, bits of earth, grains of sawdust, particles of mortar, cypress-catkins, broken leaves, dry Snail-droppings and any other material that comes her way. The pile, a real barricade this time, blocks the reed completely to the end, except about two centimetres (About three-quarters of an inch.--Translator's Note.) left for the final cotton plug. Certainly no foe will break in through the double rampart; but he will make an insidious attack from the rear. The Leucopsis will come and, with her long probe, thanks to some imperceptible fissure in the tube, will insert her dread eggs and destroy every single inhabitant of the fortress. Thus are the Manicate Anthidium's anxious precautions outwitted.

If we had not already seen the same thing with the Leaf-cutters, this would be the place to enlarge upon the useless tasks undertaken by the insect when, with its ovaries apparently depleted, it goes on spending its strength with no maternal object in view and for the sole pleasure of work. I have come across several reeds stopped up with flock though containing nothing at all, or else furnished with one, two or three cells devoid of provisions or eggs. The ever-imperious instinct for gathering cotton and felting it into purses and heaping it into barricades persists, fruitlessly, until life fails. The Lizard's tail wriggles, curls and uncurls after it is detached from the animal's body. In these reflex movements, I seem to see not an explanation, certainly, but a rough image of the industrious persistency of the insect, still toiling away at its business, even when there is nothing useful left to do. This worker knows no rest but death.

I have said enough about the dwelling of the Diadem Anthidium; let us look at the inhabitant and her provisions. The honey is pale-yellow, homogeneous and of a semifluid consistency, which prevents it from trickling through the porous cotton bag. The egg floats on the surface of the heap, with the end containing the head dipped into the paste. To follow the larva through its progressive stages is not without interest, especially on account of the cocoon, which is one of the most singular that I know. With this object in view, I prepare a few cells that lend themselves to observation. I take a pair of scissors, slice a piece off the side of the cotton-wool purse, so as to lay bare both the victuals and the consumer, and place the ripped cell in a short glass tube. During the first few days, nothing striking happens. The little grub, with its head still plunged in the honey, slakes its thirst with long draughts and waxes fat. A moment comes...But let us go back a little farther, before broaching this question of sanitation.

Every grub, of whatever kind, fed on provisions collected by the mother and placed in a narrow cell is subject to conditions of health unknown to the roving grub that goes where it likes and feeds itself on what it can pick up. The first, the recluse, is no more able than the second, the gadabout, to solve the problem of a food which can be entirely assimilated, without leaving an unclean residue. The second gives no thought to these sordid matters: any place suits it for getting rid of that difficulty. But what will the other do with its waste matter, cooped up as it is in a tiny cell stuffed full of provisions? A most unpleasant mixture seems inevitable. Picture the honey-eating grub floating on liquid provisions and fouling them at intervals with its excretions! The least movement of the hinder-part would cause the whole to amalgamate; and what a broth that would make for the delicate nursling! No, it cannot be; those dainty epicures must have some method of escaping these horrors.

They all have, in fact, and most original methods at that. Some take the bull by the horns, so to speak, and, in order not to soil things, refrain from uncleanliness until the end of the meal: they keep the dropping-trap closed as long as the victuals are unfinished. This is a radical scheme, but not in every one's power, it appears. It is the course adopted, for instance, by the Sphex-wasps and the Anthophora-bees, who, when the whole of the food is consumed, expel at one shot the residues amassed in the intestines since the commencement of the repast.

Others, the Osmiae in particular, accept a compromise and begin to relieve the digestive tract when a suitable space has been made in the cell through the gradual disappearance of the victuals. Others again--more hurried these--find means of obeying the common law pretty early by engaging in stercoral manufactures. By a stroke of genius, they make the unpleasant obstruction into building-bricks. We already know the art of the Lily-beetle (Crioceris merdigera. Fabre's essay on this insect has not yet been translated into English; but readers interested in the matter will find a full description in "An Introduction to Entomology," by William Kirby, Rector of Barham, and William Spence: letter 21.--Translator's Note.), who, with her soft excrement, makes herself a coat wherein to keep cool in spite of the sun. It is a very crude and revolting art, disgusting to the eye. The Diadem Anthidium belongs to another school. With her droppings she fashions masterpieces of marquetry and mosaic, which wholly conceal their base origin from the onlooker. Let us watch her labours through the windows of my tubes.

When the portion of food is nearly half consumed, there begins and goes on to the end a frequent defecation of yellowish droppings, each hardly the size of a pin's head. As these are ejected, the grub pushes them back to the circumference of the cell with a movement of its hinder-part and keeps them there by means of a few threads of silk. The work of the spinnerets, therefore, which is deferred in the others until the provisions are finished, starts earlier here and alternates with the feeding. In this way, the excretions are kept at a distance, away from the honey and without any danger of getting mixed with it. They end by becoming so numerous as to form an almost continuous screen around the larva. This excremental awning, made half of silk and half of droppings, is the rough draft of the cocoon, or rather a sort of scaffolding on which the stones are deposited until they are definitely placed in position. Pending the piecing together of the mosaic, the scaffolding keeps the victuals free from all contamination.

To get rid of what cannot be flung outside, by hanging it on the ceiling, is not bad to begin with; but to use it for making a work of art is better still. The honey has disappeared. Now commences the final weaving of the cocoon. The grub surrounds itself with a wall of silk, first pure white, then tinted reddish-brown by means of an adhesive varnish. Through its loose-meshed stuff, it seizes one by one the droppings hanging from the scaffold and inlays them firmly in the tissue. The same mode of work is employed by the Bembex-, Stizus-and Tachytes-wasps and other inlayers, who strengthen the inadequate woof of their cocoons with grains of sand; only, in their cotton-wool purses, the Anthidium's grubs substitute for the mineral particles the only solid materials at their disposal. For them, excrement takes the place of pebbles.

And the work goes none the worse for it. On the contrary: when the cocoon is finished, any one who had not witnessed the process of manufacture would be greatly puzzled to state the nature of the workmanship. The colouring and the elegant regularity of the outer wrapper of the cocoon suggest some kind of basket-work made with tiny bits of bamboo, or a marquetry of exotic granules. I too let myself be caught by it in my early days and wondered in vain what the hermit of the cotton wallet had used to inlay her nymphal dwelling so prettily withal. To-day, when the secret is known to me, I admire the ingenuity of the insect capable of obtaining the useful and the beautiful out of the basest materials.

The cocoon has another surprise in store for us. The end containing the head finishes with a short conical nipple, an apex, pierced by a narrow shaft that establishes a communication between the inside and the out. This architectural feature is common to all the Anthidia, to the resin-workers who will occupy our attention presently, as well as to the cotton-workers. It is found nowhere outside the Anthidium group.

What is the use of this point which the larva leaves bare instead of inlaying it like the rest of the shell? What is the use of that hole, left quite open or, at most, closed at the bottom with a feeble grating of silk? The insect appears to attach great importance to it, from what I see. In point of fact, I watch the careful work of the apex. The grub, whose movements the hole enables me to follow, patiently perfects the lower end of the conical channel, polishes it and gives it an exactly circular shape; from time to time, it inserts into the passage its two closed mandibles, whose points project a little way outside; then, opening them to a definite radius, like a pair of compasses, it widens the aperture and makes it regular.

I imagine, without venturing, however, to make a categorical statement, that the perforated apex is a chimney to admit the air required for breathing. Every pupa breathes in its shell, however compact this may be, even as the unhatched bird breathes inside the egg. The thousands of pores with which the shell is pierced allow the inside moisture to evaporate and the outer air to penetrate as and when needed. The stony caskets of the Bembex- and Stizus-wasps are endowed, notwithstanding their hardness, with similar means of exchange between the vitiated and the pure atmosphere. Can the shells of the Anthidia be air-proof, owing to some modification that escapes me? In any case, this impermeability cannot be attributed to the excremental mosaic, which the cocoons of the resin-working Anthidia do not possess, though endowed with an apex of the very best.

Shall we find an answer to the question in the varnish with which the silken fabric is impregnated? I hesitate to say yes and I hesitate to say no, for a host of cocoons are coated with a similar lacquer though deprived of communication with the outside air. All said, without being able at present to account for its necessity, I admit that the apex of the Anthidia is a breathing-aperture. I bequeath to the future the task of telling us for what reasons the collectors of both cotton and resin leave a large pore in their shells, whereas all the other weavers close theirs completely.

After these biological curiosities, it remains for me to discuss the principal subject of this chapter: the botanical origin of the materials of the nest. By watching the insect when busy at its harvesting, or else by examining its manufactured flock under the microscope, I was able to learn, not without a great expenditure of time and patience, that the different Anthidia of my neighbourhood have recourse without distinction to any cottony plant. Most of the wadding is supplied by the Compositae, particularly the following: Centaurea solsticialis, or St. Barnaby's thistle; C. paniculata, or panicled centaury; Echinops ritro, or small globe-thistle; Onopordon illyricum, or Illyrian cotton-thistle; Helichrysum staechas, or wild everlasting; Filago germanica, or common cotton-rose. Next come the Labiatae: Marrubium vulgare, or common white horehound; Ballota fetida, or stinking horehound; Calamintha nepeta, or lesser calamint; Salvia aethiopis, or woolly sage. Lastly, the Solanaceae: Verbascum thapsus, or shepherd's club; V. sinuatum, or scollop-leaved mullein.

The Cotton-bees' flora, we see, incomplete as it is in my notes, embraces plants of very different aspect. There is no resemblance in appearance between the proud candelabrum of the cotton-thistle, with its red tufts, and the humble stalk of the globe-thistle, with its sky-blue capitula; between the plentiful leaves of the mullein and the scanty foliage of the St. Barnaby's thistle; between the rich silvery fleece of the woolly sage and the short hairs of the everlasting. With the Anthidium, these clumsy botanical characteristics do not count; one thing alone guides her: the presence of cotton. Provided that the plant be more or less well-covered with soft wadding, the rest is immaterial to her.

Another condition, however, has to be fulfilled, apart from the fineness of the cotton-wool. The plant, to be worth shearing, must be dead and dry. I have never seen the harvesting done on fresh plants. In this way, the Bee avoids mildew, which would make its appearance in a mass of hairs still filled with sap.

Faithful to the plant recognized as yielding good results, the Anthidium arrives and resumes her gleaning on the edges of the parts denuded by earlier harvests. Her mandibles scrape away and pass the tiny fluffs, one by one, to the hind-legs, which hold the pellet pressed against the chest, mix with it the rapidly-increasing store of down and make the whole into a little ball. When this is the size of a pea, it goes back into the mandibles; and the insect flies off, with its bale of cotton in its mouth. If we have the patience to wait, we shall see it return to the same point, at intervals of a few minutes, so long as the bag is not made. The foraging for provisions will suspend the collecting of cotton; then, next day or the day after, the scraping will be resumed on the same stalk, on the same leaf, if the fleece be not exhausted. The owner of a rich crop appears to keep to it until the closing-plug calls for coarser materials; and even then this plug is often manufactured with the same fine flock as the cells.

After ascertaining the diversity of cotton-fields among our native plants, I naturally had to enquire whether the Cotton-bee would also put up with exotic plants, unknown to her race; whether the insect would show any hesitation in the presence of woolly plants offered for the first time to the rakes of her mandibles. The common clary and the Babylonian centaury, with which I have stocked the harmas, shall be the harvest-fields; the reaper shall be the Diadem Anthidium, the inmate of my reeds.

The common clary, or toute-bonne, forms part, I know, of our French flora to-day; but it is an acclimatized foreigner. They say that a gallant crusader, returning from Palestine with his share of glory and bruises, brought back the toute-bonne from the Levant to help him cure his rheumatism and dress his wounds. From the lordly manor, the plant propagated itself in all directions, while remaining faithful to the walls under whose shelter the noble dames of yore used to grow it for their unguents. To this day, feudal ruins are its favourite resorts. Crusaders and manors disappeared; the plant remained. In this case, the origin of the clary, whether historical or legendary, is of secondary importance. Even if it were of spontaneous growth in certain parts of France, the toute-bonne is undoubtedly a stranger in the Vaucluse district. Only once in the course of my long botanizing-expeditions across the department have I come upon this plant. It was at Caromb, in some ruins, nearly thirty years ago. I took a cutting of it; and since then the crusaders' sage has accompanied me on all my peregrinations. My present hermitage possesses several tufts of it: but, outside the enclosure, except at the foot of the walls, it would be impossible to find one. We have, therefore, a plant that is new to the country for many miles around, a cotton-field which the Serignan Cotton-bees had never utilized before I came and sowed it.

Nor had they ever made use of the Babylonian centaury, which I was the first to introduce in order to cover my ungrateful stony soil with some little vegetation. They had never seen anything like the colossal centaury imported from the region of the Euphrates. Nothing in the local flora, not even the cotton-thistle, had prepared them for this stalk as thick as a child's wrist, crowned at a height of nine feet with a multitude of yellow balls, nor for those great leaves spreading over the ground in an enormous rosette. What will they do in the presence of such a find? They will take possession of it with no more hesitation than if it were the humble St. Barnaby's thistle, the usual purveyor.

In fact, I place a few stalks of clary and Babylonian centaury, duly dried, near the reed-hives. The Diadem Anthidium is not long in discovering the rich harvest. Straight away the wool is recognized as being of excellent quality, so much so that, during the three or four weeks of nest-building, I can daily witness the gleaning, now on the clary, now on the centaury. Nevertheless the Babylonian plant appears to be preferred, no doubt because of its whiter, finer and more plentiful down. I keep a watchful eye on the scraping of the mandibles and the work of the legs as they prepare the pellet; and I see nothing that differs from the operations of the insect when gleaning on the globe-thistle and the St. Barnaby's thistle. The plant from the Euphrates and the plant from Palestine are treated like those of the district.

Thus we find what the Leaf-cutters taught us proved, in another way, by the cotton-gatherers. In the local flora, the insect has no precise domain; it reaps its harvest readily now from one species, now from another, provided that it find the materials for its manufactures. The exotic plant is accepted quite as easily as that of indigenous growth. Lastly, the change from one plant to another, from the common to the rare, from the habitual to the exceptional, from the known to the unknown, is made suddenly, without gradual initiations. There is no novitiate, no training by habit in the choice of the materials for the nest. The insect's industry, variable in its details by sudden, individual and non-transmissible innovations, gives the lie to the two great factors of evolution: time and heredity.

CHAPTER 10. THE RESIN-BEES.

At the time when Fabricius (Johann Christian Fabricius (1745-1808), a noted Danish entomologist, author of "Systema entomologiae" (1775).--Translator's Note.) gave the genus Anthidium its name, a name still used in our classifications, entomologists troubled very little about the live animal; they worked on corpses, a dissecting-room method which does not yet seem to be drawing to an end. They would examine with a conscientious eye the antenna, the mandible, the wing, the leg, without asking themselves what use the insect had made of those organs in the exercise of its calling. The animal was classified very nearly after the manner adopted in crystallography. Structure was everything; life, with its highest prerogatives, intellect, instinct, did not count, was not worthy of admission into the zoological scheme.

It is true that an almost exclusively necrological study is obligatory at first. To fill one's boxes with insects stuck on pins is an operation within the reach of all; to watch those same insects in their mode of life, their work, their habits and customs is quite a different thing. The nomenclator who lacks the time--and sometimes also the inclination--takes his magnifying-glass, analyzes the dead body and names the worker without knowing its work. Hence the number of appellations the least of whose faults is that they are unpleasant to the ear, certain of them, indeed, being gross misnomers. Have we not, for instance, seen the name of Lithurgus, or stone-worker, given to a Bee who works in wood and nothing but wood? Such absurdities will be inevitable until the animal's profession is sufficiently familiar to lend its aid in the compiling of diagnoses. I trust that the future will see this magnificent advance in entomological science: men will reflect that the impaled specimens in our collections once lived and followed a trade; and anatomy will be kept in its proper place and made to leave due room for biology.

Fabricius did not commit himself with his expression Anthidium, which alludes to the love of flowers, but neither did he mention anything characteristic: as all Bees have the same passion in a very high degree, I see no reason to treat the Anthidia as more zealous looters than the others. If he had known their cotton nests, perhaps the Scandinavian naturalist would have given them a more logical denomination. As for me, in a language wherein technical parade is out of place, I will call them the Cotton-bees.

The term requires some limiting. To judge by my finds, in fact, the old genus Anthidium, that of the classifying entomologists, comprises in my district two very different corporations. One is known to us and works exclusively in wadding; the other, which we are about to study, works in resin, without ever having recourse to cotton. Faithful to my extremely simple principle of defining the worker, as far as possible, by his work, I will call the members of this guild the Resin-bees. Thus confining myself to the data supplied by my observations, I divide the Anthidium group into equal sections, of equal importance, for which I demand special generic titles; for it is highly illogical to call the carders of wool and the kneaders of resin by the same name. I surrender to those whom it concerns the honour of effecting this reform in the orthodox fashion.

Good luck, the friend of the persevering, made me acquainted in different parts of Vaucluse with four Resin-bees whose singular trade no one had yet suspected. To-day, I find them all four again in my own neighbourhood. They are the following: Anthidium septemdentatum, LATR., A. bellicosum, LEP., A. quadrilobum, LEP., and A. Latreillii, LEP. The first two make their nests in deserted Snail-shells; the other two shelter their groups of cells sometimes in the ground, sometimes under a large stone. We will first discuss the inhabitants of the Snail-shell. I made a brief reference to them in an earlier chapter, when speaking of the distribution of the sexes. This mere allusion, suggested by a study of a different kind, must now be amplified. I return to it with fuller particulars.

The stone-heaps in the Roman quarries near Serignan, which I have so often visited in search of the nests of the Osmia who takes up her abode in Snail-shells, supply me also with the two Resin-bees installed in similar quarters. When the Field-mouse has left behind him a rich collection of empty shells scattered all round his hay mattress under the slab, there is always a hope of finding some Snail-shells plugged with mud and, here and there, mixed with them, a few Snail-shells closed with resin. The two Bees work next door to each other, one using clay, the other gum. The excellence of the locality is responsible for this frequent cohabitation, shelter being provided by the broken stone from the quarry and lodgings by the shells which the Mouse has left behind.

At places where dead Snail-shells are few and far between, as in the crevices of rustic walls, each Bee occupies by herself the shells which she has found. But here, in the quarries, our crop will certainly be a double or even a treble one, for both Resin-bees frequent the same heaps. Let us, therefore, lift the stones and dig into the mound until the excessive dampness of the subsoil tells us that it is useless to look lower down. Sometimes at the moment of removing the first layer, sometimes at a depth of eighteen inches, we shall find the Osmia's Snail-shell and, much more rarely, the Resin-bee's. Above all, patience! The job is none of the most fruitful; nor is it exactly an agreeable one. By dint of turning over uncommonly jagged stones, our fingertips get hurt, lose their skin and become as smooth as though we had held them on a grindstone. After a whole afternoon of this work, our back will be aching, our fingers will be itching and smarting and we shall possess a dozen Osmia-nests and perhaps two or three Resin-bees' nests. Let us be content with that.

The Osmia's shells can be recognized at once, as being closed at the orifice with a clay cover. The Anthidium's call for a special examination, without which we should run a great risk of filling our pockets with cumbersome rubbish. We find a dead Snail-shell among the stones. Is it inhabited by the Resin-bee or not? The outside tells us nothing. The Anthidium's work comes at the bottom of the spiral, a long way from the mouth; and, though this is wide open, the eye cannot travel far enough along the winding stair. I hold up the doubtful shell to the light. If it is completely transparent, I know that it is empty and I put it back to serve for future nests. If the second whorl is opaque, the spiral contains something. What does it contain? Earth washed in by the rain? Remnants of the putrefied Snail? That remains to be seen. With a little pocket-trowel, the inquisitorial implement which always accompanies me, I make a wide window in the middle of the final whorl. If I see a gleaming resin floor, with incrustations of gravel, the thing is settled: I possess an Anthidium's nest. But, oh the number of failures that go to one success! The number of windows vainly opened in shells whose bottom is stuffed with clay or with noisome corpses! Thus picking shells among the overturned stone-heaps, inspecting them in the sun, breaking into them with the trowel and nearly always rejecting them, I manage, after repeated attempts, to obtain my materials for this chapter.

The first to hatch is the Seven-pronged Resin-bee (Anthidium septemdentatum). We see her, in the month of April, lumbering along to the rubbish-heaps in the quarries and the low boundary-walls, in search of her Snail-shell. She is a contemporary of the Three-horned Osmia, who begins operations in the last week of April, and often occupies the same stone-heap, settling in the next shell. She is well-advised to start work early and to be on neighbourly terms with the Osmia when the latter is building; in fact, we shall soon see the terrible dangers to which that same proximity exposes her dilatory rival in resin-work, Anthidium bellicosum.

The shell adopted in the great majority of cases is that of the Common Snail, Helix aspersa. It is sometimes of full size, sometimes half-developed. Helix nemoralis and H. caespitum, which are much smaller, also supply suitable lodgings; and this would as surely apply to any shell of sufficient capacity, if the places which I explore possessed others, as witness a nest which my son Emile has sent me from somewhere near Marseilles. This time, the Resin-bee is settled in Helix algira, the most remarkable of our land-shells because of the width and regularity of its spiral, which is copied from that of the Ammonites. This magnificent nest, a perfect specimen of both the Snail's work and the Bee's, deserves description before any other.

For a distance of three centimetres (1.17 inches.--Translator's Note.) from the mouth, the last spiral whorl contains nothing. At this inconsiderable depth, a partition is clearly seen. The moderate diameter of the passage accounts for the Anthidium's choice of this site to which our eye can penetrate. In the common Snail-shell, whose cavity widens rapidly, the insect establishes itself much farther back, so that, in order to see the terminal partition, we must, as I have said, make a lateral inlet. The position of this boundary-ceiling, which may come farther forward or farther back, depends on the variable diameter of the passage. The cells of the cocoons require a certain length and a certain breadth, which the mother finds by going higher up or lower down in the spiral, according to the shape of the shell. When the diameter is suitable, the last whorl is occupied up to the orifice, where the final lid appears, absolutely exposed to view. This is the case with the adult Helix nemoralis and H. caespitum, and also with the young Common Snail. We will not linger at present over this peculiarity, the importance of which will become manifest shortly.

Whether in the front or at the back of the spiral slope, the insect's work ends in a facade of coarse mosaic, formed of small, angular bits of gravel, firmly cemented with a gum the nature of which has to be ascertained. It is an amber-coloured material, semi-transparent, brittle, soluble in spirits of wine and burning with a sooty flame and a strong smell of resin. From these characteristics it is evident that the Bee prepares her gum with the resinous drops exuded by the Coniferae.

I think that I am even able to name the particular plant, though I have never caught the insect in the act of gathering its materials. Hard by the stone-heaps which I turn over for my collections there is a plentiful supply of brown-berried junipers. Pines are totally absent; and the cypress only appears occasionally near the houses. Moreover, among the vegetable remains which we shall see assisting in the protection of the nest, we often find the juniper's catkins and needles. As the resin-insect is economical of its time and does not fly far from the quarters familiar to it, the gum must have been collected on the shrub at whose foot the materials for the barricade have been gathered. Nor is this merely a local circumstance, for the Marseilles nest abounds in similar remnants. I therefore regard the juniper as the regular resin-purveyor, without, however, excluding the pine, the cypress and other Coniferae when the favourite shrub is absent.

The bits of gravel in the lid are angular and chalky in the Marseilles nest; they are round and flinty in most of the Serignan nests. In making her mosaic, the worker pays no heed to the form or colour of its component parts; she collects indiscriminately anything that is hard enough and not too large. Sometimes she lights upon treasures that give her work a more original character. The Marseilles nest shows me, neatly encrusted amid the bits of gravel, a tiny whole landshell, Pupa cineres. A nest in my own neighbourhood provides me with a pretty Snail-shell, Helix striata, forming a rose-pattern in the middle of the mosaic. These little artistic details remind me of a certain nest of Eumenes Amadei (A Mason-wasp, forming the subject of an essay which has not yet been published in English.--Translator's Note.) which abounds in small shells. Ornamental shell-work appears to number its lovers among the insects.

After the lid of resin and gravel, an entire whorl of the spiral is occupied by a barricade of incongruous remnants, similar to that which, in the reeds, protects the row of cocoons of the Manicate Cotton-bee. It is curious to see exactly the same defensive methods employed by two builders of such different talents, one of whom handles flock, the other gum. The nest from Marseilles has for its barricade bits of chalky gravel, particles of earth, fragments of sticks, a few scraps of moss and especially juniper-catkins and needles. The Serignan nests, installed in Helix aspersa, have almost the same protective materials. I see bits of gravel, the size of a lentil, and the catkins and needles of the brown-berried juniper predominating. Next come the dry excretions of the Snail and a few rare little land-shells. A similar jumble of more or less everything found near the nest forms, as we know, the barricade of the Manicate Cotton-bee, who is also an adept at using the Snail's stercoral droppings after these have been dried in the sun. Let us observe finally that these dissimilar materials are heaped together without any cementing, just as the insect has picked them up. Resin plays no part in the mass; and we have only to pierce the lid and turn the shell upside down for the barricade to come dribbling to the ground. To glue the whole thing together does not enter into the Resin-bee's scheme. Perhaps such an expenditure of gum is beyond her means; perhaps the barricade, if hardened into a solid block, would afterwards form an invincible obstacle to the escape of the youngsters; perhaps again the mass of gravel is an accessory rampart, run up roughly as a work of secondary importance.

Amid these doubtful matters, I see at least that the insect does not look upon its barricade as indispensable. It employs it regularly in the large shells, whose last whorl, too spacious to be used, forms an unoccupied vestibule; it neglects it in the moderate shells, such as Helix nemoralis, in which the resin lid is level with the orifice. My excavations in the stone-heaps supply me with an almost equal number of nests with and without defensive embankments. Among the Cotton-bees, the Manicate Anthidium is not faithful either to her fort of little sticks and stones; I know some of her nests in which cotton serves every purpose. With both of them, the gravel rampart seems useful only in certain circumstances, which I am unable to specify.

On the other side of the outworks of the fortification, the lid and barricade, are the cells set more or less far down in the spiral, according to the diameter of the shell. They are bounded back and front by partitions of pure resin, without any en-crustations of mineral particles. Their number is exceedingly restricted and is usu-ally limited to two. The front room, which is larger because the width of the passage goes on increasing, is the abode of a male, superior in size to the other sex; the less spacious back room contains a female. I have already drawn attention in an earlier chapter to the wonderful problem submitted for our consideration by this breaking up of the laying into couples and this alternation of the males and females. Without calling for other work than the transverse partitions, the broadening stairway of the Snail-shell thus furnishes both sexes with house-room suited to their size.

The second Resin-bee that inhabits shells, Anthidium bellicosum, hatches in July and works during the fierce heat of August. Her architecture differs in no wise from that of her kinswoman of the springtime, so much so that, when we find a tenanted Snail-shell in a hole in the wall or under the stones, it is impossible to decide to which of the two species the nest belongs. The only way to obtain exact information is to break the shell and split the cocoons in February, at which time the nests of the summer Resin-bee are occupied by larvae and those of the spring Resin-bee by the perfect insect. If we shrink from this brutal method, we are still in doubt until the cocoons open, so great is the resemblance between the two pieces of work.

In both cases, we find the same lodging, Snail-shells of every size and every kind, just as they happen to come; the same resin lid, the inside gritty with tiny bits of stone, the outside almost smooth and sometimes ornamented with little shells; the same barricade--not always present--of various kinds of rubbish; the same divi-sion into two rooms of unequal size occupied by the two sexes. Everything is iden-tical, down to the purveyor of the gum, the brown-berried juniper. To say more about the nest of the summer Resin-bee would be to repeat oneself.

There is only one thing that requires further investigation. I do not see the reason that prompts the two insects to leave the greater part of their shell empty in front, instead of occupying it entirely up to the orifice as the Osmia habitually does. As the mother's laying is broken up into intermittent shifts of a couple of eggs apiece, is it necessary that there should be a new home for each shift? Is the half-flu-id resin unsuitable for the wide-spanned roofs which would have to be constructed when the diameter of the helical passage exceeded certain limits? Is the gathering of the cement too wearisome a task to leave the Bee any strength for making the numerous partitions which she would need if she utilized the spacious final whorl? I find no answer to these questions. I note the fact without interpreting it: when the shell is a large one, the front part, almost the whole of the last whorl, remains an empty vestibule.

To the spring Resin-bee, Anthidium septemdentatum, this less than half occupied lodging presents no drawbacks. A contemporary of the Osmia, often her neighbour under the same stone, the gum-worker builds her nest at the same period as the mud-worker; but there is no fear of mutual encroachments, for the two Bees, working next door to each other, watch their respective properties with a jealous eye. If attempts at usurpation were to be made, the owner of the Snail-shell would know how to enforce her rights as the first occupant.

For the summer Resin-bee, A. bellicosum, the conditions are very different. At the moment when the Osmia is building, she is still in the larval, or at most in the nymphal stage. Her abode, which would not be more absolutely silent if deserted, her shell, with its vast untenanted porch, will not tempt the earlier Resin-bee, who herself wants apartments right at the far end of the spiral, but it might suit the Osmia, who knows how to fill the shell with cells up to the mouth. The last whorl left vacant by the Anthidium is a magnificent lodging which nothing prevents the mason from occupying. The Osmia does seize upon it, in fact, and does so too often for the welfare of the unfortunate late-comer. The final resin lid takes the place, for the Osmia, of the mud stopper with which she cuts off at the back the portion of the spiral too narrow for her labours. Upon this lid she builds her mass of cells in so many storeys, after which she covers the whole with a thick defensive plug. In short, the work is conducted as though the Snail-shell contained nothing.

When July arrives, this doubly-tenanted house becomes the scene of a tragic conflict. Those below, on attaining the adult state, burst their swaddling-bands, demolish their resin partitions, pass through the gravel barricade and try to release themselves; those above, larvae still or budding pupae, prisoners in their shells until the following spring, completely block the way. To force a passage from the far-end of those catacombs is beyond the strength of the Resin-bee, already weakened by the effort of breaking out of her own nest. A few of the Osmia's partitions are damaged, a few cocoons receive slight injuries; and then, worn out with vain struggles, the captives abandon hope and perish behind the impregnable wall of earth. And with them perish also certain parasites, even less fit for the prodigious work of clearance: Zonites and Chryses (Chrysis flammea), of whom the first are consumers of provisions and the second of grubs.

This lamentable ending of the Resin-bee, buried alive under the Osmia's walls, is not a rare accident to be passed over in silence or mentioned in a few words; on the contrary, it happens very often; and its frequency suggests this thought: the school which sees in instinct an acquired habit treats the slightest favourable occurrence in the course of animal industry as the starting-point of an improvement which, transmitted by heredity and becoming in time more and more accentuated, at last grows into a settled characteristic common to the whole race. There is, it is true, a total absence of positive proofs in support of this theory; but it is stated with a wealth of hypothesis that leaves a thousand loopholes: 'Granting that...Supposing that...It may be...nothing need prevent us from believing... It is quite possible...' Thus argued the master; and the disciples have not yet hit upon anything better.

'If the sky were to fall,' said Rabelais, 'the larks would all be caught.'

Yes, but the sky stays up; and the larks go on flying.

'If things happened in such and such a way,' says our friend, 'instinct may have undergone variations and modifications.'

Yes, but are you quite sure that things happened as you say?

I banish the word 'if' from my vocabulary. I suppose nothing, I take nothing for granted; I pluck the brutal fact, the only thing that can be trusted; I record it and then ask myself what conclusion rests upon its solid framework. From the fact which I have related we may draw the following inference:

'You say that any modification profitable to the animal is transmitted throughout a series of favoured ones who, better equipped with tools, better endowed with aptitudes, abandon the ancient usages and replace the primitive species, the victim of the struggle for life. You declare that once, in the dim distance of the ages, a Bee found herself by accident in possession of a dead Snail-shell. The safe and peaceful lodging pleased her fancy. On and on went the hereditary liking; and the Snail-shell proved more and more agreeable to the insect's descendants, who began to look for it under the stones, so that later generations, with the aid of habit, ended by adopting it as the ancestral dwelling. Again by accident, the Bee happened upon a drop of resin. It was soft, plastic, well-suited for the partitioning of the Snail-shell; it soon hardened into a solid ceiling. The Bee tried the resinous gum and benefited by it. Her successors also benefited by it, especially after improving it. Little by little, the rubble-work of the lid and of the gravel barricade was invented: an enormous improvement, of which the race did not fail to take advantage. The defensive fortification was the finishing-touch to the original structure. Here we have the origin and development of the instinct of the Resin-bees who make their home in Snail-shells.'

This glorious genesis of insect ways and means lacks just one little thing: probability. Life everywhere, even among the humble, has two phases: its share of good and its share of evil. Avoiding the latter and seeking the former is the rough balance-sheet of life's actions. Animals, like ourselves, have their portion of the sweet and the bitter: they are just as anxious to reduce the second as to increase the first; for, with them as with us,

De malheurs evites le bonheur se compose.
(Bad luck missed is good luck gained.)

If the Bee has so faithfully handed down her casual invention of a resin nest built inside a Snail-shell, then there is no denying that she must have just as faithfully handed down the means of averting the terrible danger of belated hatchings. A few mothers, escaping at rare intervals from the catacombs blocked by the Osmiae, must have retained a lively memory, a powerful impression of their desperate struggle through the mass of earth; they must have inspired their descendants with a dread of those vast dwellings where the stranger comes afterwards and builds; they must have taught them by habit the means of safety, the use of the medium-sized shell, which the nest fills to the mouth. So far as the prosperity of the race was concerned, the discontinuance of the system of empty vestibules was far more important than the invention of the barricade, which is not altogether indispensable: it would have saved them from perishing miserably, behind impenetrable walls, and would have considerably increased the numbers of their posterity.

Thousands and thousands of experiments have been made throughout the ages with Snail-shells of average dimensions: the thing is certain, because I find many of them to-day. Well, have these life-saving experiments, with their immense importance to the race, become general by hereditary bequest? Not at all: the Resin-bee persists in using big Snail-shells just as though her ancestors had never known the danger of the Osmia-blocked vestibule. Once these facts are duly recognized, the conclusion is irresistible: it is obvious that, as the insect does not hand down the casual modification tending towards the avoidance of what is to its disadvantage, neither does it hand down the modification leading to the adoption of what is to its advantage. However lively the impression made upon the mother, the accidental leaves no trace in the offspring. Chance plays no part in the genesis of the instincts.

Next to these tenants of the Snail-shells we have two other Resin-bees who never come to the shells for a cabin for their nests. They are Anthidium quadrilobum, LEP., and A. Latreillii, LEP., both exceedingly uncommon in my district. If we meet them very rarely, however, this may well be due to the difficulty of seeing them; for they lead extremely solitary and wary lives. A warm nook under some stone or other; the deserted streets of an Ant-hill in a sun-baked bank; a Beetle's vacant burrow a few inches below the ground; in short, a cavity of some sort, perhaps arranged by the Bee's own care: these are the only establishments which I know them to occupy. And here, with no other shelter than the cover of the refuge, they build a mass of cells joined together and grouped into a sphere, which, in the case of the Four-lobed Resin-bee, attains the size of a man's fist and, in that of Latreille's Resin-bee, the size of a small apple.

At first sight, we remain very uncertain as to the nature of the strange ball. It is brown, rather hard, slightly sticky, with a bituminous smell. Outside are encrusted a few bits of gravel, particles of earth, heads of large-sized Ants. This cannibal trophy is not a sign of barbarous customs: the Bee does not decapitate Ants to adorn her hut. An inlayer, like her colleagues of the Snail-shell, she gathers any hard granule near at hand capable of strengthening her work; and the dried skulls of Ants, which are frequent around about her abode, are in her eyes building-stones of equal value to the pebbles. One and all employ whatever they can find without much seeking. The inhabitant of the shell, in order to construct her barricade, makes shift with the dry excrement of the nearest Snail; the denizen of the flat stones and of the roadside banks frequented by the Ants does what she can with the heads of the defunct and, should these be lacking, is ready to replace them with something else. Moreover, the defensive inlaying is slight; we see that the insect attaches no great importance to it and has every confidence in the stout wall of the home.

The material of which the work is made at first suggests some rustic wax, much coarser than that of the Bumble-bees, or rather some tar of unknown origin. We think again and then recognize in the puzzling substance the semitransparent fracture, the quality of becoming soft when exposed to heat and of burning with a smoky flame, the solubility in spirits of wine--in short, all the distinguishing characteristics of resin. Here then are two more collectors of the exudations of the Coniferae. At the points where I find their nests are Aleppo pines, cypresses, brown-berried junipers and common junipers. Which of the four supplies the mastic? There is nothing to tell us. Nor is there anything to explain how the native amber-colour of the resin is replaced in the work of both Bees by a dark-brown hue resembling that of pitch. Does the insect collect resin impaired by the weather, soiled by the sanies of rotten wood? When kneading it, does it mix some dark ingredient with it? I look upon this as possible, but not as proved, since I have never seen the Bee collecting her resin.

While this point escapes me, another of higher interest appears most plainly; and that is the large amount of resinous material used in a single nest, especially in that of Anthidium quadrilobum, in which I have counted as many as twelve cells. The nest of the Mason-bee of the Pebbles is hardly more massive. For so costly an establishment, therefore, the Resin-bee collects her pitch on the dead pine as copiously as the Mason-bee collects her mortar on the macadamized road. Her workshop no longer shows us the niggardly partitioning of a Snail-shell with two or three drops of resin; what we see is the whole building of the house, from the basement to the roof, from the thick outer walls to the partitions of the rooms. The cement expended would be enough to divide hundreds of Snail-shells, wherefore the title of Resin-bee is due first and foremost to this master-builder in pitch. Honourable mention should be awarded to A. Latreillii, who rivals her fellow-worker as far as her smaller stature permits. The other manipulators of resin, those who build partitions in Snail-shells, come third, a very long way behind.

And now, with the facts to support us, let us philosophize a little. We have here, recognized as of excellent standard by all the expert classifiers, so fastidious in the arrangement of their lists, a generic group, called Anthidium, containing two guilds of workers entirely dissimilar in character: the cotton-fullers and the resin-kneaders. It is even possible that other species, when their habits are better known, will come and increase this variety of manufactures. I confine myself to the little that I know and ask myself in what the manipulator of cotton differs from the manipulator of resin as regards tools, that is to say, organs. Certainly, when the genus Anthidium was set down by the classifiers, they were not wanting in scientific precision: they consulted, under the lens of the microscope, the wings, the mandibles, the legs, the harvesting-brush, in short, all the details calculated to assist the proper delimitation of the group. After this minute examination by the experts, if no organic differences stand revealed, the reason is that they do not exist. Any dissimilarity of structure could not escape the accurate eyes of our learned taxonomists. The genus, therefore, is indeed organically homogeneous; but industrially it is thoroughly heterogeneous. The implements are the same and the work is different.

That eminent Bordeaux entomologist, Professor Jean Perez, to whom I communicated the misgivings aroused in my mind by the contradictory nature of my discoveries, thinks that he has found the solution of the difficulty in the conformation of the mandibles. I extract the following passage from his volume, "Les Abeilles":

'The cotton-pressing females have the edge of their mandibles cut out into five or six little teeth, which make an instrument admirably suited for scraping and removing the hairs from the epidermis of the plants. It is a sort of comb or teasel. The resin-kneading females have the edge of the mandible not toothed, but simply curved; the tip alone, preceded by a notch which is pretty clearly marked in some species, forms a real tooth; but this tooth is blunt and does not project. The mandible, in short, is a kind of spoon perfectly fitted to remove the sticky matter and to shape it into a ball.'

Nothing better could be said to explain the two sorts of industry: in the one case, a rake which gathers the wool; in the other, a spoon which scoops up the resin. I should have left it at that and felt quite content without further investigation, if I had not had the curiosity to open my boxes and, in my turn, to take a good look, side by side, at the workers in cement and the workers in cotton. Allow me, my learned master, to whisper in your ear what I saw.

The first that I examine is Anthidium septemdentatum. A spoon: yes, it is just that. Powerful mandibles, shaped like an isosceles triangle, flat above, hollowed out below; and no indentations, none whatsoever. A splendid tool, as you say, for gathering the viscous pellet; quite as efficacious in its kind of work as is the rake of the toothed mandibles for gathering cotton. Here certainly is a creature potently-gifted, even though it be for a poor little task, the scooping up of two or three drops of glue.

Things are not quite so satisfactory with the second Resin-bee of the Snail-shells, A. bellicosum. I find that she has three teeth to her mandibles. Still, they are slight and project very little. Let us say that this does not count, even though the work is exactly the same. With A. quadrilobum the whole thing breaks down. She, the queen of Resin-bees; she, who collects a lump of mastic the size of one's fist, enough to subdivide hundreds of her kinswomen's Snail-shells: well, she, by way of a spoon, carries a rake! On the wide edges of her mandibles stand four teeth, as long and pointed as those of the most zealous cotton-gleaner. A. florentinum, that mighty manufacturer of cotton-goods, can hardly rival her in respect of combing-tools. And nevertheless, with her toothed implement, a sort of saw, the Resin-bee collects her great heap of pitch, load by load; and the material is carried not rigid, but sticky, half-fluid, so that it may amalgamate with the previous lots and be fashioned into cells.

A. Latreillii, without having a very large implement, also bears witness to the possibility of heaping up soft resin with a rake; she arms her mandibles with three or four sharply-cut teeth. In short, out of four Resin-bees, the only four that I know, one is armed with a spoon, if this expression be really suited to the tool's function; the three others are armed with a rake; and it so happens that the most copious heap of resin is just the work of the rake with the most teeth to it, a tool suited to the cotton-reapers, according to the views of the Bordeaux entomological expert.

No, the explanation that appealed to me so much at first is not admissible. The mandible, whether supplied with teeth or not, does not account at all for the two manufactures. May we, in this predicament, have recourse to the general structure of the insect, although this is not distinctive enough to be of much use to us? Not so either; for, in the same stone-heaps where the Osmia and the two Resin-bees of the Snail-shells work, I find from time to time another manipulator of mastic who bears no structural relationship whatever to the genus Anthidium. It is a small-sized Mason-wasp, Odynerus alpestris, SAUSS. She builds a very pretty nest with resin and gravel in the shells of the young Common Snail, of Helix nemoralis and sometimes of Bulimulus radiatus. I will describe her masterpiece on some other occasion. To one acquainted with the genus Odynerus, any comparison with the Anthidia would be an inexcusable error. In larval diet, in shape, in habits, they form two dissimilar groups, very far removed one from the other. The Anthidia feed their offspring on honey-bread; the Odyneri feed it on live prey. Well, with her slender form, her weakly frame, in which the most clear-seeing eye would seek in vain for a clue to the trade practised, the Alpine Odynerus, the game-lover, uses pitch in the same way as the stout and massive Resin-bee, the honey-lover. She even uses it better, for her mosaic of tiny pebbles is much prettier than the Bee's and no less solid. With her mandibles, this time neither spoon nor rake, but rather a long forceps slightly notched at the tip, she gathers her drop of sticky matter as dexterously as do her rivals with their very different outfit. Her case will, I think, persuade us that neither the shape of the tool nor the shape of the worker can explain the work done.

I will go further: I ask myself in vain the reason of this or that trade in the case of a fixed species. The Osmiae make their partitions with mud or with a paste of chewed leaves; the Mason-bees build with cement; the Pelopaeus-wasps fashion clay pots; the Megachiles made disks cut from leaves into urns; the Anthidia felt cotton into purses; the Resin-bees cement together little bits of gravel with gum; the Carpenter-bees and the Lithurgi bore holes in timber; the Anthophorae tunnel the roadside slopes. Why all these different trades, to say nothing of the others? How are they prescribed for the insect, this one rather than that?

I foresee the answer: they are prescribed by the organization. An insect excellently equipped for gathering and felting cotton is ill-equipped for cutting leaves, kneading mud or mixing resin. The tool in its possession decides its trade.

This is a very simple explanation, I admit, and one within the scope of everybody: in itself a sufficient recommendation for any one who has neither the inclination nor the time to undertake a more thorough investigation. The popularity of certain speculative views is due entirely to the easy food which they provide for our curiosity. They save us much long and often irksome study; they impart a veneer of general knowledge. There is nothing that achieves such immediate success as an explanation of the riddle of the universe in a word or two. The thinker does not travel so fast: content to know little so that he may know something, he limits his field of search and is satisfied with a scanty harvest, provided that the grain be of good quality. Before agreeing that the tool determines the trade, he wants to see things with his own eyes; and what he observes is far from confirming the sweeping statement. Let us share his doubts for a moment and look into matters more closely.

Franklin left us a maxim which is much to the point here. He said that a good workman should be able to plane with a saw and to saw with a plane. The insect is too good a workman not to follow the advice of the sage of Boston. Its industry abounds in instances where the plane takes the place of the saw, or the saw of the plane; its dexterity makes good the inadequacy of the implement. To go no further, have we not just seen different artisans collecting and using pitch, some with spoons, others with rakes, others again with pincers? Therefore, with such equipment as it possesses, the insect would be capable of abandoning cotton for leaves, leaves for resin, resin for mortar, if some predisposition of talent did not make it keep to its speciality.

These few lines, which are the outcome not of a heedless pen but of mature reflection, will set people talking of hateful paradoxes. We will let them talk and we will submit the following proposition to our adversaries: take an entomologist of the highest merit, a Latreille (Pierre Andre Latreille (1762-1833), one of the founders of modern entomological science.--Translator's Note.), for instance, versed in all the details of the structure of insects but utterly unacquainted with their habits. He knows the dead insect better than anybody, but he has never occupied himself with the living insect. As a classifier, he is beyond compare; and that is all. We ask him to examine a Bee, the first that comes to hand, and to name her trade from her tools.

Come, be honest: could he? Who would dare put him to such a test? Has personal experience not fully convinced us that the mere examination of the insect can tell us nothing about its particular industry? The baskets on its legs and the brush on its abdomen will certainly inform us that it collects honey and pollen; but its special art will remain an utter secret, notwithstanding all the scrutiny of the microscope. In our own industries, the plane denotes the joiner, the trowel the mason, the scissors the tailor, the needle the seamstress. Are things the same in animal industry? Just show us, if you please, the trowel that is a certain sign of the mason-insect, the chisel that is a positive characteristic of the carpenter-insect, the iron that is an authentic mark of the pinking-insect; and as you show them, say:

'This one cuts leaves; that one bores wood; that other mixes cement.'

And so on, specifying the trade from the tool.

You cannot do it, no one can; the worker's speciality remains an impenetrable secret until direct observation intervenes. Does not this incapacity, even of the most expert, proclaim loudly that animal industry, in its infinite variety, is due to other causes besides the possession of tools? Certainly, each of those specialists requires implements; but they are rough and ready implements, good for all sorts of purposes, like the tool of Franklin's workman. The same notched mandible that reaps cotton, cuts leaves and moulds pitch also kneads mud, scrapes decayed wood and mixes mortar; the same tarsus that manufactures cotton and disks cut out of leaves is no less clever at the art of making earthen partitions, clay turrets and gravel mosaics.

What then is the reason of these thousand industries? In the light of facts, I can see but one: imagination governing matter. A primordial inspiration, a talent antecedent to the actual form, directs the tool instead of being subordinate to it. The instrument does not determine the manner of industry; the tool does not make the workman. At the beginning there is an object, a plan, in view of which the animal acts, unconsciously. Have we eyes to see with, or do we see because we have eyes? Does the function create the organ, or the organ the function? Of the two alternatives, the insect proclaims the first. It says:

'My industry is not imposed upon me by the implement which I possess; what I do is to use the implement, such as it is, for the talent with which I am gifted.'

It says to us, in its own way:

'The function has determined the organ; vision is the reason of the eye.'

In short, it repeats to us Virgil's profound reflection:

'Mens agitat molem'; 'Mind moves matter.'

CHAPTER 11. THE POISON OF THE BEE.

I have discussed elsewhere the stings administered by the Wasps to their prey. Now chemistry comes and puts a spoke in the wheel of our arguments, telling us that the poison of the Bees is not the same as that of the Wasps. The Bees' is complex and formed of two elements, acid and alkaline. The Wasps' possess only the acid element; and it is to this very acidity and not to the 'so-called' skill of the operators that the preservation of the provisions is due. (The author's numerous essays on the Wasps will form the contents of later works. In the meantime, cf. "Insect Life," by J.H. Fabre, translated by the author of "Mademoiselle Mori": chapters 4 to 12, and 14 to 18; and "The Life and Love of the Insect," by J. Henri Fabre, translated by Alexander Teixeira de Mattos: chapters 11, 12 and 17.--Translator's Note.)

Admitting that there is a difference in the nature of the venom, I fail to see that this has any bearing on the problem in hand. I can inoculate with various liquids-- acids, weak nitric acid, alkalis, ammonia, neutral bodies, spirits of wine, essence of turpentine--and obtain conditions similar to those of the victims of the predatory insects, that is to say, inertia with the persistence of a dull vitality betrayed by the movements of the mouth-parts and antennae. I am not, of course, invariably successful, for there is neither delicacy nor precision in my poisoned needle and the wound which it makes does not bear comparison with the tiny puncture of the unerring natural sting; but, after all, it is repeated often enough to put the object of my experiment beyond doubt. I should add that, to achieve success, we must have a subject with a concentrated ganglionic column, such as the Weevil, the Buprestis, the Dung-beetle and others. Paralysis is then obtained with but a single prick, made at the point which the Cerceris has revealed to us, the point at which the corselet joins the rest of the thorax. In that case, the least possible quantity of the acrid liquid is instilled, a quantity too small to endanger the patient's life. With scattered nervous centres, each requiring a separate operation, this method is impracticable: the victim would die of the excess of corrosive fluid. I am quite ashamed to have to recall these old experiments. Had they been resumed and carried on by others of greater authority than I, we should have escaped the objections of chemistry.

When light is so easy to obtain, why go in search of scientific obscurity? Why talk of acid or alkaline reactions, which prove nothing, when it is so simple to have recourse to facts, which prove everything? Before declaring that the hunting insects' poison has preservative properties merely because of its acid qualities, it would have been well to enquire if the sting of a Bee, with its acid and its alkali, could not perchance produce the same effects as that of the paralyser, whose skill is categorically denied. The chemists never gave this a thought. Simplicity is not always welcome in our laboratories. It is my duty to repair that little omission. I propose to enquire if the poison of the Bee, the chief of the Apidae, is suitable for a surgery that paralyses without killing.

The enquiry bristles with difficulties, though this is no reason for abandoning it. First and foremost, I cannot possibly operate with the Bee just as I catch her. Time after time I make the attempt, without once succeeding; and patience becomes exhausted. The sting has to penetrate at a definite point, exactly where the Wasp's sting would have entered. My intractable captive tosses about angrily and stings at random, never where I wish. My fingers get hurt even oftener than the patient. I have only one means of gaining a little control over the indomitable dart; and that is to cut off the Bee's abdomen with my scissors, to seize the stump instantly with a fine forceps and to apply the tip at the spot where the sting is to enter.

Everybody knows that the Bee's abdomen needs no orders from the head to go on drawing its weapon for a few instants longer and to avenge the deceased before being itself overcome with death's inertia. This vindictive persistency serves me to perfection. There is another circumstance in my favour: the barbed sting remains where it is, which enables me to ascertain the exact spot pierced. A needle withdrawn as soon as inserted would leave me doubtful. I can also, when the transparency of the tissues permits, perceive the direction of the weapon, whether perpendicular and favourable to my plans, or slanting and therefore valueless. Those are the advantages.

The disadvantages are these: the amputated abdomen, though more tractable than the entire Bee, is still far from satisfying my wishes. It gives capricious starts and unexpected pricks. I want it to sting here. No, it balks my forceps and goes and stings elsewhere: not very far away, I admit; but it takes so little to miss the nerve-centre which we wish to get at. I want it to go in perpendicularly. No, in the great majority of cases it enters obliquely and passes only through the epidermis. This is enough to show how many failures are needed to make one success.

Nor is this all. I shall be telling nobody anything new when I recall the fact that the Bee's sting is very painful. That of the hunting insects, on the contrary, is in most cases insignificant. My skin, which is no less sensitive than another's, pays no attention to it: I handle Sphex, Ammophilae and Scoliae without heeding their lancet-pricks. I have said this before; I remind the reader of it because of the matter in hand. In the absence of well-known chemical or other properties, we have really but one means of comparing the two respective poisons; and that is the amount of pain produced. All the rest is mystery. Besides, no poison, not even that of the Rattlesnake, has hitherto revealed the cause of its dread effects.

Acting, therefore, under the instruction of that one guide, pain, I place the Bee's sting far above that of the predatory insects as an offensive weapon. A single one of its thrusts must equal and often surpass in efficaciousness the repeated wounds of the other. For all these reasons--an excessive display of energy; the variable quantity of the virus inoculated by a wriggling abdomen which no longer measures the emission by doses; a sting which I cannot direct as I please; a wound which may be deep or superficial, the weapon entering perpendicularly or obliquely, touching the nerve-centres or affecting only the surrounding tissues--my experiments ought to produce the most varied results.

I obtain, in fact, every possible kind of disorder: ataxy, temporary disablement, permanent disablement, complete paralysis, partial paralysis. Some of my stricken victims recover; others die after a brief interval. It would be an unnecessary waste of space to record in this volume my hundred and one attempts. The details would form tedious reading and be of very little advantage, as in this sort of study it is impossible to marshal one's facts with any regularity. I will, therefore, sum them up in a few examples.

A colossal member of the Grasshopper tribe, the most powerful in my district, Decticus verrucivorus (This Decticus has received its specific name of verrucivorus, or Wart-eating, because it is employed by the peasants in Sweden and elsewhere to bite off the warts on their fingers.--Translator's Note.), is pricked at the base of the neck, on the line of the fore-legs, at the median point. The prick goes straight down. The spot is the same as that pierced by the sting of the slayer of Crickets and Ephippigers. (A species of Green Grasshopper. The Sphex paralyses Crickets and Grasshoppers to provide food for her grubs. Cf. "Insect Life": chapters 6 to 12.-- Translator's Note.) The giantess, as soon as stung, kicks furiously, flounders about, falls on her side and is unable to get up again. The fore-legs are paralysed; the others are capable of moving. Lying sideways, if not interfered with, the insect in a few moments gives no signs of life beyond a fluttering of the antennae and palpi, a pulsation of the abdomen and a convulsive uplifting of the ovipositor; but, if irritated with a slight touch, it stirs its four hind-legs, especially the third pair, those with the big thighs, which kick vigorously. Next day, the condition is much the same, with an aggravation of the paralysis, which has now attacked the middle-legs. On the day after that, the legs do not move, but the antennae, the palpi and the ovipositor continue to flutter actively. This is the condition of the Ephippiger stabbed three times in the thorax by the Languedocian Sphex. One point alone is missing, a most important point: the long persistence of a remnant of life. In fact, on the fourth day, the Decticus is dead; her dark colour tells me so.

There are two conclusions to be drawn from this experiment and it is well to emphasise them. First, the Bee's poison is so active that a single dagger-thrust aimed at a nervous centre kills in four days one of the largest of the Orthoptera (An order of insects including the Grasshoppers, Locusts, Cockroaches, Mantes and Earwigs, in addition to the Stick- and Leaf-insects, Termites, Dragon-flies, May-flies, Book-lice and others.--Translator's Note.), though an insect of powerful constitution. Secondly, the paralysis at first affects only the legs whose ganglion is attacked; next, it spreads slowly to the second pair; lastly, it reaches the third. The local effect is diffused. This diffusion, which might well take place in the victims of the predatory insects, plays no part in the latters' method of operation. The egg, which will be laid immediately afterwards, demands the complete inertia of the prey from the outset. Hence all the nerve-centres that govern locomotion must be numbed instantaneously by the virus.

I can now understand why the poison of the predatory Wasps is comparatively painless in its effects. If it possessed the strength of that of the Bee, a single stab would impair the vitality of the prey, while leaving it for some days capable of violent movements that would be very dangerous to the huntress and especially to the egg. More moderate in its action, it is instilled at the different nervous centres, as is the case more particularly with the caterpillars. (Caterpillars are the prey of the Ammophila, which administers a separate stab to each of the several ganglia.--Translator's Note.) In this way, the requisite immobility is obtained at once; and, notwithstanding the number of wounds, the victim is not a speedy corpse. To the marvels of the paralysers' talent we must add one more: their wonderful poison, the strength of which is regulated by delicate doses. The Bee revenging herself intensifies the virulence of her poison; the Sphex putting her grubs' provender to sleep weakens it, reduces it to what is strictly necessary.

One more instance of nearly the same kind. I prefer to take my subjects from among the Orthoptera, which, owing to their imposing size and the thinness of their skin at the points to be attacked, lend themselves better than other insects to my delicate manipulations. The armour of a Buprestis, the fat blubber of a Rosechafer-grub, the contortions of a caterpillar present almost insuperable obstacles to the success of a sting which it is not in my power to direct. The insect which I now offer to the Bee's lancet is the Great Green Grasshopper (Locusta viridissima), the adult female. The prick is given in the median line of the fore-legs.

The effect is overwhelming. For two or three seconds the insect writhes in convulsions and then falls on its side, motionless throughout, save in the ovipositor and the antennae. Nothing stirs so long as the creature is left alone; but, if I tickle it with a hair-pencil, the four hind-legs move sharply and grip the point. As for the fore-legs, smitten in their nerve-centre, they are quite lifeless. The same condition is maintained for three days longer. On the fifth day, the creeping paralysis leaves nothing free but the antennae waving to and fro and the abdomen throbbing and lifting up the ovipositor. On the sixth, the Grasshopper begins to turn brown; she is dead. Except that the vestige of life is more persistent, the case is the same as that of the Decticus. If we can prolong the duration, we shall have the victim of the Sphex.

But first let us look into the effect of a prick administered elsewhere than opposite the thoracic ganglia. I cause a female Ephippiger to be stung in the abdomen, about the middle of the lower surface. The patient does not seem to trouble greatly about her wound: she clambers gallantly up the sides of the bell-jar under which I have placed her; she goes on hopping as before. Better still, she sets about browsing the vine-leaf which I have given her for her consolation. A few hours pass and the whole thing is forgotten. She has made a rapid and complete recovery.

A second is wounded in three places on the abdomen: in the middle and on either side. On the first day, the insect seems to have felt nothing; I see no sign of stiffness in its movements. No doubt it is suffering acutely; but these stoics keep their troubles to themselves. Next day, the Ephippiger drags her legs a little and walks somewhat slowly. Two days more; and, when laid on her back, she is unable to turn over. On the fifth day, she succumbs. This time, I have exceeded the dose; the shock of receiving three stabs was too much for her.

And so with the others, down to the sensitive Cricket, who, pricked once in the abdomen, recovers in one day from the painful experience and goes back to her lettuce-leaf. But, if the wound is repeated a few times, death ensues within a more or less short period. I make an exception, among those who pay tribute to my cruel curiosity, of the Rosechafer-grubs, who defy three and four needle-thrusts. They will collapse suddenly and lie outstretched, flabby and lifeless; and, just when I am thinking them dead or paralysed, the hardy creatures will recover consciousness, move along on their backs (This is the usual mode of progression of the Cetonia- or Rosechafer-grub. Cf. "The Life and Love of the Insect": chapter 11.--Translator's Note.), bury themselves in the mould. I can obtain no precise information from them. True, their thinly scattered cilia and their breastplate of fat form a palisade and a rampart against the sting, which nearly always enters only a little way and that obliquely.

Let us leave these unmanageable ones and keep to the Orthoperon, which is more amenable to experiment. A dagger-thrust, we were saying, kills it if directed upon the ganglia of the thorax; it throws it into a transient state of discomfort if directed upon another point. It is, therefore, by its direct action upon the nervous centres that the poison reveals its formidable properties.

To generalize and say that death is always near at hand when the sting is administered in the thoracic ganglia would be going too far: it occurs frequently, but there are a good many exceptions, resulting from circumstances impossible to define. I cannot control the direction of the sting, the depth attained, the quantity of poison shed; and the stump of the Bee is very far from making up for my shortcomings. We have here not the cunning sword-play of the predatory insect, but a casual blow, ill-placed and ill-regulated. Any accident is possible, therefore, from the gravest to the mildest. Let us mention some of the more interesting.

An adult Praying Mantis (Mantis religiosa, so-called because the toothed forelegs, in which it catches and kills its prey, adopt, when folded, an attitude resembling that of prayer.--Translator's Note.) is pricked level with the attachment of the predatory legs. Had the wound been in the centre, I should have witnessed an occurrence which, although I have seen it many times, still arouses my liveliest emotion and surprise. This is the sudden paralysis of the warrior's savage harpoons. No machinery stops more abruptly when the mainspring breaks. As a rule, the inertia of the predatory legs attacks the others in the course of a day or two; and the palsied one dies in less than a week. But the present sting is not in the exact centre. The dart has entered near the base of the right leg, at less than a millimetre (.039 inch.--Translator's Note.) from the median point. That leg is paralysed at once; the other is not; and the insect employs it to the detriment of my unsuspecting fingers, which are pricked to bleeding-point by the spike at the tip. Not until to-morrow is the leg which wounded me to-day rendered motionless. This time, the paralysis goes no farther. The Mantis moves along quite well, with her corselet proudly raised, in her usual attitude; but the predatory fore-arms, instead of being folded against the chest, ready for attack, hang lifeless and open. I keep the cripple for twelve days longer, during which she refuses all nourishment, being incapable of using her tongs to seize the prey and lift it to her mouth. The prolonged abstinence kills her.

Some suffer from locomotor ataxy. My notes recall an Ephippiger who, pricked in the prothorax away from the median line, retained the use of her six limbs without being able to walk or climb for lack of co-ordination in her movements. A singular awkwardness left her wavering between going back and going forward, between turning to the right and turning to the left.

Some are smitten with semiparalysis. A Cetonia-grub, pricked away from the centre on a level with the fore-legs, has her right side flaccid, spread out, incapable of contracting, while the left side swells, wrinkles and contracts. Since the left half no longer receives the symmetrical cooperation of the right half, the grub, instead of curling into the normal volute, closes its spiral on one side and leaves it wide open on the other. The concentration of the nervous apparatus, poisoned by the venom down one side of the body only, a longitudinal half, explains this condition, which is the most remarkable of all.

There is nothing to be gained by multiplying these examples. We have seen pretty clearly the great variety of results produced by the haphazard sting of a Bee's abdomen; let us now come to the crux of the matter. Can the Bee's poison reduce the prey to the condition required by the predatory Wasp? Yes, I have proved it by experiment; but the proof calls for so much patience that it seemed to me to suffice when obtained once for each species. In such difficult conditions, with a poison of excessive strength, a single success is conclusive proof; the thing is possible so long as it occurs once.

A female Ephippiger is stung at the median point, just a little in front of the fore-legs. Convulsive movements lasting for a few seconds are followed by a fall to one side, with pulsations of the abdomen, flutterings of the antennae and a few feeble movements of the legs. The tarsi cling firmly to the hair-pencil which I hold out to them. I place the insect on its back. It lies motionless. Its state is absolutely the same as that to which the Languedocian Sphex (Cf. "Insect Life": chapter 10.-- Translator's Note.) reduces her Ephippigers. For three weeks on end, I see repeated in all its details the spectacle to which I have been accustomed in the victims ex-tracted from the burrows or taken from the huntress: the wide-open mandibles, the quivering palpi and tarsi, the ovipositor shuddering convulsively, the abdomen throbbing at long intervals, the spark of life rekindled at the touch of a pencil. In the fourth week, these signs of life, which have gradually weakened, disappear, but the insect still remains irreproachably fresh. At last a month passes; and the paraly-sed creature begins to turn brown. It is over; death has come.

I have the same success with a Cricket and also with a Praying Mantis. In all three cases, from the point of view of long-maintained freshness and of the signs of life proved by slight movements, the resemblance between my victim and those of the predatory insects is so great that no Sphex and no Tachytes would have dis-owned the product of my devices. My Cricket, my Ephippiger, my Mantis had the same freshness as theirs; they preserved it as theirs did for a period amply sufficient to allow of the grubs' complete evolution. They proved to me, in the most conclusive manner, they prove to all whom it may interest, that the poison of the Bees, leaving its hideous violence on one side, does not differ in its effects from the poison of the predatory Wasps. Are they alkaline or acid? The question is an idle one in this connection. Both of them intoxicate, derange, torpify the nervous centres and thus produce either death or paralysis, according to the method of inoculation. For the moment, that is all. No one is yet able to say the last word on the actions of those poisons, so terrible in infinitesimal doses. But on the point under discussion we need no longer be ignorant: the Wasp owes the preservation of her grub's provisions not to any special qualities of her poison but to the extreme precision of her surgery.

A last and more plausible objection is that raised by Darwin when he said that there were no fossil remains of instincts. And, if there were, O master, what would they teach us? Not very much more than what we learn from the instincts of to-day. Does not the geologist make the erstwhile carcases live anew in our minds in the light of the world as we see it? With nothing but analogy to guide them, he describes how some saurian lived in the jurassic age; there are no fossil remains of habits, but nevertheless he can tell us plenty about them, things worthy of credence, because the present teaches him the past. Let us do a little as he does.

I will suppose a precursor of the Calicurgi (The Calicurgus, or Pompilus, is a Hunting Wasp, feeding her larvae on Spiders. Cf. "The Life and Love of the Insect": chapter 12.--Translator's Note.) dwelling in the prehistoric coal-forests. Her prey was some hideous Scorpion, that first-born of the Arachnida. How did the Hymenopteron master the terrible prey? Analogy tells us, by the methods of the present slayer of Tarantulae. It disarmed the adversary; it paralysed the venomous sting by a stroke administered at a point which we could determine for certain by the animal's anatomy. Unless this was the way it happened, the assailant must have perished, first stabbed and then devoured by the prey. There is no getting away from it: either the precursor of the Calicurgi, that slaughterer of Scorpions, knew her trade thoroughly, or else the continuation of her race became impossible, even as it would be impossible to keep up the race of the Tarantula-killer without the dagger-thrust that paralyses the Spider's poison-fangs. The first who, greatly daring, pinked the Scorpion of the coal-seams was already an expert fencer; the first to come to grips with the Tarantula had an unerring knowledge of her dangerous surgery. The least hesitation, the slightest speculation; and they were lost. The first teacher would also have been the last, with no disciples to take up her work and perfect it.

But fossil instincts, they insist, would show us intermediary stages, first, second and third rungs; they would show us the gradual passing from the casual and very incorrect attempt to the perfect practice, the fruit of the ages; with their accidental differences, they would give us terms of comparison wherewith to trace matters from the simple to the complex. Never mind about that, my masters: if you want varied instincts in which to seek the source of the complex by means of the simple, it is not necessary to search the foliations of the coal-seams and the successive layers of the rocks, those archives of the prehistoric world; the present day affords to contemplation an inexhaustible treasury realizing perhaps everything that can emerge from the limbo of possibility. In what will soon be half a century of study, I have caught but a tiny glimpse of a very tiny corner of the realm of instinct; and the harvest gathered overwhelms me with its variety: I do not yet know two species of predatory Wasps whose methods are exactly the same.

One gives a single stroke of the dagger, a second two, a third three, a fourth nine or ten. One stabs here and the other there; and neither is imitated by the next, who attacks elsewhere. This one injures the cephalic centres and produces death; that one respects them and produces paralysis. Some squeeze the cervical ganglia to obtain a temporary torpor; others know nothing of the effects of compressing the brain. A few make the prey disgorge, lest its honey should poison the offspring; the majority do not resort to preventive manipulations. Here are some that first disarm the foe, who carries poisoned daggers; yonder are others and more numerous, who have no precautions to take before murdering the unarmed prey. In the preliminary struggle, I know some who grab their victims by the neck, by the rostrum, by the antennae, by the caudal threads; I know some who throw them on their backs, some who lift them breast to breast, some who operate on them in the vertical position, some who attack them lengthwise and crosswise, some who climb on their backs or on their abdomens, some who press on their backs to force out a pectoral fissure, some who open their desperately contracted coil, using the tip of the abdomen as a wedge. And so I could go on indefinitely: every method of fencing is employed. What could I not also say about the egg, slung pendulum-fashion by a thread from the ceiling, when the live provisions are wriggling underneath; laid on a scanty mouthful, a solitary opening dish, when the dead prey requires renewing from day to-day; entrusted to the last joint stored away, when the victuals are paralysed; fixed at a precise spot, entailing the least danger to the consumer and the game, when the corpulent prey has to be devoured with a special art that warrants its freshness!

Well, how can this multitude of varied instincts teach us anything about gradual transformation? Will the one and only dagger-thrust of the Cerceris and the Scolia take us to the two thrusts of the Calicurgus, to the three thrusts of the Sphex, to the manifold thrust of the Ammophila? Yes, if we consider only numerical progression. One and one are two; two and one are three: so run the figures. But is this what we want to know? What has arithmetic to do with the case? Is not the whole problem subordinate to a condition that cannot be translated into cyphers? As the prey changes, the anatomy changes; and the surgeon always operates with a complete understanding of his subject. The single dagger-thrust is administered to ganglia collected into a common cluster; the manifold thrusts are distributed over the scattered ganglia; of the two thrusts of the Tarantula-huntress, one disarms and the other paralyses. And so with the others: that is to say, the instinct is directed each time by the secrets of the nervous organism. There is a perfect harmony between the operation and the patient's anatomy.

The single stroke of the Scolia is no less wonderful than the repeated strokes of the Ammophila. Each has her appointed game and each slays it by a method as rational as any that our own science could invent. In the presence of this consummate knowledge, which leaves us utterly confounded, what a poor argument is that of $1 + 1 = 2$! And what is that progress by units to us? The universe is mirrored in a drop of water; universal logic flashes into sight in a single sting.

Besides, push on the pitiful argument. One leads to two, two lead to three. Granted without dispute. And then? We will accept the Scolia as the pioneer, the foundress of the first principles of the art. The simplicity of her method justifies our supposition. She learns her trade in some way or other, by accident; she knows supremely well how to paralyse her Cetonia-grub with a single dagger-thrust driven into the thorax. One day, through some fortuitous circumstance, or rather by mistake, she takes it into her head to strike two blows. As one is enough for the Cetonia, the repetition was of no value unless there was a change of prey. What was the new victim submitted to the butcher's knife? Apparently, a large Spider, since the Tarantula and the Garden Spider call for two thrusts. And the prentice Scolia, who used at first to sting under the throat, had the skill, at her first attempt, to begin by disarming her adversary and then to go quite low down, almost to the end of the thorax, to strike the vital point. I am utterly incredulous as to her success. I see her eaten up if her lancet swerves and hits the wrong spot. Let us look impossibility boldly in the face and admit that she succeeds. I then see the offspring, which have no recollection of the fortunate event save through the belly--and then we are postulating that the digestion of the carnivorous larva leaves a trace in the memory of the honey-sipping insect--I see the offspring, I say, obliged to wait at long intervals for that inspired double thrust and obliged to succeed each time under pain of death for them and their descendants. To accept this host of impossibilities exceeds all my faculties of belief. One leads to two, no doubt; the Ssingle blow of the predatory Wasp will never lead to the blow twice delivered.

In order to live, we all require the conditions that enable us to live: this is a truth worthy of the famous axioms of La Palice. (Jacques de Chabannes, Seigneur de La Palice [circa 1470-1525]), was a French captain killed at the battle of Pavia. His soldiers made up in his honour a ballad, two lines of which, translated, run:

Fifteen minutes before he died, He was still alive.

(Hence the French expression, une verite de La Palice, meaning an obvious truth.--Translator's Note.)

The predatory insects live by their talent. If they do not possess it to perfection, their race is lost. Hidden in the murk of the past ages, the argument based upon the non-existence of fossil instinct is no better able than the others to withstand the light of living realities; it crumbles under the stroke of fate; it vanishes before a La Palice platitude.

CHAPTER 12. THE HALICTI: A PARASITE.

D o you know the Halicti? Perhaps not. There is no great harm done: it is quite possible to enjoy the few sweets of existence without knowing the Halicti. Nevertheless, when questioned persistently, these humble creatures with no history can tell us some very singular things; and their acquaintance is not to be disdained if we would enlarge our ideas upon the bewildering swarm of this world. Since we have nothing better to do, let us look into the Halicti. They are worth the trouble.

How shall we recognize them? They are manufacturers of honey, generally longer and slighter than the Bee of our hives. They constitute a numerous group that varies greatly in size and colouring. Some there are that exceed the dimensions of the Common Wasp; others might be compared with the House-fly, or are even smaller. In the midst of this variety, which is the despair of the novice, one characteristic remains invariable. Every Halictus carries the clearly-written certificate of her guild.

Examine the last ring, at the tip of the abdomen, on the dorsal surface. If your capture be an Halictus, there will be here a smooth and shiny line, a narrow groove along which the sting slides up and down when the insect is on the defensive. This slide for the unsheathed weapon denotes some member of the Halictus tribe, without distinction of size or colour. No elsewhere, in the sting-bearing order, is this original sort of groove in use. It is the distinctive mark, the emblem of the family.

Three Halicti will appear before you in this biographical fragment. Two of them are my neighbours, my familiars, who rarely fail to settle each year in the best parts of the enclosure. They occupied the ground before I did; and I should not dream of evicting them, persuaded as I am that they will well repay my indulgence. Their proximity, which allows me to visit them daily at my leisure, is a piece of good luck. Let us profit by it.

At the head of my three subjects is the Zebra Halictus (H. zebrus, WALCK.), which is beautifully belted around her long abdomen with alternate black and pale-russet scarves. Her slender shape, her size, which equals that of the Common Wasp, her simple and pretty dress, combine to make her the chief representative of the genus here.

She establishes her galleries in firm soil, where there is no danger of landslips which would interfere with the work at nesting-time. In my garden, the well-levelled paths, made of a mixture of tiny pebbles and red clayey earth, suits her to perfection. Every spring she takes possession of it, never alone, but in gangs whose number varies greatly, amounting sometimes to as many as a hundred. In this way she founds what may be described as small townships, each clearly marked out and distant from the other, in which the joint possession of the site in no way entails joint work.

Each has her home, an inviolable manor which none but the owner has the right to enter. A sound buffeting would soon call to order any adventuress who dared to make her way into another's dwelling. No such indiscretion is suffered among the Halicti. Let each keep to her own place and to herself and perfect peace will reign in this new-formed society, made up of neighbours and not of fellow-workers.

Operations begin in April, most unobtrusively, the only sign of the underground works being the little mounds of fresh earth. There is no animation in the building-yards. The labourers show themselves very seldom, so busy are they at the bottom of their pits. At moments, here and there, the summit of a tiny mole-hill begins to totter and tumbles down the slopes of the cone: it is a worker coming up with her armful of rubbish and shooting it outside, without showing herself in the open. Nothing more for the moment.

There is one precaution to be taken: the villages must be protected against the passers-by, who might inadvertently trample them under foot. I surround each of them with a palisade of reed-stumps. In the centre I plant a danger-signal, a post with a paper flag. The sections of the paths thus marked are forbidden ground; none of the household will walk upon them.

May arrives, gay with flowers and sunshine. The navvies of April have turned themselves into harvesters. At every moment I see them settling, all befloured with yellow, atop of the mole-hills now turned into craters. Let us first look into the question of the house. The arrangement of the home will give us some useful information. A spade and a three-pronged fork place the insect's crypts before our eyes.

A shaft as nearly vertical as possible, straight or winding according to the exigencies of a soil rich in flinty remains, descends to a depth of between eight and twelve inches. As it is merely a passage in which the only thing necessary is that the Halictus should find an easy support in coming and going, this long entrance-hall is rough and uneven. A regular shape and a polished surface would be out of place here. These artistic refinements are reserved for the apartments of her young. All that the Halictus mother asks is that the passage should be easy to go up and down, to ascend or descend in a hurry. And so she leaves it rugged. Its width is about that of a thick lead-pencil.

Arranged one by one, horizontally and at different heights, the cells occupy the basement of the house. They are oval cavities, three-quarters of an inch long, dug out of the clay mass. They end in a short bottle-neck that widens into a graceful mouth. They look like tiny vaccine-phials laid on their sides. All of them open into the passage.

The inside of these little cells has the gloss and polish of a stucco which our most experienced plasterers might envy. It is diapered with faint longitudinal, diamond-shaped marks. These are the traces of the polishing-tool that has given the last finish to the work. What can this polisher be? None other than the tongue, that is obvious. The Halictus has made a trowel of her tongue and licked the wall daintily and methodically in order to polish it.

This final glazing, so exquisite in its perfection, is preceded by a trimming-process. In the cells that are not yet stocked with provisions, the walls are dotted with tiny dents like those in a thimble. Here we recognize the work of the mandibles, which squeeze the clay with their tips, compress it and purge it of any grains of sand. The result is a milled surface whereon the polished layer will find a solid adhesive base. This layer is obtained with a fine clay, very carefully selected by the insect, purified, softened and then applied atom by atom, after which the trowel of the tongue steps in, diapering and polishing, while saliva, disgorged as needed, gives pliancy to the paste and finally dries into a waterproof varnish.

The humidity of the subsoil, at the time of the spring showers, would reduce the little earthen alcove to a sort of pap. The coating of saliva is an excellent preservative against this danger. It is so delicate that we suspect rather than see it; but its efficacy is none the less evident. I fill a cell with water. The liquid remains in it quite well, without any trace of infiltration.

The tiny pitcher looks as if it were varnished with galenite. The impermeability which the potter obtains by the brutal infusion of his mineral ingredients the Halictus achieves with the soft polisher of her tongue moistened with saliva. Thus protected, the larva will enjoy all the advantages of a dry berth, even in rain-soaked ground.

Should the wish seize us, it is easy to detach the waterproof film, at least in shreds. Take the little shapeless lump in which a cell has been excavated and put it in sufficient water to cover the bottom of it. The whole earthy mass will soon be soaked and reduced to a mud which we are able to sweep with the point of a hair-pencil. Let us have patience and do our sweeping gently; and we shall be able to separate from the main body the fragments of a sort of extremely fine satin. This transparent, colourless material is the upholstery that keeps out the wet. The Spider's web, if it formed a stuff and not a net, is the only thing that could be compared with it.

The Halictus' nurseries are, as we see, structures that take much time in the making. The insect first digs in the clayey earth a recess with an oval curve to it. It has its mandibles for a pick-axe and its tarsi, armed with tiny claws, for rakes. Rough though it be, this early work presents difficulties, for the Bee has to do her excavating in a narrow gully, where there is only just room for her to pass.

The rubbish soon becomes cumbersome. The insect collects it and then, moving backwards, with its fore-legs closed over the load, it hoists it up through the shaft and flings it outside, upon the mole-hill, which rises by so much above the threshold of the burrow. Next come the dainty finishing-touches: the milling of the wall, the application of a glaze of better-quality clay, the assiduous polishing with the long-suffering tongue, the waterproof coating and the jarlike mouth, a masterpiece of pottery in which the stopping-plug will be fixed when the time comes for locking the door of the room. And all this has to be done with mathematical precision.

No, because of this perfection, the grubs' chambers could never be work done casually from day to day, as the ripe eggs descend from the ovaries. They are prepared long beforehand, during the bad weather, at the end of March and in April, when flowers are scarce and the temperature subject to sudden changes. This thankless period, often cold, liable to hail-storms, is spent in making ready the home. Alone at the bottom of her shaft, which she rarely leaves, the mother works at her children's apartments, lavishing upon them those finishing-touches which leisure allows. They are completed, or very nearly, when May comes with the radiant sunshine and wealth of flowers.

We see the evidence of these long preparations in the burrows themselves, if we inspect them before the provisions are brought. All of them show us cells, about a dozen in number, quite finished, but still empty. To begin by getting all the huts built is a sensible precaution: the mother will not have to turn aside from the delicate task of harvesting and egg-laying in order to perform rough navvy's work.

Everything is ready by May. The air is balmy; the smiling lawns are gay with a thousand little flowers, dandelions, rock-roses, tansies and daisies, among which the harvesting Bee rolls gleefully, covering herself with pollen. With her crop full of honey and the brushes of her legs befloured, the Halictus returns to her village. Flying very low, almost level with the ground, she hesitates, with sudden turns and bewildered movements. It seems that the weak-sighted insect finds its way with difficulty among the cottages of its little township.

Which is its mole-hill among the many others near, all similar in appearance? It cannot tell exactly save by the sign-board of certain details known to itself alone. Therefore, still on the wing, tacking from side to side, it examines the locality. The home is found at last: the Halictus alights on the threshold of her abode and dives into it quickly.

What happens at the bottom of the pit must be the same thing that happens in the case of the other Wild Bees. The harvester enters a cell backwards; she first brushes herself and drops her load of pollen; then, turning round, she disgorges the honey in her crop upon the floury mass. This done, the unwearied one leaves the burrow and flies away, back to the flowers. After many journeys, the stack of provisions in the cell is sufficient. This is the moment to bake the cake.

The mother kneads her flour, mingles it sparingly with honey. The mixture is made into a round loaf, the size of a pea. Unlike our own loaves, this one has the crust inside and the crumb outside. The middle part of the roll, the ration which will be consumed last, when the grub has acquired some strength, consists of almost nothing but dry pollen. The Bee keeps the dainties in her crop for the outside of the loaf, whence the feeble grub-worm is to take its first mouthfuls. Here it is all soft crumb, a delicious sandwich with plenty of honey. The little breakfast-roll is arranged in rings regulated according to the age of the nurseling: first the syrupy outside and at the very end the dry inside. Thus it is ordained by the economics of the Halictus.

An egg bent like a bow is laid upon the sphere. According to the generally-accepted rule, it now only remains to close the cabin. Honey-gatherers--Anthophorae, Osmiae, Mason-bees and many others--usually first collect a sufficient stock of food and then, having laid the egg, shut up the cell, to which they need pay no more attention. The Halicti employ a different method. The compartments, each with its round loaf and its egg--the tenant and his provisions--are not closed up. As they all open into the common passage of the burrow, the mother is able, without leaving her other occupations, to inspect them daily and enquire tenderly into the progress of her family. I imagine, without possessing any certain proof, that from time to time she distributes additional provisions to the grubs, for the original loaf appears to me a very frugal ration compared with that served by the other Bees.

Certain hunting Hymenoptera, the Bembex-wasps, for instance, are accustomed to furnish the provisions in instalments: so that the grub may have fresh though dead game, they fill the platter each day. The Halictus mother has not these domestic necessities, as her provisions keep more easily; but still she might well distribute a second portion of flour to the larvae, when their appetite attains its height. I can see nothing else to explain the open doors of the cells during the feeding-period.

At last the grubs, close-watched and fed to repletion, have achieved the requisite degree of fatness; they are on the eve of being transformed into pupae. Then and not till then the cells are closed: a big clay stopper is built by the mother into the spreading mouth of the jug. Henceforth the maternal cares are over. The rest will come of itself.

Hitherto we have witnessed only the peaceful details of the housekeeping. Let us go back a little and we shall be witnesses of rampant brigandage. In May, I visit my most populous village daily, at about ten o'clock in the morning, when the vict-ualling-operations are in full swing. Seated on a low chair in the sun, with my back bent and my arms upon my knees, I watch, without moving, until dinner-time. What attracts me is a parasite, a trumpery Gnat, the bold despoiler of the Halictus.

Has the jade a name? I trust so, without, however, caring to waste my time in enquiries that can have no interest for the reader. Facts clearly stated are preferable to the dry minutiae of nomenclature. Let me content myself with giving a brief description of the culprit. She is a Dipteron, or Fly, five millimetres long. (.195 inch.--Translator's Note.) Eyes, dark-red; face, white. Corselet, pearl-grey, with five rows of fine black dots, which are the roots of stiff bristles pointing backwards. Greyish belly, pale below. Black legs.

She abounds in the colony under observation. Crouching in the sun, near a burrow, she waits. As soon as the Halictus arrives from her harvesting, her legs yellow with pollen, the Gnat darts forth and pursues her, keeping behind her in all the turns of her oscillating flight. At last, the Bee suddenly dives indoors. No less suddenly the other settles on the mole-hill, quite close to the entrance. Motionless, with her head turned towards the door of the house, she waits for the Bee to finish her business. The latter reappears at last and, for a few seconds, stands on the threshold, with her head and thorax outside the hole. The Gnat, on her side, does not stir.

Often, they are face to face, separated by a space no wider than a finger's breadth. Neither of them shows the least excitement. The Halictus--judging, at least, by her tranquillity--takes no notice of the parasite lying in wait for her; the parasite, on the other hand, displays no fear of being punished for her audacity. She remains imperturbable, she, the dwarf, in the presence of the colossus who could crush her with one blow.

In vain I watch anxiously for some sign of apprehension on either side: nothing in the Halictus points to a knowledge of the danger run by her family; nor does the Gnat betray any dread of swift retribution. Plunderer and plundered stare at each other for a moment; and that is all.

If she liked, the amiable giantess could rip up with her claw the tiny bandit who ruins her home; she could crunch her with her mandibles, run her through with her stiletto. She does nothing of the sort, but leaves the robber in peace, to sit quite close, motionless, with her red eyes fixed on the threshold of the house. Why this fatuous clemency?

The Bee flies off. Forthwith, the Gnat walks in, with no more ceremony than if she were entering her own place. She now chooses among the victualled cells at her ease, for they are all open, as I have said; she leisurely deposits her eggs. No one will disturb her until the Bee's return. To flour one's legs with pollen, to distend one's crop with syrup is a task that takes long a-doing; and the intruder, therefore, has time and to spare wherein to commit her felony. Moreover, her chronometer is well-regulated and gives the exact measure of the Bee's length of absence. When the Halictus comes back from the fields, the Gnat has decamped. In some favourable spot, not far from the burrow, she awaits the opportunity for a fresh misdeed.

What would happen if a parasite were surprised at her work by the Bee? Nothing serious. I see them, greatly daring, follow the Halictus right into the cave and remain there for some time while the mixture of pollen and honey is being prepared. Unable to make use of the paste so long as the harvester is kneading it, they go back to the open air and wait on the threshold for the Bee to come out. They return to the sunlight, calmly, with unhurried steps: a clear proof that nothing untoward has occurred in the depths where the Halictus works.

A tap on the Gnat's neck, if she become too enterprising in the neighbourhood of the cake: that is all that the lady of the house seems to allow herself, to drive away the intruder. There is no serious affray between the robber and the robbed. This is apparent from the self-possessed manner and undamaged condition of the dwarf who returns from visiting the giantess engaged down in the burrow.

The Bee, when she comes home, whether laden with provisions or not, hesitates, as I have said, for a while; in a series of rapid zigzags, she moves backwards, forwards and from side to side, at a short distance from the ground. This intricate flight at first suggests the idea that she is trying to lead her persecutress astray by means of an inextricable tangle of marches and countermarches. That would certainly be a prudent move on the Bee's part; but so much wisdom appears to be denied her.

It is not the enemy that is disturbing her, but rather the difficulty of finding her own house amid the confusion of the mole-hills, encroaching one upon the other, and all the alleys of the little township, which, owing to landslips of fresh rubbish, alter in appearance from one day to the next. Her hesitation is manifest, for she often blunders and alights at the entrance to a burrow that is not hers. The mistake is at once perceived from the slight indications of the doorway.

The search is resumed with the same see-sawing flights, mingled with sudden excursions to a distance. At last, the burrow is recognized. The Halictus dives into it with a rush; but, however prompt her disappearance underground, the Gnat is there, perched on the threshold with her eyes turned to the entrance, waiting for the Bee to come out, so that she may visit the honey-jars in her turn.

When the owner of the house ascends, the other draws back a little, just enough to leave a free passage and no more. Why should she put herself out? the meeting is so peaceful that, short of further information, one would not suspect that a destroyer and destroyed were face to face. Far from being intimidated by the sudden arrival of the Halictus, the Gnat pays hardly any attention; and, in the same way, the Halictus takes no notice of her persecutress, unless the bandit pursue her and worry her on the wing. Then, with a sudden bend, the Bee makes off.

Even so do Philanthus apivorus (The Bee-hunting Wasp. Cf. "Social Life in the Insect World": chapter 13.--Translator's Note.) and the other game-hunters behave when the Tachina is at their heels seeking the chance to lay her egg on the morsel about to be stored away. Without jostling the parasite which they find hanging around the burrow, they go indoors quite peaceably; but, on the wing, perceiving her after them, they dart off wildly. The Tachina, however, dares not go down to the cells where the huntress stacks her provisions; she prudently waits at the door for the Philanthus to arrive. The crime, the laying of the egg, is committed at the very moment when the victim is about to vanish underground.

The troubles of the parasite of the Halictus are of quite another kind. The homing Bee has her honey in her crop and her pollen on her leg-brushes: the first is inaccessible to the thief; the second is powdery and would give no resting-place to the egg. Besides, there is not enough of it yet: to collect the wherewithal for that round loaf of hers, the Bee will have to make repeated journeys. When the necessary amount is obtained, she will knead it with the tip of her mandibles and shape it with her feet into a little ball. The Gnat's egg, were it present among the materials, would certainly be in danger during this manipulation.

The alien egg, therefore, must be laid on the finished bread; and, as the preparation takes place underground, the parasite is needs obliged to go down to the Halictus. With inconceivable daring, she does go down, even when the Bee is there. Whether through cowardice or silly indulgence, the dispossessed insect lets the other have its way.

The object of the Gnat, with her tenacious lying-in-wait and her reckless burglaries, is not to feed herself at the harvester's expense: she could get her living out of the flowers with much less trouble than her thieving trade involves. The most, I think, that she can allow herself to do in the Halictus' cellars is to take one morsel just to ascertain the quality of the victuals. Her great, her sole business is to settle her family. The stolen goods are not for herself, but for her offspring.

Let us dig up the pollen-loaves. We shall find them most often crumbled with no regard to economy, simply frittered away. We shall see two or three maggots, with pointed mouths, moving in the yellow flour scattered over the floor of the cell. These are the Gnat's progeny. With them we sometimes find the lawful owner, the grub-worm of the Halictus, but stunted and emaciated with fasting. His gluttonous companions, without otherwise molesting him, deprive him of the best of everything. The wretched starveling dwindles, shrivels up and soon disappears from view. His corpse, a mere atom, blended with the remaining provisions, supplies the maggots with one mouthful the more.

And what does the Halictus mother do in this disaster? She is free to visit her grubs at any moment; she has but to put her head into the passage of the house: she cannot fail to be apprised of their distress. The squandered loaf, the swarming mass of vermin tell their own tale. Why does she not take the intruders by the skin of the abdomen? To grind them to powder with her mandibles, to fling them out of doors were the business of a second. And the foolish creature never thinks of it, leaves the ravagers in peace!

She does worse. When the time of the nymphosis comes, the Halictus mother goes to the cells rifled by the parasite and closes them with an earthen plug as carefully as she does the rest. This final barricade, an excellent precaution when the cot is occupied by an Halictus in course of metamorphosis, becomes the height of absurdity when the Gnat has passed that way. Instinct does not hesitate in the face of this ineptitude: it seals up emptiness. I say, emptiness, because the crafty maggot hastens to decamp the instant that the victuals are consumed, as though it foresaw an insuperable obstacle for the coming Fly: it quits the cell before the Bee closes it.

To rascally guile the parasite adds prudence. All, until there is none of them left, abandon the clay homes which would be their undoing once the entrance was plugged up. The earthen niche, so grateful to the tender skin, thanks to its polished coating, so free from humidity, thanks to its waterproof glaze, ought, one would think, to make an excellent waiting-place. The maggots will have none of it. Lest they should find themselves walled in when they become frail Gnats, they go away and disperse in the neighbourhood of the ascending shaft.

My digging operations, in fact, always reveal the pupae outside the cells, never inside. I find them enshrined, one by one, in the body of the clayey earth, in a narrow recess which the emigrant worm has contrived to make for itself. Next spring, when the hour comes for leaving, the adult insect has but to creep through the rubbish, which is easy work.

Another and no less imperative reason compels this change of abode on the parasite's part. In July, a second generation of the Halictus is procreated. The Gnat, reduced on her side to a single brood, remains in the pupa state and awaits the spring of the following year before effecting her transformation. The honey-gather resumes her work in her native village; she avails herself of the pits and cells constructed in the spring, saving no little time thereby. The whole elaborate structure has remained in good condition. It needs but a few repairs to make the old house habitable.

Now what would happen if the Bee, so scrupulous in matters of cleanliness, were to find a pupa in the cell which she is sweeping? She would treat the cumbersome object as she would a piece of old plaster. It would be no more to her than any other refuse, a bit of gravel, which, seized with the mandibles, crushed perhaps, would be sent to join the rubbish-heap outside. Once removed from the soil and exposed to the inclemencies of the weather, the pupa would inevitably perish.

I admire this intelligent foresight of the maggot, which forgoes the comfort of the moment for the security of the future. Two dangers threaten it: to be immured in a casket whence the Fly can never issue; or else to die out of doors, in the unkindly air, when the Bee sweeps out the restored cells. To avoid this twofold peril, it decamps before the door is closed, before the July Halictus sets her house in order.

Let us now see what comes of the parasite's intrusion. In the course of June, when peace is established in the Halictus' home, I dig up my largest village, comprising some fifty burrows in all. None of the sorrows of this underworld shall escape me. There are four of us engaged in sifting the excavated earth through our fingers. What one has examined another takes up and examines; and then another and another yet. The returns are heartrending. We do not succeed in finding one single nymph of the Halictus. The whole of the populous city has perished; and its place has been taken by the Gnat. There is a glut of that individual's pupae. I collect them in order to trace their evolution.

The year runs its course; and the little russet kegs, into which the original maggots have hardened and contracted, remain stationary. They are seeds endowed with latent life. The heats of July do not rouse them from their torpor. In that month, the period of the second generation of the Halictus, there is a sort of truce of God: the parasite rests and the Bee works in peace. If hostilities were to be resumed straight away, as murderous in summer as they were in spring, the progeny of the Halictus, too cruelly smitten, might possibly disappear altogether. This lull readjusts the balance.

In April, when the Zebra Halictus, in search of a good place for her burrows, roams up and down the garden paths with her oscillating flight, the parasite, on its side, hastens to hatch. Oh, the precise and terrible agreement between those two calendars, the calendar of the persecutor and the persecuted! At the very moment when the Bee comes out, here is the Gnat: she is ready to begin her deadly starving-process all over again.

Were this an isolated case, one's mind would not dwell upon it: an Halictus more or less in the world makes little difference in the general balance. But, alas, brigandage in all its forms is the rule in the eternal conflict of living things! From the lowest to the highest, every producer is exploited by the unproductive. Man himself, whose exceptional rank ought to raise him above such baseness, excels in this ravening lust. He says to himself that business means getting hold of other people's cash, even as the Gnat says to herself that business means getting hold of the Halictus' honey. And, to play the brigand to better purpose, he invents war, the art of killing wholesale and of doing with glory that which, when done on a smaller scale, leads to the gallows.

Shall we never behold the realization of that sublime vision which is sung on

Sundays in the smallest village-church: Gloria in excelsis Deo, et in terra pax hominibus bonae voluntatis! If war affected humanity alone, perhaps the future would have peace in store for us, seeing that generous minds are working for it with might and main; but the scourge also rages among the lower animals, which in their obstinate way, will never listen to reason. Once the evil is laid down as a general condition, it perhaps becomes incurable. Life in the future, it is to be feared, will be what it is to-day, a perpetual massacre.

Whereupon, by a desperate effort of the imagination, one pictures to oneself a giant capable of juggling with the planets. He is irresistible strength; he is also law and justice. He knows of our battles, our butcheries, our farm-burnings, our town-burnings, our brutal triumphs; he knows our explosives, our shells, our torpedo-boats, our ironclads and all our cunning engines of destruction; he knows as well the appalling extent of the appetites among all creatures, down to the very lowest. Well, if that just and mighty one held the earth under his thumb, would he hesitate whether he ought to crush it?

He would not hesitate...He would let things take their course. He would say to himself:

'The old belief is right; the earth is a rotten apple, gnawed by the vermin of evil. It is a first crude attempt, a step towards a kindlier destiny. Let it be: order and justice are waiting at the end.'

CHAPTER 13. THE HALICTI: THE PORTRESS.

L eaving our village is no very serious matter when we are children. We even look on it as a sort of holiday. We are going to see something new, those magic pictures of our dreams. With age come regrets; and the close of life is spent in stirring up old memories. Then the beloved village reappears, in the biograph of the mind, embellished, transfigured by the glow of those first impressions; and the mental image, superior to the reality, stands out in amazingly clear relief. The past, the far-off past, was only yesterday; we see it, we touch it.

For my part, after three-quarters of a century, I could walk with my eyes closed straight to the flat stone where I first heard the soft chiming note of the Midwife Toad; yes, I should find it to a certainty, if time, which devastates all things, even the homes of Toads, has not moved it or perhaps left it in ruins.

I see, on the margin of the brook, the exact position of the alder-trees whose tangled roots, deep under the water, were a refuge for the Crayfish. I should say:

'It is just at the foot of that tree that I had the unutterable bliss of catching a beauty. She had horns so long...and enormous claws, full of meat, for I got her just at the right time.'

I should go without faltering to the ash under whose shade my heart beat so loudly one sunny spring morning. I had caught sight of a sort of white, cottony ball among the branches. Peeping from the depths of the wadding was an anxious little head with a red hood to it. O what unparalleled luck! It was a Goldfinch, sitting on her eggs.

Compared with a find like this, lesser events do not count. Let us leave them. In any case, they pale before the memory of the paternal garden, a tiny hanging garden of some thirty paces by ten, situated right at the top of the village. The only spot that overlooks it is a little esplanade on which stands the old castle (The Chateau de

Saint-Leons standing just outside and above the village of Saint-Leons, where the author was born in 1823. Cf. "The Life of the Fly": chapters 6 and 7.--Translator's Note.) with the four turrets that have now become dovecotes. A steep path takes you up to this open space. From my house on, it is more like a precipice than a slope. Gardens buttressed by walls are staged in terraces on the sides of the funnel-shaped valley. Ours is the highest; it is also the smallest.

There are no trees. Even a solitary apple-tree would crowd it. There is a patch of cabbages, with a border of sorrel, a patch of turnips and another of lettuces. That is all we have in the way of garden-stuff; there is no room for more. Against the upper supporting-wall, facing due south, is a vine-arbour which, at intervals, when the sun is generous, provides half a basketful of white muscatel grapes. These are a luxury of our own, greatly envied by the neighbours, for the vine is unknown outside this corner, the warmest in the village.

A hedge of currant-bushes, the only safeguard against a terrible fall, forms a parapet above the next terrace. When our parents' watchful eyes are off us, we lie flat on our stomachs, my brother and I, and look into the abyss at the foot of the wall bulging under the thrust of the land. It is the garden of monsieur le notaire.

There are beds with box-borders in that garden; there are pear-trees reputed to give pears, real pears, more or less good to eat when they have ripened on the straw all through the late autumn. In our imagination, it is a spot of perpetual delight, a paradise, but a paradise seen the wrong way up: instead of contemplating it from below, we gaze at it from above. How happy they must be with so much space and all those pears!

We look at the hives, around which the hovering Bees make a sort of russet smoke. They stand under the shelter of a great hazel. The tree has sprung up all of itself in a fissure of the wall, almost on the level of our currant-bushes. While it spreads its mighty branches over the notary's hives, its roots, at least, are on our land. It belongs to us. The trouble is to gather the nuts.

I creep along astride the strong branches projecting horizontally into space. If I slip or if the support breaks, I shall come to grief in the midst of the angry Bees. I do not slip and the support does not break. With the bent switch which my brother hands me, I bring the finest clusters within my reach. I soon fill my pockets. Moving backwards, still straddling my branch, I recover terra firma. O wondrous days of litheness and assurance, when, for a few filberts, on a perilous perch we braved the abyss!

Enough. These reminiscences, so dear to my dreams, do not interest the reader. Why stir up more of them? I am content to have brought this fact into prominence: the first glimmers of light penetrating into the dark chambers of the mind leave an indelible impression, which the years make fresher instead of dimmer.

Obscured by everyday worries, the present is much less familiar to us, in its petty details, than the past, with childhood's glow upon it. I see plainly in my memory what my prentice eyes saw; and I should never succeed in reproducing with the same accuracy what I saw last week. I know my village thoroughly, though I quitted it so long ago; and I know hardly anything of the towns to which the vicissitudes of life have brought me. An exquisitely sweet link binds us to our native soil; we are like the plant that has to be torn away from the spot where it put out its first roots. Poor though it be, I should love to see my own village again; I should like to leave my bones there.

Does the insect in its turn receive a lasting impression of its earliest visions? Has it pleasant memories of its first surroundings? We will not speak of the majority, a world of wandering gipsies who establish themselves anywhere provided that certain conditions be fulfilled; but the others, the settlers, living in groups: do they recall their native village? Have they, like ourselves, a special affection for the place which saw their birth?

Yes, indeed they have: they remember, they recognize the maternal abode, they come back to it, they restore it, they colonize it anew. Among many other instances, let us quote that of the Zebra Halictus. She will show us a splendid example of love for one's birthplace translating itself into deeds.

The Halictus' spring family acquire the adult form in a couple of months or so; they leave the cells about the end of June. What goes on inside these neophytes as they cross the threshold of the burrow for the first time? Something, apparently, that may be compared with our own impressions of childhood. An exact and indelible image is stamped on their virgin memories. Despite the years, I still see the stone whence came the resonant notes of the little Toads, the parapet of currant-bushes, the notary's garden of Eden. These trifles make the best part of my life. The Halictus sees in the same way the blade of grass whereon she rested in her first flight, the bit of gravel which her claw touched in her first climb to the top of the shaft. She knows her native abode by heart just as I know my village. The locality has become familiar to her in one glad, sunny morning.

She flies off, seeks refreshment on the flowers near at hand and visits the fields where the coming harvests will be gathered. The distance does not lead her astray, so faithful are her impressions of her first trip; she finds the encampment of her tribe; among the burrows of the village, so numerous and so closely resembling one another, she knows her own. It is the house where she was born, the beloved house with its unforgettable memories.

But, on returning home, the Halictus is not the only mistress of the house. The dwelling dug by the solitary Bee in early spring remains, when summer comes, the joint inheritance of the members of the family. There are ten cells, or thereabouts, underground. Now from these cells there have issued none but females. This is the rule among the three species of Halicti that concern us now and probably also among many others, if not all. They have two generations in each year. The spring one consists of females only; the summer one comprises both males and females, in almost equal numbers. We shall return to this curious subject in our next chapter.

The household, therefore, if not reduced by accidents, above all if not starved by the usurping Gnat, would consist of half-a-score of sisters, none but sisters, all equally industrious and all capable of procreating without a nuptial partner. On the other hand, the maternal dwelling is no hovel; far from it: the entrance-gallery, the principal room of the house, will serve quite well, after a few odds and ends of refuse have been swept away. This will be so much gained in time, ever precious to the Bee. The cells at the bottom, the clay cabins, are also nearly intact. To make use of them, it will be enough for the Halictus to polish up the stucco with her tongue.

Well, which of the survivors, all equally entitled to the succession, will inherit the house? There are six of them, seven, or more, according to the chances of mortality. To whose share will the maternal dwelling fall?

There is no quarrel between the interested parties. The mansion is recognized as common property without dispute. The sisters come and go peacefully through the same door, attend to their business, pass and let the others pass. Down at the bottom of the pit, each has her little demesne, her group of cells dug at the cost of fresh toil, when the old ones, now insufficient in number, are occupied. In these recesses, which are private estates, each mother works by herself, jealous of her property and of her privacy. Every elsewhere, traffic is free to all.

The exits and entrances in the working fortress provide a spectacle of the highest interest. A harvester arrives from the fields, the feather-brushes of her legs powdered with pollen. If the door be open, the Bee at once dives underground. To tarry on the threshold would mean waste of time; and the business is urgent. Sometimes, several appear upon the scene at almost the same moment. The passage is too narrow for two, especially when they have to avoid any untimely contact that would make the floury burden fall to the floor. The nearest to the opening enters quickly. The others, drawn up on the threshold in order of their arrival, respectful of one another's rights, await their turn. As soon as the first disappears, the second follows after her and is herself swiftly followed by the third and then the others, one by one.

Sometimes, again, there is a meeting between a Bee about to come out and a Bee about to go in. Then the latter draws back a little and makes way for the former. The politeness is reciprocal. I see some who, when on the point of emerging from the pit, go down again and leave the passage free for the one who has just arrived. Thanks to this mutual spirit of accommodation, the business of the house proceeds without impediment.

Let us keep our eyes open. There is something better than the well-preserved order of the entrances. When an Halictus appears, returning from her round of the flowers, we see a sort of trap-door, which closed the house, suddenly fall and give a free passage. As soon as the new arrival has entered, the trap rises back into its place, almost level with the ground, and closes the entrance anew. The same thing happens when the insects go out. At a request from within, the trap descends, the door opens and the Bee flies away. The outlet is closed forthwith.

What can this valve be which, descending or ascending in the cylinder of the pit, after the fashion of a piston, opens and closes the house at each departure and at each arrival? It is an Halictus, who has become the portress of the establishment. With her large head, she makes an impassable barrier at the top of the entrance-hall. If any one belonging to the house wants to go in or out, she 'pulls the cord,' that is to say, she withdraws to a spot where the gallery becomes wider and leaves room for two. The other passes. She then at once returns to the orifice and blocks it with the top of her head. Motionless, ever on the look-out, she does not leave her post save to drive away importunate visitors.

Let us profit by her brief appearances outside to take a look at her. We recognize in her an Halictus similar to the others, which are now busy harvesting; but the top of her head is bald and her dress is dingy and thread-bare. All the nap is gone; and one can hardly make out the handsome stripes of red and brown which she used to have. These tattered, work-worn garments make things clear to us.

This Bee who mounts guard and performs the office of a portress at the entrance to the burrow is older than the others. She is the foundress of the establishment, the mother of the actual workers, the grandmother of the present grubs. In the springtime of her life, three months ago, she wore herself out in solitary labours. Now that her ovaries are dried up, she takes a well-earned rest. No, rest is hardly the word. She still works, she assists the household to the best of her power. Incapable of being a mother for a second time, she becomes a portress, opens the door to the members of her family and makes strangers keep their distance.

The suspicious Kid (In La Fontaine's fable, "Le Loup, la Chevre et le Chevreau."--Translator's Note.), looking through the chink, said to the Wolf:

'Show me a white foot, or I shan't open the door.'

No less suspicious, the grandmother says to each comer:

'Show me the yellow foot of an Halictus, or you won't be let in.'

None is admitted to the dwelling unless she be recognized as a member of the family.

See for yourselves. Near the burrow passes an Ant, an unscrupulous adventuress, who would not be sorry to know the meaning of the honeyed fragrance that rises from the bottom of the cellar.

"Be off, or you'll catch it!' says the portress, wagging her neck.

As a rule the threat suffices. The Ant decamps. Should she insist, the watcher leaves her sentry-box, flings herself upon the saucy jade, buffets her and drives her away. The moment the punishment has been administered, she returns to her post.

Next comes the turn of a Leaf-cutter (Megachile albocincta, PEREZ), which, unskilled in the art of burrowing, utilizes, after the manner of her kin, the old galleries dug by others. Those of the Zebra Halictus suit her very well, when the terrible Gnat has left them vacant for lack of heirs. Seeking for a home wherein to stack her robinia-leaf honey-pots, she often makes a flying inspection of my colonies of Halicti. A burrow seems to take her fancy; but, before she sets foot on earth, her buzzing is noticed by the sentry, who suddenly darts out and makes a few gestures on the threshold of her door. That is all. The Leaf-cutter has understood. She moves on.

Sometimes, the Megachile has time to alight and insert her head into the mouth of the pit. In a moment, the portress is there, comes a little higher and bars the way. Follows a not very serious contest. The stranger quickly recognizes the rights of the first occupant and, without insisting, goes to seek an abode elsewhere.

An accomplished marauder (Caelioxys caudata, SPIN.), a parasite of the Megachile, receives a sound drubbing under my eyes. She thought, the feather-brain, that she was entering the Leaf-Cutter's establishment! She soon finds out her mistake; she meets the door-keeping Halictus, who administers a sharp correction. She makes off at full speed. And so with the others which, through inadvertence or ambition, seek to enter the burrow.

The same intolerance exists among the different grandmothers. About the middle of July, when the animation of the colony is at its height, two sets of Halicti are easily distinguishable: the young mothers and the old. The former, much more numerous, brisk of movement and smartly arrayed, come and go unceasingly from the burrows to the fields and from the fields to the burrows. The latter, faded and dispirited, wander idly from hole to hole. They look as though they had lost their way and were incapable of finding their homes. Who are these vagabonds? I see in them afflicted ones bereft of a family through the act of the odious Gnat. Many burrows have been altogether exterminated. At the awakening of summer, the mother found herself alone. She left her empty house and went off in search of a dwelling where there were cradles to defend, a guard to mount. But those fortunate nests already have their overseer, the foundress, who, jealous of her rights, gives her unemployed neighbour a cold reception. One sentry is enough; two would merely block the narrow guard-room.

I am privileged at times to witness a fight between two grandmothers. When the tramp in quest of employment appears outside the door, the lawful occupant does not move from her post, does not withdraw into the passage, as she would before an Halictus returning from the fields. Far from making way, she threatens the intruder with her feet and mandibles. The other retaliates and tries to force her way in notwithstanding. Blows are exchanged. The fray ends by the defeat of the stranger, who goes off to pick a quarrel elsewhere.

These little scenes afford us a glimpse of certain details of the highest interest in the habits of the Zebra Halictus. The mother who builds her nest in the spring no longer leaves her home, once her works are finished. Shut up at the bottom of the burrow, busied with the thousand cares of housekeeping, or else drowsing, she waits for her daughters to come out. When, in the summer heats, the life of the village recommences, having nought to do outside as a harvester, she stands sentry at the entrance to the hall, so as to let none in save the workers of the home, her own daughters. She wards off evilly-disposed visitors. None can enter without the door-keeper's consent.

There is nothing to tell us that the watcher ever deserts her post. Not once do I see her leave her house to go and seek some refreshment from the flowers. Her age and her sedentary occupation, which involves no great fatigue, perhaps relieve her of the need of nourishment. Perhaps, also, the young ones returning from their plundering may from time to time disgorge a drop of the contents of their crops for her benefit. Fed or unfed, the old one no longer goes out.

But what she does need is the joys of an active family. Many are deprived of these. The Gnat's burglary has destroyed the busy household. The sorely-tried Bees abandon the deserted burrow. It is they who, ragged and careworn, wander through the village. When they move, their flight is only a short one; more often they remain motionless. It is they who, soured in their tempers, attack their fellows and seek to dislodge them. They grow rarer and more languid from day to day; then they disappear for good. What has become of them? The little Grey Lizard had his eye on them: they are easily snapped up.

Those settled in their own demesne, those who guard the honey-factory wherein their daughters, the heiresses of the maternal establishment, are at work, display wonderful vigilance. The more I see of them, the more I admire them. In the cool hours of the early morning, when the pollen-flour is not sufficiently ripened by the sun and while the harvesters are still indoors, I see them at their posts, at the top of the gallery. Here, motionless, their heads flush with the earth, they bar the door to all invaders. If I look at them closely, they retreat a little and, in the shadow, await the indiscreet observer's departure.

I return when the harvesting is in full swing, between eight o'clock and twelve. There is now, as the Halicti go in or out, a succession of prompt withdrawals to open the door and of ascents to close it. The portress is in the full exercise of her functions.

In the afternoon, the heat is too great and the workers do not go to the fields. Retiring to the bottom of the house, they varnish the new cells, they make the round loaf that is to receive the egg. The grandmother is still upstairs, stopping the door with her bald head. For her, there is no siesta during the stifling hours: the safety of the household requires her to forgo it.

I come back again at nightfall, or even later. By the light of a lantern, I again behold the overseer, as zealous and assiduous as in the day-time. The others are resting, but not she, for fear, apparently, of nocturnal dangers known to herself alone. Does she nevertheless end by descending to the quiet of the floor below? It seems probable, so essential must rest be, after the fatigue of such a vigil!

It is evident that, guarded in this manner, the burrow is exempt from calamities similar to those which, too often, depopulate it in May. Let the Gnat come now, if she dare, to steal the Halictus' loaves! Let her lie in wait as long as she will! Neither her audacity nor her slyness will make her escape the lynx eyes of the sentinel, who will put her to flight with a threatening gesture or, if she persist, crush her with her nippers. She will not come; and we know the reason: until spring returns, she is underground in the pupa state.

But, in her absence, there is no lack, among the Fly rabble, of other batteners on the toil of their fellow insects. Whatever the job, whatever the plunder, you will find parasites there. And yet, for all my daily visits, I never catch one of these in the neighbourhood of the summer burrows. How cleverly the rascals ply their trade! How well aware are they of the guard who keeps watch at the Halictus' door! There is no foul deed possible nowadays; and the result is that no Fly puts in an appearance and the tribulations of last spring are not repeated.

The grandmother who, dispensed by age from maternal bothers, mounts guard at the entrance of the home and watches over the safety of the family, tells us that in the genesis of the instincts sudden births occur; she shows us the existence of a spontaneous aptitude which nothing, either in her own past conduct or in the actions of her daughters, could have led us to suspect. Timorous in her prime, in the month of May, when she lived alone in the burrow of her making, she has become gifted, in her decline, with a superb contempt of danger and dares in her impotence what she never dared do in her strength.

Formerly, when her tyrant, the Gnat, entered the house in her presence, or, more often, stood face to face with her at the entrance, the silly Bee did not stir, did not even threaten the red-eyed bandit, the dwarf whose doom she could so easily have sealed. Was it terror on her part? No, for she attended to her duties with her usual punctiliousness; no, for the strong do not allow themselves to be thus paralysed by the weak. It was ignorance of the danger, it was sheer fecklessness.

And behold, to-day, the ignoramus of three months ago knows the peril, knows it well, without serving any apprenticeship. Every stranger who appears is kept at a distance, without distinction of size or race. If the threatening gesture be not enough, the keeper sallies forth and flings herself upon the persistent one. Cowardice has developed into courage.

How has this change been brought about? I should like to picture the Halictus gaining wisdom from the misfortunes of the spring and capable thenceforth of looking out for danger; I would gladly credit her with having learnt in the stern school of experience the advantages of a patrol. I must give up the idea. If, by dint of gradual little acts of progress, the Bee has achieved the glorious invention of a janitress, how comes it that the fear of thieves is intermittent? It is true that, being by herself in May, she cannot stand permanently at her door: the business of the house takes precedence of everything else. But she ought, at any rate as soon as her offspring are victimized, to know the parasite and give chase when, at every moment, she finds her almost under her feet and even in her house. Yet she pays no attention to her.

The bitter experience of her ancestors, therefore, has bequeathed nothing to her of a nature to alter her placid character; nor have her own tribulations aught to do with the sudden awakening of her vigilance in July. Like ourselves, animals have their joys and their sorrows. They eagerly make the most of the former; they fret but little about the latter, which, when all is said, is the best way of achieving a purely animal enjoyment of life. To mitigate these troubles and protect the progeny there is the inspiration of instinct, which is able without the counsels of experience to give the Halicti a portress.

When the victualling is finished, when the Halicti no longer sally forth on harvesting intent nor return all befloured with their spoils, the old Bee is still at her post, vigilant as ever. The final preparations for the brood are made below; the cells are closed. The door will be kept until everything is finished. Then grandmother and mothers leave the house. Exhausted by the performance of their duty, they go, somewhere or other, to die.

In September appears the second generation, comprising both males and females. I find both sexes wassailing on the flowers, especially the Compositae, the centauries and thistles. They are not harvesting now: they are refreshing themselves, holding high holiday, teasing one another. It is the wedding-time. Yet another fortnight and the males will disappear, henceforth useless. The part of the idlers is played. Only the industrious ones remain, the impregnated females, who go through the winter and set to work in April.

I do not know their exact haunt during the inclement season. I expected them to return to their native burrow, an excellent dwelling for the winter, one would think. Excavations made in January showed me my mistake. The old homes are empty, are falling to pieces owing to the prolonged effect of the rains. The Zebra Halictus has something better than these muddy hovels: she has snug corners in the stone-heaps, hiding-places in the sunny walls and many other convenient habitations. And so the natives of a village become scattered far and wide.

In April, the scattered ones reassemble from all directions. On the well-flattened garden-paths a choice is made of the site for their common labours. Operations soon begin. Close to the first who bores her shaft there is soon a second one busy with hers; a third arrives, followed by another and others yet, until the little mounds often touch one another, while at times they number as many as fifty on a surface of less than a square yard.

One would be inclined, at first sight, to say that these groups are accounted for by the insect's recollection of its birthplace, by the fact that the villagers, after dispersing during the winter, return to their hamlet. But it is not thus that things happen: the Halictus scorns to-day the place that once suited her. I never see her occupy the same patch of ground for two years in succession. Each spring she needs new quarters. And there are plenty of them.

Can this mustering of the Halicti be due to a wish to resume the old intercourse with their friends and relations? Do the natives of the same burrow, of the same hamlet, recognize one another? Are they inclined to do their work among themselves rather than in the company of strangers? There is nothing to prove it, nor is there anything to disprove it. Either for this reason or for others, the Halictus likes to keep with her neighbours.

This propensity is pretty frequent among peace-lovers, who, needing little nourishment, have no cause to fear competition. The others, the big eaters, take possession of estates, of hunting-grounds from which their fellows are excluded. Ask a Wolf his opinion of a brother Wolf poaching on his preserves. Man himself, the chief of consumers, makes for himself frontiers armed with artillery; he sets up posts at the foot of which one says to the other:

'Here's my side, there's yours. That's enough: now we'll pepper each other.'

And the rattle of the latest explosives ends the colloquy.

Happy are the peace-lovers. What do they gain by their mustering? With them it is not a defensive system, a concerted effort to ward off the common foe. The Halictus does not care about her neighbour's affairs. She does not visit another's burrow; she does not allow others to visit hers. She has her tribulations, which she endures alone; she is indifferent to the tribulations of her kind. She stands aloof from the strife of her fellows. Let each mind her own business and leave things at that.

But company has its attractions. He lives twice who watches the life of others. Individual activity gains by the sight of the general activity; the animation of each one derives fresh warmth from the fire of the universal animation. To see one's neighbours at work stimulates one's rivalry. And work is the great delight, the real satisfaction that gives some value to life. The Halictus knows this well and assembles in her numbers that she may work all the better.

Sometimes she assembles in such multitudes and over such extents of ground as to suggest our own colossal swarms. Babylon and Memphis, Rome and Carthage, London and Paris, those frantic hives, occur to our mind if we can manage to forget comparative dimensions and see a Cyclopean pile in a pinch of earth.

It was in February. The almond-tree was in blossom. A sudden rush of sap had given the tree new life; its boughs, all black and desolate, seemingly dead, were becoming a glorious dome of snowy satin. I have always loved this magic of the awakening spring, this smile of the first flowers against the gloomy bareness of the bark.

And so I was walking across the fields, gazing at the almond-trees' carnival. Others were before me. An Osmia in a black velvet bodice and a red woollen skirt, the Horned Osmia, was visiting the flowers, dipping into each pink eye in search of a honeyed tear. A very small and very modestly-dressed Halictus, much busier and in far greater numbers, was flitting silently from blossom to blossom. Official science calls her Halictus malachurus, K. The pretty little Bee's godfather strikes me as ill-inspired. What has malachurus, calling attention to the softness of the rump, to do in this connection? The name of Early Halictus would better describe the almond-tree's little visitor.

None of the melliferous clan, in my neighbourhood at least, is stirring as early as she is. She digs her burrows in February, an inclement month, subject to sudden returns of frost. When none as yet, even among her near kinswomen, dares to sally forth from winter-quarters, she pluckily goes to work, shine the sun ever so little. Like the Zebra Halictus, she has two generations a year, one in spring and one in summer; like her, too, she settles by preference in the hard ruts of the country roads.

Her mole-hills, those humble mounds any two of which would go easily into a Hen's egg, rise innumerous in my path, the path by the almond-trees which is the happy hunting-ground of my curiosity to-day. This path is a ribbon of road three paces wide, worn into ruts by the Mule's hoofs and the wheels of the farm-carts. A coppice of holm-oaks shelters it from the north wind. In this Eden with its well-caked soil, its warmth and quiet, the little Halictus has multiplied her mole-hills to such a degree that I cannot take a step without crushing some of them. The accident is not serious: the miner, safe underground, will be able to scramble up the crumbling sides of the mine and repair the threshold of the trampled home.

I make a point of measuring the density of the population. I count from forty to sixty mole-hills on a surface of one square yard. The encampment is three paces wide and stretches over nearly three-quarters of a mile. How many Halicti are there in this Babylon? I do not venture to make the calculation.

Speaking of the Zebra Halictus, I used the words hamlet, village, township; and the expressions were appropriate. Here the term city hardly meets the case. And what reason can we allege for these innumerable clusters? I can see but one: the charm of living together, which is the origin of society. Like mingles with like, without the rendering of any mutual service; and this is enough to summon the Early Halictus to the same way-side, even as the Herring and the Sardine assemble in the same waters.

CHAPTER 14. THE HALICTI: PARTHENOGENESIS.

The Halictus opens up another question, connected with one of life's obscurest problems. Let us go back five-and-twenty years. I am living at Orange. My house stands alone among the fields. On the other side of the wall enclosing our yard, which faces due south, is a narrow path overgrown with couch-grass. The sun beats full upon it; and the glare reflected from the whitewash of the wall turns it into a little tropical corner, shut off from the rude gusts of the north-west wind.

Here the Cats come to take their afternoon nap, with their eyes half-closed; here the children come, with Bull, the House-dog; here also come the haymakers, at the hottest time of the day, to sit and take their meal and whet their scythes in the shade of the plane-tree; here the women pass up and down with their rakes, after the hay-harvest, to glean what they can on the niggardly carpet of the shorn meadow. It is therefore a very much frequented footpath, were it only because of the coming and going of our household: a thoroughfare ill-suited, one would think, to the peaceful operations of a Bee; and nevertheless it is such a very warm and sheltered spot and the soil is so favourable that every year I see the Cylindrical Halictus (H. cylindricus, FAB.) hand down the site from one generation to the next. It is true that the very matutinal, even partly nocturnal character of the work makes the insect suffer less inconvenience from the traffic.

The burrows cover an extent of some ten square yards, and their mounds, which often come near enough to touch, average a distance of four inches at the most from one another. Their number is therefore something like a thousand. The ground just here is very rough, consisting of stones and dust mixed with a little mould and held together by the closely interwoven roots of the couch-grass. But, owing to its nature, it is thoroughly well drained, a condition always in request among Bees and

Wasps that have underground cells.

Let us forget for a moment what the Zebra Halictus and the Early Halictus have taught us. At the risk of repeating myself a little, I will relate what I observed during my first investigations. The Cylindrical Halictus works in May. Except among the social species, such as Common Wasps, Bumble-bees, Ants and Hive-bees, it is the rule for each insect that victuals its nests either with honey or game to work by itself at constructing the home of its grubs. Among insects of the same species there is often neighbourship; but their labours are individual and not the result of co-operation. For instance, the Cricket-hunters, the Yellow-winged Sphex, settle in gangs at the foot of a sandstone cliff, but each digs her own burrow and would not suffer a neighbour to come and help in piercing the home.

In the case of the Anthophorae, an innumerable swarm takes possession of a sun-scorched crag, each Bee digging her own gallery and jealously excluding any of her fellows who might venture to come to the entrance of her hole. The Three-pronged Osmia, when boring the bramble-stalk tunnel in which her cells are to be stacked, gives a warm reception to any Osmia that dares set foot upon her property.

Let one of the Odyneri who make their homes in a road-side bank mistake the door and enter her neighbour's house: she would have a bad time of it! Let a Megachile, returning with her leafy disk in her legs, go into the wrong basement: she would be very soon dislodged! So with the others: each has her own home, which none of the others has the right to enter. This is the rule, even among Bees and Wasps established in a populous colony on a common site. Close neighbourhood implies no sort of intimate relationship.

Great therefore is my surprise as I watch the Cylindrical Halictus' operations. She forms no society, in the entomological sense of the word: there is no common family; and the general interest does not engross the attention of the individual. Each mother occupies herself only with her own eggs, builds cells and gathers honey only for her own larvae, without concerning herself in any way with the upbringing of the others' grubs. All that they have in common is the entrance-door and the goods-passage, which ramifies in the ground and leads to different groups of cells, each the property of one mother. Even so, in the blocks of flats in our large towns, one door, one hall and one staircase lead to different floors or different portions of a floor where each family retains its isolation and its independence.

This common right of way is extremely easy to perceive at the time for victualling the nests. Let us direct our attention for a while to the same entrance-aperture, opening at the top of a little mound of earth freshly thrown up, like that accumulated by the Ants during their works. Sooner or later we shall see the Halicti arrive with their load of pollen, gathered on the Cichoriaceae of the neighbourhood.

Usually, they come up one by one; but it is not rare to see three, four or even more appearing at the same time at the mouth of one burrow. They perch on the top of the mound and, without hurrying in front of one another, with no sign of jealousy, they dive down the passage, each in her turn. We need but watch their peaceful waiting, their tranquil dives, to recognize that this indeed is a common passage to which each has as much right as another.

When the soil is exploited for the first time and the shaft sunk slowly from the outside to the inside, do several Cylindrical Halicti, one relieving the other, take part in the work by which they will afterwards profit equally? I do not believe it for a moment. As the Zebra Halictus and the Early Halictus told me later, each miner goes to work alone and makes herself a gallery which will be her exclusive property. The common use of the passage comes presently, when the site, tested by experience, is handed down from one generation to another.

A first group of cells is established, we will suppose, at the bottom of a pit dug in virgin soil. The whole thing, cells and pit, is the work of one insect. When the moment comes to leave the underground dwelling, the Bees emerging from this nest will find before them an open road, or one at most obstructed by crumbly matter, which offers less resistance than the neighbouring soil, as yet untouched. The exit-way will therefore be the primitive way, contrived by the mother during the construction of the nest. All enter upon it without any hesitation, for the cells open straight on it. All, coming and going from the cells to the bottom of the shaft and from the shaft to the cells, will take part in the clearing, under the stimulus of the approaching deliverance.

It is quite unnecessary here to presume among these underground prisoners a concerted effort to liberate themselves more easily by working in common: each is thinking only of herself and invariably returns, after resting, to toil at the inevitable path, the path of least resistance, in short the passage once dug by the mother and now more or less blocked up.

Among the Cylindrical Halicti, any one who wishes emerges from her cell at her own hour, without waiting for the emergence of the others, because the cells, grouped in small stacks, have each their special outlet opening into the common gallery. The result of this arrangement is that all the inhabitants of one burrow are able to assist, each doing her share, in the clearing of the exit-shaft. When she feels fatigued, the worker retires to her undamaged cell and another succeeds her, impatient to get out rather than to help the first. At last the way is clear and the Halicti emerge. They disperse over the flowers around as long as the sun is hot; when the air cools, they go back to the burrows to spend the night there.

A few days pass and already the cares of egg-laying are at hand. The galleries have never been abandoned. The Bees have come to take refuge there on rainy or very windy days; most, if not all, have returned every evening at sunset, each doubtless making for her own cell, which is still intact and which is carefully impressed upon her memory. In a word, the Cylindrical Halictus does not lead a wandering life; she has a fixed residence.

A necessary consequence results from these settled habits: for the purpose of her laying, the Bee will adopt the identical burrow in which she was born. The entrance-gallery is ready therefore. Should it need to be carried deeper, to be pushed in new directions, the builder has but to extend it at will. The old cells even can serve again, if slightly restored.

Thus resuming possession of the native burrow in view of her offspring, the Bee, notwithstanding her instincts as a solitary worker, achieves an attempt at social life, because there is one entrance-door and one passage for the use of all the mothers returning to the original domicile. There is thus a semblance of collaboration without any real co-operation for the common weal. Everything is reduced to a family inheritance shared equally among the heirs.

The number of these coheirs must soon be limited, for a too tumultuous traffic in the corridor would delay the work. Then fresh passages are opened inwards, often communicating with depths already excavated, so that the ground at last is perforated in every direction with an inextricable maze of winding tunnels.

The digging of the cells and the piercing of new galleries take place especially at night. A cone of fresh earth on top of the burrow bears evidence every morning to the overnight activity. It also shows by its volume that several navvies have taken part in the work, for it would be impossible for a single Halictus to extract from the ground, convey to the surface and heap up so large a stack of rubbish in so short a time.

At sunrise, when the fields around are still wet with dew, the Cylindrical Halictus leaves her underground passages and starts on her foraging. This is done without animation, perhaps because of the morning coolness. There is no joyous excitement, no humming above the burrows. The Bees come back again, flying low, silently and heavily, their hind-legs yellow with pollen; they alight on the earth-cone and at once dive down the vertical chimney. Others come up the pipe and go off to their harvesting.

This journeying to and fro for provisions continues until eight or nine in the morning. Then the heat begins to grow intense and is reflected by the wall; then also the path is once more frequented. People pass at every moment, coming out of the house or elsewhence. The soil is so much trodden under foot that the little mounds of refuse surrounding each burrow soon disappear and the site loses every sign of underground habitation.

All day long, the Halicti remain indoors. Withdrawing to the bottom of the galleries, they occupy themselves probably in making and polishing the cells. Next morning, new cones of rubbish appear, the result of the night's work, and the pollen-harvest is resumed for a few hours; then everything ceases again. And so the work goes on, suspended by day, renewed at night and in the morning hours, until completely finished.

The passages of the Cylindrical Halictus descend to a depth of some eight inches and branch into secondary corridors, each giving access to a set of cells. These number six or eight to each set and are ranged side by side, parallel with their main axis, which is almost horizontal. They are oval at the base and contracted at the neck. Their length is nearly twenty millimetres (.78 inch.--Translator's Note.) and their greatest width eight. (.312 inch.--Translator's Note.) They do not consist simply of a cavity in the ground; on the contrary, they have their own walls, so that the group can be taken out in one piece, with a little precaution, and removed neatly from the earth in which it is contained.

The walls are formed of fairly delicate materials, which must have been chosen in the coarse surrounding mass and kneaded with saliva. The inside is carefully pol-ished and upholstered with a thin waterproof film. We will cut short these details concerning the cells, which the Zebra Halictus has already shown us in greater perfection, leave the home to itself and come to the most striking feature in the life-history of the Halicti.

The Cylindrical Halictus is at work in the first days of May. It is a rule among the Hymenoptera for the males never to take part in the fatiguing work of nest-building. To construct cells and to amass victuals are occupations entirely foreign to their nature. This rule seems to have no exceptions; and the Halicti conform to it like the rest. It is therefore only to be expected that we should see no males shoot-ing the underground rubbish outside the galleries. That is not their business.

But what does astonish us, when our attention is directed to it, is the total ab-sence of any males in the vicinity of the burrows. Although it is the rule that the males should be idle, it is also the rule for these idlers to keep near the galleries in course of construction, coming and going from door to door and hovering above the work-yards to seize the moment at which the unfecundated females will at last yield to their importunities.

Now here, despite the enormous population, despite my careful and incessant watch, it is impossible for me to distinguish a single male. And yet the distinction between the sexes is of the simplest. It is not necessary to take hold of the male. He can be recognized even at a distance by his slenderer frame, by his long, narrow ab-domen, by his red sash. They might easily suggest two different species. The female is a pale russet-brown; the male is black, with a few red segments to his abdomen. Well, during the May building-operations, there is not a Bee in sight clad in black, with a slender, red-belted abdomen; in short, not a male.

Though the males do not come to visit the environs of the burrows, they might be elsewhere, particularly on the flowers where the females go plundering. I did not fail to explore the fields, insect-net in hand. My search was invariably fruitless. On the other hand, those males, now nowhere to be found, are plentiful later, in September, along the borders of the paths, on the close-set flowers of the eringo.

This singular colony, reduced exclusively to mothers, made me suspect the existence of several generations a year, whereof one at least must possess the other sex. I continued therefore, when the building-who was over, to keep a daily watch on the establishment of the Cylindrical Halictus, in order to seize the favourable moment that would verify my suspicions. For six weeks, solitude reigned above the burrows: not a single Halictus appeared; and the path, trodden by the wayfarers, lost its little heaps of rubbish, the only signs of the excavations. There was nothing outside to show that the warmth down below was hatching populous swarms.

July comes and already a few little mounds of fresh earth betoken work going on underground in preparation for an exodus in the near future. As the males, among the Hymenoptera, are generally further advanced than the females and quit their natal cells earlier, it was important that I should witness the first exits made, so as to dispel the least shadow of a doubt. A violent exhumation would have a great advantage over the natural exit: it would place the population of the burrows immediately under my eyes, before the departure of either sex. In this way, nothing could escape from me and I was dispensed from a watch which, for all its attentiveness, was not to be relied upon absolutely. I therefore resolve upon a reconnaissance with the spade.

I dig down to the full depth of the galleries and remove large lumps of earth which I take in my hands and break very carefully so as to examine all the parts that may contain cells. Halicti in the perfect state predominate, most of them still lodged in their unbroken chambers. Though they are not quite so numerous, there are also plenty of pupae. I collect them of every shade of colour, from dead-white, the sign of a recent transformation, to smoky-brown, the mark of an approaching metamorphosis. Larvae, in small quantities, complete the harvest. They are in the state of torpor that precedes the appearance of the pupa.

I prepare boxes with a bed of fresh, sifted earth to receive the larvae and the pupae, which I lodge each in a sort of half-cell formed by the imprint of my finger. I will await the transformation to decide to which sex they belong. As for the perfect insects, they are inspected, counted and at once released.

In the very unlikely supposition that the distribution of the sexes might vary in different parts of the colony, I make a second excavation, at a few yards' distance from the other. It supplies me with another collection both of perfect insects and of pupae and larvae.

When the metamorphosis of the laggards is completed, which does not take many days, I proceed to take a general census. It gives me two hundred and fifty Halicti. Well, in this number of Bees, collected in the burrow before any have emerged, I perceive none, absolutely none but females; or, to be mathematically accurate, I find just one male, one alone; and he is so small and feeble that he dies without quite succeeding in divesting himself of his nymphal bands. This solitary male is certainly accidental. A female population of two hundred and forty-nine Halicti implies other males than this abortion, or rather implies none at all. I therefore eliminate him as an accident of no value and conclude that, in the Cylindrical Halictus, the July generation consists of females only.

The building-operations start again in the second week of July. The galleries are restored and lengthened; new cells are fashioned and the old ones repaired. Follow the provisioning, the laying of the eggs, the closing of the cells; and, before July is over, there is solitude again. Let me also say that, during the building-period, not a male appears in sight, a fact which adds further proof to that already supplied by my excavations.

With the high temperature of this time of the year, the development of the larvae makes rapid progress: a month is sufficient for the various stages of the metamorphosis. On the 24th of August there are once more signs of life above the burrows of the Cylindrical Halictus, but under very different conditions. For the first time, both sexes are present. Males, so easily recognized by their black livery and their slim abdomen adorned with a red ring, hover backwards and forwards, almost level with the ground. They fuss about from burrow to burrow. A few rare females come out for a moment and then go in again.

I proceed to make an excavation with my spade; I gather indiscriminately whatever I come across. Larvae are very scarce; pupae abound, as do perfect insects. The list of my captures amounts to eighty males and fifty-eight females. The males, therefore, hitherto impossible to discover, either on the flowers around or in the neighbourhood of the burrows, could be picked up to-day by the hundred, if I wished. They outnumber the females by about four to three; they are also further developed, in accordance with the general rule, for most of the backward pupae give me only females.

Once the two sexes had appeared, I expected a third generation that would spend the winter in the larval state and recommence in May the annual cycle which I have just described. My anticipation proved to be at fault. Throughout September, when the sun beats upon the burrows, I see the males flitting in great numbers from one shaft to the other. Sometimes a female appears, returning from the fields, but with no pollen on her legs. She seeks her gallery, finds it, dives down and disappears.

The males, as though indifferent to her arrival, offer her no welcome, do not harass her with their amorous pursuits; they continue to visit the doors of the burrows with a winding and oscillating flight. For two months, I follow their evolutions. If they set foot on earth, it is to descend forthwith into some gallery that suits them.

It is not uncommon to see several of them on the threshold of the same burrow. Then each awaits his turn to enter; they are as peaceable in their relations as the females who are joint owners of a burrow. At other times, one wants to go in as a second is coming out. This sudden encounter produces no strife. The one leaving the hole withdraws a little to one side to make enough room for two; the other slips past as best he can. These peaceful meetings are all the more striking when we consider the usual rivalry between males of the same species.

No rubbish-mound stands at the mouth of the shafts, showing that the building has not been resumed; at the most, a few crumbs of earth are heaped outside. And by whom, pray? By the males and by them alone. The lazy sex has bethought itself of working. It turns navvy and shoots out grains of earth that would interfere with its continual entrances and exits. For the first time I witness a custom which no Hymenopteron had yet shown me: I see the males haunting the interior of the burrows with an assiduity equalling that of the mothers employed in nest-building.

The cause of these unwonted operations soon stands revealed. The females seen flitting above the burrows are very rare; the majority of the feminine population remain sequestered under ground, do not perhaps come out once during the whole of the latter part of summer. Those who do venture out go in again soon, empty-handed of course and always without any amorous teasing from the males, a number of whom are hovering above the burrows.

On the other hand, watch as carefully as I may, I do not discover a single act of pairing out of doors. The weddings are clandestine, therefore, and take place under ground. This explains the males' fussy visits to the doors of the galleries during the hottest hours of the day, their continual descents into the depths and their continual reappearances. They are looking for the females cloistered in the retirement of the cells.

A little spade-work soon turns suspicion into certainty. I unearth a sufficient number of couples to prove to me that the sexes come together underground. When the marriage is consummated, the red-belted one quits the spot and goes to die outside the burrow, after dragging from flower to flower the bit of life that remains to him. The other shuts herself up in her cell, there to await the return of the month of May.

September is spent by the Halictus solely in nuptial celebrations. Whenever the sky is fine, I witness the evolutions of the males above the burrows, with their continual entrances and exits; should the sun be veiled, they take refuge down the passages. The more impatient, half-hidden in the pit, show their little black heads outside, as though peeping for the least break in the clouds that will allow them to pay a brief visit to the flowers round about. They also spend the night in the burrows. In the morning, I attend their levee; I see them put their head to the window, take a look at the weather and then go in again until the sun beats on the encampment.

The same mode of life is continued throughout October, but the males become less numerous from day to day as the stormy season approaches and fewer females remain to be wooed. By the time that the first cold weather comes, in November, complete solitude reigns over the burrows. I once more have recourse to the spade. I find none but females in their cells. There is not one male left. All have vanished, all are dead, the victims of their life of pleasure and of the wind and rain. Thus ends the cycle of the year for the Cylindrical Halictus.

In February, after a hard winter, when the snow had lain on the ground for a fortnight, I wanted once more to look into the matter of my Halicti. I was in bed with pneumonia and at the point of death, to all appearances. I had little or no pain, thank God, but extreme difficulty in living. With the little lucidity left to me, being able to do no other sort of observing, I observed myself dying; I watched with a certain interest the gradual falling to pieces of my poor machinery. Were it not for the terror of leaving my family, who were still young, I would gladly have departed. The after-life must have so many higher and fairer truths to teach us.

My hour had not yet come. When the little lamps of thought began to emerge, all flickering, from the dusk of unconsciousness, I wished to take leave of the Hymenopteron, my fondest joy, and first of all of my neighbour, the Halictus. My son Emile took the spade and went and dug the frozen ground. Not a male was found, of course; but there were plenty of females, numbed with the cold in their cells.

A few were brought for me to see. Their little chambers showed no efflorescence of rime, with which all the surrounding earth was coated. The waterproof varnish had been wonderfully efficacious. As for the anchorites, roused from their torpor by the warmth of the room, they began to wander about my bed, where I followed them vaguely with my fading eyes.

May came, as eagerly awaited by the sick man as by the Halicti. I left Orange for Serignan, my last stage, I expect. While I was moving, the Bees resumed their building. I gave them a regretful glance, for I had still much to learn in their company. I have never since met with such a mighty colony.

These old observations on the habits of the Cylindrical Halictus may now be followed by a general summary which will incorporate the recent data supplied by the Zebra Halictus and the Early Halictus.

The females of the Cylindrical Halictus whom I unearth from November onwards are evidently fecundated, as is proved by the assiduity of the males during the preceding two months and most positively confirmed by the couples discovered in the course of my excavations. These females spend the winter in their cells, as do many of the early-hatching melliferous insects, such as Anthophorae and Mason-bees, who build their nests in the spring, the larvae reaching the perfect state in the summer and yet remaining shut up in their cells until the following May. But there is this great difference in the case of the Cylindrical Halictus, that in the autumn the females leave their cells for a time to receive the males under ground. The couples pair and the males perish. Left alone, the females return to their cells, where they spend the inclement season.

The Zebra Halicti, studied first at Orange and then, under better conditions, at Serignan, in my own enclosure, have not these subterranean customs: they celebrate their weddings amid the joys of the light, the sun and the flowers. I see the first males appear in the middle of September, on the centauries. Generally there are several of them courting the same bride. Now one, then another, they swoop upon her suddenly, clasp her, leave her, seize hold of her again. Fierce brawls decide who shall possess her. One is accepted and the others decamp. With a swift and angular flight, they go from flower to flower, without alighting. They hover on the wing, looking about them, more intent on pairing than on eating.

The Early Halictus did not supply me with any definite information, partly through my own fault, partly through the difficulty of excavation in a stony soil, which calls for the pick-axe rather than the spade. I suspect her of having the nuptial customs of the Cylindrical Halictus.

There is another difference, which causes certain variations of detail in these customs. In the autumn, the females of the Cylindrical Halictus leave their burrows seldom or not at all. Those who do go out invariably come back after a brief halt upon the flowers. All pass the winter in the natal cells. On the other hand, those of the Zebra Halictus move their quarters, meet the males outside and do not return to the burrows, which my autumn excavations always find deserted. They hibernate in the first hiding-places that offer.

In the spring, the females, fecundated since the autumn, come out: the Cylindrical Halicti from their cells, the Zebra Halicti from their various shelters, the Early Halicti apparently from their chambers, like the first. They work at their nests in the absence of any male, as do also the Social Wasps, whose whole brood has perished excepting a few mothers also fecundated in the autumn. In both cases, the assistance of the males is equally real, only it has preceded the laying by about six months.

So far, there is nothing new in the life of the Halicti; but here is where the unexpected appears: in July, another generation is produced; and this time without males. The absence of masculine assistance is no longer a mere semblance here, due to an earlier fecundation: it is a reality established beyond a doubt by the continuity of my observations and by my excavations during the summer season, before the emergence of the new Bees. At this period, a little before July, if my spade unearth the cells of any one of my three Halicti, the result is always females, nothing but females, with exceedingly rare exceptions.

True, it may be said that the second progeny is due to the mothers who knew the males in autumn and who would be able to nidify twice a year. The suggestion is not admissible. The Zebra Halictus confirms what I say. She shows us the old mothers no longer leaving the home but mounting guard at the entrance to the burrows.

No harvesting- or pottery-work is possible with these absorbing doorkeeping-functions. Therefore there is no new family, even admitting that the mothers' ovaries are not depleted.

I do not know if a similar argument is valid in the case of the Cylindrical Halictus. Has she any general survivors? As my attention had not yet been directed on this point in the old days, when I had the insect at my door, I have no records to go upon. For all that, I am inclined to think that the portress of the Zebra Halictus is unknown here. The reason of this absence would be the number of workers at the start.

In May, the Zebra Halictus, living by herself in her winter retreat, founds her house alone. When her daughters succeed her, in July, she is the only grandmother in the establishment and the post of portress falls to her. With the Cylindrical Halictus, the conditions are different. Here the May workers are many in the same burrow, where they dwell in common during the winter. Supposing that they survive when the business of the household is finished, to whom will the office of overseer fall? Their number is so great and they are all so full of zeal that disorder would be inevitable. But we can leave this small matter unsettled pending further information.

The fact remains that females, females exclusively, have come out of the eggs laid in May. They have descendants, of that there is no room for doubt; they procreate though there are no males in their time. From this generation by a single sex, there spring, two months later, males and females. These mate; and the same order of things recommences.

To sum up, judging by the three species that form the subject of my investigations, the Halicti have two generations a year: one in the spring, issuing from the mothers who have lived through the winter after being fecundated in the autumn; the other in the summer, the fruit of parthenogenesis, that is to say, of reproduction by the powers of the mother alone. Of the union of the two sexes, females alone are born; parthenogenesis gives birth at the same time to females and males.

When the mother, the original genitrix, has been able once to dispense with a coadjutor, why does she need one later? What is the puny idler there for? He was unnecessary. Why does he become necessary now? Shall we ever obtain a satisfactory answer to the question? It is doubtful. However, without much hope of succeeding we will one day consult the Gall-fly, who is better-versed than we in the tangled problem of the sexes.

INDEX.

Archimedes.
Augustus, the Emperor.
Bee.
Beetle.
Bembex.
Black, Adam and Charles.
Black Plant-louse.
Black Psen.
Black-tipped Leaf-cutter.
Blue Osmia.
Book-louse.
Brown Snail.
Bulimulus radiatus.
Bumble-bee.
Calicurgus (see Pompilus).
Capricorn.
Carpenter-bee.
Cat.
Cemonus unicolor.
Cerambyx (see Capricorn).
Ceratina (see also the varieties below).
Ceratina albilabris.
Ceratina callosa.
Ceratina chalcites.
Ceratina coerulea.
Cerceris.
Cetonia.
Chaffinch.
Chalicodoma (see Mason-bee).
Chrysis flammea.
Cockroach.
Coelyoxis caudata.
Coelyoxis octodentata.

www.bookjungle.com *email: sales@bookjungle.com fax: 630-214-0564 mail: Book Jungle PO Box 2226 Champaign, IL 61825*

The Codes Of Hammurabi And Moses
W. W. Davies

QTY

The discovery of the Hammurabi Code is one of the greatest achievements of archaeology, and is of paramount interest, not only to the student of the Bible, but also to all those interested in ancient history...

Religion   **ISBN: *1-59462-338-4***   **Pages:132**
MSRP $12.95

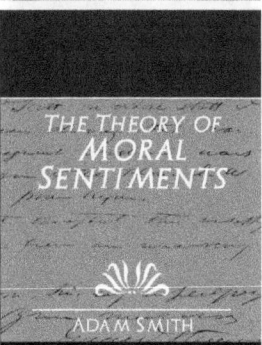

The Theory of Moral Sentiments
Adam Smith

QTY

This work from 1749. contains original theories of conscience amd moral judgment and it is the foundation for systemof morals.

Philosophy **ISBN: *1-59462-777-0***   **Pages:536**
MSRP $19.95

Jessica's First Prayer
Hesba Stretton

QTY

In a screened and secluded corner of one of the many railway-bridges which span the streets of London there could be seen a few years ago, from five o'clock every morning until half past eight, a tidily set-out coffee-stall, consisting of a trestle and board, upon which stood two large tin cans, with a small fire of charcoal burning under each so as to keep the coffee boiling during the early hours of the morning when the work-people were thronging into the city on their way to their daily toil...

Pages:84

Childrens   **ISBN: *1-59462-373-2***   *MSRP $9.95*

My Life and Work
Henry Ford

QTY

Henry Ford revolutionized the world with his implementation of mass production for the Model T automobile. Gain valuable business insight into his life and work with his own auto-biography... "We have only started on our development of our country we have not as yet, with all our talk of wonderful progress, done more than scratch the surface. The progress has been wonderful enough but..."

Pages:300

Biographies/   **ISBN: *1-59462-198-5***   *MSRP $21.95*

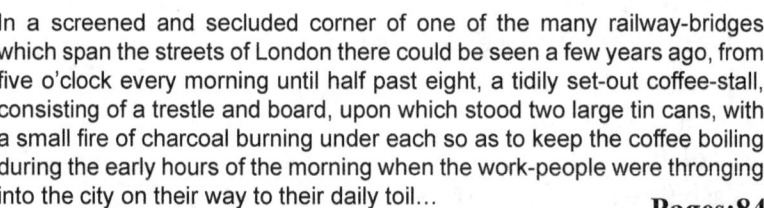

The Art of Cross-Examination
Francis Wellman

QTY

I presume it is the experience of every author, after his first book is published upon an important subject, to be almost overwhelmed with a wealth of ideas and illustrations which could readily have been included in his book, and which to his own mind, at least, seem to make a second edition inevitable. Such certainly was the case with me; and when the first edition had reached its sixth impression in five months, I rejoiced to learn that it seemed to my publishers that the book had met with a sufficiently favorable reception to justify a second and considerably enlarged edition. ..

Reference   **ISBN:** *1-59462-647-2*

Pages:412

MSRP $19.95

On the Duty of Civil Disobedience
Henry David Thoreau

QTY

Thoreau wrote his famous essay, On the Duty of Civil Disobedience, as a protest against an unjust but popular war and the immoral but popular institution of slave-owning. He did more than write—he declined to pay his taxes, and was hauled off to gaol in consequence. Who can say how much this refusal of his hastened the end of the war and of slavery ?

Law   **ISBN:** *1-59462-747-9*

Pages:48

MSRP $7.45

Dream Psychology Psychoanalysis for Beginners
Sigmund Freud

QTY

Sigmund Freud, born Sigismund Schlomo Freud (May 6, 1856 - September 23, 1939), was a Jewish-Austrian neurologist and psychiatrist who co-founded the psychoanalytic school of psychology. Freud is best known for his theories of the unconscious mind, especially involving the mechanism of repression; his redefinition of sexual desire as mobile and directed towards a wide variety of objects; and his therapeutic techniques, especially his understanding of transference in the therapeutic relationship and the presumed value of dreams as sources of insight into unconscious desires.

Pages:196

Psychology   **ISBN:** *1-59462-905-6*

MSRP $15.45

The Miracle of Right Thought
Orison Swett Marden

QTY

Believe with all of your heart that you will do what you were made to do. When the mind has once formed the habit of holding cheerful, happy, prosperous pictures, it will not be easy to form the opposite habit. It does not matter how improbable or how far away this realization may see, or how dark the prospects may be, if we visualize them as best we can, as vividly as possible, hold tenaciously to them and vigorously struggle to attain them, they will gradually become actualized, realized in the life. But a desire, a longing without endeavor, a yearning abandoned or held indifferently will vanish without realization.

Pages:360

Self Help   **ISBN:** *1-59462-644-8*

MSRP $25.45

www.**bookjungle**.com *email: sales@bookjungle.com fax: 630-214-0564 mail: Book Jungle PO Box 2226 Champaign, IL 61825*

QTY

The Rosicrucian Cosmo-Conception Mystic Christianity *by Max Heindel*   ISBN: *1-59462-188-8*   **$38.95**
The Rosicrucian Cosmo-conception is not dogmatic, neither does it appeal to any other authority than the reason of the student. It is: not controversial, but is: sent forth in the, hope that it may help to clear...   New Age/Religion Pages 646

Abandonment To Divine Providence *by Jean-Pierre de Caussade*   ISBN: *1-59462-228-0*   **$25.95**
"The Rev. Jean Pierre de Caussade was one of the most remarkable spiritual writers of the Society of Jesus in France in the 18th Century. His death took place at Toulouse in 1751. His works have gone through many editions and have been republished...   Inspirational/Religion Pages 400

Mental Chemistry *by Charles Haanel*   ISBN: *1-59462-192-6*   **$23.95**
Mental Chemistry allows the change of material conditions by combining and appropriately utilizing the power of the mind. Much like applied chemistry creates something new and unique out of careful combinations of chemicals the mastery of mental chemistry...   New Age Pages 354

The Letters of Robert Browning and Elizabeth Barret Barrett 1845-1846 vol II   ISBN: *1-59462-193-4*   **$35.95**
by Robert Browning and Elizabeth Barrett   Biographies Pages 596

Gleanings In Genesis (volume I) *by Arthur W. Pink*   ISBN: *1-59462-130-6*   **$27.45**
Appropriately has Genesis been termed "the seed plot of the Bible" for in it we have, in germ form, almost all of the great doctrines which are afterwards fully developed in the books of Scripture which follow...   Religion/Inspirational Pages 420

The Master Key *by L. W. de Laurence*   ISBN: *1-59462-001-6*   **$30.95**
In no branch of human knowledge has there been a more lively increase of the spirit of research during the past few years than in the study of Psychology, Concentration and Mental Discipline. The requests for authentic lessons in Thought Control, Mental Discipline and...   New Age/Business Pages 422

The Lesser Key Of Solomon Goetia *by L. W. de Laurence*   ISBN: *1-59462-092-X*   **$9.95**
This translation of the first book of the "Lemegton" which is now for the first time made accessible to students of Talismanic Magic was done, after careful collation and edition, from numerous Ancient Manuscripts in Hebrew, Latin, and French...   New Age/Occult Pages 92

Rubaiyat Of Omar Khayyam *by Edward Fitzgerald*   ISBN:*1-59462-332-5*   **$13.95**
Edward Fitzgerald, whom the world has already learned, in spite of his own efforts to remain within the shadow of anonymity, to look upon as one of the rarest poets of the century, was born at Bredfield, in Suffolk, on the 31st of March, 1809. He was the third son of John Purcell...   Music Pages 172

Ancient Law *by Henry Maine*   ISBN: *1-59462-128-4*   **$29.95**
The chief object of the following pages is to indicate some of the earliest ideas of mankind, as they are reflected in Ancient Law, and to point out the relation of those ideas to modern thought.   Religion/History Pages 452

Far-Away Stories *by William J. Locke*   ISBN: *1-59462-129-2*   **$19.45**
"Good wine needs no bush, but a collection of mixed vintages does. And this book is just such a collection. Some of the stories I do not want to remain buried for ever in the museum files of dead magazine-numbers an author's not unpardonable vanity..."   Fiction Pages 272

Life of David Crockett *by David Crockett*   ISBN: *1-59462-250-7*   **$27.45**
"Colonel David Crockett was one of the most remarkable men of the times in which he lived. Born in humble life, but gifted with a strong will, an indomitable courage, and unremitting perseverance...   Biographies/New Age Pages 424

Lip-Reading *by Edward Nitchie*   ISBN: *1-59462-206-X*   **$25.95**
Edward B. Nitchie, founder of the New York School for the Hard of Hearing, now the Nitchie School of Lip-Reading, Inc, wrote "LIP-READING Principles and Practice". The development and perfecting of this meritorious work on lip-reading was an undertaking...   How-to Pages 400

A Handbook of Suggestive Therapeutics, Applied Hypnotism, Psychic Science   ISBN: *1-59462-214-0*   **$24.95**
by Henry Munro   Health/New Age/Health/Self-help Pages 376

A Doll's House: and Two Other Plays *by Henrik Ibsen*   ISBN: *1-59462-112-8*   **$19.95**
Henrik Ibsen created this classic when in revolutionary 1848 Rome. Introducing some striking concepts in playwriting for the realist genre, this play has been studied the world over.   Fiction/Classics/Plays 308

The Light of Asia *by sir Edwin Arnold*   ISBN: *1-59462-204-3*   **$13.95**
In this poetic masterpiece, Edwin Arnold describes the life and teachings of Buddha. The man who was to become known as Buddha to the world was born as Prince Gautama of India but he rejected the worldly riches and abandoned the reigns of power when...   Religion/History/Biographies Pages 170

The Complete Works of Guy de Maupassant *by Guy de Maupassant*   ISBN: *1-59462-157-8*   **$16.95**
"For days and days, nights and nights, I had dreamed of that first kiss which was to consecrate our engagement, and I knew not on what spot I should put my lips..."   Fiction/Classics Pages 240

The Art of Cross-Examination *by Francis L. Wellman*   ISBN: *1-59462-309-0*   **$26.95**
Written by a renowned trial lawyer, Wellman imparts his experience and uses case studies to explain how to use psychology to extract desired information through questioning.   How-to/Science/Reference Pages 408

Answered or Unanswered? *by Louisa Vaughan*   ISBN: *1-59462-248-5*   **$10.95**
Miracles of Faith in China   Religion Pages 112

The Edinburgh Lectures on Mental Science (1909) *by Thomas*   ISBN: *1-59462-008-3*   **$11.95**
This book contains the substance of a course of lectures recently given by the writer in the Queen Street Hall, Edinburgh. Its purpose is to indicate the Natural Principles governing the relation between Mental Action and Material Conditions...   New Age/Psychology Pages 148

Ayesha *by H. Rider Haggard*   ISBN: *1-59462-301-5*   **$24.95**
Verily and indeed it is the unexpected that happens! Probably if there was one person upon the earth from whom the Editor of this, and of a certain previous history, did not expect to hear again...   Classics Pages 380

Ayala's Angel *by Anthony Trollope*   ISBN: *1-59462-352-X*   **$29.95**
The two girls were both pretty, but Lucy who was twenty-one who supposed to be simple and comparatively unattractive, whereas Ayala was credited, as her Bombwhat romantic name might show, with poetic charm and a taste for romance. Ayala when her father died was nineteen...   Fiction Pages 484

The American Commonwealth *by James Bryce*   ISBN: *1-59462-286-8*   **$34.45**
An interpretation of American democratic political theory. It examines political mechanics and society from the perspective of Scotsman James Bryce   Politics Pages 572

Stories of the Pilgrims *by Margaret P. Pumphrey*   ISBN: *1-59462-116-0*   **$17.95**
This book explores pilgrims religious oppression in England as well as their escape to Holland and eventual crossing to America on the Mayflower, and their early days in New England...   History Pages 268

QTY

The Fasting Cure *by Sinclair Upton*   ISBN: *1-59462-222-1*   **$13.95**
In the Cosmopolitan Magazine for May, 1910, and in the Contemporary Review (London) for April, 1910, I published an article dealing with my experiences in fasting. I have written a great many magazine articles, but never one which attracted so much attention... New Age/Self Help/Health Pages 164

Hebrew Astrology *by Sepharial*   ISBN: *1-59462-308-2*   **$13.45**
In these days of advanced thinking it is a matter of common observation that we have left many of the old landmarks behind and that we are now pressing forward to greater heights and to a wider horizon than that which represented the mind-content of our progenitors... Astrology Pages 144

Thought Vibration or The Law of Attraction in the Thought World   ISBN: *1-59462-127-6*   **$12.95**

by William Walker Atkinson   Psychology/Religion Pages 144

Optimism *by Helen Keller*   ISBN: *1-59462-108-X*   **$15.95**
Helen Keller was blind, deaf, and mute since 19 months old, yet famously learned how to overcome these handicaps, communicate with the world, and spread her lectures promoting optimism. An inspiring read for everyone... Biographies/Inspirational Pages 84

Sara Crewe *by Frances Burnett*   ISBN: *1-59462-360-0*   **$9.45**
In the first place, Miss Minchin lived in London. Her home was a large, dull, tall one, in a large, dull square, where all the houses were alike, and all the sparrows were alike, and where all the door-knockers made the same heavy sound... Childrens/Classic Pages 88

The Autobiography of Benjamin Franklin *by Benjamin Franklin*   ISBN: *1-59462-135-7*   **$24.95**
The Autobiography of Benjamin Franklin has probably been more extensively read than any other American historical work, and no other book of its kind has had such ups and downs of fortune. Franklin lived for many years in England, where he was agent... Biographies/History Pages 332

Name	
Email	
Telephone	
Address	
City, State ZIP	

☐ **Credit Card**   ☐ **Check / Money Order**

Credit Card Number	
Expiration Date	
Signature	

Please Mail to: Book Jungle
PO Box 2226
Champaign, IL 61825
or Fax to: 630-214-0564

ORDERING INFORMATION

web*: www.bookjungle.com*
email*: sales@bookjungle.com*
fax*: 630-214-0564*
mail*: Book Jungle PO Box 2226 Champaign, IL 61825*
or PayPal *to sales@bookjungle.com*

Please contact us for bulk discounts

DIRECT-ORDER TERMS

**20% Discount if You Order
Two or More Books**
Free Domestic Shipping!
Accepted: Master Card, Visa,
Discover, American Express

www.ingramcontent.com/pod-product-compliance
Lightning Source LLC
Chambersburg PA
CBHW080727020726
47503CB00010B/2821